More praise for
THE NEON SMILE

"THE NEON SMILE is as colorful and entertaining as any police thriller ever inspired by the fascinating and fantastical Big Easy. This big story would make a great miniseries."
—JOSEPH WAMBAUGH

"Lochte's evocative writing and complex plot are enormously satisfying, and despite my vow that I was going to read for only an hour or two, I never started my Saturday errands once I sat down with this book."
—*The Houston Chronicle*

"Lochte more than doubles the cerebral challenges and literary pleasures in this second appearance of New Orleans P.I. Terry Manion. . . . Over a dozen richly drawn characters populate this story—from a madame-turned-P.I. to a black artist who renders Mona Lisa in neon—all set against the delightfully grotesque and corrupt backdrops of 1965 and 1995 New Orleans. Chockful of dark humor, wordplay, and subtle clues, the novel is rich enough to reward multiple readings."
—*Publishers Weekly* (starred review)

Please turn the page
for more reviews. . . .

By Dick Lochte

SLEEPING DOG
LAUGHING DOG
BLUE BAYOU*
THE NEON SMILE*

*Published by Ivy Books

THE NEON SMILE

Dick Lochte

IVY BOOKS • NEW YORK

Ivy Books
Published by Ballantine Books
Copyright © 1995 by Dick Lochte

All rights reserved under International and Pan-American Copyright Conventions. Published in the United States by Ballantine Books, a division of Random House, Inc., New York, and distributed in Canada by Random House of Canada Limited, Toronto.

Library of Congress Catalog Card Number: 94-34248

ISBN 0-8041-1405-6

This edition published by arrangement with Simon & Schuster, Inc.

Manufactured in the United States of America

First Ballantine Books Edition: May 1996

10 9 8 7 6 5 4 3 2 1

Acknowledgments

I would like to thank Captain Linda Buczek and Officer Ronnie Brink of the New Orleans Police Department for their time and patience and for whatever accurate law enforcement information that may exist amid the fiction.

With special thanks to Mel Berger, agent extraordinaire.

For the Bradys, the Brysons, the Carbines, and the Lochtes, particularly the two at my house.

"Lawdy Lawd, she up and died.
An' left poor me in the lurch.
I did what I could
To make her soul feel good,
But I never went near the church."

—from *LADY BIRD BLUES*
    by *Colgate, James and Weiss*

ONE

New Orleans Louisiana

The Present

1

THE MARDI GRAS Lounge of the New Orleans International Airport was dark and crowded and noisy, and it was only, according to Terry Manion's wristwatch, 3:42 P.M. He wasn't surprised by all the activity. He had always felt that flying drunk was the preferable way to go. But he didn't drink anymore. And he wasn't going anywhere.

He took a sip of Abita Springs water and looked at the lovely young woman seated across from him. "I'll miss you," he said.

The words brought tears to her dark eyes, which was not their intent. At least he didn't think so.

Her name was Lucille Munn and for nearly eight months she had been the center of his life, holding together its comparatively unimportant other bits and pieces. The euphoria that their romance produced in him had ended two nights before when she'd informed him that she'd heard from an old lover.

To Manion, one of the least competitive of God's creatures, the words had the ring of doom.

She'd told him about her history with the guy. A bright young executive in a thriving Boston advertising agency, Mark Benton had seemed the ideal marriage prospect. Except for one tiny problem he'd neglected to mention at the start of their romance—he already was married. His refusal to divorce his wife and marry her had been one of the reasons Lucille had decided to return to New Orleans, the city of her birth. She hadn't heard a word from him in over a year. Until the phone call.

When she'd told Manion about it later that same night, he'd felt the dinner she'd fixed him, whatever it had been, turning to concrete within his chest.

3

"He wants me to marry him."

"Bigamy isn't all that popular in Boston," he'd replied, trying to fast-freeze his emotions.

"He's getting a divorce." Had the expression on her face been sorrow? Pain? Pity?

"And you said . . . ?" he'd asked.

"I told him about us."

"Fine. Now that that's settled, let's see what's on TV."

She'd put a hand to his cheek. "I do love you."

"And Benton?"

She'd shrugged. "I don't know. I'm a little confused right now."

"What is it you want?" he'd asked.

"To be certain."

"Do you have your plane ticket already?"

She'd nodded. "He arranged it. I just have to pick it up."

"I bet he didn't pop for a round-trip."

"You must be a detective," she'd said with a wan smile.

"Because it's a profession love laughs at?"

"You know what I mean, Terry . . . Please, tell me what I should do."

He'd wanted to tell her to forget the son of a bitch. Benton had had his chance and let it pass. It was *their* turn now. If there was any marrying to be done . . .

But Manion still had the scars from his first marriage. And the idea of taking that leap again, even with someone he loved, seemed beyond his capability.

"What should I do?" she'd asked again.

"Whatever you feel you have to."

She'd reached across the table to hold his hand. They sat like that for a few minutes. Then: "I'm going to Boston."

"When?"

"In two days."

He'd nodded and offered to drive her to the airport.

And there they were.

"Time I was boarding," she said.

He paid the check and they walked out to a busy corridor brightly lit by fluorescence and the afternoon sun.

At the gate, she began to weep again. He gave her his handkerchief. Squeezing it in her hand, she hugged him fiercely. He felt each sob through her body. They remained clinging to each other until the rest of the passengers had boarded.

They did not kiss good-bye.

Lucille's eyes were red as she presented her pass to the anxious attendant at the ramp. Before boarding, she turned and waved his mangled handkerchief.

Then she was gone.

Driving back home along the Airline Highway, Manion was disgusted with himself. He wanted her to stay. He wanted them to be together. He didn't know what he wanted.

In the old days, he would have driven to the nearest bar and ordered something other than Abita Springs water. But that was behind him now, like so much else. Instead, he selected his second most favorite way of escaping reality. He went to the movies.

He arrived at his home-office in the French Quarter at nine that night. There were two messages on the phone machine. The first was from Eben Munn, Lucille's brother, a lieutenant with the New Orleans Police Department, recently reassigned to the new statewide Organized Crime Combat Squad. "Manion, I hear Lucy's off to see the Boston bullshit artist. Too bad. I thought you two deserved each other. Now you'll probably go back to being a morose, depressing asshole again. But give me a ring, anyway. We can go trolling for catfish, or somethin'."

The second call was from a man named Elliott Rubin. A stranger. His voice had an East Coast accent, with words tumbling fast into one another, full of hard "r"s. "I co-produce the television series, *Crime Busters*, Mr. Manion," he said. "We're planning a special segment from New Orleans and I'd like to secure your services in connection with an investigation we are pursuing. Call me anytime before midnight. I work late."

The number Rubin left belonged to the Hotel St. Regis on Royal. Rubin answered, clearly drunk. "Sorry, Manion, but I seem to have been seduced . . ." A woman giggled in the background, and Rubin moaned and went on, ". . . seduced by this freaking, incredible city of yours. Could we get together tomorrow, when I'm sane? Lunch wherever you want."

2

THE LUNCHEON CROWD had just started to gather at the neighborhood restaurant known as Mandina's when Manion strolled in. He nodded to Tommy Mandina, third-generation owner of the tavern, and took a quick survey of the room. Long bar to the left. Main dining room to the right. There was a smaller room behind the bar area, but Manion found it vaguely depressing.

Following a preference passed on by the late J.J. Legendre, a cranky, cynical law enforcement veteran who had served as his mentor, he selected a table that allowed him to sit with his back to the wall.

By the time Elliott Rubin sauntered in, the tavern was alive with diners, drinkers, talkers and aproned waiters gliding gracefully through the crowd at maximum speed, carrying plates of fried trout, pork chops, chicken.

Rubin was a short, wide man wearing a black, shoulder-padded Armani jacket that made him look shorter and wider. Clean-shaven. Dirty-blond hair tied in a ponytail. Wraparound blackout sunglasses. Gold ID bracelet. Smelling of some musky aftershave. Not Manion's idea of a priority client. But his one-man detective agency, like most businesses in the country, especially in that part of the country, had not exactly been thriving. "Have a good night?" he asked Rubin.

"Ouch." The little man removed his sunglasses and parked them in his jacket's outer pocket. His eyes looked as if they belonged on Dracula's dog.

Their waiter, a big African-American named Harmon, arrived. He asked Rubin if he wanted a cocktail, causing the short man to grimace and point to Manion's cup of coffee. "That's the kind of cocktail I need," he said.

They both ordered the trout, and as soon as Harmon left them, Rubin said, "I don't know how any work gets done in this goddamn town, Manion. All everybody does is eat, drink and fuck."

"Some call *that* work," Manion said. "Depends on which side of the bed you're on."

Rubin's head rose and his red-veined eyes studied the thin, bespectacled blond sitting across from him. Then he said, "Yeah, well, like I told you, I co-produce the *Crime Busters* show. I'm sure you've seen it. We're in three hundred and sixty markets. You're cable-rich down here, so we're on maybe three times a week, one station or another."

When Manion did not reply, Rubin continued, "I produce the show with Pierre Reynaldo." He seemed disappointed that the dropped name evoked no awed reaction.

"You know who he is, right?" Rubin asked.

"Of course," Manion said. "Wears bow ties." Judging by the few times he'd seen Reynaldo in action, the glib television performer seemed a rather pestilent presence who specialized in a fast-cut sensationalism, character assassination and the trumpeting of scandal large and small.

"Yeah." Rubin gave a little chuckle. "Bow ties. Anyway . . ." He waited for Harmon to deposit a cup of coffee in front of him. "Anyway, Pierre has taken an uncommon interest in an incident that happened down here back in the Swinging Sixties."

He had a sip of the coffee and frowned. "Jesus, this is strong stuff."

"Cut it with some milk," Manion told him.

"I like it black," Rubin complained.

"You've come to the wrong city for weak black coffee," Manion said.

"The hell with the coffee. Look, back in the mid-sixties, there was this guy they called the Panther Man. Head of this cult of militants. Slipped the pipe to every broad who was in the cult. You familiar with any of this?"

"In the mid-sixties," Manion said, "I would have been seven or eight years old. I wasn't all that aware of black militants and their sexual habits."

"Gotcha," Rubin said. "I wasn't even born yet. So here's the take. This Panther Man, real name Tyrone Pano, supposedly offed his main squeeze and when they nailed him on it, he hung himself in his cell before the case could come to trial."

"So far, it sounds a little . . . historical for *Crime Busters*," Manion said.

"Maybe. But Pierre's got a nose for this stuff. The black TV audience is goddamned awesome and they get a lot of comedy crap, but not much in the way of serious material like this."

"Serious," Manion repeated.

"We're talking cults. We're talking sex and murder. And we're talking tense race relations thirty years ago that aren't that much different than they are now in this city."

Manion didn't have much to say to that. He nodded his head toward Harmon, who was waltzing their way with two fried-trout lunches.

Rubin traded his untouched coffee for a glass of iced tea and sat poised, staring at his plate. Manion watched the ponytailed man take a bite of fish. "Taste okay?" Manion asked, with only a hint of sarcasm.

"Not bad," Rubin said, as if he were making a major concession. "Now, about this Panther Man character . . ."

"Let's eat first," Manion told him. He didn't wait for the other's reaction. He didn't much care what it was.

They completed the meal without a word of conversation. When they'd finished, Rubin asked testily, "Now, can we get to business?"

Manion nodded. "What stirred up Reynaldo's interest in the Panther Man?"

"A kid, a fan of the show, sent him a letter, telling him about Pano. This kid's been studying the case in school and he raises a few interesting questions."

"Tell me about him," Manion said. "How old is he?"

Elliott Rubin looked sheepish. "His name's Louis deMay. His great-aunt was sort of a surrogate mother to Pano. And she used to talk a lot about him to the kid."

"Louis is in college?"

"Not exactly," Rubin said. "He's thirteen years old. But he's very, ah, precocious. Check this out."

He pulled a Xeroxed sheet from his inside jacket pocket and handed it to Manion. It was a neatly typed letter addressed to Pierre Reynaldo. It described a project its writer, Louis deMay, had undertaken for his junior high African-American studies course. It involved the Southern Cross, a militant organization begun in Louisiana by Tyrone Pano in the 1960s while Malcolm X was delivering his inflammatory speeches in other parts of the country.

According to Louis deMay, Pano had named his group for "the most conspicuous astronomical constellation of the southern hemisphere. The white press had bestowed the racial epithet Panther Man on Pano, but he had chosen for himself the pseudonym 'Coalsack,' the name of the dark nebula within the constellation. It was under this name that he kept a diary of his life and times."

"A little precocious," Manion agreed.

"Keep reading."

The letter went on to explain that deMay's great-aunt, Shana Washington, had been close to Pano and had been his only heir. In addition to nearly a hundred thousand dollars in various savings and loan accounts, she also received his effects. Beneath the dust jacket for a popular novel of the day, she had discovered the final volume of Coalsack's diary. Leafing through it, she saw something that surprised and pleased her. She confided it to young Louis. "What my grand-aunt Shana told me was that Tyrone Pano had written in his diary that he was merely playing the role of black militant, that he was in fact an agent of the Federal Bureau of Investigation. The Bureau had been looking into a rumor that several of the most outspoken black organizations were gathering under one banner for a major demonstration of terrorism that would shock the world. His assignment had been to discover whatever he could about the people behind this new movement. It is my thesis," Louis deMay concluded his letter, "that Tyrone Pano was murdered to keep whatever he had discovered a secret."

Rubin took back the Xeroxed letter, folded it carefully and slipped it into his jacket pocket. "Neat, huh? We got a couple angles here. First, an FBI agent working undercover goes off the deep end and kills his girlfriend. Then, the group he's infiltrating bumps him off in his jail cell and makes it look like suicide. And the Feds have to back off and play dumb."

"You weave a wondrous tale," Manion said.

"Yeah." Rubin accepted what he assumed was a compliment. "But if we're going to come on strong with an exposé that'll embarrass the FBI, we're gonna need evidence slightly more solid than Louis's memory of something his great-aunt told him. We'd like you to provide us with backup for the kid's story, Manion. Talk to people who knew Pano, who worked with him. Maybe there are still some members of the Southern Cross around." He smiled. "There's a bonus in it, if you can come up with the diary."

Manion smiled back. "Suppose it turns out Louis deMay or his great-aunt made up the story?"

Rubin leaned forward, frowning. "Why even think that?"

"If Pano was killed to keep him quiet, why didn't the world-shaking act of terrorism take place?"

"Hell," Rubin said, folding his napkin, "Pano died in nineteen sixty-five. Pick any major blast after that. The King assassination. Bobby Kennedy."

"I thought they caught those killers," Manion said.

Rubin waved a hand. "These days, people are willing to believe anything you tell 'em. Pierre can spin any connection he wants. We're not going for a goddamn Pulitzer here, just a major share of the audience."

"How'd you get my name, Elliott?" Manion asked.

"You were recommended by this guy we use on the Coast. Leo Bloodworth."

"You told him what the job was?"

"Not in so many words," Rubin said. "Leo's done a few little things for us. What we told him was that we needed a good P.I. in the New Orleans area and he recommended you." When Manion made no comment, he went on, "Think of the publicity when Pierre blows the lid off this FBI cover-up and you're named as the investigator who did the groundwork."

"It's my experience," Manion replied, "that when you screw with the FBI, they always get the last word. And that's usually in the ear of the IRS." He stood up. "Thanks for the lunch, Elliott."

The producer tossed several bills on the table and rushed after Manion. He caught up just as the detective was getting into his old Mustang convertible. "What's the deal?" he whined. "We haven't even talked money."

"How much should I ask, Elliott? What's the going rate for finding some bogus diary or turning up a ringer you and Reynaldo have planted?"

"Who's talking bogus or ringers?"

"Just because the literacy rate in Louisiana is below sea level, don't think we're all dead between the ears. Isn't Pierre Reynaldo the same guy who was going to confront the devil at a televised black mass, only the devil was a no-show? Didn't Pierre dig up a grave that was guaranteed to contain the body of Jimmy Hoffa, only to find that the carcass was a female?"

"Talk to the kid," Rubin pleaded. "If he strikes you as anything but a hundred percent legit, then I write you a check for a thousand bucks and we call it quits. But if you sign up for the full package, there's a minimum of ten grand in it for you."

Manion stared at him.

"If you need any extra grease money, we'll provide that, up to a point," Rubin said. "And, if you should stumble on the diary, there'll be a bonus of another ten grand. Whadaya say?"

"I say you give me the grand right now before I meet with Louis deMay. If I agree to go further, it'll serve as an advance on the ten thousand."

"That's copa," Rubin said, removing a snakeskin-covered checkbook from a pocket. "I appreciate your doing this, Manion. Now I can fly out of here this evening. Got this segment shooting in Tampa I want to oversee. Schoolgirl hookers. Great-looking little babes, all of 'em teenagers. High society. Terrific story."

Manion sighed and was reminded of one of J.J. Legendre's favorite truisms: "There's no such thing as a free lunch."

LOUIS DEMAY, AGE thirteen and a half, stood at a window that looked down on the cement yard surrounding the three-story brick-and-mortar building that served as the Huey P. Long Junior High School. Past the chain-link fence he could see Shoo-Bear's black Jaguar parked down the block, which meant that it was nearly time for the ten-fifteen morning recess.

Shoo-Bear would appear as if by magic just before the school bell rang, sell his crack and nickel bags of hi-ho and disappear before Louis's classmates were summoned back inside the brick building.

Louis often wondered if the teachers knew about Shoo-Bear. It seemed impossible they didn't. They probably didn't care one way or the other. Louis was not yet jaded enough to assume that they were sharing in Shoo-Bear's profits.

When he heard Mrs. Hilmette call his name, he turned from the window and entered the office of the principal, Mr. Weyman, a large black man with white hair and a white goatee, whose breath invariably smelled of Tic Tacs mixed with whiskey. Weyman pushed back from his battered and scarred desk and sighed. He indicated an open folder on the desktop and said, "We seem to have a problem here, Louis."

Louis knew what the problem was, but he responded with, "Like what, Mr. Weyman?"

"How do I inform your mother, who was one of Long's brightest students, that her son is in danger of flunking out? What's going on, boy?"

"Nothing's going on, Mr. Weyman."

"You're just tired of school, eh?"

"No, sir. I like school."

"What then? Drugs? Are you on drugs, boy?"

Louis shook his head impatiently.

Weyman scowled. "Then maybe you won't mind peeing in a bottle?"

Louis shrugged. " 'F that's what you want."

Weyman sighed again and said, "I know something's wrong. A straight-A student doesn't just turn stupid overnight."

"Maybe I got somethin' on my mind, Mr. Weyman. Soon's it's straightened out, I'll be okay again."

"Tell me about it."

"I . . . can't."

"Is it the Chops?"

Adults sure as hell followed a course, Louis thought. Drugs and gangs—the only two things a black man of thirteen and a half would worry about. "No, Mr. Weyman. I got no problem with the Chops." The Chops were a black gang that had begun in the Tchoupitoulas area and then branched out, picking up a few white members along the way. The blocks surrounding Long Junior High fell between the territory of the Chops and that of their rivals, the Olays—light-skinned blacks whose name was a diminution and a corruption of the term café au lait.

Louis's daddy had been one of the founders of the Olays when he was younger. Louis's daddy was over thirty and beyond such things now, or so the boy surmised.

Though Louis was not an official Olay, on occasion he

would wear his daddy's hand-me-down jacket, brown in the body, with tan and white stripes along the sleeves. The colors protected him from the petty bullshit that most of his classmates had to suffer at the hands of the older boys. But those same colors had a reverse effect when he walked home through Chops territory. After school, before leaving the concrete yard, he would take care to remove the jacket and bundle it up, so that only its satin lining showed.

Mr. Weyman looked at him, a boy barely five feet tall, and saw the same dullness of eye that he had seen on so many students. "Okay, Louis. You can go back to homeroom now."

Louis almost leaped from the chair. He raced for the door, but before he made it, Mr. Weyman said, "You used to be the best student in your class."

"I will be again," Louis said over his shoulder. He believed it. The principal didn't.

The rest of the school day was unbearably drawn out, if not without its distractions. A young girl cut off the left ear of another girl in the lavatory, presumably because of a boy they both fancied. The mathematics teacher gave a surprise quiz and two male students, older and bigger than the rest of the class, stood up and walked out of the room, grumbling.

The teacher, a fat, perspiring man named Flood, told the others, "Well, those fellas are just gonna get an 'F.'" And Marie Ann Brown, near the front of the class replied, "That's better than they'da got if they stayed. They'da got a 'F' minus, they so ignorant." And everybody laughed. Except for Louis. As he had told Mr. Weyman, he had something on his mind.

At three o'clock, the final bell rang and the classroom emptied immediately. In days gone by, Louis would have taken his time, plotting out his exact needs for the night's homework and stacking the nonessential books and paraphernalia neatly in his locker. That day, he led the mass exodus, pausing only as long as it took to grab a chocolate-brown schoolbag from his jumbled locker. He checked to make sure its contents were intact and slipped its straps over his shoulders until the bag rested snugly but comfortably against his back like a parachute. Then he rushed to catch the Louisiana Avenue bus.

He made it with seconds to spare and headed for an empty seat. Before he could claim it, a hand grabbed his schoolbag and jerked him back. "Don't dis your elders," a large boy said, grinning down at him from a height of at least five-ten. The large boy, who wore rimless glasses, took the empty seat. He was not much older than Louis. He removed a paperback from his pocket and smiled at Louis over it. He said, genially, "Fuck off now. Get out of my face."

Louis stood up for the twenty minutes it took the bus to arrive at St. Charles Avenue. He made sure that a streetcar was waiting and stepped backward, bumping against the tall boy's hand. He grabbed the paperback book and raced through the open bus door. The boy jumped up and followed him. He paused at the door, evidently wondering if a used paperback was worth getting off the bus and paying another fare.

The book hit him in the forehead and fell to the floor of the bus. He scowled out at Louis, who was disappearing into the Canal streetcar. "Little bastard," he shouted.

The name didn't bother Louis. He knew he wasn't a bastard. His mama and daddy were married. What worried him was how long they were going to stay married.

The streetcar rocked and clattered to a halt on Royal. Louis grabbed the safety pole and swung out through the door, bouncing down onto the neutral ground. He had all but forgotten the boy on the bus, was thinking instead about his daddy. He wished Big Louis was around, so that he could talk to him about Shoo-Bear. He felt quite sure his daddy would have gathered some of the older Olays and paid the Bear a visit, suggesting that he take his drugs on down the road. But Daddy wasn't around, not to help him with Shoo-Bear and not to tell him what to do about this thing he'd started with the TV people.

He raced across Canal and strolled down Royal into the heart of the Vieux Carré. It was three-thirty, and the tourists were still walking off their Brennan's lunches. Skirting them, Louis paused from time to time to take furtive peeks into dark, empty striptease joints that smelled of stale booze and Mackey's Pine Oil.

Barely noticing that a tall henna-haired white woman clutched her purse fearfully as he passed, Louis turned right onto Conti, moving faster now to Merchant Place, a three-block street generally unknown to the tourist trade.

Anxiety pushed him faster along the narrow street. He felt like running, but he knew better. The easiest way for a young black boy to bring the police down on him was to run full out down the streets of the French Quarter.

He could see his destination now, sandwiched between the Crescent City Finance Company and Plauche's Old Gold. The former was a syndicate front, the latter a repository for stolen merchandise, but there was no reason for Louis to take them at anything but face value. He was only interested in their neighboring building with its odd window display—a poster from the film *The Third Man*, which rested on an easel in front of a black curtain.

He hopped up the steps to the midnight blue front door and used the dull brass knocker. He waited and, when nothing seemed to be happening inside, used the knocker again.

Frowning, he stepped back. He saw movement out of the corner of his eye and turned. A big, flabby, weird-looking white dude in a red silk gown was standing in front of the Old Gold shop. In his arms was a little mutt, the ugliest Louis had ever seen. Its pink skin shone where tufts of dirty brown hair had fallen out.

"There's no one there," the man informed him.

"I ... I got an appointment," Louis replied.

"This is a protected neighborhood," the fat man warned. "You try something in this neighborhood and you're in trouble."

"I ain't gonna try nothin'," Louis said defensively.

The man said to his dog, "Tokay, you take a good look at that boy. If he does something stupid you'll have to punish him."

The dog licked his lips and seemed to stare hungrily at Louis.

Then the boy heard his name being called. A tall white man in a tan suit was walking toward him. The man was blond and thin and wore glasses. He looked like a college professor or maybe an announcer on the TV. He sure as hell didn't look like any private detective.

The owner of Plauche's Old Gold watched them both for a second, then returned to his shop with a raised eyebrow. "Sorry to keep you waiting," Manion said to the boy as he unlocked his front door.

" 'S okay," Louis deMay replied.

Manion led the way to his office, where Louis refused milk or iced tea but said yes to a Dr Pepper. While the detective poured the soft drink in his kitchenette, Louis shrugged his schoolbag from his back and placed it on Manion's desk. He undid the straps and pulled out a stack of papers. Then he hopped onto the red leather client chair.

Louis slowly drank his Dr Pepper while Manion flipped through Xeroxes of the *Times-Picayune*'s coverage of the fatal shooting of a woman named Lillian Davis, the arrest of her supposed lover and murderer, Tyrone Pano, and his eventual suicide in the cell where he was awaiting trial. There were also Xeroxed newspaper accounts pertaining to Pano's organization, the Southern Cross, including sit-ins, a disturbance at a Ku Klux Klan rally, a red-beans-and-rice charity picnic to benefit the SC.

Manion's eye was drawn to a report detailing Pano's arrest. He leaned forward in his chair.

"You see something?" Louis asked.

"One of Tyrone Pano's arresting officers," Manion said.

"Officer Legendre or Officer Guillory?"

The boy had memorized every detail, apparently.

"Legendre," Manion said.

"Tante Shana met him," the boy said. "She thought he was a weird kind of cop. Tyrone an' him gettin' on. He musta been all right, Officer Legendre."

"Yeah," Manion said, "he was that."

"You knew him?"

"He was my teacher."

"No shit?" Louis exclaimed.

"No shit."

"He was a policeman *an'* a teacher?"

"This was after he stopped being a policeman," Manion said. "He taught me how to be a detective."

"Man got hisself shot just last year," Louis said. "I looked him up in the papers at the liberry. They thought at first Officer Legendre killed himself, but they found out later somebody else shot him. You were close to him, huh?"

Manion nodded. Close enough to know the story of J.J. Legendre's death only too well.

"Maybe he kept some kinda records about Tyrone?" the boy asked hopefully.

"We'll see," Manion told him. "But first I have all this to read."

Louis nodded. "I better be goin', then," he said.

"I'll probably have a bunch of questions to ask you," Manion told him. "Could I drop by your house tomorrow after your school lets out?"

Louis hesitated. "Uh . . . I'll come here."

"If you'd rather."

The boy jumped up from his chair and awkwardly presented his hand to be shaken. Manion shook it, then saw him to the front door.

He stayed there for a minute, watching the boy make his way down Merchant Place. He was certain that Louis was not a Pierre Reynaldo ringer. And in spite of his initial skepticism, he began to wonder if there might not be something to the boy's story.

He returned to his desk and spent an hour going through Louis's notes, after which he picked up the phone and called the one person who might know some of the details concerning J.J. Legendre's involvement with the Panther Man, Tyrone Pano.

The conversation was short. A breakfast meeting was set for the following morning. Manion replaced the receiver and looked at his watch. Nearly eight o'clock in Boston. Lucille would probably be at dinner. It was too early for him to even think about eating.

He left the house, strolled to Canal and then over to the Riverwalk. He turned his back on the construction of a new casino-hotel and found an empty bench where he sat and watched the tugboats and commercial paddle wheelers moving along the Mississippi.

Once the sun had set, he drove to a revival house to see the 1940s movie *The Lady Eve*. He loved the film and knew most of its bright, witty dialogue by heart. It had never failed to amuse him. Until that night.

4

MANION WAS NOT fond of breakfast meetings, mainly because he didn't eat breakfast. He looked at the redwood picnic table and sighed. On it rested a large silver tureen filled with Scottish oatmeal, sweet cream, bowls of brown sugar, cut bananas and raisins, frosty glass pitchers containing freshly squeezed juices. One platter offered at least a dozen eggs sunny-side up, while another presented a parade of crisp bacon strips and links of tiny sausages. There were two baskets, one containing a loaf of toast, the other an assortment of sweet rolls and pastries. There were also two tall silver pots of chicory coffee at either end of the table.

The formidable display seemed at odds with its piney, out-of-doors setting, with the morning sun peeking through the trees and the gently flowing Bayou St. John murmuring a hundred yards away.

The other, considerably more eager, participants in the cholesterol-rich repast drifted his way from a nearby two-story home of antique brick and gray wood. Buddy Lapere, a short, stocky Cajun, greeted him good-naturedly, slapped his back and immediately lost himself in the task of piling food onto a plate. His partner, a thin, leather-skinned ancient named Felix, kept his salutation to a nod and opted for the oatmeal and two slices of dry toast. Both men wore suits and shirts without ties. Felix's shirt was buttoned at the neck; Buddy's was open, exposing a few inches of undershirt and a gold crucifix.

"Ain't you eatin', T-man?" Buddy asked Manion as he took a seat.

"It's a little early for food," Manion said.

Buddy frowned. "Early? It's eight-thirty. What time you gonna eat breakfast? Noon?"

"Terry was just making a joke," Felix told him solemnly. "You know how he likes his little jokes."

Next to join them was a buxom woman of some sixty-odd years with a flat, wide-eyed, elaborately made-up face. The only thing tiny about her—her nose—looked as if she'd stolen it from someone much more demure. She wore a white silk blouse, pale green slacks and matching turban. She always struck Manion as a character who might have stepped from a panel of the *Steve Canyon* comic strip. "Well, hi there, Terry," she said in her raspy smoker's voice. "It's been ages. Oh, my, are those Jones's sausages? They sure as hell look like Jones's. Stop me before I eat 'em all."

Her name was Olivette, and for several decades she'd served as secretary and assistant to Nadia Wells, the owner and operator of one of the largest investigative agencies in the South. The two men had been with Nadia for almost as long, performing many tasks from chauffeuring to bodyguarding. They were the ones who'd found Manion in a drunken stupor eight years earlier and dragged him to a private hospital on River Road, where the late Dr. Louis Farber supervised his drying out.

On what Manion called his Final Day of Atonement, Felix and Buddy had escorted him from the clinic to that very same house on Bayou St. John. He had never met Nadia Wells before. He had heard of her, of course. A former madam turned private investigator, she had not kept a low profile. But he could think of no reason why she should have interfered with him or with his drinking.

He'd felt he was entitled to stay as skunk drunk as he desired. Through no fault of his own, his seemingly blessed life had taken a downturn. His father, a banker, had committed suicide, leaving behind many bills and a clouded reputation. Manion's bride of only three months, reacting to his suddenly impoverished state, had left him cold. Alcohol provided the warmth he needed.

He'd been surly and definitely ungrateful at that first meeting with Nadia. She, with her fine-boned features and prim Laura Ashley outfit, had responded with a tongue-lashing that had shocked him, ending with a statement that if he didn't shape up, she'd forget that his father had been an old friend and have Buddy and Felix drown him in the nearby bayou.

Manion shaped up, and Nadia put him to work at the Wells Agency as an apprentice to J.J. Legendre. And when she'd felt he was ready to move out on his own, she'd fired him.

Sitting at the massive outdoor breakfast table and watching the seemingly frail but cast-iron Nadia walking toward him with a smile on her radiant face, Manion wondered again, for perhaps the thousandth time, what sort of relationship she'd had with his father. He was more or less convinced he'd never know the answer.

"Sonny," she called brightly, as he stood to kiss her cheek, "I hope this isn't too early for you. I know you like to sleep in."

"As long as I get my five hours," he told her.

She rolled her eyes, as she always did at his attempts at sarcasm. Then she turned to the food. "Well," she said, "it appears Olivette left us a couple pork saussies. Fill your plate, boy. You look like you haven't eaten in days."

She beamed at her husband, George, as he hobbled stiffly toward them. He was dressed in his usual blue blazer, gray slacks and club tie. He nodded to Manion, smiled to the others and took his chair at the head of the table.

George Wells muttered a prayer over the food and they dug in. Manion nibbled on a sweet roll and gazed in wonder as Nadia polished off two eggs, bacon, sausage and several slices of toasted homemade French bread, pausing to regale them with reminiscences of her early days in the detective business in the late 1940s.

When he'd phoned her the evening before, to tap her memory for information about J.J.'s involvement in the Tyrone Pano matter, not surprisingly, she'd replied that she knew quite a lot about it. And so he sat, waiting for the breakfast to end.

"Whatcha got on th' docker?" Buddy asked him suddenly.

"Docker?" Manion replied.

"Whatcha workin' on, T-man? I got my nights off. Maybe give ya a han'."

Nadia eyed the stocky Cajun skeptically. "This your subtle way of suggesting you're being underemployed, you ungrateful beast of bayou?"

"Whoa," Buddy whined. "Didn't mean nothin' like that, ma'am. Just thought Terry could use a little assist from a man of mah exper'ence."

"The only *exper'ence* you got," Felix drawled, "is taking orders and bustin' out at bourree."

"Who was it caught the Marigny Mauler?" Buddy replied.

"What you did was drive your car into his headfirst," Nadia snapped. "A very silly thing for a grown man to do. Not to say dangerous. And expensive. Our insurance rates are on the moon."

"Well, I caught the guy," Buddy insisted. "The *Times-Picayune* called me 'a brave passerby.' "

"But you wasn't a passerby," Felix said. "You was stationed there to follow the guy, not crash into him."

"The lady"—Buddy indicated Nadia with his big hand—"tol' me to tell the reporter I was just a passerby."

"We did a job the cops couldn't," Nadia explained to Manion. "No sense playing it up big and getting their noses out of joint." She paused, then asked, "That all you're going to have, that sweet roll?"

He nodded.

"Well then, let's us go inside for our talk."

He rose from his chair, but she was already headed up the

path to the house. Over her shoulder she said, "I'm worried about you, sonny. You don't eat enough to keep a bird alive."

She led him through the house to a small wood-paneled office with soft tan suede-covered furniture and lipstick-red filing cabinets stacked against a far wall. When she had seated herself behind her antique desk, Manion picked the nearest chair and said, "I haven't been in this room since the night you told me about J.J.'s death."

She sighed and then brightened. "This time, we're on a subject a little more upbeat. The business about J.J. and Tyrone Pano. While it didn't work out so well for Mr. Pano, our old pal often referred to that particular period as 'the best goddamned year' of his life."

TWO

New Orleans Louisiana

1965

1

J.J. LEGENDRE, GARBED in a slightly tatty black silk robe that had been a Christmas gift from long ago, sat at a weather-beaten wooden table on the second-story balcony of his Vieux Carré apartment, sipping chicory coffee and scanning the morning *Times-Picayune*.

Though only two days old, the riots in the Watts section of Los Angeles had been bumped from the *Picayune*'s front page by a story of violence that had struck closer to home. The headline read: "Meddler Slays Number Five." Accompanying it was a high school graduation portrait of an attractive young woman facing the future with a determined smile.

J.J. folded the paper and put it aside. He swallowed the dregs of his coffee and pushed his cane-back chair away from the table.

He was tall, three inches over six feet, with not much meat on his bones. His long, angular face was topped by a hairline that was receding into a widow's peak so dramatic it gave him a slightly Satanic appearance. This effect was enhanced by a thin mustache that he mistakenly thought made him resemble the actor William Powell. Mistake or not, some women found him handsome.

He yawned and stared down into a neighbor's courtyard filled with brightly hued bromeliads and white magnolias and flowers he did not recognize, glowing from the previous night's rain. It was as calm and unattended as a church on Mardi Gras Day.

He looked at his watch. Nearly nine. He tore himself away from the colors of the morning to carry his empty coffee cup and the paper into a bedroom that was monochromatic by dis-interest rather than design. The walls, originally a pale yellow, had faded to a dingy off-white. The dark finish had worn off most of the oak floor except for untrodden corners, which still held a mild gloss.

There were only two points of brightness in the room. The one of lesser interest was a framed color photograph of a Mardi Gras float paying homage to Uncle Sam, a welcome-home-from-Italy gift from a friend since deceased. The other was the golden-haired woman asleep in his bed, her body barely covered by a red nightshirt they'd discovered in his chest of drawers eight hours before.

Madeleine. He didn't think she'd told him her last name. He was good at remembering names.

He'd picked her up—or maybe it had been the other way around—at the Perdido Lounge, a Quarter hangout with a dirt floor that catered to dwarfs, off-duty call girls, upper-class pimps and drug dealers, lower-class thieves, musicians, transvestites and college students. She'd been at a table with two other women, all of them wearing black felt derbies.

Madeleine was being crowded by a doubles team—a mean-spirited midget pimp called Tidy Boy and an aging stripper named Bobbie Hope (aka "the Bobber"). J.J. had crossed their paths before.

Madeleine's eyes caught his in what he took to be an imploring gesture. He was right. She was out of her chair while he was still two strides away from the table.

Tidy Boy and Bobbie were not pleased by his interference, but they didn't make a big thing of it, a fact that impressed Madeleine. She and J.J. walked straight out of the lounge without a word being exchanged.

On the street, avoiding a puddle from the recent rain, he said, "I like the derby, but I hope you don't smoke cigars."

"A corncob pipe," she told him, and took his arm.

He steered her into Lafitte's Blacksmith Shop, a low-key bar with subdued lighting and a sound system devoted exclusively to classical music. There, with Seiber's *Sonata da Camera* not exactly wailing in the background, he discovered that Madeleine was from Mobile, Alabama, the eldest offspring of a pulp paper manufacturer. Her mother was one of the leaders of the Alabama Planned Parenthood Association and the whole large family—sons, daughters, aunts and uncles—was violently antipapist because "the nuns at a hospital gave my nephew, Jerry, too many ccs of something when he was born and turned him into a sort of large lump—very sweet, but a lump who faintly resembles Elvis."

Madeleine and her two friends had spent the early part of the evening going to parties and mocking Derby Day, a tradition of the Tulane School of Law where they were the only women in a graduating class of thirty-five.

"Getting out of law school this year," J.J. said. "That would make you . . . ?"

"Legal," she replied.

"Yes, legal," he repeated, liking her more and more. "That leaves only one other important question."

"I can't wait to hear it," she said.

"How far will I have to drive to take you home?"

"Oh, you are a smoothie," she said. "I could always catch the streetcar. They're only seven cents one way."

"Then you're an uptown girl?"

"At the moment I'm sharing an apartment on Henry Clay with a girlfriend. But she's been living with this Kappa Alpha southern gentleman for about two months and that seems to be working for her. So she isn't coming back. And, since I can't handle the rent by myself, I'm not sure where I'll be living twelve days from now."

"Find a new roommate," he suggested.

"I've discovered I sorta like living on my own. Maybe I'll just scrounge around and find a place I can afford." She grinned and shook her head. "Here I am, nattering on, and you haven't told me word one about yourself."

"What do you want to know?"

"Who you are, where you come from. The usual."

J.J. sipped his Pimm's Cup, a specialty of the house, wondering whether to lie or tell the truth. "I'm French. I was born in Bordeaux," he said, "no brothers or sisters." The truth.

"My father brought us to New Orleans when I was four years old." The truth. "I grew up in Metairie." A little lie. The Legendres had lived in the comfortable, middle-class suburb of Metairie for only one year before moving on to the lower half of a duplex shack near the Chef Menteur where his father fished the lakes for a living.

"I went to public schools." A lie. He was not about to tell a "violent antipapist" of his Catholic education.

"College?"

"LSU on the GI Bill." True.

"You were in Korea?"

"I used a fake birth certificate to enlist when I was only seventeen," he said. That part was true. But his war had been in Europe and the Philippines, quite a few years before the Korean Conflict.

"What do you do?" she asked.

"What do you think I do?"

She narrowed her eyes. "It's probably the mustache, but I'd say you were a jewel thief."

"Close," he said, and signaled for another couple of Pimm's Cups.

She was asleep on her side, curved into a "C." But when he moved closer, his shadow covered her face and she stirred. Her pale long lashes fluttered. She looked up at him, made a sleepy grimace, and asked, "Do I have to?"

He chuckled. "Stay as long as you want. We'll go to dinner at Charlie's." It was a popular steak house in the Uptown area.

"Mmmm," she said dreamily, then hugged the pillow to herself and closed her eyes again.

He went into the kitchenette and rinsed his spoon and coffee cup. Then he strolled into the other room, a combination living room–dining room–office. At his dark wooden desk, he reached down and opened its bottom right drawer. He withdrew a handgun nestled in a clip-on holster.

He hooked the device onto his belt, put on his suit coat, and went to work.

2

THOUGH HE DIDN'T feel particularly cheery, he was humming the Louis Armstrong arrangement of "Hello, Dolly!" as he strolled through the Burglary section of the Bureau of Detectives. His dark blue suit seemed too big for him everywhere but in the shoulders.

As he neared the door to the offices that Homicide shared with Robbery, he was approached by a wild-haired man with a permanently blue chin, whose wide-striped jacket made him look like a gandy dancer in search of a cakewalk. He was J.J.'s occasional partner, Marty Boyle. He sidled up to the thin cop and informed him, *sotto voce,* that Lieutenant Lamotta was looking for him. What Boyle said specifically, in his Ninth Ward accent, was, "Hey, Lejern, Lamotta's been axing for you, and not in a fren'ly way."

J.J. stopped humming. He gave Boyle a nod of thanks and entered Homicide.

It was a large space with a high ceiling. Most of the activity that day was centered around a bulletin board against the far wall, where photos and other bits of information about last night's Meddler victim were being added to the already crowded display. Like the latest addition, the others had been females, Caucasians, ages twenty-three to thirty-eight. All stabbed and mutilated and left where they died in the French Quarter.

The police had found a conjure doll wrapped in a swatch of black satin beside each body. As soon as that information had been leaked to the press, a local historian named Henry Marnet had risen to the occasion. Gleefully, he'd informed an already edgy populace that in the mid-1800s a mysterious figure known only as the Meddler had challenged New Orlean Voodoo Queen, Marie Laveau, by slaying several of her more affluent white female followers. He'd left behind just that sort of doll on black satin. The Meddler's true identity had never been discovered, but Marnet didn't really think he, or she, could still be alive.

The handful of homicide detectives who had been assigned to the newly formed Meddler Squad studied the fresh material with poker faces. One of them made a joke that broke the tension.

J.J. would have forfeited a month's pay to have been with them, but long ago he had given up the hope of ever being tapped for anything but the most routine, or the most impossible, homicides. As he headed for his desk, he asked himself once again why he continued to carry a badge. He still had no idea. November would mark his fifteenth year on the force. A decade and a half of being odd man out.

He was at his desk, draping his coat over the back of his chair, when Lamotta spotted him. The lieutenant was just under six feet, a lean, permanently tanned man with the profile, flat yellow hair and disposition of a mountain lion. He was several years younger than Legendre, a graduate of Loyola with considerably more ambition than street experience. He was carrying a manila folder in his right hand.

"You better get yourself a new alarm clock, Cajun," Lamotta said, pointing the folder at him like a weapon.

J.J. looked at him without expression. He'd once taken the trouble to explain to the lieutenant that he was not a Cajun, that he'd never spent more than a few days in the Cajun sections of Louisiana. But guys like Lamotta thought anybody with a French name and a mustache had to hail from Bayou Tech.

"What can I do for you, Lieutenant?"

"I want you and . . ." Lamotta looked right and left, then turned and shouted across the big room, "Hey, Guillory . . . get your butt over here."

Pat Guillory was in his late twenties, with thick, curly black hair and sideburns that were at least an inch lower than regulation. He had a flat, pale face, dark green eyes and a full-lipped mouth set in a permanent smirk. He responded to Lamotta's rude request by heading toward them at a pace leisurely enough to show the other detectives he was no suckass.

A yawn snuck up on J.J. before he could stifle it.

"We keeping you up, Cajun?" Lamotta asked. "Before you go beddy-bye, maybe you and Guillory can bring in Mr. Tyrone Pano and find out what he knows about a Nigra named Lillian Davis who got herself shot last night. You know who Ty-rone is, Cajun?"

"I've heard of him," J.J. answered. Pano, the militant leader of the Southern Cross, a group "dedicated to the complete and total freedom of all peoples of color by whatever means necessary," was on the news more often than the mayor.

"Then you know it's a delicate matter," Lamotta said. "Everything by the book. We wouldn't want to start any Watts deal down on Rampart."

"Yeah," Guillory said sarcastically, "like that could happen here."

"That's what they thought in L.A.," J.J. said.

"Just do it right," Lamotta ordered. He handed the folder to the tall detective. "The info's all in there. Woman he was intimate with got cut down on Burgundy. Three shots, centered in the chest. Good shootin'."

J.J. opened the folder and noted the address. He frowned. "This isn't far from where they found the Meddler's number four."

"So?" Lamotta said. "You think there's a connection between a serial killer who cuts up white women and some spade shooting?"

J.J. didn't reply. There had probably been three or four other crimes of violence in the Quarter last night. None related.

"The victim was Pano's latest pump," Lamotta said. "She musta pissed him off in some major way. Find out. Guillory's got the Panther Man's address and some of his hangouts."

"Any other suspects?" J.J. asked.

Lamotta smiled again. "It's your case. Yours and Guillory's. Find any other suspects, bring them in, too. Just like it says in the manual. Only kick things off with the Panther Man."

J.J. nodded. He grabbed his coat and started away. But Lamotta wasn't quite finished. "Don't think about this one too much, Cajun. Whenever you think too much you get yourself in trouble."

J.J. wasn't sure of the reference.

"Just bring the bastard in without frills. And Guillory, for God's sake, don't go cutting up his face with that ring of yours. The guy's lawyer'll probably send over a photographer for a head-to-toe."

Guillory nodded and grinned agreeably, like a dog that'd just been kicked but was still hungry.

J.J. headed out fast, trying to distance himself from Lamotta.

"Hey, wait up, Cajun," Guillory yelled, missing a step as he pulled the rough-edged gold ring from his finger and dropped it into his jacket pocket.

3

TYRONE PANO'S ADDRESS was a small apartment over Loretta's Gris-Gris Shop on South Rampart. He answered the door, a man not more than five feet six, but wiry, with a grizzled beard and an angry scowl that didn't jibe with his coolly passive behavior.

He wore a bright, rainbow-colored madras shirt over his pipe-cleaner-thin black chino pants. His rather dainty bare feet were partially covered by sandals with leather straps and thick rubber soles that might have been carved from an automobile tire.

He stood beside his open door and said, "Come in, Officers," with a strained courtliness. They entered a room that had been freshly painted a bright purple. Purple walls. Purple floor. White ceiling and trim. The furniture was old, but had been repainted in movie cartoon colors, too. Red chairs. A yellow coffee table. An orange book case filled with potted plants and five uniform black untitled volumes. Generic books from the Acme Company? J.J. half-expected to see Bugs Bunny or Daffy Duck sitting on the pea-green leatherette couch. Instead, he found a young white woman perched nervously on its edge.

She had light brown hair and just a touch of makeup. She was dressed in an expensive dark blue linen dress suit that the couch did nothing for.

Pano said, "This is Miss Kelly Dolwin. She's from the law firm represents me." He sat down on one of his red chairs, his small hands grasping his knees. Kelly Dolwin smiled nervously, her eyes not quite meeting theirs but resting instead on the barely used tan briefcase that lay on the yellow table in front of her.

J.J. wasn't surprised that Pano had been expecting them. He

would have someone in the department to keep him informed of such things. What surprised him was the apparent inexperience of his attorney.

"I want you gentlemen to note that my client, Mr. Pano, is meeting with you of his own volition," she said sternly. "In order to make this exchange of information as stressless as possible, he has dismissed other members of the Southern Cross, including his personal assistants."

"We're takin' him with us," Guillory said. "Hope that's okay with you, honey."

Kelly Dolwin's face reddened. "There's no need for that, Officer. Mr. Pano wishes to cooperate with you. He wants very much to provide you with whatever information he has that can assist you in your investigation of the murder of . . ."

While she was still talking, Guillory walked over to Pano and grabbed the collar of the madras shirt and yanked upward. "On your feet, Panther Boy. We're goin' over to Homicide."

Kelly Dolwin shot up from the couch, then realized she wasn't quite sure what to do next. J.J. supposed she was a year or two older than Madeleine. Maybe she'd gone to Tulane Law School, too. He wondered how Madeleine would have handled the situation. Better than Kelly Dolwin, he hoped.

"This is absolutely . . ." But she really didn't know what it absolutely was.

Pano took a somewhat more useful approach. He didn't fight Guillory; he just didn't cooperate. He slumped. The policeman had to struggle to lift him from the chair.

Kelly Dolwin reached out and grabbed Guillory's hand.

It was more than the cop had hoped. He dropped Pano onto the chair and pulled the woman to him. She struggled in his arms. "I know you weren't trying to interfere with an officer carrying out his duty," he said. "No lawyer would be that stupid. It must be somethin' else." He grinned. "You wanna get close to ol' Guillory? Well, honey, here I am." He pressed his body against hers. She struggled, panicked. He released her suddenly and she staggered backward against the couch, sat down on it and began to whimper. Guillory sat next to her and she leaped away.

"That's enough," J.J. said.

Guillory looked up at him. "Screw you, Cajun."

"You made your point. It's enough."

Guillory stared at him for a beat, then shrugged. "Sure

'nuf," he said. His hand suddenly shot out and found Kelly Dolwin's right breast, giving it a squeeze.

She shrieked and jumped from the couch, backpedaling out of his reach. Her teary eyes met Pano's. But instead of sympathy she found cold annoyance. "I . . ." she began.

He turned away from her, obviously disgusted. She fled from the apartment in tears, leaving the door open behind her. The three men listened to her high heels clicking down the stairwell.

"Aw, she forgot her nice, shiny briefcase," Guillory said. "You shoulda hired yourself a nigger lip, Panther Piss. They're used to a little terrorizin'."

"The lady was just sittin' in for my man, who's in Baton Rouge, helping out the guv'nor," Pano said, rather bored. "Mr. Kiel Nathan, maybe you heard of him." Nathan, an attorney with strong ties to the statehouse, had been successful the previous year in forcing Lamotta to dismiss two officers for extreme brutality, one of them the chief's own cousin.

"He'll be back tonight," Pano said. "Then we see who does the terrorizin', Officer Guillory."

The smile left Guillory's face. "You threatenin' me, you black sonbitch?" He drew back his fist.

J.J. stepped between the two men. "We'll take him in, like we were told," he said, leading Pano to the door.

Guillory rushed forward and kicked the door shut. "I'm questioning him first. Layin' a little groundwork."

J.J. stared at the younger officer, staying close to the black man. Guillory shifted his weight, facing J.J. now, jaw thrust out.

"You officers want to duke it out," Pano said, "I be happy to hold your coats."

J.J. raised his eyebrows at the black man. "Okay, brother," he said. "My mistake." He took a few steps backward and leaned against the purple wall.

Guillory, frowning, looked from him to Pano. Then, without warning, he drove his fist into the black man's stomach.

Pano grunted and folded simultaneously.

"Why'd you wanna kill your girlfriend, Panther Man?"

"I . . . didn't . . ." Pano replied between gasps. "Want . . . my lawyer."

"What'd you do with the gun?"

"I don't have a—"

Guillory stepped behind the black man and delivered a kidney punch. Pano straightened and made a sound like "Uhhhh."

"Screw this," J.J. said. He opened the front door, then grabbed Pano's belt and pulled him from the apartment.

"Damnit, Cajun," Guillory shouted, lumbering after them. "We can get our confession right here and now. Lamotta'll back us up."

"Lamotta'll back us till Kiel Nathan begins to complain about your unique interrogation technique. And the *Picayune* will add its ten cents. Then the story just might make the TV news. And Lamotta'll suddenly go on one of his extended fishing trips. And it'll be every man for himself."

He led Pano down the stairwell. Guillory didn't try to stop them.

THE MAN WHOM Henry Marnet and the newspapers had labeled the Meddler watched as the two policemen escorted Tyrone Pano from the building and into an unmarked black Ford sedan. From his position at the corner of Rampart and Union, where he'd been parked for nearly a half hour, he could clearly see the building with the gris-gris shop. But until the infamous Panther Man was dragged from it, the address had meant nothing to him.

His interest had been elsewhere, with the men in the car parked across Rampart, the car registered to Vieux Carré Rentals. They had murdered Lillian Davis the night before and were absolutely certain they'd made a clean getaway. But the Meddler had been there.

He'd seen it all. Sitting in his parked car on Burgundy, enjoying the night after a heavy downpour. Soaking up ions. He'd been fifteen minutes early for one of those endless, purposeless civic affairs meetings at the League for Black Advancement.

Suddenly, the door to the League's offices had opened and the woman—the morning paper had named her Lillian Davis—rushed out, dressed in some kind of multicolored, full-length nightgown and sandals. The Meddler didn't quite understand the significance of the Mardi Gras outfits the blacks were starting to wear.

The woman was followed by the pompous idiot who ran the League, Thayer Coy, a tall black man with pomaded hair like Adam Clayton Powell's. He yelled to her to take care. The French Quarter was dangerous. A homicidal maniac was on the loose!

Oh indeed he was.

For some reason, the lady was furious with Coy. Instead of paying heed to his words, she shot him the finger.

Bravo, the Meddler thought. But as much as he applauded her spirit, he realized the folly of her impetuosity. No sooner had Coy retreated in a huff inside the building than a sedan started up. It pulled abreast of the black woman. The cretinous gunman in the passenger seat placed three bullets into her body. And she'd fallen, her tentlike multicolored dress draping her like the sail from a broken mast.

It was not bad marksmanship, the Meddler had to admit, but the whole thing had annoyed him greatly. As soon as he'd laid eyes on the Davis woman, he'd selected her for himself. He felt it was time he made his statement on behalf of racial equality. But those careless thugs had punctured that balloon. He found a slip of paper in the glove compartment and he copied down the license plate number of their car.

Then he started his engine. With a dead woman lying on the sidewalk only a few yards from the League of Black Advancement there probably wouldn't be a meeting that night after all. Not with him in attendance, at any rate. His absence would not be noted. Attendance records were not kept. He drove down the empty street headed for home. But nine or ten blocks away he spotted another potential victim. This one was white, young, very attractive. And all by her lonesome.

He drove past her and quickly parked the car. In the glove compartment he carried a sharp knife and a few voodoo dolls for just such a spontaneous occasion. He got out of the car and waited for the woman to come to him.

* * *

Much later that night, his annoyance at the team of hit men was joined by curiosity. Why had the black woman been killed? Who was poaching on his territory? One phone call informed him that the sedan was owned by Vieux Carré Rentals. He convinced the night counter girl at the airport branch of Vieux Carré, a rather naive and trusting young woman, to provide him with copies of all the agency's rental contracts for the past three days.

He could have made her job easier by telling her the killers' license-plate number. But he wasn't sure where his investigation might take him. And he didn't want to have to return to kill the counter girl just because she knew precisely which of her customers had been of interest to him.

He found the killers' contract easily enough. The sedan had been rented by a Murray Lattimer from an address in Fort Lauderdale, Florida. Residing locally at the Carnival Motel on the Airline Highway.

He returned all of the contracts, thanked the dull young woman and drove immediately to the neon-bedecked red brick edifice posing as the Carnival Motel. He didn't really think that Lattimer had given the rental agency a legitimate New Orleans address. But there it was, the death sedan—parked behind the motel near an acre or more of high grass. God, was it possible that they were even using their real names? Their audacity and/or stupidity amazed him.

He'd kept watch on the car until he was confident that the two men were in for the night. Then he'd gone home.

That morning, he called his office to say that he wouldn't be in until afternoon. The secretary he hated, the one who pronounced oil "earl," informed him of a meeting he'd scheduled at eleven that day. Annoyed, he told her he'd take care of it.

His presence at the meeting was, regrettably, a necessity. That gave him barely two hours. He hated being rushed.

Armed with a thermos of coffee and a box of beignets from Café du Monde, he camped out in his car, parked on a shell shoulder along the Airline Highway a hundred yards or so from the motel.

Less than twenty minutes later, he was focusing his binoculars on a red-haired man exiting one of the units and walking toward the rental car. The redhead was lanky, in his forties, with a long nose, lifeless blue eyes and the worst teeth the Meddler had seen this side of the Atlantic.

Behind him scurried a human spider monkey. Pale face rimmed with blond downy beard. Coke-bottle glasses. And the delicate hands of a painter.

The monkey had been the trigger man, but they both shared the guilt under the law, of course. The Meddler grinned. Who was calling *whom* guilty?

The rental parked briefly at the Dixie Doughboy fast-food stop on the Airline, where the redheaded driver retrieved a Dixie Dozen and two quart cardboard containers of coffee. The Meddler shook his head sadly. These boys were definitely not natives or they wouldn't have dreamt of eating anything from Dixie Doughboy, a shop that had been exposed on WDSU-TV as having had rat feces in its ovens.

The rental's next stop was a spot across the street from Loretta's Gris-Gris, where, the Meddler was amused to note, the two hit men wolfed down their rat-shit sinkers with gusto.

The arrival of the unmarked police car did nothing to diminish their appetites. But when the two officers left with Tyrone Pano, the spider monkey got out of the sedan and brushed crumbs from his trousers while he waited for the driver to join him.

He said something to the tall redhead, who unlocked the trunk and removed an overnight bag. The spider monkey was cool and rather detached as he strolled to Pano's building. If it had not been for the driver's furtive glances up and down the street, the two men would have inspired not even a hint of curiosity. As it was, the Meddler was certain that only he, on that bright morning, was aware of their existence. He assumed that they were breaking into Pano's apartment to plant the murder weapon in some location that would be neither too obvious nor too inconspicuous for a disinterested cop to find it.

Their task took about ten minutes. When they left the building the driver carried something in his hands. It looked like a bunch of black books. They returned to the rental and drove away. The Meddler followed. He decided to have a chat with the driver, who seemed the more nervous of the two. Maybe he'd have a chat with both of them.

5

IN THE UNMARKED black police car, Guillory drove in silence, with Pano slumped on the rear seat next to J.J. The younger officer seemed to have something on his mind. Eventually, he growled, "I don't understand what the fuck you think you're doin' on the force, Cajun."

"That makes two of us," J.J. replied.

Initially, he'd believed that becoming a policeman was a smart career move. But on his first day on the job he'd discovered that a few of his fellow lawmen were more crooked than some of the criminals they were supposed to arrest. A month later, he'd concluded that it wasn't just a few; the New Orleans Police Department, from bottom to top, was thoroughly corrupt.

Corruption was what he'd been trying to avoid, and so he'd steadfastly stayed off Mafia payrolls and refused even the most accessible graft. This alone would have made his fellow officers uneasy enough, but he also decided to keep his own counsel. He did not mingle. He barely spoke with his co-workers.

The others initially disliked him, assuming his aloofness to be a criticism of their free and easy approach to the job. As time went on, they grew to distrust him, too. Conversations would stop when he entered a room. Schedules would be shifted to keep him from witnessing any serious miscarriage of justice.

His fellow officers had no way of knowing, of course, that before joining the force, J.J. Legendre had spent nearly a year on the con, selling worthless land to people with more money than sense.

Was it perversity, then, that he chose to refuse the graft? A priest might call it penance. J.J. thought of it as a form of

payback. On his final, disastrous score, he and his partner—a
beguiling son of Erin named Fran O'Fallon—had nicked the
wrong mark and then compounded the error by taking too long
to clear town. J.J. still had the tiny scars on his back from the
mark's shotgun blast. His wounds had been minor. Fallon had
taken his shot square in the face and chest. If the mark hadn't
stopped to make sure that the Irishman was dead, J.J. might
not have escaped. He saw the whole thing as a sign. Time to
change direction.

Maybe it was time again, he thought, as Guillory rounded a
corner on two wheels. The young cop's fierce green eyes were
glaring at him in the rearview. "Goddamn Cajun," he mumbled. "Don't know whose side he's on anyway."

"This isn't a ball game," J.J. said heatedly. "It's a job. We're
told to go pick the guy up, we pick him up. No sides. And I'm
not a Cajun. My family comes from Bordeaux, France."

"Oh, then that explains it."

Sensing a setup, J.J. didn't respond.

Undaunted, Guillory continued. "You're French." He waited
for a reply and when none came, he continued. "They say all
frogs got a little coon blood in 'em. That'd explain why you
feel so kindly to your brother back there."

"Let me make a wild guess," J.J. said. "You didn't exactly
graduate from grammar school did you, Guillory?"

"Fuckhead," Guillory replied, and slammed his foot on the
gas pedal.

From the corner of his eye, J.J. saw that Pano was staring at
him with curiosity.

6

IT WAS NEARLY eleven o'clock by the time the two detectives deposited Pano in the interrogation room. J.J. was surprised, but grateful, that Lieutenant Lamotta was not waiting for them.

He discovered why when he went to his desk. The lieutenant was in his glass-enclosed fishbowl of an office locked in conversation with two men. J.J. recognized them both. The plump, perspiring figure in the shiny gray suit was Jamey Fontineau, a genuine Cajun from La Place who was in charge of the Meddler investigation. Fontineau was mopping the sweat from his round, dark face and nodding in agreement to whatever the other man was saying.

That one was in his fifties, an imposing, stocky man wearing a starched seersucker suit that seemed impervious to the humidity or his hostility. His normally impassive face was crimson with anger. His name was Theodore Glander, and J.J. had first met him in the mid-fifties, when police corruption had become so pervasive that the city council felt compelled to go against the wishes of the mayor and bring in a hired gun to clean house.

They brought in Glander, a former FBI investigator who had spent the previous decade getting rid of rotten apples in police department barrels across the country. J.J. was one of the first people he called to the St. Charles Hotel room he was using as a temporary office.

"Let me tell you what I'm doing here in New Orleans," he'd said by way of introduction. "I'm a sharp, serrated knife and I'm here to cut away the rot. If that includes Police Chief Nodella and his buddy, the mayor, then so be it."

J.J. looked at the colorless middle-aged man who considered himself a sharp, serrated knife. He said nothing.

41

"Rumor is Chief Nodella hates you because you're incorruptible," Glander told him.

"I've never heard that rumor," J.J. replied. "As far as I know, the chief thinks I'm a great guy."

Glander gawked at him for a moment, then said, "I'm not going to beat around the bush, Officer Legendre. I need all the honest cops I can find and I'd like you to help me find them."

"I'm not the man for that job," J.J. said.

"Why not?"

"Because I see both sides of what you want."

"I don't understand," Glander said.

"I tell you who the honest men are," J.J. replied. "Then you put an 'X' on the guys who didn't make my list. I'm not looking for that kind of responsibility."

"Nobody wants responsibility. It's forced on them."

J.J. stood, smiling. "I'd better be going. You've got a lot of cutting to do."

"In this game, you're either on my team or you're the opposition," Glander said.

"I'm just a guy sitting in the stands," J.J. told him. "But, if it means anything, I'll be rooting for you."

Evidently, Glander must have found the helper he was seeking. By the time he was finished nearly half the force had been let go and Chief of Police Nodella had resigned, the official reason being ill health. Only the mayor seemed to have escaped Glander's knife, but he died in a boating accident shortly after a reorganization of the NOPD, so J.J. was forced to give the reformer a grade of 100 percent.

Instead of moving on to another den of bent lawmen, Glander decided to settle in New Orleans. His wife was from one of the city's oldest and wealthiest families; that had been one of the main reasons he'd taken the job—her desire to return to familiar surroundings and old friends. She didn't want to leave. And so they stayed put with their young daughter in one of the better homes in the Garden District.

Though they never spoke again, J.J. did send Glander a sympathy card when his wife passed away in 1959 and another, quite recently, when his daughter, Mrs. Lee Ann Keller, became the third victim of the Meddler.

J.J. watched Glander angrily shaking an accusing finger at Lamotta. The policeman didn't like it, but he took it because

Glander was a local hero and, possibly, because the guy's daughter had been murdered in a particularly grisly manner.

J.J.'s interest shifted from the contretemps in Lamotta's office to a stack of messages on his desk. He ignored all of them and phoned his apartment.

She answered on the third ring. "Legendre residence."

"Is this the maid?" he asked.

"No. It's only me, Madeleine DuBois, wondering how I can make biscuits without flour."

"I don't have any flour and I can't believe I've got any of the other ingredients, either."

"You have now," she said. "I went out and did some shopping. I just assumed you'd have flour. Everybody has flour."

He looked up as a man he did not recognize passed his desk headed toward Lamotta's office. He was young, late twenties, probably, conservative Terry & Juden midnight blue gabardine suit, blue button-down oxford shirt, green-and-black striped tie, black loafers. Ruddy face, clean-cut, handsome, freshly barbered brown hair. J.J. thought he walked like an athlete. Tennis, maybe. Or basketball. Not beefy enough for football.

"The last flour sack I had," J.J. told Madeleine DuBois, "the weevils ran away with it."

"You don't have any magazines, either," she complained. "If I hadn't found a little packet of letters, I would have begun to doubt you really lived here."

In Lamotta's office, Glander paused mid-rant to greet the newcomer, hugging him. J.J. supposed that made the young man his widowed son-in-law, John Keller. "What packet of letters?" he asked.

"Juicy stuff *en français*," she replied enthusiastically. "From somebody named Lulu."

"That's my cousin's little girl. In Bordeaux," he said.

"My French is a bit rusty," she replied. "But doesn't *'caresses buccales'* mean 'oral sex'?"

"No, no, no," he said. "She's saying she polishes her buckles."

"Oh, and this—*'un super baiseur'*?"

John Keller was giving Lamotta an indignant look and Glander's rage was building again. "The French word *baisse* means 'to fall,' " J.J. said into the phone, "so I suppose a rough translation would be 'a great fall.' "

She laughed, then rattled off a sentence in French so fast not even he could catch all of it. "You speak the language," he said.

"I lived in Paris for four years," she informed him. "Fortunately, I can tell a *baisse* from a *baiseur*, and tonight, after dinner, I'll be glad to demonstrate the difference."

"As eager as I am, I may be a little late," he said. "There are a few things here that require my special skills. . . ."

Lamotta opened his door. Glander, Keller, and Jamey Fontineau walked through it.

"Take your time," she told him. "I'll be here polishing my buckles."

In those days, the interrogation of a suspect was referred to as "GTT," or "Gumbo Tak Tak." The term slipped into usage during the reign of a much-loathed Cajun chief of detectives named Chenevet, who in the late 1930s had created almost a second language that the officers had been expected to use. Since his sudden death in 1943, caused by a cerebral hemorrhage (his only act that had been in any way cerebral, according to his secretary), his imposed patois had all but disappeared from the department. Except for the Gumbo Tak Tak, which was, in J.J.'s day, conducted in a closed room not far from the lockup.

In the room were a gray metal table and three gray chairs—one for the suspect, two for the detectives. The walls were white; the tile on the floor was gray.

On one wall was a large mirror. Only the dimmest suspect would have failed to realize that, on the other side of the mirror, officers and sometimes invited civilians would watch and listen to the proceedings.

That day, Guillory was alone in the observation room, sleeves rolled up, holding a phone to his ear. He saw J.J. and said, "He's here now," and replaced the receiver.

J.J. looked questioningly at the phone.

"Lamotta," Guillory said. "Looking for you. He's coming over."

J.J. stared through the one-way mirror at Tyrone Pano, slumped on his gray metal chair, alone. His head lolled forward, his chin resting on his chest. He looked as if he was sleeping.

J.J. turned and glanced at Guillory's hands. The younger cop nervously shoved them into his pockets.

"Better than sex, is it?" J.J. asked.

Guillory glared at him. He opened his mouth, but before he could form a reply, Lamotta entered the room. With him was a black plainclothes cop named Marcus Dudley. He was about six-four and no more than a hundred pounds over the NOPD weight limit. Both men looked through the mirror at Pano. "He give you guys trouble?" Lamotta asked.

J.J. looked at Guillory, who grinned and said, "Naw. He's a sweetie pie."

Dudley stared at him, unblinking. J.J. didn't know much about the black cop, except to recognize him as a fellow pariah.

"Is he unconscious?" the lieutenant inquired, staring through the glass.

"Faking," Guillory said.

"Let's get going on it," J.J. said.

"Not you, Cajun," Lamotta told him. "I got another assignment for you. Dudley'll take over this interrogation."

Guillory looked at Lamotta in utter disbelief. "Dudley takin' over? Jesus, Loot, I just assumed—"

"Assumed what, Guillory? That I'd put *you* in charge? After you grab a lawyer from Kiel Nathan's office by the tit?"

Guillory turned the glare of his green eyes on J.J. Lamotta followed his stare. "The Cajun didn't mention the broad. Nobody around here tells me shit. I gotta get the news from that smartass coon lawyer who works for Nathan."

Dudley didn't bat an eye. He'd heard the word before.

"She attacked me first," Guillory offered in his defense.

Lamotta shook his head. "Jesus, Guillory, you're pathetic. Shape up, or I'll stick your ass back in uniform and see you get a South Rampart beat."

"C'mon, Loot," Guillory whined, "I just about got the Panther Man ready to sing."

"You do what Dudley tells you, nothing more, nothing less. He's calling the shots."

Guillory mumbled something.

"What?" Lamotta asked.

"Nothing, Loot," Guillory said.

Dudley lumbered to the door and entered the interrogation room. They watched him approach Pano. "You 'wake?" he asked.

Pano's eyes fluttered open, but his chin remained pressed into his chest.

"You know this bitch got killed, Lillian Davis?"

Pano said nothing.

Dudley yanked Pano's chair out from under him as easily as if he were removing a chocolate from a candy box. Pano hit the cement with a thud. "Don' mess with me, boy," Dudley said, tossing the chair carelessly behind him. "I ask you nice, you answer. Easy or hard, it up to you."

Lamotta said, "C'mon, Cajun, you got work to do."

Walking back to his office Lamotta told J.J., "Take Boyle and go back to Pano's place and see what you can turn up."

"You booking him?" J.J. asked.

"You're doing it again, Cajun. Thinking. I haven't booked him yet. I want to book him. Therefore, I would appreciate it if you would get your Cajun butt over to his domicile and find me some evidence."

"Do I get a warrant?"

Lamotta stared at him. "Uh-huh. With any luck, it'll be on my desk when we get there. Satisfied?"

"Not often enough," J.J. replied.

7

MARTY BOYLE WAS not happy with the assignment. "This is one of them fuckin' hot potatoes," he said for the fifth or sixth time, as they approached Pano's apartment. "I don't want us to find nothing, 'cause if we find somethin', we're gonna wind up on the fuckin' stand with that fuckin' lawyer, what the fuck's his name?"

"Nathan. Kiel Nathan," J.J. answered.

"Yeah, that guy. With him makin' us look like donkeys, 'cause we ain't got no cause to be searching the guy's place."

"Judge Basile issued the warrant," J.J. said.

Boyle rolled his eyes and ran his fingers through his wild

mane. "But Judge Basile ain't gonna be on the stand facin' what's-his-name. Shit, I hate workin' with you, Lejern. Nothin' personal, it's just you get the shittiest de-tails. Christ, I can't believe I'm sayin' this, but I hope the nigger's innocent and we don't find nothin'."

It took them less than fifteen minutes to discover letters in Pano's closet indicating that the murder victim, Lillian Davis, had been blackmailing him. Ten minutes later, a cache of unused bullets turned up in an ice tray in the refrigerator, the same caliber as those recovered from the body of the dead woman.

Within the hour, the murder weapon, complete with silencer, surfaced, taped behind a dresser in the bedroom. By then, J.J. had called in a full-investigation team that was bagging and marking the various items. He'd tell Lamotta about the missing black books later.

It was evening when he arrived back at headquarters.

Lamotta was playing host to Pano and two other men. He spotted J.J. through the glass partition and waved him in.

The newcomers were Pano's lawyers. Kiel Nathan was a tall, pale man of middle age, dressed in a suit of dark blue with a white pinstripe. His hair was cut close in a Julius Caesar forward brush. His associate, James Billins, a couple of decades his junior, was a slightly shorter black man in a light gray suit, with alert brown eyes and an inappropriate twisted grin on his face. J.J. wondered whether he had suffered some sort of nerve damage or if he found the proceedings humorous.

Nathan's mood was far from giddy. "So tell me about this so-called 'evidence,' " he demanded of J.J. after their introduction.

J.J. looked at Lamotta, who nodded.

"Murder weapon, silencer, incriminating letters," J.J. said without emotion. "Also a notebook outlining a plan to place explosives near the capitol building in Baton Rouge."

Pano jumped to his feet. "You didn't find no gun in my place."

"Taped to the back of a dresser in the bedroom," J.J. said.

"Fuckin' plant!" Pano shouted.

Billins moved to him and eased him back into his chair. The lawyer's smile was gone. No nerve problem, then. "Any prints found on the gun?" he asked.

"I don't know," J.J. replied. "They're checking on that now."

"What was the nature of the letters?" Billins asked.

"There were four. I only saw one. From Lillian Davis, handwritten to your client, requesting money to keep from notifying the authorities of the plan to blow up the capitol."

"Lillian didn't send me no letters," Pano said. "We both right here in town. Why would she send me letters?"

"Please keep quiet, Tyrone," Nathan ordered, in a tone usually reserved for schoolteachers at the end of day and the end of their rope. To Lamotta, he said, "My client states that he had no gun, had no letters."

"But he ain't denying he was gonna blow up the goddamn capitol."

Pano started to reply, but Nathan fixed him with a deadly glare and he stayed quiet. "Scrawls in a notebook don't mean much," Nathan said archly, "unless you can prove my client made them and intended to use them for some criminal purpose. As for the other items, my client says they do not belong to him. Ergo, they must have been placed in his apartment without his knowledge or permission."

"If you're suggesting—" Lamotta began.

"What I am suggesting," Nathan interrupted, "is that someone must have entered my client's apartment illegally and planted the items. Now, unless you plan on charging Mr. Pano based on this ridiculous trumped-up evidence, we'll be going."

Lamotta smiled. "Not today, counselor. I got a weapon and I got motive. Your boy belongs to me."

Nathan was quiet for a few seconds, then said, "Unwise of you, Lieutenant. You've already denied Mr. Pano's civil rights by dragging him down here and abusing him physically."

"He doesn't look very abused to me," Lamotta said. "Anyway, counselor, my job is to collect evidence and to make arrests based on that evidence. That's what I'm doing now."

"If you or your thugs do any more damage to him," Nathan warned him, "you'll be the one paying the price."

Pano stared glumly at the floor. Billins put his hand on his shoulder. "We'll get bail set first thing in the morning," he said.

Pano didn't look at him. "I shouldn't be in this mess," he grumbled. "They had no cause to take me down here. You know they got the wrong man, Jimmy. You shoulda been at my place, 'stead of that dumb bitch you sent. This is your fault."

Billins's eyes flickered to his boss. Nathan said, "We'll take care of it, Tyrone. I'm sure Lieutenant Lamotta will make a special effort to insure your spending a comfortable night here."

The two lawyers exited without a backward glance.

Lamotta called for an officer to escort Pano to booking. As soon as the prisoner had been led away, Lamotta scowled at J.J. "Don't you have some work to do?"

"You were complaining earlier about people not telling you anything," J.J. said. "So I thought I'd better mention the missing books."

"So mention 'em."

"When we picked Pano up there were these books on a shelf. Small with black binding. They're not there now. Somebody had to have entered his apartment after we left."

Lamotta digested this news, then said, "You musta made a mistake."

J.J. stared at him.

"Just shut up about the books, okay?" Lamotta said.

"Then there's the salesgirl at Loretta's Gris-Gris Shop."

"What about her?" Lamotta asked warily.

"Pano's apartment is directly above the shop. She says she heard somebody up there after we took him in."

"Damnit, Cajun, who the devil told you to go stirrin' up the neighbors?"

J.J. shrugged. "Ever wonder why people don't tell you things, Lieutenant?"

"Don't red-ass me, pal," Lamotta said. "You're already on the top of my list."

"Nathan will surely be checking the gris-gris shop," J.J. said. "This way, you have an idea what he'll find."

Lamotta considered it. "Yeah. You're right. Okay, just keep quiet about the missing books. If Boyle noticed 'em, tell him to button it, too. Tomorrow, you and him spend the morning in the neighborhood. See if you can get a line on whoever might've gone into Pano's place. Not that I'm sayin' anybody did."

J.J. left Lamotta's office and strolled in the direction of Boyle's desk.

Boyle, who'd been squinting at an information sheet, looked

up and was dismayed to see that J.J. was smiling. "What the fuck now?" Boyle whined.

PRECISELY AT SUNSET, a naked lightbulb flashed on at the rear of the Carnival Motel, covering a small section of the rectangular parking lot that separated the red brick building from an acre or so of untended weeds and grass. The Meddler had already noted that the foliage had grown high—if not quite enough to reach an elephant's eye, then certainly enough to conceal the body of a man for a day or two.

He sat in his newly leased sedan, his attention focused on unit number seven. His main distraction came from an ice machine and a soft-drink dispenser that were noisily humming and crunching in an alcove, mid-building.

The Meddler had been there a while. At first, he'd kept his air-conditioner purring. But the night was certainly pleasant enough for him to give the car engine a rest and enjoy the magnolia-scented air wafting through his open driver's window.

An occasional mosquito would drift in with the breeze, but he'd always been amused rather than annoyed by the little bloodsuckers. As he'd done in his youth, he made a game of testing his hand-ear coordination. *Buzzzz. Whap.* And another bug bit the dust.

He'd rid the world of eight mosquitoes by the time the door of number seven opened with a loud clack and the redheaded driver exited carrying an empty cardboard ice bucket. His shirt was unbuttoned and draped over his pants. His bare feet slapped the cement.

The Meddler stepped from his car soundlessly. In his left

hand he carried a leather sap, New Orleans Police Department issue.

The driver bent over the ice bin and began shoveling cubes into his bucket. He was humming a song so badly that the Meddler, who prided himself on knowing just about every popular tune except that crap by the British longhairs, had no idea what it was. If only the driver would continue filling his bucket ... Ah *yesss*. The sap plowed through red hair and pounded against scalp.

Dazed, the driver started to turn. The tub of ice fell to the concrete.

Slamming the sap against the driver's forehead, the Meddler took a step to grab the unconscious body. Ice cubes crunched under his shoe and he felt himself slide forward. He regained his footing by grabbing hold of the ice bin. The driver landed on his side on the cold ice and recovered a bit. The Meddler, annoyed at his own brief awkwardness, hit the man twice more, very hard.

As thin as Lattimer was, his unconscious body was difficult to manage. The Meddler dragged him across the parking lot and into the weeds and wild grass. There, with the grass brushing his neck and face and tiny humming insects flitting by, he jammed his palm against the driver's slack mouth, using the thumb and index finger to pinch off the nostrils.

Within a few seconds, the driver began to buck, and the sap was again applied.

There'd been no artistry to it, the Meddler admitted, looking at the driver's dead body in the weeds. But in the world he had created for himself, art always took a back seat to necessity.

He was in motel room seven, closing the door behind him, before the little man who'd shot Lillian Davis looked up from the book he'd been reading and whispered, rather ingenuously, "You're not Murray."

"No, thank God," the Meddler replied.

The human spider monkey was sitting in a chair, one of Tyrone Pano's little black books open on his lap. The other books were scattered at his feet.

His hand dropped beside the chair, but not before the Meddler had his heel on the gun resting on the floor. The Meddler plucked the book from the little man's lap. It was filled with precise handwriting.

"What do you want?" the spider monkey asked in a hushed voice.

"Let's start with this," the Meddler said, indicating the book. "Good reading?"

"Sorta boring."

"Then why'd you take it from the building on Rampart?"

The little man blinked. "I, uh ... somebody hired me to pick 'em up."

"The same somebody who hired you to kill Lillian Davis?"

"I didn't kill—"

The Meddler hit him across the face with the book, putting some force behind it. The spider monkey's glasses flew from his head. "I saw you kill her," the Meddler said. "You have lousy technique."

"Wh-who are you?"

"Police."

The spider monkey stared at him and hope fluttered out of his soul. "No you're not," he said.

"Wrong again," the Meddler said. "But enough about me. We were talking about your employer."

"I don't ..."

The Meddler sighed and dropped the book back onto the spider monkey's lap. He grabbed the small man's delicate right hand and, without hesitation, broke the little finger.

The spider monkey screeched, and the Meddler had to clamp a hand over his mouth to muffle the sound. He said, "Nineteen little piggies to go. Why not cut to the wee-wee-wee and save us a lot of bother?"

The little man calmed, and the hand was removed from his mouth. His finger hurt like hell, but he didn't whimper. He stared at the Meddler, recognized the unblinking gaze of a murderer. He knew the look. Saw it every morning when he shaved. "You're going to kill me," he said. "If I tell you or if I don't, you're going to kill me."

"True," the Meddler replied. "You're history." He wiggled his fingers. "It's the relative ease with which you'll die that we're negotiating."

9

J.J. AND MADELEINE sat at a table for two in a rear corner of Charlie's Steak House. They appeared to be engaged in some weird ritual, lifting their heavy white napkins to their chins by two corners. It was a familiar sight in the restaurant, the only way to intercept the sizzling specks of butter gravy that leaped from hot pewter dishes on which rested charred filets mignons the size of softballs.

"Where do they get filets this size?" Madeleine asked. It was a question Charlie's patrons had been asking for decades.

"Voodoo," he said. "The filets are sprinkled with a powder that clouds our minds into thinking they're three times their real size."

"Ah. That must be the reason some people, like yourself, can stay thin in this city. They eat at Charlie's."

"Damn," he said, his knife slicing through the filet's dark crust and soft pink interior. "One of my best secrets exposed."

"About your other secrets . . ." she said.

He paused, the sliver of meat on his fork just inches from his mouth. She was no longer smiling. He lowered his fork and asked, "What about them?" Ready for anything.

"Lannie dropped by your apartment this evening. She was surprised to find me there."

"Umm," he replied. Lannie Dufosset was a blond and bubbly salesgirl he'd met in the housewares section of the D. H. Holmes department store.

"How old is she?"

"Almost twenty," he said, his appetite heading south.

"She told me she was glad to see you'd found somebody closer to your age. I didn't take that as a compliment. How old are you, anyway?"

The question annoyed him, but he figured she had a right to ask. "Thirty-five," he lied.

"Your neighbor, the one with the white face, says she's never seen you with a girl who wasn't young enough to be your daughter."

"A slight exaggeration," he said. "But, as you may have guessed from her face powder, she's prone to exaggeration."

"Still," Madeleine said, "men your age who prefer the company of young girls often do so because they're not interested in any sort of long-lasting relationship."

He stared at her blankly. It was true, of course. "Well ..." he began, not sure what he was going to say.

She didn't give him a chance. "I hope that's the case. Because I sure as hell don't plan on spending too much of my youth with an old fart like you. Maybe a month or two, if you keep feeding me this well." She grinned and deposited a tiny bite of filet into her mouth.

He ate, too. He was starting to relax when she asked, "Is it true what Lannie said about you?"

It was the innocent way she posed the question that put him on guard. "What'd she say?"

"That you were a goddamned NOPD cop."

Ah well. "That's true," he said. "Not the 'goddamned' part, necessarily, but—"

"Why didn't you mention it last night? You let me believe you were a jewel thief."

"You'd prefer that?"

"Jewel thieves don't bash in the skulls of black people who are just trying to get along like the rest of us."

Romance could be so difficult at times. "How many black students are there in your classes at Tulane?" he asked.

"None, but—"

"How many have been in any of your classes?"

"None, but you know—"

"Does that make you a racist?"

She didn't answer.

"Are all Negroes alike?" he asked.

"Of course not."

"Are all policemen?"

"Damnit," she said.

"Thank you," he replied. "Now can we eat?"

"What kind of police work do you do? Lannie didn't know."

"I collect the pennies from parking meters."

"Don't make fun of me," she said. "What do you do?"

He had never spoken of his occupation to the women he'd spent time with. He didn't feel it was a subject conducive to romance.

Madeleine was staring at him, eyes glistening, eager. Someone he'd known for less than twenty-four hours. Maybe it was better to slow things down right now. End them, if necessary. Clear the air. "I work Homicide," he said.

She was silent for a few seconds. Then she leaned across the table and whispered, "What's the real skinny on the Meddler?"

He laughed and his heart opened up to her. "Why aren't you eating your meat?" he asked. "Not bloody enough for you?"

Much later that night, as they lay in his bed, a faint breeze cooling their perspiring bodies, she gave a little shiver and again brought up the subject of the Meddler.

Trying to keep from his mind the photos of the Meddler's victims, he traced her profile with his fingertips and said, "If you've been reading the *Picayune*, you know as much as I do. It's not my case."

"Oh," she said, rolling closer to him, pressing against him, shoulder to ankle, "then tell me about your cases."

"They're ongoing. I don't talk about them."

"God, but you're impossible," she said, not at all angrily. "What about one of your cases that isn't ongoing. Don't hold back any gruesome details."

"Are you having any luck finding a place to live?" he asked.

"I looked at three apartments today. Fleapits, all of them. But don't change the subject. I want to hear about one of your investigations."

"There was the Praying Mantis case," he said. "A woman, the Mantis. She'd pick up a guy in a bar and bring him back to her place in the Knoll Apartments on the Avenue and literally screw him to death. She'd steal his money and valuables, drag him down to her car, drive him to some deserted street and throw him out, naked and dead."

"My God." Madeleine was silent for a moment, then moved closer to him and asked, "What did she look like?"

"Sort of like you. A natural blonde. Used a little more makeup." He ran his hand over her breasts. "Not quite as full here as you." He moved his hand further down. "Very similar here. Very, very similar."

She was breathing faster. "Are you making this up?" she whispered.

"No, indeed," he said, turning to face her, continuing to caress her.

"You are the worst liar I ever met," she said.

"True story," he insisted. "You can look it up."

"She screwed men to death?"

"Yes."

"How did you catch her?"

"I used myself as a decoy."

"Oh, come *on*."

"Policeman's honor."

"And what happened?"

"We kissed. Like this."

"Ummm."

"And then she . . ." He took her hand and placed it on his body. "And then I . . ."

"Uh . . . you . . . are . . . making . . . this . . . up. . . ."

"No, I swear I . . ."

"Shut up . . . and . . . don't . . . stop doing that . . . you bastard."

Later, she mumbled sarcastically, "Praying Mantis."

"Taught me everything I know," he said.

"Cops," she said and rolled away from him. "They don't prepare you for them in law school."

In a minute she was asleep.

J.J. eased out of the bed, threw on his tatty silk robe. He stepped onto the porch. He sat down at the wooden table and stared at the full moon until he could make out its sad-angry fat man's face. He wondered if there was any remote possibility that Tyrone Pano had actually murdered Lillian Davis.

10

BARRING HURRICANES, FLOODS, plagues and the sudden presence of a Russian submarine at the foot of Canal Street, any news that might have been deemed upsetting to tourists and potential tourists was downplayed in New Orleans. The short article briefly noting the "apparently unprovoked murder of Herman E. Barr, fifty-three, and Murray Lattimer, forty-nine, two businessmen from Fort Lauderdale, Florida," appeared on page nine of the metropolitan section of the *Times-Picayune*, dwarfed by an appropriately huge ad for Schwegmann's Giant Supermarket's specials of the day.

J.J. Legendre missed the story. If the deaths had occurred in his jurisdiction, he would have heard about them, might even have been sent by Lamotta to investigate them, since they were the sort of cases he got—confusing, hopeless and of seemingly small consequence. Instead, he and Boyle spent the morning poking around Tyrone Pano's neighborhood and turning up nothing, except for the curious fact that two other men had canvassed the area before them. Black men. They'd identified themselves as lawyers for Mr. Pano, but they'd presented no business cards. Nor had they been very precise about their names. Lincoln and James, according to some neighbors. Wilkins and Jones, according to others.

James Billins at the law offices of Nathan and Burns informed J.J. that the firm's investigation had not yet begun. "Is someone claiming to be an employee of Nathan and Burns?"

"Not in so many words. Sorry to have bothered you," J.J. said, and broke the connection before Billins's questions grew more specific.

He mentioned the fake lawyers to Lamotta.

"So?" the lieutenant asked. "They're black. Pano is black.

So maybe they're his people. So who cares? I got my case and it's tight as a drum."

"It could tear apart."

"How?" Lamotta asked.

J.J. knew better than to bring up the missing books again. He said, "If Nathan and Billins put the woman in the gris-gris shop on the stand, she'll talk about hearing somebody in Pano's place after we grabbed him. The evidence will be classified as tainted. And the evidence is all we've got."

Lamotta grinned. "We got more."

He led J.J. to the window that looked into the interrogation room. Guillory and the mountainous Marcus Dudley were questioning a tall, well-dressed black man while a poker-faced steno clicked the keys of her machine.

"His name's Thayer Coy," Lamotta told J.J. "He was with the Davis woman up till the time she was popped."

J.J. stared at Coy's dark, unlined face. "I can't say for sure that Tyrone Pano killed poor Lillian," Coy enunciated clearly, sounding more properly British, J.J. thought, than Rex Harrison in *My Fair Lady*. "All I can say is that she seemed . . . restive . . . not fearful but . . . concerned . . . distracted."

"Who is this guy?" J.J. asked.

"Another of those fucking, carpetbagging shines. He's set up shop on Burgundy. Calls his grift the League for Black Advancement, the LBA. Preaches 'peaceful demonstration.' What horseshit."

"I have no intention of speaking ill of the dead," Thayer Coy was telling a scowling Marcus Dudley, "but Lillian was not an easy person to be around. She was an angry, often vindictive woman. She could . . . drive a violent man to do something he might later regret."

"You a violent man, Mr. Coy?" Marcus wondered sleepily.

"I am a man in control of his emotions," Coy replied.

"She worked for the LBA for how long?" Marcus asked.

"Nearly a year." Coy's placid face rippled a bit. "But she was too impatient. The LBA, adhering to the teachings of Gandhi and, of course, the Reverend Martin Luther King, was moving too slowly for her. So she joined the Southern Cross and embraced the militancy of Tyrone Pano. She hath sown the wind and reaped the whirlwind."

"Jesus," Lamotta said, "what a two-bit phony asshole! But, he's *our* two-bit phony asshole."

"Has he said anything solid?"

"This guy wouldn't know solid if you hit him in the face with it. But he's black, and a leader of the community—the chief dragged me to a meeting at his place, once—and Coy thinks the Panther Man did it to the broad and that's the main thing."

"Christ, Lieutenant—"

Lamotta cut him off furiously. "Pano was planning on bombing the goddamned state capitol. Fuck him and fuck you and your friends."

"What friends?" J.J. asked.

Lamotta waved a dismissive hand. "Just get outta here and do your work, Cajun. You and Boyle got a couple new assignments. On the board."

The first assignment concerned a mid-morning knifing at Toochy's Wonder Spa, a bar on Dauphine, one block up from Canal, where the twelve customers, the three weary B-girls, the bartender, the bouncer, the fifteen-year-old sweeper and a surviving victim, who had endured twenty-two stitches without a murmur, claimed to have seen and heard nothing.

The second assignment sent the two detectives to the columned, milk-white Garden District home of a noted realtor who was convinced that his wife had tried to murder him. The man, whose age J.J. placed in the high sixties or low seventies, was dressed in dry baggy striped swim trunks and a thick yellow terry cloth robe with a crest of some sort over the top pocket. He led them down a lint-covered carpeted hall and through a dusty but bright and airy day room to a garden that was going to seed and a rectangular, emerald-green swimming pool in which swam a nutria—a large, rodentlike animal with pointed, bright yellow front teeth.

If the water had been a few inches higher, the nutria might have been able to jump to dry ground. Instead, it was having to make do with a rubber raft on which it hopped and relaxed briefly before leaping again into the drink.

The elderly man was certain his wife had purposely given the nutria access to the pool, assuming that it would attack him during his morning dip and thereby lead to his death by drowning. "Or possibly blood poisoning from a vermin bite," he added.

"Why would she do that, sir?" J.J. asked, wondering how big a part senility was playing in the man's scenario.

The realtor hesitated only briefly before replying, "Because she's a greedy little minx who's thirty years my junior. And she doesn't want to wait until my heart gives out, which could be never, the doctors tell me."

"Did she threaten you?"

"Isn't that damn rat a big enough threat?"

"Did your wife say she put the rat in your pool?" a slightly confused Boyle asked. His hair seemed even more unkempt than usual. He'd been pulling at it nervously since the old man began his story.

"My wife and I have not discussed the matter."

"Well, then—" Boyle began.

"How else would it have gotten in there, if *she* didn't do it?" the old man snapped. "It's just the two of us. We used to have servants all over this place. Servants steal from you. I shitcanned 'em all the day I sold the business. Lou—that's my wife—Lou claims she can't do all the work herself, but I say the hell she can't. She's barely forty. I worked an eighty-hour week when I was forty."

During this diatribe, the old man seemed to be noticing Boyle for the first time, taking in the mismatching of his gray sports jacket and powder blue trousers and wrinkling his nose at it. "Son," he said suddenly, "I wouldn't wear that outfit to a dogfight."

Before Boyle could react to the insult, J.J. explained that the nutria population had entered the heart of New Orleans several years before and that there had been numerous examples of their presence throughout the city. "But," he concluded, "if you are right and your wife is behind this, we'll find out. Officer Boyle will return with a net to apprehend the nutria and take it into custody. Once we get it down to the lab, we'll be able to see if it's been living in the wilds or if it's been in training to do damage. I'll give you a call later in the day with the results."

"Thank you, Officer," the old man said, grabbing his hand and pumping it in gratitude. "You've relieved my mind. But what should I do if she returns before I hear from you?"

"Play dumb," J.J. told him.

He was starting up the steps to City Hall when someone called, "Hey, you Officer Lejern?"

He knew enough not to acknowledge such a question when it was asked from behind. He continued walking.

"Hey," the man shouted. "Hey, Officer Lejern."

One of two cops walking down the front steps grinned and said, "Cajun, your cousin wants you."

J.J. turned.

A black man was standing on the sidewalk staring up at him. He resembled a very tall anvil wrapped in a green-and-white striped T-shirt and workman's khaki trousers. J.J. noted that beyond him, a Pontiac stripped to its dark gray primer was parked parallel to the curb. A small black man wearing round glasses was in the passenger seat, looking his way.

The big man's hands were hanging at his side. Relaxed. Weaponless.

J.J. descended the steps warily.

"We been waitin' here for a while for you," the big man said.

"What's up?"

"My name's Tank. That's Luther in the car. We members of the Southern Cross, you know."

J.J. stared at him blankly.

"We visited Tyrone this morning," Tank said, wincing at the memory.

"I heard he didn't make bail," J.J. said.

"He want to speak with you," Tank said.

"What about?"

"He didn't say. Just that I should tell you he want to speak with you."

It seemed as if this was going to be one of those days. "You ought to go see his lawyers about this," J.J. told the big man. "They may not want him talking to cops."

"Ac'shally," Tank said, "Tyrone sorta down on the legal profession just now. Says they screwed this whole thing up from the jump. He wants to talk with *you*."

"Speaking of lawyers, you and Luther haven't been going around telling people you're Tyrone's lawyers and asking questions?"

Tank gave him a lopsided grin. "Hey, man, we look like we could pass for lawyers?"

J.J. wondered. There was something about Tank that suggested he wasn't as slow as he pretended. "Thanks for delivering the message," the policeman said.

" 'S what we do," Tank replied.

11

"I DON'T SEE why not," Lamotta said when J.J. had told him of Pano's request. He grinned. "He's pissed at Nathan, huh? That's good. I like that. Talk to him."

J.J. was walking away when Lamotta added, "Better get fixed up with a wire. No sense trusting that Cajun memory of yours."

Pano was alone in his small cell in the lockup. He looked ill. He could barely sit up on his cot.

"What's the matter with you, Tyrone?" J.J. asked.

"Don't agree with the food here."

"What's wrong with it?"

The Panther Man smiled, then winced. "Don't trust it. Won't eat it."

"How long have you been without food?"

"Tank brung me some candy bars," Pano said. "I don't want to talk about food."

"You're clear that anything you tell me might be used against you, okay?"

Pano's forehead wrinkled in confusion, then smoothed as J.J. outlined the microphone taped under his shirt.

"Yeah. That's cool."

"Did you kill Lillian Davis?" J.J. asked.

"No, man. Not me," Pano said. "It was probably her boyfriend."

"I thought *you* were her boyfriend."

"No. That was somebody else."

"You don't know his name?"

"Nope."

"Is there anybody who can tell me more about it?"

The thin black man stared at the spot on J.J.'s chest where the mike was. He nodded his head yes. Then he said, "I don't know anything about it."

"Okay."

"I just want to make it clear I didn't do it." He leaned forward. "Got a pencil?"

J.J. patted his pockets. "No pencil or pen."

"They won't give me one," Pano said. He got to his feet and walked slowly to the dirty washbasin near the toilet at the rear of the cell. "They don't want me to have nothing to use to defend myself."

He picked up a small bar of soap and scrawled on the dirty mirror the words, "Find Sister Shana."

He looked at J.J.

"Who—" the policeman began to ask.

But Pano put a finger to his lips, winked and pointed to the name on the mirror. Then he wet his hand and smeared the writing until it was indecipherable. He wrote another word: "Coalsack." And under it: "tell Shana."

He smeared those words, too.

J.J. was confused.

"That's all I got to say to you," Pano said, walking back to his cot with difficulty and easing himself onto it.

"Two black men are snooping around, claiming to be your lawyers," J.J. said. "Any idea who they are?"

"Ask Jimmy Billins."

"I did. He says he doesn't know."

"Probably the fucking FBI. Wouldn't put it past 'em to have done Lillian in. They believe the end justifies the means."

"Unlike the members of the Southern Cross," J.J. said.

Pano shrugged.

"Anything else?" J.J. asked.

"Just that I want all my last requests to be followed to the letter."

"And that's it?"

"What else you expectin', ofay? A tip?"

J.J. started to go. Suddenly, Pano said angrily, "And tell the other officers they can beat my ass all they want, that ain't gonna get them any closer to the guy who killed Lillian. Now get the hell out of my face." He winked and grinned feebly at J.J.

J.J. nodded but did not grin back. He was too perplexed to be in a grinning mood.

* * *

Lamotta waved him into his office. With the lieutenant were Marcus Dudley and Pat Guillory, seated on Lamotta's maroon leather couch and staring at J.J. Guillory ran a hand through his oily hair and gave him a half-smile. The big black policeman looked bored.

They listened to the tape in silence.

When the noisy recording ended, Guillory roared, "What horseshit. The FBI killed Lillian Davis. Right."

Ignoring him, Dudley asked, "What was all that about his last requests?"

J.J. shrugged. "All I know is what we just heard on the tape."

"And that guff about defending himself?" Lamotta asked.

"Just what it sounded like. He's afraid."

"Of what?" Lamotta asked.

J.J. shrugged again.

Lamotta leaned back in his chair and asked, "What made you and the Panther Man such buddy-roos, Cajun?"

"I don't have any idea, unless it was because I stopped Guillory from beating on him."

"That's a goddamned lie. I wasn't beatin' on him, exactly, Loot. The bastard was smartin' off, and I was settin' him straight. Cajun, here, lets the fuckin' scum of the earth spit all over him *and the NOPD* and don't even lift a finger."

Lamotta waited for Guillory to finish, but he didn't seem to have heard anything the young cop said. "You ever meet him before?" he asked J.J., continuing his original line of thought. "I mean, before you arrested him?"

J.J.'s mind groped for an appropriately sarcastic answer. But Lamotta was staring at him so intently that he merely replied, "No. Never met him before."

"Okay, Cajun, that's all," Lamotta said. "Back to work."

Guillory stood and started for the door behind J.J.

"Stick around, Guillory," Lamotta said. "You and Dudley and me still got things to go over."

J.J. walked from the office to his desk. He turned to find all three of the men staring at him through Lamotta's partition window.

He sighed. He'd spent nearly fifteen years of his life on the force. He'd had hopes of hanging in long enough for his pension to kick in. But that possibility seemed to be growing more and more remote. He'd be lucky to last till the end of the month.

12

THE SOUTHERN CROSS was officed in a disreputable-looking pale orange brick apartment building on Basin Street, not far from St. Louis Cemetery. J.J. was relieved to see the primer-painted sedan parked in front. If Tank were there, it would simplify matters. He filled the empty space behind the Pontiac.

A name had been carved in the granite over the front door of the building at least a century before. The name was "Plagenet." J.J. knew nothing of its significance. Probably the original owner. If so, the detective doubted the late Mr. Plagenet would care for the other, less professional, carvings on the wooden front door, slogans like "Freedom For All" and "Fuck Oppression." The door was unlocked. The hall beyond it was empty of everything but dust and dirt. Except for the black scuffs of rubber-soled shoes on the floor, the building seemed unoccupied.

J.J. paused, listened. From somewhere above he heard a whirring sound and the low murmur of voices. He began to climb the shadowy stairwell.

Just before he reached the first level, a board creaked beneath his foot. A door opened and he was staring into the twin barrels of a shotgun held by a black boy who appeared to be in his late teens. Very dark skin. Shaved head under a round cap of many colors. His shirt was a pink-and-orange pullover. Black trousers. Sandals. "Whatchu want?" he asked.

"I'm here to see Tank. My name's J.J. Legendre."

The boy called out, "Latita, go tell Tank. Say his name La John."

A shadow shifted in a doorway and a girl even younger than the boy glided down the hall and through a rear passageway. J.J. stood where he was, two steps from the landing. He was in an uncomfortable, slightly bent position, but the boy looked frightened and inexperienced and he decided to remain still for as long as he could.

Latita was back almost immediately. "Tank says fo' me to bring him in."

The boy let out his breath and raised the shotgun. He nodded at J.J., who straightened and climbed the remaining steps. Latita was waiting for him. Barely over five feet. Pretty, in Levi's and some kind of lacy white top. She asked, "You a cop, right?"

"Tank knows I am."

"I don't need Tank to tell me," she said harshly. "I can see what you look like. This way."

There was a mustiness in the hall, mixed with the odor of cooked vegetables. The whirring sound grew louder. "Down here," Latita said, and led him to a closed door.

Beyond it was a large room with a bank of open windows that might once have served as a loft. Now it was a busy work space. A woman in her forties, with a cigarette dangling from her bright red lips, was standing beside a mimeograph machine. She was wearing a bright tie-dyed shirt over tight denim trousers. She'd been turning the handle of the mimeo, causing the whirring noise. Now the machine was silent, its operator staring at him. He couldn't tell if she was hostile or merely curious.

Elsewhere, a line of eight or nine black men and women, most wearing cotton shirts, tie-dyed and otherwise, were talking on the telephone. They continued their conversations, but their eyes were on him, too. And their voices dropped a decibel as he passed.

He and Latita rounded a partition and found three more men and two women at a table, dressed in what appeared to be the uniform of the day, extracting cash and checks from envelopes. They paused in their work. This time he was sure of the hostility behind their stares. Latita didn't seem to notice. "Donations," she told him, and gestured him onward.

Tank and his pal Luther were at the far end of the floor, in a newly constructed, boxlike office, watching television on a tiny set resting on a filing cabinet. On the screen, young white teenagers danced to rock and roll. Tank turned the sound down and faced J.J. "You see Tyrone?" he asked.

"Uh-huh," J.J. said. Luther reached down beside his chair and picked up a Polaroid camera. He pointed it at J.J.

"Should I smile?" the detective asked.

"Do what you want," Luther said. "I outta film anyway."

"Luther used a whole roll on me," Latita said, winking at the little man.

Tank wasn't interested in photography. "How'd Tyrone look?" he asked J.J.

"Not good. He's not eating."

Tank nodded his head. "We working on getting him out." He smiled. "Legal, I mean. Anyways, what you need?"

"Who's Sister Shana?"

"Sister who?"

"Shana?"

Tank frowned and turned to Luther. "You know any Sister Shana?"

"She a nun or something?" Luther wondered, cradling his boxy camera in both hands like an objet d'art.

"I was hoping you'd know."

Tank and Luther both shook their heads. Latita didn't seem to have heard the question.

"Tyrone has no sister?"

"Not likely," Tank said.

"What about Lillian Davis? She have any sisters?"

"She wasn't from aroun' here," Tank said. "Maybe she got family back where she comes from, wherever that be. What's this Sister Shana got to do with Tyrone?"

J.J. realized that if Tank knew nothing about Sister Shana, that was the way Tyrone wanted it. He said, "I don't know if she's got anything to do with him. It's just a name that came up. She may have some information about Lillian Davis's murder."

"She can't know nothing that'll hurt Tyrone," Tank said, " 'cause he didn't do that killin'."

J.J. tended to agree with him, but he didn't say so. Instead, he turned to Latita. "You ready to take me back?"

"Can't you find the way y'self, Mister Cop?" she asked.

"I think so," J.J. told her. "But if you'd warned me I'd be on my own, I could have dropped bread crumbs."

He headed out past the donation table with its mountains of cash. No one said a word. When the door shut behind him, he felt as if a lead weight had been removed from his chest. The boy with the shotgun did not reappear at the top of the stairs to bid him good-bye.

His car was parked not more than fifty feet from the front of the Plagenet Building, but before he could reach it, two young, well-dressed black men cut him off. "Could you walk with us, please, Officer Legendre?" the one wearing the dark brown suit asked.

"I don't think so," J.J. answered, his hand moving toward his gun.

"Please," the dark gray suit said. "We're on the same side."

"Same side of what?"

The brown suit looked up at the Plagenet Building nervously. "Not out here," he said. "Come on."

J.J. knew immediately who they were. Well groomed. Conservatively dressed. Average height. Smelling of Old Spice. Arrogant. "Shouldn't you be waving something in my face?" he asked. "Like an ID?"

"All right," dark gray suit said, "but let's keep walking."

His name was Edgar Reel. Brown suit's name was Harold White. They were agents representing the Federal Bureau of Investigation.

Their tan sedan was parked at the end of the block on the other side of the street. Before getting into the back seat, J.J. scanned the area, pausing to note a closed van a few parked cars away. That would be the observation vehicle, housing another agent or two, a tape recorder and a camera trained on the front of the Plagenet Building.

Inside the tan sedan, Agent White sat next to J.J. on the rear seat. Agent Reel was in front, twisting his upper trunk to join the discussion. Agent White asked, "Just what the hell do you think you're doing, Legendre?"

"I was about to ask you the same question."

"Don't smart-mouth us," Agent White replied, tensing up. "You're in the shitcan right now. Cooperate or we flush."

J.J. reached for the door handle. "Flush away, pal, if that's how you earn your dollar."

"Just a minute, Officer," Reel said.

J.J. paused.

"You have to understand something," Reel went on. "We don't want another Watts riot right here in this city, okay?"

"I'm with you so far," J.J. said.

"I . . . Agent White and I have been working on this for about sixteen months."

"Working on what?" J.J. asked.

White's eyes moved to his partner's, then back to J.J.'s. "We're investigating the Southern Cross for possible firearms violations, insurrection, terrorism," he said.

"And that gives you the right to go around passing yourself off as lawyers for Tyrone Pano?" J.J. asked.

"What's your deal with Pano?" White asked.

"I don't have any deal with him."

"Then what were you doing in there just now?"

J.J. shrugged. "I'm investigating the murder of Lillian Davis."

"That's finished," White said. "You got Pano."

"He may not have done it."

"We can just about guarantee that he did," White said. "We've been told that the NOPD is satisfied that Pano is guilty. Why aren't you?"

"Somebody planted a number of incriminating items in his apartment," J.J. said.

"I hope you don't think we do that sort of thing," Reel said.

"Somebody did."

"That still doesn't mean Pano's innocent," White said. "We know he's guilty."

"How?"

"None of your business," White replied testily.

"Inside man?" J.J. asked.

"We didn't say that," White responded sharply.

"Pano suggested that maybe the FBI killed the Davis woman," J.J. said.

"That little prick," White said.

"I hope you realize how absurd that charge is," Reel said. "You have the right man in jail, Officer. So, there's no reason for you to visit the Southern Cross anymore. Unless you're there for some . . . *personal* reason."

"Like what?" J.J. asked.

Reel shrugged. "It doesn't matter. Our next move is to go to Lamotta and tell him you're undermining his case while you're screwing up our investigation. Unless, of course, you behave yourself to our satisfaction."

J.J. gave them both a polite smile. It was time to mess with their heads a little. "You guys have told me the name of your inside agent," he said.

Reel blinked. White said, "Like shit . . ."

"Your agent's not inside anymore," J.J. replied.

"No?" Reel asked.

"No. If she were, you wouldn't be having this talk with me. She'd be giving you all the answers."

"You said 'she,' " Reel said, staring hard at the policeman.

"The only person I can think of who recently ended her membership in the Southern Cross is Lillian Davis."

Reel and White exchanged glances.

J.J. opened the door and stepped out.

"Hold on," White shouted, "we're not through here."

"I'm leaving before you guys screw up and tell me some *really* big secret," J.J. said. "I wouldn't want that kind of responsibility."

13

J.J. HAD JUST settled in at his desk when Boyle lumbered toward him.

"What a goddamn day," Boyle said.

"Nab that nutria?"

"Hell yeah. Had to jump into the goddamned pool, but I got the fucking rat, nutria, whatever. I felt like slippin' it down that fruitcake's skivvies."

"Give him a call," J.J. said. "Tell him we put the nutria through every test in the book. Totally harmless. His wife isn't homicidal."

"Okay," Boyle said. "But the way I see it, if she does bump him off, I'm in her corner."

J.J. waited for Boyle to leave, then unlocked his desk drawer and removed a small address book. He turned to the "W"s, found the phone number he was looking for. He dialed with one hand and used the other to replace the book and lock the drawer.

"Wells Detective Agency," a deep but feminine voice answered. J.J. gave his name and said that he wanted to speak with Nadia Wells.

There was a pause, then he heard her cool, dry voice.

He wasn't quite sure what to make of her, a handsome woman in her forties, who looked for all the world like an overprivileged, well-educated lady of taste and refinement. Some of that was true, he knew, but he also understood that at one time she had been a French Quarter madam as famous locally as Gertie Yost and Norma Wallace.

J.J.'s association had come from her current, not her former, profession. They'd met in the course of a homicide in the late fifties—the mugging and murder in the Quarter of a college boy whose wealthy Hattiesburg parents hired the Wells Agency because the NOPD seemed to be dragging its feet. J.J. had uncovered the name of a likely suspect, but it was Nadia's people who tracked the guy down in the fishing town of Grande Isle.

"Well?" she asked. "Decided to make an honest living on our side of the tracks?" In the past, when she'd offered him a job, he'd thanked her politely and said he was happy to remain as a part of the ever-vigilant NOPD. This time, he deviated from that routine.

"Maybe we should have a little talk about that some day."

"Why not now, Slim?" she asked.

"Now isn't the right time."

"Okay. Then suppose you enlighten me on why you *did* call."

He told her he wanted to find a woman named Sister Shana. Anticipating her questions, he'd sorted out in his mind exactly how much information he would disclose. Nothing about Pano nor the Lillian Davis murder. It wasn't that he distrusted Nadia. She was, however, in the information business, and he had no way of knowing if any of her clients were even peripherally touched by the Davis murder.

She surprised him by not questioning him at all. Instead, she said, "Ordinarily, J.J., the agency charges three hundred smackers a week for a Mr. Keene," a missing persons case. "But for you, a professional in the field, we'll do it for twenty-five or a lunch at some fine restaurant, whichever costs more."

"That'll be the lunch," he said. He'd dined with her before and had been astonished at the amount of food she could put into her small, thin body. "But you're still letting me off cheap. And that's not like you."

"I happen to know the lady, hon'. Our paths crossed briefly when I was still working with the girls. But she had even less heart for it than I did. When she quit, she went in the other direction. Last I heard she was at the Donlevy Mission on Constance Street."

"A vagrant?"

"Nothing like that, hon'. A sister of mercy. You see her, you give her my best."

"As long as you're on a streak," he said, "does the word 'Coalsack' mean anything to you?"

"You got me on that one. Sorry. But that doesn't let you off the hook for lunch."

"Where do you want to go?" J.J. asked.

"Oh hell. Antoine's. Arnaud's. Galatoire's. Somewhere expensive. Surprise me."

J.J. was getting ready to leave when he heard his name being called from across the room. The speaker was James Billins, Pano's erstwhile lawyer. He was scowling.

J.J. waited, unperturbed, while the man strode toward him angrily. "Officer Legendre," Billins said furiously, "I don't like being hung up on and I don't like you talking with my client without my being present."

J.J. moved his head slightly and glanced in the direction of Lieutenant Lamotta's office. He didn't want to talk to Billins or any other lawyer on the warpath without plenty of backup. "Maybe you should take this up with the Lieut—"

"You're the one who talked with Tyrone."

"Yes, but—"

"Why'd he want to talk with you?"

Lamotta was in the doorway of his office, observing them.

Great, J.J. thought. Now the bastard will assume I'm cutting a deal with Nathan. He waved his arm at Lamotta. "Lieutenant, I think Mr. Billins wants to speak with you."

Lamotta took his time crossing the room. When he arrived, he asked, "How can I help you, counselor?"

"You can tell me what my client had to say to Officer Legendre."

Lamotta smiled his lion's grin. "Since your client was present at the interview, I suggest you ask him," he said.

Billins was off balance, but he tried to recover. "If anything

Mr. Pano said will be used in court, I demand the right to know what it is."

"Counselor," Lamotta said with mock sincerity, "you know we bend over backward to cooperate with members of the legal profession. But in this case, we don't want to infringe on the rights of Mr. Pano. If it's okay with him for us to provide you with a transcript of his conversation with Officer Legendre, we will be happy to do so."

Billins teetered slightly on his feet, then did an about-face and marched from the room. "You know, Cajun," Lamotta said, placing a friendly hand on J.J.'s shoulder, "sometimes this job's got its moments."

The hand was an unconscious gesture. When the lieutenant became aware of it, he withdrew it quickly. J.J. watched him, bemused. "You don't have any work?" Lamotta asked angrily. "I sure as hell can hunt some up."

He turned and loped across the room to the water fountain. J.J. yawned and looked at his watch. It was an hour or so to quitting time, but he decided to take a short day.

14

IN THE 1830s, Irish immigrants poured into New Orleans to dig through fetid swamp, building a commercial waterway that would rival the railroad in transporting goods and machinery. When the New Basin Canal was finally completed, the Irishmen who hadn't left or perished from sunstroke, malaria or yellow fever, settled in an area that became known as the Irish Channel. It was on the edge of the Channel, on Constance Street, that the Donlevy Mission opened its leaded-glass doors to the poor and the needy.

Inside the three-story building, which had once housed the wealthy shipper Padraig Donlevy and his family, there were still touches of architectural elegance like coved ceilings and a graceful stairwell in the center of the circular entry room, leading to the two upper floors. But the paint on the ceilings was dingy and cracked, and the balustrade was scratched and gouged and missing a few newel posts.

Not that the present inhabitants cared about such things. In what had once been a huge, well-appointed living room, thirty or more welfare cases—more men than women—wandered about aimlessly or sat on dusty, stained velvet settees or formerly plush sofas. They didn't talk. Their eyes didn't seem to leave the floor.

J.J. passed them by in favor of an elderly man standing at a table. He was dressed in fresh but worn shirt and trousers. His long white hair and matching full beard were clean but slightly unruly, as if they hadn't been treated to a barber's expertise in some time. He was pouring red liquid from a clear plastic pitcher into small Dixie cups that he handed to the others as they shuffled by. He held out a cup of red to J.J.

"Maybe later," J.J. told him. "Where can I find Sister Shana?"

"Don' know no *sister* Shana. But plain ol' Shana Washington's on t'ird floah up, champ," the old man said, his voice rougher than sandpaper. " 'S where we deal with the nigras."

J.J. took the stairs quickly. The second floor was quiet, the third very active. Pregnant black women. Sick black men. Some rested on chairs, couches, the floor, their eyes closed in an unsuccessful attempt to shut out the cruel world.

Three females, wearing street clothes and nurses' caps, worked the room. J.J. correctly picked out Shana, a big woman in her late forties standing more than six feet high and carrying upward of two hundred pounds on her sturdy frame. She was examining a red and angry ragged cut on the right arm of a man whose toes showed through his shoes.

"This ain't doing you no good at all, Davis," she scolded him with a deep voice. "You gotta keep putting that salve on it or it ain't never gonna scab over and get well." She was preparing to coat the wound with an unguent, when she noticed J.J.

"Sorry, sir, but this area for colored. They fix you up downstairs."

"You Sister Shana?"

"My name's Shana Washington," she said, frowning.

J.J. said, "Tyrone asked me to come see you."

She eyed him skeptically.

"He said to tell you 'Coalsack.' "

She relaxed and rewarded him with a brief smile. "Wait just a minute and lemme do this."

She applied a clear salve to the man's wound, then covered it with a fresh bandage. As he moved away without thanking her, she said to J.J., "Come with me."

She led him to a room that might once have been a kitchen. Three ancient refrigerators stood side by side. One of them was open. A young woman was removing medicine bottles and placing them on a long table. There were other items on the table—gauze, adhesive tape, spatulas, Band-Aids. Patch-up stuff. A hospital aroma permeated the room. It was the only smell J.J. could think of that was both reassuring and nauseating.

Shana Washington moved swiftly to a long metal sink that ran almost the length of one wall. She used one of four sets of water faucets to scrub her oddly delicate hands. When she'd dried them, she said, "I hear Tyrone is in jail."

"Yes."

"What they sayin' he did?"

J.J. hesitated, then said, "The charge is murder."

"OhmahGod," she said. "That poor boy."

J.J. thought it an amusing way to describe a revolutionary firebrand.

She gave him a stern look. "I didn't know Tyrone trusted any white folks. You part of that crowd of his?"

J.J. shook his head. "No. I'm a police officer. I arrested Tyrone."

Her chin dropped. Then she began to laugh. It was the sort of laugh that rattles glassware. The other women stared at Shana in surprise. J.J. didn't imagine they heard much laughter in that place.

Shana calmed down and said, "You must be some kind of policeman, Tyrone to trust you with his secret name, Coalsack."

He shrugged.

"And I know you couldn't beat on him enough for him to send you to me, much less call me *sister*. Not many know about my sistering with the Carmelites. Tyrone's mama, Phyllis Ann, she with me in the convent way back then when we was girls with no idea what we was doing. As soon as we found out, we left the convent. If we hadn't left together, maybe we couldn't have left at all. But it wasn't our kind of life."

"Tyrone's mother passed on?" J.J. asked.

"Oh, many years ago."

Continuing to talk, she led him to the stairs. "She was my sweet best friend, Phyllis Ann. She had to be operated on, and didn't have the money for that. So I did what I had to and got all she needed." That would have been the time spent with Nadia Wells.

"The doctors fixed her, but later, when she found out Tyrone was on the way, they told her she might be having more trouble. I was studying nursing by then and put her with some very good doctors, and she had Tyrone. But her poor body paid the price. And she died when he was still a little boy. I was a qualified nurse and was making myself some fair money taking care of folks. So it only seemed right that Tyrone come to live with me. He always call me Sister, just like his mama did. And some others I knew back when."

On the second floor, she left the stairwell and turned right, down a dimly lit hall. Several doors lined both sides of the hall. The last one on the right led to Shana's living quarters, a small, neat room with a fold-down bed and a kitchenette that looked too small to hold a lady her size.

"You wait here," she told J.J.

She walked into the bathroom and shut the door behind her. J.J. observed the polished wood floor, the pictures of various saints and members of the Holy Family on the walls, all in uniform black wooden frames, a maple chest of drawers, an end table decorated by a round shiny black pot filled with water and floating magnolias that scented the air.

In the corner was a cushioned chair and a lamp. Beside it was a waist-high bookcase. Resting on the top shelf was a framed photograph of two young women seated on a bench, dressed in frilly summer dresses. One of them was Shana, twenty years younger and fifty pounds lighter. The other woman could have been her twin.

His attention moved on to the books. Most were hardbound, medical or religious. But there was a long row of black volumes similar to the ones that had disappeared from Pano's apartment.

J.J. plucked one from the shelf. He was about to open it when Shana emerged from the bathroom, clutching a white envelope. She paused, staring at the book. "That's personal," she said.

Embarrassed, he replaced it. "I'm sorry," he said.

"My diaries. I been keeping them for a long time."

"Did Tyrone keep diaries, too?" he asked.

She smiled. "I started him on it when he was a little boy."

"Any of these his?"

She hesitated, then replied, "No, sir. None of these." He suspected she wasn't being totally candid. Maybe she had one of Tyrone's diaries somewhere else in the apartment.

She handed J.J. the white envelope. It was sealed.

"He give me this a few days ago. Said for me to keep it until he comes to get it hisself or he sends somebody who'll give me the name he uses sometimes, 'Coalsack.' "

"I was wondering what the name means," J.J. said.

"I don't rightly know." She looked away. "He also told me that if I heard he passed on, I was to open the envelope and use my own judgment on what's inside."

"Any idea what it is?" J.J. asked. She shook her head. "Maybe *you*'d better hang on to it."

He held out the envelope.

"You say that's not what Tyrone wants," she said. "Fact is, as much as I love the boy, I'm glad to be rid of it, whatever it be."

"I know what you mean," J.J. said. "And not only do I *not* love the guy, I barely know him."

She smiled. "You a very strange policeman."

"So everyone seems to think," he said.

In the privacy of his car, he removed the envelope from his pocket. He felt it, judged the thickness of whatever was inside. A piece of paper. A canceled check? A folded confession to Lillian Davis's murder? "Follow my request to the letter," Tyrone had said. And, according to Shana Washington, that request was for him to hang on to the envelope until Tyrone asked for it back or wound up dead.

He returned it to his pocket, seal intact.

He started the car and pulled out into the evening traffic. No cars started up after him. The FBI evidently had more important leads to follow.

15

GATOR PLAUCHE WATCHED while Junior, his ancient, arthritic black assistant, corner-walked a stack of unsold *Racing Forms* inside the door of his Claiborne Avenue newsstand. Gator was an overweight, unkempt man in his fifties. His pale, round face had worn a scowl for at least twenty-five years that had deposited bags of flesh under the corners of his full lips. He wore a stained Pelican baseball cap that covered most of his oily gray hair and a faded plaid shirt and black pants with suspenders—a few steady customers thought it was the same shirt and pants—every day of the week except Sunday, when the stand was shuttered.

"Good day today, Mr. Gator?" Junior asked, as he had every night at eight, just before closing, for more than two decades.

"Good enough," Gator replied as he invariably did. He assumed that, by this time, Junior had realized he wasn't keeping the newsstand open for a gross profit of about twenty bucks a day. The old guy might be a couple scoops low in the smarts department, but he must have figured it out that Gator had something else going for himself. The thing that Gator liked about Junior was that he didn't seem to give a damn as long as he got his sixty bucks a week. A lack of curiosity passed for loyalty in Gator's book.

He studied the covers of a lineup of men's magazines that he kept at the rear of the shop, near the hot paperbacks—*Playboy, Nugget, Adam, Dude, Titter, Swank.* He turned his nose up at the *Playboy*. The women looked too wholesome. Wholesome didn't do it for Gator.

With a copy of the new British magazine *Penthouse* under his arm, he shuffled from the stand, locking up behind him. He turned away from the sight of Junior struggling to step up into the Claiborne bus and walked toward his car. It was a big Olds that held the heat from the sun for hours, so he was careful to park under trees whenever he could. That evening it was waiting for him half a block from the newsstand.

The car was actually cool when he entered it. And there was something strange about it. Something not usual. He settled in behind the wheel and tried to figure it out.

The smell. The car usually carried the scent of stale perspiration. It smelled of him. But in addition to that odor, Gator was sniffing a good cologne, even better than the kind he had sampled in the K & B Drug Store and always promised to buy for himself but never did.

He had just realized that the pleasant cologne odor might indicate something not so pleasant when he felt a cold, hard object pressing against the back of his neck.

"Oh Jesus, Mary and Joseph," Gator exclaimed so quickly it sounded like one word.

"Relax, Gator," a voice whispered in his ear. "This won't take long."

"Oh Lord o'mercy," Gator went on. "Wh-who are you?"

"Stu Bailey, private eye."

"Who?"

"Don't you watch TV, Gator?"

"Not if I can he'p it," Gator replied truthfully. "You on TV?"

"In a way."

"Wh-what you want with me?"

"What do you think?"

"Money. I don't have much money."

"Who needs money when you've got the latest *Penthouse* magazine?" the voice said.

"You ain't gonna hurt me, Mistah Bailey, are you?" Gator asked.

"That depends on how quickly you tell me who asked you to hire Barr and Lattimer."

"Oh sweet Jesus," Gator exclaimed, tears coming to his eyes. "I didn't have nothing to do with them boys, Mistah Bailey."

"Barr sung a different tune," the voice told him. "And considering the . . . pressure he was under, I'm inclined to believe him."

Gator realized from the size of the prod that it wasn't just the muzzle of a gun pressing against his flesh. It was bigger than that. A silencer. Who the hell was this guy Bailey who used a gun with a silencer? "Whatcha want, man?" Gator whined.

"The name."

"I mean *why*? Why you doing all this?"

The figure on the back seat hesitated. "I don't know why I'm bothering to explain," he said, "but a man follows his instincts and in this particular instance I sense an outcome that will more than repay me for my time and effort."

"If it's just money we talkin' about . . ." Gator began.

"No, you fat gob of slime," the figure said. "Money has nothing to do with it."

Gator knew better than to try to chance a glance at the rearview mirror. But he was a curious man. And the guy in the back seat wouldn't notice if he just casually were to look up and . . .

The stranger's eyes seemed to glow in the shadows and they were staring right at him. Jesus!

Gator had been in a few hard places over the years. You don't act as a middleman in contract killings without catching a little flak. The talent—he'd heard a pimp named Biloxi Bob refer to his hookers as "talent" and he thought the term so classy he used it in lieu of "shooter" or "mechanic" or whatever horseshit word the tough guys thought was cool—the talent would mess up the job and the client would be pissed. Or the client would try to renege on a final payment and the talent would get restless. But Gator always managed to calm the troubled waters because he was not without connections. People he dealt with knew that.

The problem here was that the guy sitting behind him, pressing the nose of a silenced gun to his neck, was a stranger. Gator said, "I . . . I'm protected, you know."

"By whom?"

"By the Benedetto family," Gator answered hopefully.

"Did the Benedettos order the death of Lillian Davis?" the stranger asked.

One of the things Gator's father had told him, back in the days when the old man had just opened the newsstand on money he'd made by gunning down some New Jersey reporter for the publisher of a rival paper, was that you don't answer any questions, not even if you can't see a way in the world it could get you in Dutch.

But he didn't think his father meant you should keep zipped

with a gun against your spine. "Naw. It wasn't the Benedettos."

"Who was it, then?"

Gator was silent. You didn't stay in business by fingering
your clients. On the other hand, what good is business if you
wind up with your head in your lap? It was a difficult decision.

And Gator took a few seconds too long making it. He felt
a momentary relief when the pressure of the gun left his neck.
But then the stranger whispered, "Time's up."

The tinny bang and the flash of a bright light in the closed
car nearly stopped Gator's heart. Then came the pain. Searing,
horrible, fucking incredible pain. The sonbitch had shot his
right foot, which was flapping uncontrollably against the floor-
board.

The pain wasn't staying in the foot but coursed up his leg
like a hunk of lava all the way to his right buttock. Gator was
so taken over by the shock and torture that he couldn't catch
his breath.

The stranger's voice somehow penetrated the layer of agony.
"One more foot to go."

Gator sucked in air, trying to get enough in his lungs to project his client's name past his throat.

It took him several tries, but when he finally was able to
speak the words, the stranger said, "That *is* interesting. As long
as we've broken the ice, maybe you'd like to tell me what
other little jobs you've assigned lately."

Gator wailed and whined and told. And cried out for a
painkiller.

"One painkiller, coming right up," the stranger said.

16

MADELEINE DUBOIS HAD spent most of the day viewing apartments for rent that were small, shabby and overpriced. The current offering was shabbier than most, but she hadn't quite noticed it. "Well, honey, you want the place?" the short, elderly woman in the print dress and droopy white socks asked between puffs on her Lucky Strike. "You been looking at that wall for five minutes and it ain't gonna change."

Madeleine suddenly realized that the wall was a disgusting purple and the window trim was an even more disgusting yellow. How could she have been looking at it for five minutes without seeing it? Probably because her mind had been on the night before.

She'd wanted to go to a movie, but J.J. talked her into a candlelit dinner at the Vieux Carré restaurant, not far from his apartment. That suited her; she'd been worried about their deepening relationship and she wanted to talk about it.

But the restaurant had been too damned comfortable and they'd had several bourbons and J.J. had said the most romantic things and she'd wound up staying over at his place yet another night with absolutely no conversation about their future.

He was gone when she awoke in the morning. But he'd made a trip to the little bakery down the street, and sweet rolls were waiting for her on the kitchen table, with a pot of coffee on the stove. Okay, so he was thoughtful. And rather sweet. She still could not figure out what she was doing getting involved with a homicide detective who was not only old enough to be her father but secretive and evasive. And paranoid. She noticed that he never entered a room without examining the faces of everyone present. Nor would he stay unless a table was available in a corner where he could sit with his back to the wall.

On the other hand, he was oddly handsome and, according to her limited experience, an excellent lover. But he had this thing for very young women, which was not exactly a sign of emotional maturity. Of course, if he hadn't liked young women, he would not have been interested in her. But there was young like that salesgirl, Lannie, and J.J.'s other teen bimbos. And there was young like her; *she* had a brain. But if she really had a brain, what in the world was she doing getting involved with J.J. Legendre?

"Do you want the place or not?" the landlady asked again.

"Colors are sort of strong, aren't they?"

"Mardi Gras colors," the elderly woman said. "What's wrong with Mardi Gras colors? But if you don't like 'em, change 'em. Do whatever you want, except play music or the TV after ten. Walls are too thin. My old man needs his sleep."

Madeleine thanked her for showing the room and returned to her car. Dutifully, she drew a line through the corresponding ad in the classifieds. She glanced at her watch. Nearly four.

She didn't want to spend another minute moping around. Better to do something, even if it was wrong.

The uniformed policeman at the front desk was middle-aged and balding, and he scowled as if something painful—a tooth, a joint, his back, something—perpetually bothered him. His eyes were weary and red-rimmed. He called her "ma'am."

"Just take a chair, ma'am," he said. "Officer LaJohn'll be here shortly."

The chair, metal with a Naugahyde seat, faced the desk and the moderately clean hall beyond it that led to a series of offices. She sat there for nearly fifteen minutes, during which time men and women came and went. Some stared at her. Some stared through her. Some didn't even glance her way. To kill time, she played the game of guessing which ones were plainclothes police and which were just ordinary citizens and which were crooks.

A thickset man with unruly hair and the worst clothes sense she'd ever encountered appeared beside the desk officer. Definitely a petty thief, she thought. Then the policeman at the desk pointed her way and the thickset man asked, "Hey, you Madeleine DuBois?"

She nodded.

"I'm Marty Boyle, Miz DuBois," the man said. "I work with J.J. He's tied up. Can I help?"

"It's personal," she said.

Boyle grinned. "Most of life is." He was standing in front of her now. "Is he expectin' ya?"

"Yes," she lied, and stood up. He looked at her purse. It was a bulky, black leather bag with long leather straps. "Miz DuBois," Boyle said, "you wouldn't be carryin' anything lethal in there?"

Annoyed, she opened the bag on a hairbrush, notebook, cosmetics, pills, cuticle scissors and a Moon Pie that she'd bought for lunch and forgotten. Boyle shrugged good-naturedly. "Sorry," he said, "but seein' how it's personal, I had to ask. Sometimes personal is a good thing. Sometimes, not so good."

She shut the purse. "Now that you know I'm harmless, can I see him?"

"Sure." He stepped back to let her go past the desk in front of him. "Harmless, huh? I didn't say that, now. You're too good-lookin' to be harmless."

She didn't put much importance in a compliment from a man who, if his clothes were any indication, had the taste of a Bourbon Street drag queen.

Boyle took her to the Homicide-Robbery area. "J.J.'s over deah," he said, pointing to a section of the room near the far wall. Several men were gathered at a bulletin board on which were photos of ... It was at least fifty yards away. She squinted. Oh God, the pictures were of dead women.

She averted her eyes.

Boyle was staring at her. "I'm sorry," he said. "It's the Meddler victims. We sorta operate out in the open here. I shoulda warned you."

He pulled out a chair and seated her beside J.J.'s desk.

"Is he working on that?" she asked, indicating the bulletin board with her chin.

"J.J. on the Meddler? Hmm, looks that way, don't it? You want some coffee or a Coke or somethin'?"

She shook her head.

"Jus' lemme know," Boyle said, and went to his desk.

J.J. remained in the huddle near the bulletin board. There were four others with him: a smaller man with long, neatly combed blond hair, a plump man who was perspiring through his shiny suit, an older scowling man, very smartly dressed, with sad eyes and dewlaps that gave him a bloodhound look, and a young guy who might have been in his thirties, handsome, hair cut like the late president's—full on top but neatly barbered off the neck and around the ears.

J.J. seemed to be listening while the fat, sweaty man did most of the talking. The JFK haircut shifted from one foot to the other. He was either bored or he had to go to the bathroom. Unconsciously or not, the blond man seemed to be edging J.J. out of the circle. She wished that J.J. had told her something about his work. Then maybe she could have figured out the dynamics of the scene.

Two hours earlier, J.J. had been at the main offices of the Century National Bank shaking hands with its thirty-seven-year-old president, John Caden Manion.

Manion was just over six feet tall, a dark Irishman with a winning smile and a confident air. J.J. said, "Actually, Mr. Manion . . ."

"Call me Jack, please."

"Jack. This is a simple thing. I didn't want to bother you with it."

"Nonsense. It's no bother. Come on into my office."

He ushered J.J. past several secretaries into a room of muted colors, oil paintings, thick carpet and antique furniture. One side of the space was given over to a row of floor-to-ceiling windows that provided a view of rooftops and, in the near distance, the mighty Mississippi.

Manion offered J.J. a chair beside his splendid desk. "Can I get you anything? A Jax? A gin fizz?"

"I've got to get back to work."

"A Coke, then?"

"No. Really." J.J. was feeling anxious. He'd decided to put Tyrone Pano's envelope into a bank's safety deposit box. But he wasn't sure how that worked and, since Nadia Wells had been the one who convinced him years ago to open a checking account with Century National, he'd called her to find out. He was beginning to think that had been a mistake; he was now sitting in the office of the president of the bank, killing time that he didn't have to spare.

"Nadia doesn't usually speak so highly of anyone," Jack Manion was saying. "So I wanted to meet you myself. Hope you don't mind?"

J.J. didn't want to offend the man, so he merely smiled.

"Nadia said you needed a safety deposit box. What size?"

"The smallest you have, probably," J.J. said.

"Done," Jack Manion told him. "Now on to other matters. I'm looking for a new security officer for the bank. Any interest?"

J.J. was taken completely by surprise. "I'm not sure what to say," he finally got out.

"If the answer's a definite 'no,' I can take it."

"I suppose I am interested," J.J. said. "But I'm not sure how interested."

"Think about it," Manion suggested. "The man I've got now is approaching retirement age. Personnel hasn't started a search yet. But we may have to get that in gear by the end of the month. Till then, bounce the idea around."

"You don't know anything about me," J.J. said.

"Nadia Wells says she'd like to hire you, and that's recommendation enough for me."

There ensued a brief discussion of what the new position would pay. It was more than enough to compensate for the loss of his retirement benefits from the force.

His head swimming, J.J. allowed himself to be led by Manion from the president's office down the elevator to the first subbasement, where the safety deposit boxes were located.

The bank president shook his hand heartily and placed him in the care of a small Frenchwoman of middle years named Gendron who guided him through the necessary paperwork. She buzzed him past a counter and together they walked to the room where the deposit boxes were housed. She presented him with a key, suggested he place it in a lock to the right of box number 1143. She placed a similar key in a lock to the left of the box. When both keys were turned, the long, narrow metal box was freed.

Mrs. Gendron handed it to him and showed him to a private room. Alone in the room, he removed the envelope from his coat pocket. He stared at it, toyed with temptation and, finally, dropped it into the box unopened.

He arrived back at his desk at Robbery-Homicide so focused on Jack Manion's offer that he didn't even notice that Lamotta was not alone in his office. J.J. rolled back his chair and sat staring at the folders piled on his desktop without seeing any of them.

He was speculating on the sort of work required of a bank's security officer when he heard someone clear his throat, someone standing very near his desk. He looked up at the handsome, troubled face of John Keller.

Lee Ann Keller's widower introduced himself and offered his hand. As J.J. shook it, Keller said, "My father-in-law would appreciate it if you would join us in Lieutenant Lamotta's office. We've been waiting for you."

J.J. looked in that direction. Glander and Lamotta were both staring at him through the glass partition. Grudgingly, Lamotta raised a hand and a beckoning finger.

In the office, Glander offered a nod of welcome rather than his hand. Lamotta told J.J. to sit.

"Mr. Glander was impressed by the speed with which you wrapped up the Davis killing," Lamotta said.

"Is it wrapped up?" J.J. asked.

"The lieutenant tells us you brought in the woman's killer, Tyrone Pano," Glander said.

"He hasn't been to trial yet," J.J. said. " 'Killer' may be a little premature."

"Quite right," Glander said. "But I'm not really interested in Pano. I'm interested in you."

J.J. stared back at the man and waited to hear where they were headed. After Manion's offer, anything was possible.

"My son and I"—Glander paused, gave John Keller a brief smile and corrected himself—"my son-in-law and I are a bit underwhelmed by the efforts that have been made to bring my daughter's murderer to justice. I've . . . *suggested* to Lieutenant Lamotta that you be assigned to the Meddler team. Perhaps then we might see a bit more progress."

J.J. turned to Lamotta, keeping his face innocent and his inner amusement bottled up. Lamotta stood. "Why don't we all go discuss this with Sergeant Fontineau?"

If the head of the Meddler team was unhappy at having J.J. shoved down his throat, he kept it to himself. With remarkable patience, Fontineau agreed to go over the investigation "in broad strokes," as much for Glander's benefit as for the newcomer to the team.

That briefing was winding down when J.J. noticed Madeleine sitting at his desk. Ordinarily, he'd have been furious with one of his girlfriends for entering his closely guarded professional world. Instead, he found himself sexually charged by her presence. Sitting there in her black slacks and white shirt, chewing on a pencil and studying what looked like the classified ad page, she appeared poised, cool, natural. She was more handsome than beautiful, he decided. She looked like the kind of woman who knew her way around.

J.J. had to force his eyes and his thoughts away from her and back on Jamey Fontineau's murder tour. While the perspiring cop's nasal voice droned on, J.J. began to assimilate the information, tucking away biographical facts about each of the five victims.

When Lee Ann Keller's turn came, J.J. focused his attention on Glander and Keller. The latter sat in his chair, staring at the floor with a blank expression. Glander's dark eyes were wet, but his furled brow suggested that the tears were from anger and frustration rather than sorrow.

When the meeting broke up, and Glander and Keller began to take their leave, J.J. stopped the older man.

"The department has been working hard to get this guy off the streets," he said. "My joining the team won't result in any miracles, but I thank you for your confidence."

Glander stared at him. "I tell you, Legendre, I can't remember how I filled my days before this monstrous thing happened. My wife ... was sick for a long time before she ... This is something different. It's taken over my life. I have no life. I have no family." He looked across the room and almost smiled. "Except for John, of course. If it weren't for John, I don't think revenge would be enough to keep me going."

Without another word, the older man headed for his son-in-law, who had paused by J.J.'s desk to say something to Madeleine DuBois. Whatever it was made her grin. Glander lumbered up to them.

"Cajun, when you have a minute," Lamotta yelled from the doorway to his office, distracting him.

J.J. responded to the call. Lamotta stood aside for him to enter, then shut the door. He paused a minute, staring through his glass partition. "Who the hell is the broad at your desk, Cajun?" he asked.

"A friend."

"You been around long enough to know the squad room is no place for 'friends.'"

J.J. nodded. He agreed with Lamotta. The lieutenant gave him a hard stare. "So the other shoe finally dropped, huh?"

"What other shoe?" J.J. asked, genuinely innocent.

"You and Glander, damnit!" Lamotta said, reddening. "I been wondering how long it'd take him to bring his fucking *stooge* in."

"What are you talking about?"

"You thought it was a secret who gave up Chief Nodella to Glander and his witch-hunters?"

J.J. shook his head. "Me? I gave up nobody. Not even an old thief like Nodella."

"Nodella wasn't any saint. But he treated us damn good and he deserved better than to go out in disgrace like that."

"I had nothing to do with it."

"Don't fucking lie to me, Cajun. Everybody knew Glander picked you for his snitch. You were seen with him way back when."

Suddenly, the antagonism he'd encountered all those years made sense. He felt both relieved and resentful. "It would have been nice if somebody had asked me about it to my face," he said evenly. "I never worked for Glander. I met with him. He offered me the job and I turned it down."

Lamotta scowled. "Is that the truth?"

"I said it," J.J. told him, and when Lamotta didn't seem convinced, added: "Believe what you want. It's history, anyway. Glander's been retired for a long time."

"Not exactly retired," Lamotta snapped. "His old lady may have died and left him a couple million bucks, but he keeps an office on Canal and he still carries a shield and he has lunch with the mayor once a month. With his cash and his contacts he still has more clout than you, me and the chief put together. Enough clout to get his dim-bulb son-in-law a job with Jim Garrison. Enough clout to get you on the Meddler investigation."

"If Glander's so strong, then the guy who was snitching to him all these years wouldn't still be an officer in Homicide," J.J. said. "By now, he'd probably be *your* boss."

Lamotta stared at him again. "Okay. If I owe you an apology, consider it given," he said grudgingly. "In any case, Glander's got you on the Meddler. But if he hears anything about what we're doin' before I give the okay, I'll cut your fucking heart out."

"That's sort of the Meddler's M.O., isn't it?" J.J. asked.

"Are you mocking me, Cajun?"

"No, indeed," J.J. replied. But he was smiling on the way out of the office. What the hell, he had another job on tap. And a lovely young woman waiting for him.

17

THE MEDDLER DECIDED it was time to add another victim to his list. He was not thrilled at the prospect, he told himself. He did not feel compelled to commit acts of murder. He was not insane. He could stop whenever he wanted.

But he needed at least one or two more additions to his tab before he could give the old cutlery a rest.

He sat on his favorite chocolate leather chair, feet up on the ottoman, facing a console television set. He was contemplating his next victim, what she would be like, how she would react, when something on the TV's screen caught his attention.

In an interview filmed earlier in the day, Mel Levitt, the dean of New Orleans newsmen, was questioning Chief of Police Lewis Mathern about the sudden upswing of murders in the city.

The Meddler was amused to note that Levitt had not added Herman Barr and Murray Lattimer to his gallery of recently departed, although the unfortunate Gator Plauche did make the cut.

As soon as the newsman uttered the name of Lillian Davis, the chief interrupted. "As for Miss Davis, Mel, I want to assure your listeners that we already have a prime suspect in custody. Not only that, he was picked up by the men of our Homicide Division not twenty-four hours after the vicious crime was committed."

Mathern treated his audience to a confident smile. He was as big and thoughtful and formidable as the boss of the Ponderosa, and he looked almost as good on TV as he thought he did.

"Anything new on the Meddler case?" the bespectacled Levitt asked.

90

"We're following some very promising leads, but I'm sorry, Mel, I just can't be more specific at this time."

"The Meddler has already claimed five female victims, Chief Mathern," Levitt persisted. "Naturally, people are nervous and con—"

"I don't mean this as criticism, Mel," the chief said, "but the media keeps feeding people's fears. And the publicity you give crazies like this Meddler may be one of the reasons they do the terrible things they do. Don't worry about the Meddler. He's made mistakes and we'll nab him soon. What I'm proud of, and what I'm here today to talk about, is the fact that there are fewer unsolved murders in this city at this time than there have been since before World War Two."

Chief Mathern then went on to spiel out facts and figures while the broadcast newsman stared at him stoically.

The Meddler made a circle with his thumb and forefinger and blew a raspberry through it at the chief's image. Then he grinned. "Better watch out, big boy," he said, "or they'll be saying *you're* the Meddler. I could make it happen. I've got the power."

He turned down the TV's sound so that he could use the phone. When his party answered, he said, "It's me again. Stu Bailey, Private Eye."

The voice on the other end was tense. "What do you want?"

"I want us to make beautiful murder together," the Meddler said.

"What the hell . . . ?"

"I know you hired two men to kill Lillian Davis," the Meddler said. "And by now you must realize that I killed those men."

"I don't know what you're talking about."

"Keep giving me that sort of nonsense and I'll just have to punish you myself for your sins."

"I don't know anything about any two killers," the other party whined with sudden emphasis.

"Maybe you didn't know the two men who actually did the job. Brothers Lattimer and Barr. Strictly B grade. But surely you know the go-between, the fellow who hired them for you. Poor ol' Gator Plauche. Page three of the Metro section, under the heading, 'Local News Dealer Shot to Death.' They're calling it a senseless crime, because none of Gator's money was taken. Otherwise, what would it be, a sensible crime?"

"I . . . saw the story," the other party said.

"In an effort to salvage Gator's reputation as a man of discretion, I should tell you that he held out through some rather heady torture. It was not until he realized the utter futility of keeping your name a secret that he let it escape his lips. That and a few other helpful items."

There was silence on the other end.

"Oh," the Meddler added, "I also have this interesting collection of diaries from someone who calls himself Coalsack."

"What do you want?" the voice asked from the other end of the line.

"Justice," the Meddler replied. "Of a sort."

18

AT 2 A.M., Madeleine awoke to find J.J. at his desk in the living room, scribbling in a spiral notebook. The top of the desk was covered by the contents of an open manila folder—papers, notes, photos. Bits and pieces of the Meddler puzzle.

His silk robe hung open on his thin frame like a scarf on a hook. He was wearing glasses far down on his nose and his head was angled back so that he could stare down through them at a typewritten sheet resting before him. Without moving from that position, he asked, "Did I wake you?"

"Yes," she replied.

He took off the glasses and faced her, his tired eyes taking in the shape of her body under the thin T-shirt. "I was trying to be quiet."

"You were," she said. "You've been quiet all night. I don't want quiet. I want conversation. I want to talk about us."

Several times that evening he'd sidestepped the dreaded discussion about "us." He rubbed his eyes and gave it one more try. "You remember what Louis Armstrong told the reporter who asked him to define jazz? 'If you gotta ask, you'll never know.' "

"That's the sort of evasive bullshit you delight in," she said, more frustrated than angry. "I'm not asking you to define jazz."

"I'm lousy when it comes to talking about my feelings."

"That's because you have to analyze them a bit before you talk about them. Do you know how you feel about me?"

"Not completely," he admitted. "The best I can do is tell you that you mean more to me than anyone else I know."

Slightly mollified, she said, "That's a start."

She wanted him to continue and was dismayed when he didn't. She turned to go back into the bedroom, and he said, "Talking isn't always the best thing."

"It's the way most humans communicate."

He moved from behind the desk. When he drew near her, she held up her hands to keep him away. "I'd better go," she said.

He followed her into the bedroom, not really expecting to improve the situation. It was headed downhill too fast. She grabbed her clothes and took them into the bathroom, shutting the door behind her. They'd made love only hours before, but that was then.

He began dragging on his clothes. He knew all she wanted was a few words of encouragement to ease her own uncertainty about their relationship. He considered telling her about Jack Manion's offer of a white-collar job with sensible hours and a fat paycheck and even the prospect of a safe and secure future—the things that made it so much easier to marry and start a family. But he didn't have the job, didn't know if he was going to take it, wasn't sure that it would change things all that much if he did.

He didn't want to lose her, but he couldn't lie to her, either. Maybe that was what true love was all about. You wanted someone so much you'd lie to them. Or you'd lie to yourself. And then what? Might the lie come true? There's nothing sadder, he thought, than a con man trying to con himself.

She exited the bathroom, fully dressed. Tears in her eyes.

"I'll drive you," he said.

"I've got my car." Not looking at him. Heading out.

"Then we'll take your car and I'll cab back."

"That's silly."

"No," he said. "Silly is taking unnecessary chances."

"Damn you," she screamed, wheeling on him in such full fury that he was momentarily startled. "Damn you and your *unnecessary* chances."

And she was gone, the front door of his apartment slamming behind her as a parting shot.

19

ONLY A FEW blocks from where Madeleine stormed angrily to her car, the Meddler spotted another woman rushing from an apartment building and heading down Royal Street. Most of the bars had served their last rounds, and the late patrons were straggling home or on to establishments that never slept.

The Meddler wondered what the blonde thought she was doing out alone at that time of night. One would have imagined that a young woman who so perfectly fit the specifications of his other victims would at the very least look around her as she trod upon his hunting ground. But this one seemed to have her mind on something other than her own mortality.

That was the beauty part, he thought. No woman really believed it could happen to her. It made his task so much easier.

The blonde turned down Dumaine Street. Headed for what? An apartment? A parked car? No matter. It would be a goal unattained.

He closed the distance, his rubber soles making no sound at all as he moved. In his pocket he carried a section of black silk and two dolls, one blond, one brunette. He was giving redheads a free pass. His knife was kept in a sheath on his belt, hidden by his suit coat.

He could smell the blonde's perfume, the spray on her hair. She was younger than he'd thought at first. Mid-twenties, perhaps. Solidly built. He liked a full-figured girl.

If only the street remained unoccupied for just another few minutes. Yes, it was going to happen. Just a few . . .

The girl stopped suddenly and turned to face him.

She was quite attractive. An intelligence in her eyes. She was startled at his nearness, but, taking in his disarming face and figure, she relaxed. "I'm sorry," she said. "I suddenly felt . . . I'm being silly." She smiled and awkwardly turned to continue walking.

He grabbed a fistful of her blond hair and yanked her backward, bringing the flat of his hand down against her neck so forcefully that her vocal cord popped and her knees gave way. She was barely conscious, but he kept his hand clamped over her mouth as he dragged her through the half-opened door of a poorly kept apartment building.

In the dimly lit hall, he hit the girl once more, then dropped her unconscious body to the dusty floor. He reached up and unscrewed the weak bulb, making the darkness in the hall nearly total.

He paused, kneeling beside the unconscious girl, listening. One of the tenants was watching a movie on TV. He could hear snatches of dialogue but could not identify the film. A musical, perhaps.

He looked down at the girl. She was even more beautiful in repose, all tension gone from her face. He removed the weapon from its sheath. Without hesitation, he used the razor-thin blade to cut the woman's throat.

He did not think she experienced any pain. He hoped not. He felt her pulse to make sure she was dead. Then he breathed deeply and began to use the knife to remove various parts of her body.

It took him nearly fourteen minutes, and by that time he was sweating profusely.

He put the knife and the bloody gloves into a plastic bag. He placed the blond voodoo doll, wrapped in a satin swatch, beside the woman's mutilated body and stuck the plastic bag under his coat, holding it hidden and in place between his elbow and his side.

Then he went out onto Dumaine Street.

No one noticed him.

As he approached his sedan, he began to hum a tune he'd heard the great Ella Fitzgerald singing on the car radio less than an hour before. When he realized that the song was

"Mack the Knife," he ceased humming immediately. He might have his little flaws, but being obvious was not one of them.

20

J.J. STUDIED THE pictures of the Meddler's latest victim and wondered if she really resembled Madeleine or if he was thinking about the law student so much that all women looked like her.

It had been three days, and he hadn't heard a word from her. He'd thrown himself into the Meddler investigation, spending much of his free time going over the folders of each of the victims. The newest, number six, was named Loretta Sprague. Beaten, murdered and disemboweled in the lobby of an apartment building just blocks from his own residence.

In life she'd been a single white female, born in New Orleans twenty-five years before, a natural blonde, standing five feet seven inches, weighing one hundred and forty-two pounds. A Catholic, a graduate of Sacred Heart Academy and Loyola University, employed for the past three years by Lemir and Bosatty, the ad agency responsible for the "Save the Quarter for a Dollar" fund-raising campaign to clean up sections of the French Quarter. Father deceased. Mother living in Gentilly with the victim's seventeen-year-old sister.

Loretta Sprague had been engaged to a young man named Raymond Boudreaux, whose background had been probed extensively by other members of the squad. J.J. was going through Boudreaux's folder when Jamey Fontineau paused beside his desk.

"You been workin' them files pretty good," the perspiring man said. "Up to date yet?"

"Just about."

"Good. I got a special assignment for you. Go talk to this

guy." He handed J.J. an embossed card that read, "Henry Marnet, author-historian." There was a phone number and an address on Octavia Street.

J.J. frowned. "What's it about?"

"Guy claims he's got some information about the Meddler we should know," Fontineau said. He could barely keep from snickering.

"He's the guy who named the Meddler, isn't he?"

Fontineau nodded. "Yeah. I think that's part of what's on his mind. I couldn't exactly follow what he was tellin' me on the phone. He speaks kinda fast."

"This is sort of a fool's errand, huh?" J.J. asked.

"Sort of. But we gotta keep this Marnet happy on account of he's good friends with a friend of the chief."

"And who would that be?" J.J. asked.

"Theodore Glander." Fontineau gave him a Cheshire grin. "That's what made me think of you, Legendre."

Henry Marnet's residence on Octavia Street was a single shotgun dwelling fronted by three columns. It was at least a decade overdue on a new paint job. The short iron fence that separated the house and its cement yard from the sidewalk was rusted. The front gate was nowhere to be seen.

Walking up the creaking steps to the small porch, J.J. noticed that one side of the center column had fallen off, exposing rotting lumber underneath. He wondered what that said about the rest of the house.

He pressed the doorbell, heard it ring inside and waited. No sound from within. But fifteen minutes before, on the phone, Marnet had seemed eager for his visit. It was unlikely that the man would have just gone off. . . .

"Ah, Officer Legendre?"

The pseudo-British accent was the same he'd heard on the phone. He turned to see Marnet, a rather ordinary-looking man in his thirties, passing through his gateless fence. He wore his gray hair long. His rimless glasses seemed to be wired to his thin face. His nose and lips were too large for the rest of his features. He was carrying a purple paper bag in one pale hand, an umbrella in the other. It didn't look much like rain.

"Sorry," he said. "I just stopped off at K & B for a pint of ice cream for us."

J.J. smiled. Marnet was not interested in shaking hands and that was fine with him.

The historian unlocked his front door, and they entered a hall littered with stacks of magazines and newspapers. "Research, Officer Legendre, research," Marnet told him.

Their destination was a dingy dining room dominated by a dark table with a round top that was covered with opened volumes, dirty dishes and glasses, cans of film and boxes of audio tape.

"Please take a chair, Officer," Marnet said. He piled up the dishes and juggled them and the purple bag into the kitchen.

J.J. surveyed his surroundings. An ancient sideboard and a cabinet, both of the same ugly dark wood as the table. On the walls were etchings and lithographs and paintings. Many of them seemed to be of the same light-skinned black woman, her hair covered by a colorful bandanna.

He was still studying the pictures when Marnet returned with two gobs of ice cream in chipped china bowls. "Ah, the divine Queen," he said, aiming his pointy chin at the lithographs.

"Beg your pardon?"

"Marie Laveau, queen of all the voodoos," Marnet said. "Although I do believe the particular litho before you may be of her daughter, Marie the Second. She was almost identical to her mother, a fact that both of them used to great advantage in perpetuating the Laveau mystique. They would appear simultaneously at locations miles apart, making it seem as if Marie could be in two places at the same time."

"You seem quite taken with the ladies," J.J. said, indicating all the portraits.

"I was only sixteen when I lost my heart to her," Henry Marnet said. "I've written one book about her and probably will write at least one more. So she definitely has me in thrall. Please, join me."

J.J. took a seat at the table across from the historian. Marnet provided him with a tarnished silver spoon for the ice cream.

"You mentioned some information you had that might help us find the Meddler," J.J. prompted.

"Try some of the ice cream. It's delicious."

J.J. poked at the melting mound, sampled it suspiciously. It had an odd, sour taste. "Is this vanilla?"

"No, no, no. It's a favorite of mine. Cream cheese. An acquired taste. I hope you like it."

"It's . . . different," J.J. told him. "Mr. Marnet, I'll have to be getting back to headquarters soon, so . . ."

"Of course." Marnet stood and walked to the corner of the room. He picked up a sheaf of papers and brought them to the table. Sitting again, he said, "These are copies of records kept by Parish prison back at the turn of the nineteenth century. Have you heard of the murderers Jean Adam, Anthony Deslisle and Philippe Swan?"

"From the eighteen-fifties?" J.J. asked. "No. Our lists are slightly more current."

"There were public executions in those days. Anyway, by then the divine Marie had renounced Satan and all his blandishments and begun a life of ... restitution. She visited the condemned prisoners, brought them food and prayer. She even built a small chapel for them."

J.J. found the cream cheese winning him over. He scooped it up, hoping it would have as little effect on his digestion as Marnet's history lesson would have on the Meddler investigation.

"When it came time for Adam, Deslisle and Swan to pay for their crimes, they were led out to the gallows," the historian informed him. "Adam's hood was in place, the noose circled his neck, but ... the trap refused to open. Adam was led away and a carpenter was summoned to test the trap. It worked perfectly, so Deslisle's turn came. Again, the trap jammed. The assembled crowd thought they knew why—Marie Laveau had put her *gris-gris* on the gallows."

J.J. had finished the ice cream. He smiled at Marnet and said, "That's pretty amazing, but I'm not sure—"

"Allow me just a few more minutes, Officer," Marnet said. "I'll make my point. The third murderer, Philippe Swan, had killed a number of women with a knife. Sound familiar?"

J.J. nodded.

"When Swan stepped up to the gallows, the crowd was expecting a repeat of the first two attempts. But this time the trap opened smoothly and Swan dangled at the end of the rope and paid for his crimes." Marnet's bland face seemed to be glowing red. "And here's my discovery, Officer Legendre. The Meddler began his murders the day after Philippe Swan died on the gallows."

"I still don't see ..."

Marnet raised a hand. He winked at J.J. "According to the warden's notes, Philippe Swan swore he was innocent until the day he died. Now here"—he thumped a dusty volume that had been on the table—"from the supposed but not fully authenticated diary of Marie's namesake daughter—this is merely a copy, mind you—comes the information that the Voodoo Queen had been paid by a young man named Raymond Swan to care for his brother whilst in Parish prison. So, you see, by making a simple deduction, I have solved the crime."

"You had me," J.J. said, "but you've lost me."

"Raymond Swan was the Meddler, of course," Marnet replied impatiently. "When Marie Laveau let his brother die on the gallows, Swan, under the guise of the Meddler, began murdering her female clients as a form of vengeance. He chased away a large number of Marie's wealthy supporters."

"That would seem to suggest that Raymond Swan killed the other women, too," J.J. said, "the ones his brother took the fall for."

"Brilliant deduction," Henry Marnet exclaimed. "Eminently logical. And quite dramatic. Good brother. Bad brother."

"But I still don't see what bearing this has on *our* Meddler," J.J. said.

Some of the glow left Marnet's face. "Bearing? I just assumed the more you knew about the original, the more you'd know about this one. I mean, he must have some reason for aping the original with the mutilations, the voodoo dolls and silk cloths."

J.J. nodded. "But according to what you've just told me, the identity of the old Meddler has been a secret until right now, that you've just figured it out."

"That's correct."

"Then our Meddler wouldn't really have known anything about the Swan brothers, unless he'd beaten you to the punch."

Marnet slumped in his chair. "I suppose that's true."

"Unless, of course, you're the Meddler," J.J. said, neither serious nor joking.

"Quite," Marnet said with a little grin, taking it as a bit of whimsy. "I'm hardly the man for that sort of grisliness."

"What's the significance of the name Meddler, anyway?" J.J. asked.

"It has to do with the way the old voodoos would refer to little gewgaws or knickknacks that had no real name. If a child would point to a chicken claw resting on a shelf and ask what it was, the mammy would say, 'It's a layover to catch a meddler.' In other words, it's an object placed on a shelf whose sole purpose is to fall to the floor or give alarm if someone is meddling with the shelf."

J.J. filed the information away, but, like the identity of the first Meddler, it seemed of little consequence to the ongoing investigation.

He rose and thanked Henry Marnet for the ice cream and his help.

"My pleasure," Marnet said as he led the police detective to the front door.

"I understand you're a friend of Theodore Glander," J.J. said.

"Oh yes. For many years now. Both Theo and his wife Alice were part of our little group."

"Group?" J.J. asked.

"People interested in the more arcane aspects of New Orleans history," Marnet said. "I arrange dinners every so often. We discuss books, trade bits of information. Sometimes there's a guest speaker. It's been a while since our last get-together. I've been rather busy, with my books and other things."

"Does Glander share your interest in Marie Laveau?"

"Of course," Marnet said. "We are all under Marie's spell."

"Have you and he talked about the Meddler?"

"I paid my condolences, of course. It was a horrible thing, his poor daughter," Marnet said. "And today, I called his home to tell him about my discovery. It was he who suggested I inform your office."

"Did his daughter and son-in-law ever attend any of your dinners?" J.J. asked.

Marnet shook his head. "No. Alas, most young people don't seem to be interested in history. Unfortunately, as George Santayana once noted, those who ignore the past are doomed to repeat it."

It was not until he was back in his car that J.J. began to wonder if Marnet's mentioning the Santayana quote was a direct reference to the reappearance of the Meddler.

"Find out anything to break the case?" Fontineau asked when J.J. joined him at the Meddler board. Another member of the squad, a short detective named Wilson, whose cherubic, freckled face was hardened by an eyebrow-to-lip scar, was marking something in chalk. A doctor's name.

"Uh-huh," J.J. said. "Marnet gave me the name of the Meddler. Raymond Swan."

Fontineau's jaw dropped, and Wilson pressed the chalk so hard against the board it broke.

"Is that for real?" Fontineau asked.

"Sure," J.J. answered. "Problem is, it all took place over a hundred years ago."

"Not funny, Cajun," Wilson said, and picked up another piece of chalk.

"What's the new name on the board?" J.J. asked.

"Ray Boudreaux, the guy who was dicking the Sprague woman, has been seein' a headshrinker," Wilson said. "Roussou's with the shrink now."

"Anything else come in while I was getting my history lesson?" J.J. asked.

"Nothing worth spit," Fontineau said. "Raymond Swan, huh? That's funny. Raymond Swan. Raymond Boudreaux. Maybe history's repeatin' itself."

J.J. wondered if he should mention Theodore Glander's fondness for New Orleans history, particularly that period in which the original Meddler roamed. He asked, "Who was it who talked to Glander about his daughter's murder?"

"I did," Fontineau said.

"There's no transcript in the files," J.J. said.

"The lieutenant told me to make it quick and painless and I did," Fontineau replied, yawning. "There wasn't nothing worth transcribing. Why?"

"Just curious."

"I did him and the Keller guy. Double zero. Did Glander say something about it?"

"Say something to *me*?" J.J. asked. "I haven't talked to Glander since we were all here in this office."

"Right. Where would I get such a dumb idea?" Fontineau asked sarcastically.

Roussou returned less than an hour later. He hadn't done so well with the doctor, who'd refused to answer any specific questions about Raymond Boudreaux's mental state. Roussou thought that meant that the suspect was a serious nut case, or why wouldn't the shrink say he was harmless?

The Meddler squad called it a day at about 5 P.M. J.J. went back to his cubicle and pawed through the files once again. He was still at it when Lamotta said, "It's nearly eight o'clock, Cajun. Give it a rest."

J.J. looked up to discover that, indeed, the sun had set and the day crew had sidled off to what they considered to be their real lives. Lamotta had his coat on, which meant he was heading home. "Just checking a few odds and ends," J.J. told him.

"Yeah, well, you're pissing Fontineau off. He thinks you're—how'd he put it?—undermining his authority by spending so much free time on the case."

"That's his problem," J.J. said.

"Get out of here, Cajun. You're pissing me off, too. You make me feel guilty *I'm* leaving."

"None of it makes sense," J.J. said, indicating the open files on his desk. "Except for the fact that they're all young women, the victims seem to have been selected at random."

"So? The guy's a psycho."

"Even psychos have some plan. What's the Meddler's plan? Why does he leave the voodoo dolls? The original Meddler was probably trying to scare all of Marie Laveau's customers away. Who's this guy trying to scare?"

"Young broads. The guy's a ding-dong who doesn't like women. So he kills 'em. He doesn't think about it. He doesn't put in as much time planning it as you do reading those files. He just gets his little voodoo dolls and his knife and goes out and cuts up."

"Why does he pick one woman and not another?" J.J. asked.

"It's like that guy that climbed the mountain. The Meddler kills a broad because she's there. Now, why don't you call your broad and go to a movie or something? I don't want you blowing a fuse on me and I don't want to hear any more complaints out of Fontineau."

J.J. nodded, and Lamotta headed out, satisfied he'd made his point.

J.J. skimmed the Sprague woman's file once more and closed it. Then he gathered it with the other files and slipped them into his deep desk drawer, the only one with a lock.

He stared at the phone. Don't think so much, he ordered himself. He grabbed the phone.

No one answered at Madeleine's apartment. Not even after eleven rings.

He could always drive to her place, park in front like a high school jerk. He wondered if she was out looking for a new apartment. Or a new lover, a younger, more talkative one.

He could phone Lannie Dufosset, but his heart definitely wasn't in that.

Instead he wound up eating alone in a small, undistinguished tavern squeezed between a topless bottomless strip joint and a jazz club where the Dixieland was so synthetic it sounded as if there were kazoos mixed in with the brass.

With a soggy roast beef sandwich resting uncomfortably under his rib cage, he had a third Falstaff for the road. But, once he was on it, he realized he didn't want to go home to an empty apartment.

He strolled south to the Perdido Lounge.

At ten o'clock the place was just beginning to come alive. The neighborhood crowd was being replaced by night crawlers of infinite variety. J.J. took a seat at the bar between a mustachioed man in a gold lamé cocktail dress and a chimpanzee that belonged to a middleweight fighter named Stolla, who had passed out on the next stool over.

While he sipped another Falstaff, two hookers got into a fight over a college student, then joined forces to beat on him when they discovered he was broke. A trio of sailors from a South American ship began screaming something about Castro and the death of John Kennedy. A lady thief that J.J. knew dropped by to say hello. He stopped her in the midst of lifting the transvestite's purse, slapped her hand and sent her on her way.

Two young black boys did a brilliant tap dance in one door, around the bar and out the other. Three couples who looked as if they'd come directly from the symphony ordered drinks and tried to brave it out, probably so that they could tell their friends at the New Orleans Country Club that they'd spent the evening at the infamous Perdido. But a regular known only as Adolph, a legless man who rarely if ever bathed, rolled his wheelchair up to one of the women and asked her to dance. When she politely refused, he grabbed her hand and began to suck her fingers. The couples couldn't get out of there fast enough, and Ramon, the skinny barkeep, chuckled good-naturedly as he handed their untouched drinks to Adolph and his pals.

J.J. waited and watched and drank. By eleven-thirty, the place was so crowded and noisy it seemed like everybody in the city was there. Except for Madeleine DuBois, of course.

He left the bar and began his walk across the French Quarter, staggering only slightly. In the middle of a quiet block, just a few yards from his building, he realized that someone was following him. He turned and saw that it was a woman. "Madeleine?" he asked dully.

"If that's who you want," the woman replied. He blinked.

She was a tall, modestly dressed redhead. She smiled and asked him if he had a light. She couldn't have been out of her twenties but he saw by the street lamp that her pretty Irish face was already starting to take on the hard lines of her profession.

"I don't smoke," he told her.

"That's 'cause you don't know me," she said, smiling suggestively. "I could set you on fire."

He was tempted. He'd succumbed to similar propositions in the past. She was attractive and young. And he was lonely and drunk. But the pictures of the Meddler's victims flashed before his eyes with all the effect of an icy shower.

"Aw Jesus," he said, conscious that he was slurring, "don't you read the goddamn papers?"

She looked at him, confused, losing her confidence rapidly.

"Don't you know women are being murdered out here, cut up like lunch meat, for Christ's sake?"

She was moving away now, lips curled in disgust. "What're you? Some kinda freak?"

"Yeah, a reality freak," he said, but she was moving on to greener pastures. Running, in fact.

He got through the front door, up the stairs and into his apartment with relatively little trouble. He pulled off his tie and removed his coat, in that order, then lifted the phone.

There was no answer at Madeleine's apartment.

He found half a bottle of chardonnay in the fridge.

An hour later, there was still no answer.

Another hour after that, he had fallen into a fitful sleep, sprawled over his desktop, the silent phone only inches from his hand.

21

IT WAS A little after 5 A.M. when he woke up, hung over, stiff, with his right eye blurry where it had pressed against the desk blotter for most of the night. Worse yet, he felt as though something dreadful had taken place while he slept.

He'd had feelings like that before. His associates called it cop instinct. But he'd had it back when he was on the con and it had served him well every time but that final, bloody one.

He lifted last night's wine bottle to his lips and shivered as the sour dregs rolled down his throat. Then he dropped the bottle into the wastebasket beside the desk, stood up and stretched until his bones popped and cracked.

By the time he'd shaved and showered, he felt nearly awake, if not precisely human. Two cups of Café du Monde coffee and a half-dozen beignets injected him with the stamina he needed to meet the day.

At six-thirty, the bullpen was quiet and nearly empty except for the surprising presence of Pat Guillory. Red-eyed and fuming, he sat at his desk, pecking out a report and grumbling. "Well, well," he sneered, "look 'ut the cat dragged in, so fucking early in the morning."

J.J. ignored him, heading for his own desk.

" 'Mr. Integrity' Legendre, the Cajun Creeping Jesus. Here to make sure I dot the 'I's and cross the 'T's."

"What's your problem?" J.J. asked, running a hanger inside his coat and hooking the result on a hat tree.

"My problem? Well, shit, Cajun, my problem is that Dudley calls me at four goddamn o'clock in the morning and tells me I gotta come in here and get this done before Lamotta shows up."

"What's so important?"

106

Guillory closed his bleary green eyes for a second, then waved a hand through the air and returned to his awkward typing. "Your nigger pal killed himself."

"Pano?" J.J. asked. But he already knew the answer.

"I ain't talking about Martin Luther King. Fucking A, Pano. Guard found him this mornin' swinging from the light fixture in his cell like a big-ass black spider."

Guillory grinned as he looked up at J.J.'s grim expression. "Yeah," he said. "Dust to fucking dust, huh?"

He held up a clear evidence bag with a sheet of paper inside. "You might find this interestin', Cajun. He probably wrote this just before he tore his shirt into strips and used 'em to do the chicken walk off his cot."

J.J. rose as if in a dream and moved to Guillory's desk. He looked down at a piece of jailhouse toilet paper on which were written Pano's last words. "This isn't working out. I killed Lillian and I must pay. By hanging myself, I know whose hand is on the rope." It was signed "Tyrone Pano."

J.J. read the note twice.

"So, you still got any doubts the son of a bitch scragged that Davis woman?" Guillory asked.

"I suppose not. Assuming he wrote this. Assuming he killed himself."

"You saying somebody went into his cell, tore up his shirt, tied it around his neck and strung him up to the light fixture, sat down and wrote the goddamned note? And nobody saw 'em or heard 'em?"

"No," J.J. replied. "I guess I'm not. Got a list of the contents of his cell?"

Guillory had just finished typing it. J.J. looked it over and asked, "Where's the pen?"

"Huh?"

"The pen. The one he used to write the note."

Guillory grabbed the sheet from J.J.'s hand and read through each entry, moving his lips. Breathing heavily, he picked up his phone and dialed three numbers.

"Lemme speak to Cady," he snarled into the receiver. "I don't care. Wake the fucker up."

J.J. went back to his desk, but he remained facing Guillory.

"Cady, you stupid sack of shit," Guillory shouted, "you told me that list of Pano's contents was complete. . . . Yeah, well where's the fucking ballpoint pen . . . the fucking ballpoint pen he used to write the fucking note, you lamebrain. . . . Yeah. Well you do that little thing. And call me back pronto."

He slammed the receiver down onto the cradle and stared at J.J. "Cady. Some genius they got in charge of the lockup."

Forty minutes later, Cady notified Guillory that the pen had been found stuck in Pano's cot.

When Guillory passed on the information, J.J. suggested, "You ought to check it for prints and also to make sure the ink matches the note."

"Yeah, sure," Guillory said, and returned to his typing.

J.J. leaned back in his chair. The Century National Bank didn't open until nine.

He was there at 9:07, heading directly down the stairs to the safety deposit box area, where Mrs. Gendron helped him retrieve his box. In the seclusion of a private room, he lifted the metal lid and removed Pano's envelope.

He stared at it for a few seconds, then used his penknife to slice the flap neatly across the top.

He removed a single sheet of paper, folded twice. It read, in neat handwriting, "To Whom It May Concern: I, Tyrone Clement Pano, being of sound mind, do hereby bequeath the full and complete sum of all my worldly goods to the Southern Cross to be used in the crucial, continuing fight for equality and freedom for black men everywhere."

It had been signed by Tyrone Pano and witnessed by James Billins, acting as Pano's attorney.

J.J. was confused. It was a simple will. Why had Pano gone to the effort of hiding it with Sister Shana, then getting J.J. to further safeguard it?

He looked at the paper again. Then he studied the envelope. Nothing out of the ordinary. The sealed edge was warped as if Pano had used too much water, or possibly saliva to wet the glue. There was nothing else in or on the envelope.

J.J. folded the paper and put it back into the envelope, which he slipped into his pocket. He returned the box to its slot and left the bank considerably more confused than he'd been when he arrived.

22

"WHAT I HONESTLY and truly love," Nadia Wells said to J.J., "is a man who pays his debts with a smile."

They were seated in the corner of the main dining room of Arnaud's Restaurant. Nadia turned her head slightly, swept the area with a glance and declared, "I haven't been here since the strike. All these waiters look brand-new." Three years earlier, under instructions from the AFL-CIO, 95 percent of the Arnaud's staff had struck for higher wages. It had been a bitter battle, and while the union eventually was defeated, the cost had been a decline in the restaurant's prestige and popularity. Most of Arnaud's beloved waiters moved on to other dining rooms.

"We could have gone to Galatoire's," J.J. said.

"This is fine," she said. "I like this place and Germaine's an old pal of mine."

"That doesn't surprise me," J.J. said. Germaine Cazenave Wells, no relation to Nadia, was a flamboyant woman whose theatrical manner and hair-trigger temper had made her the best-known restaurateur in a city of well-known restaurateurs.

Nadia sliced through a plump oyster, speared it with a fork and dragged it through a mound of rich sauce Bienville. "Anyway, it's the food that counts, and I understand that the kitchen crew stuck with her," she said, and plopped the oyster into her mouth.

J.J., who'd opted for the slightly more conservative Businessman's Lunch, sipped iced tea and allowed his sinuses to calm down before his next bite of shrimp Arnaud, with its blend of mustard and horseradish and a dozen or so more secret ingredients. He was happy for the excuse that the Sister Shana business had given him to have lunch with Nadia. She was intelligent, funny, beautiful and apparently without affectation, except for her fondness for dated tough-guy slang.

Staring at that pale patrician face framed by short, copper-colored hair, the delicate lips, the alert, playful blue eyes, he wondered if he might be just the least bit in love with her. It was an odd thought for a man who spent so much time courting youth. Though she looked his age or younger, according to some of the city's better-informed historians she would have to be in her middle to late fifties.

At any age, he thought, she was a tremendously alluring woman. And he began to fantasize. . . .

"What's on your mind, hon?" she asked. "Last time a man looked at me like that, I had to use a tire iron on him."

"Actually," he lied with a smile, "I was thinking about a dead man."

She raised an eyebrow. "I've been observing you birds for a long time, J.J., and I can usually read all of you pretty well. But rather than seem unduly immodest, I'll play your game and ask: 'What dead man?' "

So he told her most of the Tyrone Pano story.

She listened intently without ignoring her remaining oysters Bienville. She interrupted him only once, to inquire about the health and welfare of her old friend Shana.

When J.J. came to his wrap-up, she asked him what was in the will.

He hesitated. "Until I've figured out how to handle it, maybe it's better if you don't know the contents. But I did bring the envelope. I'd like your opinion on whether it's been tampered with."

She removed a pair of granny glasses from her purse and studied the envelope, running her fingers over the glued flap. She handed it back to J.J.

"Well?" he asked.

Instead of replying, she turned and signaled for the waiter. "What's your name, hon?" she asked the handsome young man.

"Juan," he said.

"Well, Juan, I'd think very kindly of you if you'd get me another of these Ojen frappes." She indicated the glass in front of her.

He picked up the glass and started to make his exit. "And ask Mr. Herman to ease off a little on the simple syrup," Nadia added, referring to the restaurant's legendary bartender.

Once again, the waiter tried to make his exit, but she called out, "And, Juan, do you think you could do something about these dirty dishes in front of us?"

The waiter turned red and nodded. He stormed across the room and grabbed a busboy who was leaning against a pillar, shaking him and pointing toward their table.

Nadia waited for the busboy to clear the dishes, then said to J.J., "It looks like that envelope's been steamed open and re-sealed. What does that tell you?"

"I'm not sure. Only that the will is suspect."

"Why do you want any part of this Pano business?" she asked.

He shrugged. "I don't. But the guy evidently trusted me to do . . . something. And I can't figure out what."

She stared at the tablecloth for a few seconds, then said, "There are some questions worth answering. Did your Mr. Pano really kill himself?"

"I assume so," J.J. replied. "Along with the fact that he left a suicide note, he was alone in a cell."

"My God, how long have you been a cop in this town?" she asked, almost angrily. "For the right kind of money, you can get anything done anywhere."

Juan returned with her pretty pink Ojen and placed it in front of her with a proud smile, as if daring her to find anything wrong with this part of his service. She smiled at him. "Thanks, hon," she said. "How're our entrees coming along?"

He snapped to attention and went to find out.

J.J. waited until she'd taken a sip of her drink, then asked, "Why would someone want him dead?"

"Because he was a militant black man. Because he made somebody mad. Because somebody was afraid of him or something he knew. Because he had something they wanted."

"That certainly narrows it down," he said.

She chuckled, then leaned forward and patted his hand. "You know, J.J., some folks believe you can solve any crime by one rule: *cherchez la femme*. To me that is the most preju-diced, obnoxious, totally incorrect idea some dumb son of a bitch male ever came up with. I'll tell you my cardinal rule, and it holds true for men, women, the old, the young, the white, the black—*cherchez l'argent*. I follow the money, honey."

J.J. frowned. "What money?" And the answer came to him as soon as he'd asked the question.

"How much is Pano's estate worth?" she wondered.

He shrugged.

"That's what you've got to find out," she said, just as their entrees arrived. She attacked her chicken Rochambeau with what J.J. thought of as graceful determination. He himself wasted no time in devouring his trout meunière.

They spoke of nothing but the food until it was gone. Then, with demitasse cups of black coffee in front of them, Nadia asked, "What'll you do if Tyrone was fat as a goose when he died?"

"I'm not sure," he said.

"You might want to check that will. Make sure it's the real McCoy."

J.J. shook his head. "Look, I only have so much time I can spend on this. I barely knew the guy."

"Okay, okay," she said, grinning. " 'Course, there's the suicide note to use for a handwriting sample."

He nodded.

"Here's another question," she said. "What if he died poor as a church mouse?"

"Then I'll put the will into a new envelope and mail it to the lawyer who witnessed it, being careful not to leave any evidence that it was ever in my possession."

She nodded and asked, with more than a hint of sarcasm, "And you'll be satisfied that Pano bumped himself off because he murdered the Davis woman and was feeling the pangs of guilt?"

"You can be a very annoying woman," he said. "But, yes, I'll be satisfied, because there won't be anything else I can be. I've got other things to keep me busy."

"Like what?" she asked.

He had no intention of telling Nadia about his crisis of the heart. He said, "I'm working on the Meddler case."

She was quiet for a few seconds. Then she said, "So things are picking up for you at Homicide?"

"Maybe."

"You won't be taking Jack's offer?"

He should have assumed that she knew about his conversation with Jack Manion, since it had been she who sent him to the banker. He wondered what their relationship was—a proper boy genius bank president and a colorful former madam. He thought it might be a romantic one, regardless of the disparity in their ages. After all, Manion was only a few years younger than he.

He said, "It's a very generous offer. I may not be able to turn it down."

She nodded and looked at her watch. "Well, can't run a business sitting here," she said. "Thanks for the lunch, J.J. And I don't want you tipping Juan any more than fifteen percent, the quality of service he provides."

"I'll keep that in mind." He stood, pulled back her chair.

She leaned forward and kissed him on the cheek. It was not a very intimate kiss, but it surprised him. She said, "If you decide not to go with Jack, please give me a call. Maybe *we* can work something out."

He sat down again and watched her move gracefully through the restaurant. Then she was gone. It was time for him to be getting back to work, too, but he picked up the coffeepot and poured himself another demitasse.

"Cherchez l'argent," Nadia had told him. That was exactly what he was going to do.

23

SERGEANT JAMEY FONTINEAU responded to J.J.'s knocking on his cubicle door with a look that was half annoyed, half wary. He was seated behind a desk on which folders and typewritten pages threatened to push brass-framed photos of his wife and children onto the floor. He was sweating through a short-sleeved light blue shirt open at the neck, with a silver-and-blue tie at half-mast. He leaned back in his wooden chair and asked, "What's up, Legendre?" as if he didn't particularly care.

J.J. entered the cubicle, picked Fontineau's seersucker coat off the only chair, draped it on the back of the chair and sat down. "I want to bounce an idea off you," he said.

Fontineau stared at him, waiting.

"I've been trying to figure out the Meddler's motive," J.J. said.

"Motive? He likes to spill blood. That's his motive."

"Lamotta thinks he hates women," J.J. said.

"I would say so," Fontineau replied. "Look, we been through all this with the headshrinkers before you got . . . before you came aboard. The guy was a mama's boy. Or he was forced into sex stuff when he was a little baby. Or he had his brains shuffled by something in grammar school."

"Okay," J.J. said. "So let's keep going with that. We've got this screwed-up guy. Nine weeks ago, he decides he has to kill a waitress. Why did he pick her?"

Fontineau lifted the folder marked "Downs, Mae Rita." According to the information inside, she'd been murdered shortly after leaving her place of employment, Dujeau's Bar, a Bourbon Street dive. She'd been a waitress, but she'd done a little hooking at the request of management. She'd been an attractive brunette with "an upbeat personality," according to one of her co-workers. Twenty-four, brunette, five feet three, divorced, with a three-year-old daughter who was now residing with the victim's parents. Ex-husband living in Atlanta with a new wife.

"The guy sees her on the street," Fontineau said. "Something she says or does pisses him off and he cuts her."

"And he just happens to be carrying a voodoo doll with him to leave behind," J.J. said.

Fontineau sighed. "We been at this for nine weeks, Legendre. And we got two theories on that. First, he carries the fucking doll—and the fucking knife—for weeks, months, years, maybe. Then, one night, bingo. Or, second, he goes bingo and decides to go out stalking, armed with the knife and the doll, and the Downs woman just happened to be unlucky enough to bump into him. We know she left the bar alone."

J.J. looked at the other folders on the desk, each devoted to a victim. "There's a third possibility," he said.

"I'm all ears."

"The Meddler isn't crazy at all."

Fontineau gave him a patronizing smile and leaned forward in his chair. "Thanks for the suggestion, Legendre. Now lemme get back to work, huh?"

"I mean, he's *crazy*. Anybody who'd carve up six women would have to be crazy. But suppose he's got a reason we can all understand."

"Like what?"

"Money," J.J. said. "Lots of money."

For the first time since J.J. entered the room he could sense that he'd piqued Fontineau's interest. "You think what?" the sergeant asked. "That some guy sliced up five strangers just so he could get rid of his wife or his girlfriend and make some money?"

"It's possible. Did any of the victims leave big bucks?" J.J. asked.

"The Downs woman didn't have a pot to piss in." Fontineau picked up the file labeled "Jeanaud, Leslie." Victim number two. "This one had some bucks," he said. "But I don't know what good it'll do anybody."

J.J. recalled her data sheet. Thirty-eight. An attractive honey blonde. Very social. Member of the Junior League. When her parents died in a car crash in 1959, she'd inherited her father's real estate business. Which she'd run with his former assistant, a woman by the name of Mildred Tarrant. Leslie Jeanaud had never married. The investigating officer, Roussou, had suspected her of being romantically involved with the Tarrant woman.

"What happened to her estate?"

"It's all fucked up," Fontineau said. "There wasn't a will anybody could find. Her lawyers had been after her to make one, but she was young and didn't dream she'd be winding up in a morgue before she hit the big four-O. So there's a search on for distant relatives. And the Tarrant woman is treading water with the company while the whole thing gets ground out by the court."

Victim number four, Georgia Blum, a strapping redhead in life, was the youngest of the group, twenty-three. She'd been an assistant comptroller for the Coast Guard at the Maritime Building on Canal. Lived at home with mother and father. Very middle class. Popular with boys. No big romance.

Victim five, Theresa Liverdais, had been a clerk at the Poinsettia Hotel in the Quarter. Thirty-one. Married to a Delta pilot. She'd left behind two boys, age five and seven. No money there. The same was true of the most recent victim, Loretta Sprague.

"But if you're talking money money," Fontineau said with a

wide grin, "here's the best bet." He dropped the folder he'd been holding back onto the desk in front of J.J.

J.J. knew which one it was. The third victim. Lee Ann Keller. The daughter of Theodore Glander, the man who'd shoehorned him into the Meddler investigation, the man who was so fond of Marie Laveau.

J.J. had known that Glander's wife had been wealthy, but he hadn't spent as much time on that file as he had on the others. He asked, "What was it? Oil money?"

"Gushers and gushers. More bread coming in every day than you and me can count. When old lady Glander died, her estate was split between the daughter, the only child, and hubby. Worth about a hunerred million."

"No wonder Glander retired," J.J. said. "I'm surprised that Keller didn't settle for a life of leisure, too."

"The Kellers didn't live like zillionaires," Fontineau said. "There was a kicker in the will. Glander got all the money he could spend, free and clear, but the way the will was written, all the daughter wound up with was some kind of trust fund, a paltry five grand a month for as long as Glander was still alive."

"Does her death change any of that?" J.J. asked.

"You want to call the lawyer, be my guest," Fontineau said, enjoying himself.

24

EDGAR MORGAN PENDLER, founder of the legal firm of Pendler, Pendler and Gallen, was the attorney of record for Tessier Oil, the company that had fueled the Tessier family fortunes for three generations, including the present. The senior Pendler took J.J.'s call without much ado. His dry, cultured

Southern voice told the officer that he was eager to help out in whatever way he could.

"I understand that Mrs. Lee Ann Keller was an extremely wealthy woman."

There was a brief silence, then the lawyer replied, "I shall try to answer that, Officer Legendre. But I'm afraid I cannot discuss such matters via the telephone with someone who may or may not be a member of the New Orleans Police Department. If you'd care to come to the law firm's offices before five o'clock with proper identification . . ."

It was barely four-thirty when J.J. was shown into Edgar Pendler's surprisingly modern office on the seventeenth floor of the Petroleum Building. There wasn't an antique or a law book to be seen. Just a brilliant oriental rug, several de Koonings on the dark green walls, a tan leather sofa and chairs and a clean kidney-shaped desk that probably had been designed by Herman Miller.

Pendler, a tanned, carefully barbered man of average height, in his sixties, was wearing, in addition to lovingly tailored chocolate-brown slacks, a brown houndstooth coat that made him look more like a successful gambler than a respected corporation lawyer.

He studied J.J.'s identification, then handed it back to him with a smile. "Take a chair, Officer. Care for coffee or a soda? Or something stronger?"

"Nothing, thanks."

Pendler caught the detective studying the room. He smiled. "My wife's the decorator," he said. "She likes to take little trips to Chicago and New York and comes back with all sorts of stuff that she drags in here. My son's office looks like the library at the Athletic Club, but I never cared for dark wood. Too gloomy."

"It's very handsome," J.J. said.

"Yes, I think so, too. Well, what is it you want to know, exactly?"

"How much money did Mrs. Keller have when she died and who gets it?"

Pendler leaned against his desk. "If you'll indulge an old man, I'd like to wait a bit before answering your question."

"Wait for what?"

"For whom, actually," Pendler said, consulting the red digital readout on the gold Pulsar on his wrist. "He should be here in a moment."

As if on cue, a soft buzzing sound emanated from Pendler's phone. He reached back, lifted the receiver and punched a button. "Yes," he said. "Send him in, please."

The door opened and John Keller entered the room.

"John," Pendler said, shaking the young man's hand. "I believe you know Officer Legendre."

John Keller smiled at J.J. as they shook hands. The smile seemed to say that he didn't really mind the detective's nosing into his late wife's finances. But of course he did.

"Officer Legendre just asked me to describe the nature of Lee Ann's estate," Pendler said.

The smile hardened on Keller's face. "Please do," he said. "Lee Ann's father has a great deal of confidence in Officer Legendre. I want him to have as much information as he needs."

Having neatly lobbed the ball of responsibility into Keller's court, the attorney said, "Mrs. Keller was an extremely wealthy woman, in point of fact, if not in practicality."

"I don't understand," J.J. said.

"She was wealthy, but she was not allowed to spend the money. Mrs. Keller's mother had been the sole owner of the Tessier Oil Refinery. When she passed on, her holdings, in accordance with Napoleonic law, were split equally between her husband, Theodore Glander, and their only child, Lee Ann."

"How much is the refinery worth?" J.J. asked.

The lawyer's eyes went to Keller, who nodded. "Today? Sixty-five million. Maybe seventy."

J.J. wondered what was going through Keller's head. Sorrow over his wife's death? Confusion? Concern? Surely he understood where J.J. was going with his questions. Why was that smile still on his face? Perhaps unreasonably, J.J. wanted to wipe it away. He asked, "So Mrs. Keller was worth somewhere in the neighborhood of forty-five million dollars?"

"Roughly," Pendler replied. "But you must understand, while Mrs. Keller owned the shares, she was not able to benefit from them. According to the terms of her mother's will, her father, Theodore Glander, had usufruct of her shares. That is, he controlled the shares and any profits they accrued."

"Then Mrs. Keller had no money of her own?" J.J. asked.

"My wife had a trust fund that had been established by her mother," Keller said. "She received five thousand dollars a month. With my salary from the district attorney's office, we lived . . . comfortably."

"What happens now?" J.J. asked.

"Now," Keller replied, "I'll probably have to sell the house and move into an apartment."

J.J. turned to the lawyer, puzzled.

Pendler said, "Had Lee Ann lived another two years, at age thirty she would have inherited the bulk sum of the trust, four hundred thousand and some odd dollars. My suggestion, of course, would have been for her to continue to live off the interest. In any case, in accordance with the will of Alice Tessier Glander, since her daughter was deceased prior to her thirtieth birthday, and since the daughter issued no offspring, the funds formerly held in trust will be shared equally by three charities specified by Mrs. Glander."

"I'm not one of them," Keller said without rancor. His smile had gone, replaced by a look of genuine despair. "My wife had a twenty-thousand-dollar life insurance policy, which will come in handy. My father-in-law insisted that we both take out small policies. I'm not sure why. It seemed silly at the time. Lee Ann and I joked about them. The jokes seem sort of sour now. I realize you have to do your job, but I hope you can understand that these questions are not answered without a degree of pain."

Tears gathered in his eyes, but he didn't cry.

J.J. suddenly felt sorry for him. But that didn't stop him from asking, "What about her shares in Tessier Oil?"

Keller shook his head. Lawyer Pendler, his former sprightliness a bit wilted, said, "In accordance with her mother's will, when Lee Ann Keller passed away, the ownership to all shares in Tessier Oil automatically passed on to Theodore Glander."

It was a stunning piece of information. J.J. was considering its ramifications when John Keller stood and said, "If that's all, I think I'll go now."

J.J. stood, too.

"Walking out with me?" Keller asked.

"I have a question or two more for Mr. Pendler."

"Ah," John Keller said, then put out his hand for J.J. to shake. "If you need anything else, Officer, give me a call."

When the door had shut behind Keller, the attorney said, "I hope you don't mind my asking him to join us. Tessier Oil is our biggest client."

"Considering that, why didn't you call Theodore Glander?" J.J. asked.

"I will. But Theodore and John are very close, and of the

two I thought there'd be a better chance of our finishing our business here if John were the one responding to your questions. Theodore can be ... volatile ... in certain situations."

"I imagine he can."

"I know how you policemen think," the lawyer said. "If for any reason you didn't get all your questions answered—if Theodore Glander had kicked you out of this office, say—you might have harbored the wrong impression and wasted even more of your time. This way, we clear the air and you can move on to greener pastures in search of your criminal."

"Multiple murderer," J.J. said.

"Yes, I wasn't trying to demean the importance of your task." The lawyer took a few steps to the door, suggesting that the interview was over. J.J. asked, "Was there a reason Lee Ann's mother took such pains to keep money out of John Keller's hands?"

"You are a persistent fellow," Edgar Pendler said, shaking his head in mock awe. "Alice Glander was dead and gone before Lee Ann even met John. Lee Ann was always a very young person. Younger than her years, I mean. When Alice made out her will, I don't imagine she gave a thought to Lee Ann having a husband. The girl was only eighteen then and she behaved like fourteen. The will was designed to protect her, I guess."

J.J. thought that Alice Glander hadn't been off the mark, exactly. Lee Ann had needed protecting.

The lawyer added, "I hope you catch the scum that did it. She was a sweet little girl." He opened his office door, but J.J. didn't leave.

"Did John Keller know about the contents of Alice Glander's will before his wife died?"

"You are something," the lawyer said. "Yes, he knew. He and Lee Ann were looking forward to her thirtieth birthday."

"Which charities are getting the money held in trust?"

"You *are* a suspicious cuss," the lawyer said.

"Was one of them the Southern Cross?" J.J. asked.

"The black militants?" Pendler asked. "Hardly. No. As I can recall, it's Hotel Dieu Hospital, the Jesuits and the Heart Association. The Southern Cross? Now that would have been a unique bequest."

J.J. wasn't sure why he'd mentioned it. Just another weird twist his brain took. "One final question," he said.

"I hope it is," Pendler said, obviously tiring of the game.

"Is Tessier Oil in any trouble that you know of?"

"Lord no!" Pendler replied, punctuating it with a mock shudder. "Last week it pushed to a new high."

"So there's no reason why Theodore Glander would need money?"

"You mean, any reason why he'd need another forty-five million dollars? No sir! I can't think of a reason in God's green world."

So, J.J. mused, while waiting for the elevator to take him to the parking level, maybe following the money hadn't been such a good idea after all.

25

THE MEDDLER HELD the phone to his ear, weighing the words of attorney Edgar Pendler. He wondered if he'd pushed his luck by suggesting J.J. Legendre become part of the team investigating his crimes.

His feeling was that the detective would apply the sort of creative thinking to the investigation that would eventually make it possible for the proper sort of justice to be done. And this, according to Pendler, was exactly what was happening. But how predictable was Legendre, really?

"The man's like a terrier," Pendler was saying on the other end of the line, with a bit more agitation than usual. "But in the end, he found nothing because there was nothing to be found."

There was a hint of a question in that statement, so the Meddler replied, "Of course not."

"I'm glad you're taking it so well. I wasn't sure if you'd approve—"

The Meddler cut him off. "You handled the whole thing admirably."

Pendler was a weasel, of course, the Meddler thought as he replaced the receiver. But he was the family's weasel, one who lived in fear that his firm might belly up without Tessier Oil's annual billings. Well, maybe the law firm would be put to that test anyway, when the right time came. For the present, however, he could count on Pendler to keep him apprised of any other questions Legendre might think of.

Pendler said the man was like a terrier. In this instance, the cupboard had been bare. Nothing there at all. Except for the odd eighty-seven million dollars.

The Meddler laughed. He felt it was just a matter of tidying up and waiting for Legendre to make it possible for him to enjoy the fruits of his labors. With luck, he would have to kill only once more.

26

MADELEINE DUBOIS HAD thought she'd put J.J. Legendre from her mind by filling every spare moment with schoolwork or the ceaseless, still fruitless, search for a new apartment. But that afternoon, on consulting her notebook, she discovered that the only notations she'd made during the last three days were the doodled initials, "J.J." Pages of them. Some with hearts, some with daggers and guns. Worse yet, she could not recall a word that she'd heard in any of the classes she'd so dutifully attended.

Annoyed with what she considered her "schoolgirl bullshit behavior," she took her thoughts and her books to the Law Library. But even there her mind continued to meander. What was it that she really wanted from J.J.? A commitment? What in God's name for? She liked him. She was infatuated with him. Perhaps she even, well, loved him. But it certainly wasn't the kind of eternal love that you really needed before you decided to spend the rest of your lives together. Even if he was so old the rest of his life might be a matter of just a few years.

God! Schoolgirl bullshit behavior! Wasn't she beyond this?

Her friend Eileen, sensing the seriousness of her condition, had fixed her up with a very attractive, very socially prominent doctor the night before. He'd taken her to dinner at Berdou's, just over the bridge in Gretna. He'd been rather good company until, after his third old-fashioned, he began complaining that she wasn't drinking enough and didn't seem terribly interested in what he had to say.

Madeleine had been guilty on both counts, she supposed. Not that that gave him any cause to try and rape her in his new Mustang convertible while they were parked in front of her building and, failing that, to shove his way into her apartment to try again.

He had torn her blouse and she'd been forced to butt him in the chin with her head and push him down a flight of stairs. But even during the brief fight, her thoughts had not been free of J.J. Legendre. Damn the man!

So what to do? Give in?

But give in to what? J.J. hadn't asked her for anything. She'd done the asking. Or had she? She couldn't remember.

She looked at the clock on the library wall and discovered to her dismay that she'd been sitting there, with her books unopened on the table before her, for nearly two hours. That left her with barely enough time to grab a quick burger at the Camellia Grill, then get to the Prytania in time for the seven-thirty screening of *Sweet Bird of Youth*, part of a Tennessee Williams Film Festival. If Paul Newman didn't make her forget J.J. Legendre, nothing would. But, if she remembered the play well enough, Newman would wind up getting castrated. . . .

No matter, she told herself. The Camellia Grill for a hamburger—and maybe a slice of pecan pie—and then on to Paul Newman.

It was dark when she left the library and started across campus at a fast clip. As she skirted the line of cars waiting for the light to change on Freret Street, she began to have a weird sensation that someone was watching her.

Safe on the other side of Freret, she glanced over her shoulder. There seemed to be nothing unusual in the night. Just other pedestrians going here and there.

She continued on to her car, moving faster. The feeling grew stronger. Somebody was . . .

She spun suddenly, but again saw nothing to give her pause.

I'm turning into a nut case, she told herself as she hurried on to her car.

Almost running, she found the entrance to the path beside Gibson Hall that led to the small lot where she'd parked. It had seemed so cheery in daylight. Night had turned it into a mugger's paradise.

In the near distance, the St. Charles streetcar scraped and clanged by, on its slow, irrevocable journey downtown. Inside Gibson Hall, the grating school bell notified students that the 7:00 P.M. classes were beginning.

That explained why she was alone on the path. Classes had convened.

She could see her car, parked four spaces from the path.

Behind her, a footstep. Someone moving closer. She should go, she thought. But not to the car. No way could she unlock the door in time. Run to St. Charles Avenue. Or into Gibson Hall. Or any goddamn place. Just don't stand there like a . . . like a . . .

It was too late. The figure was behind her now. She could feel its presence. She dropped all of her books except for the heaviest one. That she hefted in her right hand, turning to face her attacker.

She drew back the book. Then her arm fell to her side.

J.J. Legendre said, gulping air, "Damn it, Madeleine, but you set a fast pace. I've been racing to catch up to you since you left the library."

They dined at Casamento's, a popular neighborhood oyster house on Magazine where, unlike the Camellia Grill, they could sit at a table instead of a counter and drink beer with their food—fried soft shell crabs for her, an oyster po'boy for him.

They didn't talk much. J.J. told her he'd missed her. She said she was sorry she'd gotten angry. Neither made any promises. He asked if she'd found a new place to live. She said no, but that she thought she had a line on something that might work.

They ate their fill, passed on after-dinner coffee, paid the tab and drove immediately to his apartment in the Quarter. They didn't talk much there, either.

27

THE NEXT MORNING, when he stepped from the shower, J.J. was surprised to find her awake and rattling pans in the kitchenette. He was stepping into his shoes when she passed on her way to the bathroom.

"Your coffee and the paper are on the back-porch table," she said, not waiting for a reply.

He was halfway through the *Picayune* and his first cup of café au lait when she joined him, fully dressed in her clothes from the night before, her cheeks pink and her hair damp. "Up kind of early, aren't you?" he asked.

"Going to see about an apartment at nine. Actually, not an apartment. A private suite, if you please. At less than I was paying when I had a roommate."

He sipped the coffee. He'd been turning her living situation over in his mind. Should he ask her to move in with him? Was that what she wanted? More important, was it what *he* wanted? He decided to try and have it both ways.

"You know," he told her, "you could move in here for a while, see how it goes."

She smiled. "Let's see how it goes if I don't move in," she said.

"It's your call."

She leaned over and kissed him on the cheek. He turned and gave her a proper kiss. The morning sun felt warm and comforting.

When they separated, she started to say something but seemed to think better of it.

"What?" he asked.

"Nothing. Sort of a secret, though I'm not sure why."

He frowned. "You're not gonna go off and leave me hanging like that."

"I'll tell you all about it over dinner tonight," she said. "In fact, I'll even make dinner if you want."

"I definitely want," he said. "But we have to cut a deal, here. Keep all the secrets you have to, but just don't let me know you're keeping secrets. We cops are sort of curious."

She nodded. "Deal," she said. And she was gone.

He was putting on his coat to leave when the front buzzer rang. Thinking it was Madeleine returning for something she'd forgotten, he opened the door without looking through the peephole. The black man known as Tank stood in the hall.

"G'mornin', Officer Lejern," he said pleasantly.

J.J. wished him good morning right back, stepping into the hall. He shut his apartment door, double-locking it. "You just caught me heading out. What can I do for you?"

"Um, the lawyer, Billins, says that Tyrone made out this will—about who was supposed to get his money and all. The Southern Cross, mainly."

J.J. looked blankly at the big man.

"And, well, we was wonderin' if Tyrone said somethin' about it to you."

"No," J.J. replied truthfully, "he didn't mention any will."

"Problem is," Tank said as they started down the stairs, "the lawyer don't know where it is. And the Southern Cross can use the bread."

"You looked like you were doing all right."

Tank shrugged. "All right is all right. But money is money."

They exited on St. Ann. J.J. saw Luther in the unpainted Pontiac parked across the street next to a fireplug. J.J. paused to give Tank a long look. "Now that Tyrone's gone," he asked, "who's running things?"

The big man ducked his head, indicating a humility that didn't seem quite real. "I guess that'd be me," he said. "I was Tyrone's second-in-command. I know what things he wanted done and how he wanted 'em to get done."

"That include blowing up parts of Baton Rouge?"

"Oh, that." Tank grinned. "That was just, you know, tough talk. We not blowin' up nothin'. We just want black people to get what's their due. That's why I'm askin' around about Tyrone's will."

"Was Tyrone a wealthy man?"

"The lawyer says he had some money."

"How much?" J.J. asked.

"Maybe, ah, fifty . . ." Tank said.

"Fifty thousand?"

Tank winced. "Maybe," he replied. "Anyway, that kind of money buys a lot of, uh, food and clothes."

And guns and explosives, J.J. thought. "Well, if Tyrone left a will, it should turn up."

Tank looked as if he were in pain. "Uh, you see, the lawyer thinks maybe Tyrone gave you the will to hold for him."

"He say where he got that idea?" J.J. started walking toward his car parked halfway down the block.

"No," Tank replied, trotting behind.

"Think about it," he said to Tank. "Would Tyrone have had his will with him in his cell? Even if he'd wanted it there, how would he get it? Did you bring it to him?"

Tank twisted his large head side to side, indicating that he hadn't. "Maybe Billins," he said.

"Then ask him," J.J. said.

Tank nodded and flashed a quick smile. "Yeah, maybe we'll go have another talk with the lawyer. Like you say, Tyrone makes a will, it's gonna turn up."

The big man waved at Luther and the Pontiac started with a deep rumble. When it was parallel to Tank, Luther reached over and opened the passenger door. Tank faced J.J., nodded and got into the car.

As the two men drove away, another sedan followed it. Its driver, FBI agent White, glared at J.J. as it passed. The detective gave him a salute.

Getting into his own car, J.J. wondered what a man of principle would do about Tyrone's will.

28

THE SUNSHINE CAFETERIA was a depressing place, with lighting that wasn't subdued enough to hide the patina of dust and mildew on its red-flocked walls and purple carpet. The cafeteria's day manager, a small man named Floyd, whose shiny gray wash-and-wear suit accentuated his potbelly, led J.J. past the smeared glass display cases and the mainly empty dark wood tables.

Fontineau and the other three detectives assigned to the Meddler squad were seated at a table in the rear, in front of an assortment of dirty dishes. Their conversation stopped as Floyd and J.J. approached.

J.J. took an empty chair. Floyd asked, "Will you be breaking fast with us this morning, Officer?"

"I've already eaten," J.J. said.

Floyd dropped his smile and grabbed the dull metal knives and forks that had been in front of J.J. and left the table with them. Wilson, his angelic, scarred face without expression, said, "You piss Floyd off, coming in here and turnin' down his fine food."

"I'll keep that in mind," J.J. said. "What's going on, Fontineau? I had a note on my desk telling me to come over here."

"This is our usual Thursday morning meeting," Fontineau replied. "Started an hour ago."

"I didn't know anything about it," J.J. said.

"No? I musta forgot to mention it," Fontineau said. "Anyway, we been going over what we got."

"Squat," said a slack-jawed detective named Roland whose eyes needed a shot of Murine as much as his face needed a razor.

"Roland here's a little p.o.ed 'cause his last lead on the voodoo dolls went nowhere," Fontineau said.

"The reports say they're handmade," J.J. said. "By somebody named Rina."

"Maman Rina," Roland said, lighting a cigarette and casually flicking the spent match onto the soiled carpet. "But none of the crap tourist places who peddled the dolls had an address for her. Didn't even know her last name. Said she just came around when she was finished sewing. Problem was, last anybody saw of her was nearly a year ago, and lots can happen to you in a year if you're a real old black woman."

"Roland found her yesterday," Fontineau said with a pinched smile.

"Yeah, she been waitin' for me all this time. In plot 117 of the Adams Street Cemetery in Uptown."

"Dead how long?" J.J. asked.

"Five months ago," Roland said, stubbing out the cigarette in what was left of his grits. "Full name: Florine Pousson. Ninety-one years young, like that guy Lescoulie says on the *Today Show*. Died of heart failure, 'cording to the death certificate. Lived in one of those shacks over on Willow near Broadway for the past thirty years. Talked to the neighbor who found her body. The old woman just died. No disturbance. No signs of struggle. Hell, this was months before the Meddler started anyway."

"But he's using her dolls," J.J. said.

"You got it," Jamey Fontineau said, moving his fork to poke through the remains of his corned beef hash for something that might be edible. "And none of the shops sold the dolls in any quantity. So unless the Meddler's been going around from shop to shop to build his collection, he probably got 'em from ol' Rina."

"What happened to her possessions?" J.J. asked.

Roland gave a brief, sarcastic snort and turned to Fontineau. "This guy cuts right through to the heart of things, don't he?" he asked.

"So tell him," Fontineau said.

"There wasn't no relatives anybody could find. The neighbor, a Mrs. Camilla Shadrow, just sorta razooed everything. Says there wasn't any voodoo dolls but there was some quilts and doilies and that kinda crap that she sold off to pay for Rina's funeral. Rina's clothes she gave to the Salvation Army. The old lady's sewing machine was a real relic that you can find in the window of the Singer store on Oak Street—a before-and-after deal. The neighbor is now sleepin' on Rina's nice oak bed. The neighbor's daughter has the dresser and some of the living-room furniture. The rest went to the Salvation Army, too."

"What happened to Rina's papers, letters, bills of sale?"

"Gawd damnit," Roland said. "You're a real de-tek-a-tive, sure enough."

J.J. had had his fill of him. He turned to Fontineau. "You got anything for me here?"

"Uh-huh." It was still morning and the cafeteria was air-conditioned, but Fontineau was already starting to sweat. He reached down beside his chair and hoisted up a tall, thin book with thick green cloth covers—a very old ledger book.

"Here's Maman Rina's records," Fontineau said. "Her business transactions for the past ten years. Should make good readin'."

J.J. opened the cover, saw the name Florine Pousson on the opening page in precise handwriting. "Roland got it from the neighbor," Fontineau said, as J.J. leafed through page after page of dense, tiny handwriting.

"This isn't English," J.J. said.

Roland snorted again. "Yessir, a real de-tek-a-tive."

"It's French, or maybe Cajun," Fontineau said. "Rina, according to the neighbor, was related to the Judge Pousson family. Her mama was the old judge's back-door punch. Anyway, she was brought up speaking Cajun. Or French. So, naturally, I thought of you."

"You're more Cajun than I am," J.J. said.

"But I don't know nothing about the language. And I got other things to do today. So you go through the ledger and if anything looks promising, you and Roland check it out."

The remaining member of the squad, a ferret-faced man in his forties named Roussou, said, "Our guy'll be at his office now, Chief. Good time to pick him up."

Fontineau sighed, took a last look at his dirty plate and pushed away from the table.

"You're making an arrest?" J.J. asked.

"Yeah," Fontineau said casually. "After we had that talk yesterday, about the money-motive thing, I made a few calls around about this guy Boudreaux. Turns out that there were two life insurance policies taken out on the Sprague girl. One was part of her company's health plan. Just ten grand. The other was a fairly new policy she took out herself. This one for fifty grand. The beneficiary of both policies is none other than . . ."

"The psycho, Raymond Boudreaux," Roussou said. "Only he don't mention nothing to me about insurance policies."

Maybe that's because you didn't ask him, J.J. thought, but didn't say. He was already the squad's pariah.

"Anyway, the guy's supporting his mother and she had some pretty heavy hospital bills about six months ago," Fontineau said. "With double indemnity, he could be collecting over a hundred grand."

Roussou grinned. "If the son of a bitch did kill the broad, the insurance company is gonna be very grateful to the squad for saving a lot of their dough."

Fontineau blinked. "Forget that bullshit. We don't take money. We don't take nothing for doing our jobs. Anyway, Legendre, your idea about this being a murder-for-profit deal is sounding better and better. Especially if the suspect's got a mental history. And, like your historian pal points out, his name is Raymond."

"So you think Boudreaux killed six women, including his fiancée, so he could pay his mother's hospital bills?" J.J. asked.

Fontineau's face turned florid. "The guy's not right in the head," he said, his voice rising to a whine. "And he's profiting big from his girlfriend's death. Hell, this was *your* goddamned idea."

He and Roussou started out of the restaurant. He turned suddenly and ordered, "You find the name Boudreaux in that ledger, you tell me about it right away."

Cherchez l'argent, huh, J.J. thought. What a dumb fucking idea.

When he returned to Homicide, J.J. asked Guillory for another look at Tyrone Pano's suicide note. He studied it carefully, remembering the curls, the flourishes. He returned to his desk and got out Pano's will. It looked like a match. Damnit. Apparently Pano had killed the Davis woman and taken his own life. And he wanted the Southern Cross to get his money.

He folded the will and placed it back in the envelope. Then he went looking for Marty Boyle.

He found the wild-haired policeman in the Gumbo Tak Tak observation room with a couple of others, watching one of the detectives grill a petite brunette. The woman looked as if she'd been up all night. Her yellow silk dress was creased and her elaborately marcelled hair was unspooling over her forehead.

"It's the Lambino dame," Boyle told him. "Fed her old man rat poison, got all dressed up and went out on the town."

"Dainty little thing," J.J. said. "How do I get hold of Pen Libideau?"

Boyle cocked his head. "The scratch man? Is he inside or out?"

"If he was in, I could probably locate him myself."

"If he's out," Boyle said, "his sister would know. Marcella—what's her married name?—Zabisa. In the phone book."

"Jesus, look at that."

The Lambino woman had removed a stiletto shoe and was pelting the interrogator with it. "Good swing," J.J. said, walking away.

Marcy Zabisa wanted to know why J.J. was looking for her brother. "Larry doesn't do forgery anymore. He's going straight." J.J. said that was good news. He wanted Larry to do a straight job for him.

The address on Magazine Street the sister provided belonged to a print shop run by an old German who wore bib overalls over fish-white bare skin. Larry Libideau, his assistant, was garbed more conventionally in a white T-shirt and Levi's. He was of average height and girth, prematurely balding, with slightly sunken cheeks and an aquiline nose. Both he and the old man looked like they'd been rolling around in ink.

Libideau was not happy to see him. "Hi, Legendre," he said halfheartedly. His quick blue eyes went to the ledger under J.J.'s arm, but he didn't seem too interested. He indicated with his head that the detective follow him through the rear door. "Grabbin' a smoke, Mister Zoller," he called to the old man, who glared at J.J.

Behind the store was a scrub-grass yard and several large metal bins filled with cardboard boxes and discarded printed matter. Libideau shook out a Camel and offered J.J. the pack, which he refused.

"What do you need?" Libideau asked.

"You read Cajun, don't you, Pen?"

"So?"

He held out the ledger to the ex-forger, who cleaned his hands on his pants before accepting it. He flipped a few pages.

"Looks like some kind of business records," he said. "Names of customers, addresses, quantities, delivery dates. Like that."

"I couldn't make any sense of it," J.J. said.

"The woman who wrote this"—he looked at the cover—"Florine Pousson, didn't set it up like a business ledger. More like a notebook. She describes how her customers look, the stuff they sell, their markup. She still with us? Naw, I guess not, or she could be telling you all this. What's the deal? You looking for the guy who did her?"

"Maybe. How much for you to go through the book and make me a list of all the names in there?"

"Just the names?" Libideau asked.

J.J. nodded.

"Some of these customers, she doesn't seem to know their names. Just nicknames and descriptions and addresses."

"Make me a list of each customer, with a name and address or a description or whatever."

"For you, fifty bucks," Libideau said.

"Thirty," J.J. said. "And there's one other little thing I'd like you to do."

"Oh?" Libideau said. "Like what?"

"The thing you do best."

"Yeah?" Libideau gave him a crooked grin. "That bein' the case, thirty-five's the lowest I go."

MADELEINE CONSULTED HER daily schedule. Yes, the house she was parked in front of was the correct address. She hadn't realized that Philip Street was in the Garden District. She got out of the car and looked at the house again. It was an imposing two-story, recently painted a medium gray with white trim and dark green shutters. The galleries were cast iron, intricately patterned. A large front yard was visible behind a five-foot wrought-iron fence. The oak trees in the yard looked like they'd been shading the house since the last century and, barring hurricanes and floods, might be shading it a century hence.

The front gate was unlocked.

She walked toward the steps that led to the porch. The air was filled with the scent of magnolias. At the door, a dull gold frame rimmed a buzzer and beneath it was a sedate rectangle bearing the family name "Glander." Madeleine pressed the buzzer and heard its signal sound deep inside the house.

In hardly any time there were footsteps approaching the front door. It opened and Theodore Glander saw her and took a backward step so she could enter.

He was fully dressed for the day, but was still wearing his slippers. He said, "Miss DuBois, come in."

"Call me Madeleine, please," she said.

"Would you like some coffee, Madeleine, or shall we begin the grand tour?"

"The tour, please," she said, her eyes taking in the hallway with its dark wood floors and peach-colored walls.

To their right was an amazing living room with high coved ceilings, elaborately carved beams and other woodwork all painted a creamy off-white. The ceiling supported one large crystal chandelier. The walls were the same off-white, broken by silk drapes of similar hue adorning four floor-to-ceiling windows. A rich, pale green carpet covered most of the floor. And on it rested an assortment of French antiques. A champagne-colored sofa and matching armchairs surrounded a fireplace topped by a large mirror with a yellow metal frame. Could it have been gold? Madeleine wondered.

Glander entered the room, displaying no small amount of pride in its expensive furnishings. Madeleine saw that another section had two pale blue silk-covered chairs flanking a series of wooden tables, each table a few inches shorter and narrower than the other and telescoping across the carpet.

Glander said, "My wife loved this room."

Madeleine nodded, trying to keep the smile on her face. She hated the room. It reminded her of a museum.

Next was a formal dining room with a table that seated four-teen comfortably, then a kitchen no smaller than that needed by Antoine's and beyond that a neat room and bath used by someone named Anna who cooked and took care of the housekeeping chores but who was away visiting a cousin in Alexandria.

Glander escorted Madeleine up a flight of stairs, and down a short hall running from front to back. He nodded to a closed door and proclaimed it his bedroom, then moved her past it and two other closed doors to one that was open at the end of the hall.

Inside was an alcove leading to a large, bright, feminine bedroom with a four-poster, a matching vanity, several tufted chairs, and a small television set on a table.

"I had Anna dust things off before she left," he told her. "My daughter lived here when she was still single. Here's the bath and off that is a little room that I suppose you could use for whatever you care to. Lee Ann did her studying in there."

"This is very nice," Madeleine told him. It was the only section of the house that seemed real to her. Not only real, but comfortable—livable.

"There's a private entrance," he said, pointing to a door at the end of the small extra room.

She walked over to it and looked down through its mullioned windows to a landscaped garden filled with lilies, roses, violets and poppies. Bright yellow buttercups surrounded a lap pool.

"It's everything you said it was on the phone, Mr. Glander," she told him. "But I'm still a bit confused as to how you knew I was in the market for an apartment."

"When my son-in-law introduced us at Homicide, you were circling rentals in the Classified."

"So I was," she said, oddly relieved. "You're a very observant man."

"Actually, it was John who noticed your paper and mentioned it to me. We were discussing Lee Ann's rooms and . . . anyway, I'd be most pleased if you decide to live here."

"It's a charming house," she said, "and the price is certainly right."

"I'm not renting the rooms for the money," he told her. "We . . . I felt the place was so big for just me and Anna. And I think it'll do us both good to have someone young in the house."

"John doesn't live here?" she asked.

"No. He prefers to live on his own. If you decide to move in, you may use any part of the house you care to, except the two rooms down the hall, my bedroom and my . . . den."

"How would we work the kitchen?"

"Work? Oh yes, of course. I haven't really thought all of this through. Anna fixes my breakfast at eight-fifteen each morning and dinner at seven-thirty. I'd be happy to have you join me whenever you care to. Just tell her what to prepare. Other than that, feel free to use the kitchen whenever you want."

"What about guests?"

He frowned. "Yes, of course, you may have guests," he said, but his face didn't seem to agree with his words. "You and J.J. Legendre, I assume you're keeping company."

She liked the expression. "Yes, we are."

"Is it serious?"

"I don't really know," she replied.

"He's an interesting man," Theodore Glander said. "The reason I asked you not to mention your coming here to him is that I feel a bit strange about the world knowing I'm taking in a boarder. John said he thinks that it may even be illegal to rent in this neighborhood."

"But if I decided to move in . . . ?"

"Oh, if you do, then of course J.J. and your other friends would have to know. But if not, I'd appreciate your keeping it to yourself."

She thought it a bit odd. In fact, the whole thing seemed less and less appealing. Possibly her face showed some negative sign, because Glander said, "Please, take your time before making up your mind. I have a few things to work on in the den, but you stay here and get the feel of the place. Visit the garden. If you'd like a swim, the pool is heated. Use one of Lee Ann's suits in the closet. I imagine they'd fit you a bit snugly, but—"

"I really don't have much time," she said.

"Spend a few minutes by yourself. Then come get me and give me the verdict."

He turned and left her.

She looked at her watch. She had over an hour before her next class. Not enough time to look at any of the other availabilities. Too much time to drive to the campus immediately. So she dallied a bit in the rooms where Glander's deceased daughter had grown up. She slipped off her loafers and hopped onto the bed, testing its firmness. It seemed very inviting.

Then, shod once again, she revisited the bathroom, poked into a medicine cabinet that contained an unopened jar of deodorant, an unwrapped bar of Sweetheart soap, Mercuro-chrome, cotton balls, Band-Aids, all in pristine condition. In a half closet were washcloths, hand towels, bath mats in matching pink.

She continued on to the small extra room, where she satisfied her curiosity about a metal filing cabinet in one corner by opening it and discovering a pile of 45 r.p.m. records. Pop music played by big bands, mostly.

Madeleine unlocked the back door and stepped out onto the platform at the top of the stairwell. She descended to the garden, made her way to the pool, bent and ran a hand through the pleasantly warm water. It was all very nice, but not for her. Besides, Glander didn't really want a boarder, he wanted a daughter.

As she climbed the stairs, she thought she heard the old man call out. But when she entered, the house was still.

She walked down the hall to the second door before the stairwell, the one leading to Glander's den. She knocked.

No answer.

"Mr. Glander," she called.

Nothing.

So he wasn't in the den.

She began a search of the house but couldn't find him, although when she entered the kitchen she had the sensation that someone had just left.

She returned to the den and knocked again.

When Glander did not answer, she began to wonder if something might have happened to him. Could the cry she thought she'd heard have been a heart attack or a seizure?

She opened the door.

Two things struck her immediately. One, Theodore Glander was not in the room. Two, it didn't look like a den. More an office, with desk, typewriter, cabinets. It had pale yellow walls and dark wood trim and beams. A tinted photograph of a teenaged girl—she assumed it was the murdered daughter, Lee Ann—was attached to the wall above the rolltop desk. The tint job wasn't very good. The girl's skin tone was too pink, her lips too red.

To the right of the desk was a bookshelf. Madeleine barely glanced at the titles. Louisiana and New Orleans histories ranging from George Augustin's *The History of Yellow Fever* to Harnett T. Kane's *Queen New Orleans*. Biographies—*Beauregard, the Great Creole* by Hamilton Basso, Gladys

Bumstead's *Louisiana Composers*, *The Life and Work of John McDonogh* by William Allan, and possibly fifty others, including at least a dozen studies of the Long family. A special section contained a number of volumes devoted to Marie Laveau, including Henry Marnet's locally published biography, as well as an assortment of voodoo titles by Robert Tallant and others.

On the desk was a stack of papers, a lighted brass lamp with a green shade and a telephone.

She turned to leave. And saw the doll.

It was resting on a wooden cabinet against the wall near the door. A small white doll, crudely sewn to resemble a woman with blond hair. Madeleine had read about the Meddler's dolls. God, she thought, could this be the one that the killer left beside Glander's daughter? Why would he keep such a thing? Wasn't it evidence that the police would hang onto until the case was solved?

The cabinet on which the doll rested had double doors that weren't quite closed. She hesitated, then opened them.

Inside were ten or more dolls, some with yellow hair, some with black, some with red. There were even a few black dolls.

She recoiled from the sight, as if the figurines had been alive. She could think of only one reason for their presence in Glander's den.

In semipanic, she somehow managed to get out of the room, racing for the stairs.

At the bottom of the stairwell, she could see the front door. The morning sun, filtered through a white linen curtain, gave the door a strange, ethereal glow.

She started for it.

Something brushed her hair, then fingers grasped it. She was yanked backward off her feet. Out of control. Helpless. Terrified.

The hallway wall rushed toward her face. Then nothing.

30

J.J. HAD SPENT his last hour on the job that day standing with a few other detectives at the one-way glass, watching the interrogation of Raymond Boudreaux. Fontineau and Roussou had been at the frail young man all day, the latter playing a convincing prone-to-violence hothead, Fontineau doing his best to bring calm and reason to the questioning. Roussou bullied Boudreaux. Fontineau befriended him.

In fact, both officers were convinced that Boudreaux was their man and all of their questions, hard or soft, were guided by that preconception.

When Boudreaux first arrived, he asked if he should get a lawyer. Fontineau responded with another question: Did he have something to hide? Boudreaux waived his right to a lawyer.

At first, he'd tried answering them calmly and coolly. But after an hour of intensifying pressure, he began to frazzle.

By 6 P.M. Boudreaux's answers had begun to take on a vague quality. He no longer remembered exactly where he'd been when his fiancée had been brutally murdered. He didn't know when or why she'd made him the beneficiary of her insurance. He asked for a glass of water.

Standing beside J.J. was Officer Roland, his eyes even more bloodshot than they'd been at breakfast. He chuckled and gleefully announced, "They got the fucker now."

At six-thirty, Lieutenant Lamotta entered the observation room looking cheerier than usual. "How's it goin'?" he asked.

"They got him sweatin' good, Lieutenant," Roland said.

"Boudreaux looks sick," J.J. said. "Maybe somebody ought to call his doctor."

"Jesus, why not call the fucker's lawyer, too?"

"I don't expect Roland to read the papers," J.J. said to Lamotta, "but you must know about the Escobedo decision."

"Nobody's robbing anybody of his rights here," Lamotta said.

J.J. stared through the one-way at Boudreaux, who had leaned forward to rest his head on the table. Roussou grabbed his collar and yanked him upright. "No sleeping, asshole, until we hear those magic words," the cop said.

J.J. nodded to Lamotta and left the room.

Back in his cubicle, he dialed his apartment number. He wanted to tell Madeleine that she could start the dinner.

But she didn't answer.

Maybe he'd misdialed. He tried again. Again, no answer.

He assumed she was at the grocery. Or maybe she'd been held up at school.

He was on his way out when a group led by Lamotta and Fontineau burst into the room, laughing and patting one another on the back. Boudreaux had just broken down and confessed to all the murders.

"C'mon, Legendre," Lamotta said to him. "Drinks on me at the Magnolia."

Fontineau said, "I told the loot it was you who gave me the idea to check the money angle. C'mon. Let's celebrate."

"My girl's fixing me dinner," he told them.

They didn't twist his arm.

31

HIS GIRL WAS definitely not fixing him dinner.

Apparently she hadn't even been back to the apartment since morning. He found the mail still in a pile under the slot. The stove was cold. The fridge was empty.

By eight, he was pacing the floor. He'd cautioned her not to walk in the Quarter after nightfall. Maybe Boudreaux was the Meddler, but J.J. did not want to gamble Madeleine's life on it.

Where the hell was she?

He phoned her apartment for the fourth or fifth time without connecting.

At eight-twenty, *his* phone rang. He grabbed it like a drowning man grabs a life preserver.

It was not Madeleine. The caller was a man. His voice was purposely muffled but there was something vaguely familiar about its cadence. "Officer Legendre, do you know what a layover is?"

"What? Who is this?"

"Oh, please. You know who I am. You're the only one who has any idea what's going on."

J.J.'s mouth was dry. He closed his eyes, his mind whirling. "Don't give me too much credit," he said.

"I could be wrong. Maybe you are as dense as the others."

"What was it you asked me?" J.J. wished he could be more glib. He wanted to keep the man talking. The more he talked, the better the chances of him giving something away. "Do I know *what*?" J.J. asked.

"Do you know what a layover is?"

The policeman frowned. He remembered Henry Marnet's little lecture. "An overnight stay?" he asked.

"I'm talking history, here, Officer Legendre. Old New Orleans history. When the little Creole urchins would point to a glittering gee-gaw in the voodoo shop and ask 'What's that?' the standard reply was, 'A layover to catch a meddler.' You understand?"

J.J. understood, but he wanted to keep the man talking. He said, "You mean, it's a word they used when they didn't know what else to call an object."

"No, no, no. You miss the point. A *layover* to catch a *meddler*. The thing—whatever it is—*lays* on a shelf or a table like a trap to catch whoever tries to meddle with it."

Was he suggesting that a trap be laid for him? Did he want to be caught?

"Of course, as you point out, a layover could also have another meaning," the caller said. "It could mean a woman of easy virtue, who *stays* over, who *lays* herself open to any man. These women I seek out. I ... cleanse them. I remove their impure parts."

The caller paused, obviously expecting J.J. to make some reply. But he hadn't any idea what to say.

Nearly a minute of silence passed and the caller growled, "All right," impatiently. "All right, here it is, Officer Legendre: your layover almost caught me. But she got caught instead."

J.J. felt his stomach flip over. "Who are we talking about?" he asked.

"We? I like that. Enlist the enemy. Well, *we*'re talking about a young woman named Madeleine DuBois."

"Is she with you?" J.J. asked.

"I'm looking at her right now. Looking at that lovely blond hair, that sweet face. Those firm, splendid breasts with just a tint of brown in their aureoles . . ."

"Can I . . ." J.J. interrupted, but his voice broke before he could complete the question.

"Can you what?"

"Speak with her?" Pictures of the Meddler's other victims flashed through his mind.

"I'm afraid not," the Meddler said. "She's resting. Had a very eventful morning. Hmmm. Isn't this interesting. She's unconscious, but if you touch her nipple with something cold, like the blade of this knife, it gets as hard as if it were feeling a lover's kiss."

J.J.'s body was struck by a chill so profound he had to press the phone tight to his ear to keep it from shaking. He'd never felt so helpless in his life. Never felt so many emotions attack and confound his brain.

"Are you still with me, Officer?" the voice asked. "Sorry if I was too . . . graphic. No offense meant."

J.J. took a deep breath. Stop fucking around, he told himself. Think like a con man, not like a cop. The guy had called *him*. That meant he wanted something. "What's on your mind?" he asked the Meddler in a voice so calm he surprised himself.

"Let me explain," his caller said, growing more intense in counterpoint to J.J.'s coolness. "I see the problem, just as my predecessor saw it more than a hundred years ago. Women of easy virtue. In those days, they were allowed to indulge in their sins at the Voodoo Queen's closed gatherings. Now we have fornication in the parks. Free love in the doorways of the French Quarter! Only love is a misnomer. Sex is today's substitute. And sex rots the social fabric. I am a sharp serrated knife that cuts away this rot."

J.J. frowned. The analogy was familiar, but not enough for him to pin it down.

"You're not up to date on your predecessor," J.J. said. "He killed those women because Marie Laveau allowed his brother to hang."

There was a brief silence. Then, "What the hell are you talking about?"

"New discovery," J.J. said, his mouth dry. Trying to keep his mind clear of the image of Madeleine. "The Meddler has been identified as a man named . . . But that's not why you called."

"Who *have* you been talking to, Officer Legendre?" the Meddler asked, his voice showing signs of strain.

Scams danced through J.J.'s head. He could drop Henry Marnet's name, then run a trace on the historian's phone, have round-the-clock surveillance on his home. Or, he could create a fake historian. . . .

But the madman had Madeleine. There wasn't enough time to set up a trap. And Lamotta was convinced the Meddler was in a prison cell, so there would be no help from that quarter.

"Just something I read," J.J. finally replied.

"Read where? You can appreciate my interest."

"There was a nice long article. Full of details. About a diary belonging to a warden at Parish prison. I've got a copy of the article. We could meet and—"

The Meddler laughed. "Actually," he said, "I was going to suggest that we do get together. Madeleine will awake soon and rather than simply purify her, as I have the others, I might listen to arguments on her behalf from someone whose integrity I respect. And I'm most anxious to hear about my predecessor."

"Where should we meet?" J.J. asked.

"Here would be nice."

"Where are you?"

The Meddler laughed again. "You're the detective," he said, and broke the connection.

32

THERE WAS NOT enough information.

J.J. knew Madeleine had had an appointment to look at an apartment—no, a suite—at 9 A.M. The Meddler had said she'd had "an eventful morning." She "almost caught me . . . but she got caught instead."

Did Madeleine almost catch him on her way to the appointment? Was he following her? Could he have been at the suite waiting for her?

Instead of killing her immediately, as he had the others, the Meddler had called *him*. The Meddler was someone who knew of his connection to Madeleine. What was his point? Madeleine had not been arbitrarily chosen. But if her role was not that of victim, what was she? The bait? The contest object? What did the Meddler really want from him? His information about Raymond Swan? His cooperation? His life?

J.J. closed his eyes and very carefully replayed everything Madeleine had said that morning. Immediately he remembered their discussion of the "secret." Had it been about the suite? Probably. Then there was something about her destination that held some significance for *him*. Was it the location? The prospective landlord?

He had to find out the address.

He tore through the bedroom, but she'd left nothing behind.

He might have better luck at her apartment. There could be a newspaper with an address circled, a note she'd written to herself. Something.

He paused on his way out. He might get to her faster if he had help. But there was no time. Even if he could convince Lamotta that the Meddler was still at large and about to kill again, the debate would take forever. He'd have to do this alone.

The drive to Madeleine's apartment on Camp Street took less than fifteen minutes. Hers was the left side of a shotgun duplex. The dark side. The right was brightly lit and noisy. Rock and roll. Dishes rattling. Laughter. There were enough cars parked along the narrow street to indicate a big party that would grow bigger.

J.J. followed the brick walkway around the left side of the duplex, checking window screens. They were all locked. He picked up a rock from the flower bed lining the property and carried it to the back door.

The sound of a glass pane being knocked out of the mullioned window was lost in the general racket issuing from the other side of the duplex. He reached in through the broken window, found the lock clasp and turned it.

He eased the back door open and entered a kitchen that smelled of coffee and cantaloupe. There was not enough moonlight for him to see the way to the rest of the apartment, but he'd brought a flashlight and he used it.

A phone was attached to the wall next to the refrigerator. But no pad. No notes.

A hall ran from back to front. The first door off it led to a room empty of furniture and everything else except for a pile of dust somebody had left in the middle of the floor. The former roommate's domain. He moved on.

Madeleine's bedroom was tidy and feminine. Ruffles. Bed neatly made with one rag doll resting on a pillow. Clothes put away. There was a pad next to the telephone beside the bed. Blank. Not even indentations of previous scribbles. The wastebasket was empty.

He found what he was looking for in the living room. On a coffee table in front of a corduroy couch. It was a lined yellow tablet on which Madeleine had written that day's date and under it three addresses.

The first one seemed familiar, but he wasn't sure why. He hoped he'd find out.

He left by the front door. Two young men were headed for the duplex as he walked away. They swayed enough to indicate they'd gotten an early start on the party.

"Good ginch inside?" one of them asked J.J.

The look he got in reply was enough to sober him for the rest of the night.

33

HER CAR WAS parked on Philip Street, directly in front of the first address on the yellow pad.

The two-story house looked dark and empty. J.J. studied the yard for some sign of a dog. Finally, he decided to chance it.

The front gate was unlocked. It had been oiled recently and opened effortlessly and without sound. No dog.

Inside the well-kept grounds, he drew his service revolver and began a careful study of the house from the outside, moving as close to the French windows as he dared, straining to see what the interior held.

As he passed the front of the house, he noticed something curious. Moonlight glittered on a shiny brass mailbox near the door. The lid was raised.

J.J. went to it. The day's mail—bills, coupons, several weekly magazines—was still in the box. All pieces were addressed to Theodore M. Glander.

J.J. was not surprised. Instead, he was annoyed with himself for not having pushed his investigation of Glander harder, especially after Henry Marnet mentioned the Marie Laveau connection. Just because the man hadn't needed his daughter's money, J.J. had ignored the obvious other possibility, that a deranged murderer didn't really need a genuine motive.

The detective paused, momentarily disturbed by the vague memory of something that happened at his meeting with Marnet. The odds on Glander's being the Meddler were improving by the second. But something didn't fit, and J.J. couldn't quite focus on the inconsistency. Not with Madeleine probably inside the house. Undoubtedly in danger.

He replaced the mail and tried the handle of the front door. Locked.

For the second time that night, he tested windows on his way to the rear of a house. For the second time, he found all the windows secured.

The bolted back door was solid wood.

But there was a rear stairwell leading to the second story.

Cautiously, he climbed the stairs.

On a landing at the top he looked through the door's mullioned windows at a small room. It was in shadows, but a light shone through an open doorway, throwing a square of pale yellow across a portion of a throw rug on the floor. On the edge of the rug, a crudely sewn voodoo doll with blond hair lay on its back.

He was staring at the doll when something else caught his eye. Something pale stirring on the floor, extending through the lighted doorway.

He pressed his face closer to the back door's glass panel. The stirring something was a naked foot. Not particularly small, but delicate. A length of cloth seemed to be wrapped around the ankle.

He shivered. A rabbit jumping over his grave.

He reached out to the door handle. Turned it.

The door was locked.

The wood frame was thick, hung to open outward. He wondered how long it would take to kick in enough glass panels to get inside the house. Too long. Especially if the Meddler were in the other room with Madeleine.

He stared at the bare foot helplessly for a moment, then descended the back stairs.

He began a search of the other side of the house. This time he was more successful. A casement window at knee height had been left unlatched. But it was paint-stuck. The night was cool, but he was perspiring freely as he used his penknife to slowly work the window free with a minimum of squeaks.

Kneeling, he edged the upper part of his body past the sill. He was staring at a dark cement basement that was damp and smelled of detergent. There were in fact two large boxes of soap flakes on a counter beside a double sink directly beneath the window. Not far away was an old washing machine with a drying apparatus on its top, the kind in which water is squeezed out of clothes as they move between two rollers.

He lowered himself carefully to the sinks. Convinced they

were sturdy enough, he shifted his weight onto them, then slipped over their side to the cement floor.

There was enough moonlight for him to see and mount several cement steps to the next level and another cement floor where an ironing board and a wooden table shared space with shelves filled with various household tools. A girl's bicycle was parked in a far corner, gathering dust.

A much higher flight of stairs, wooden this time, led to a closed door. J.J. approached it cautiously, his gun again in his hand.

The door was unlocked. Beyond it was a large kitchen filled with the pleasant odor of baked bread. Clean, waxed linoleum made a soft popping noise under his rubber soles as he crossed the room to a pantry and through that into a hall.

It, like most of the house, was in darkness. But his night sight had kicked in and, with the moonlight, was enough to keep him from bumping into walls and furniture.

He paused before entering the hall. There were several open doorways, which meant that as soon as he stepped from the relative safety of the pantry, knowing that the house behind him was secure, he would be exposing himself to attack from every side.

With this in mind, he hugged one wall all the way to the stairwell. The stairs were dark wood, solid, heavily padded. They smelled of furniture wax and dust. He shifted his full weight onto the first stair. No loud creak. No creak at all.

He strained his ears but couldn't hear a sound except his own heartbeat. Then he was up two steps. Four. Ten. His head cleared the top of the well.

The upstairs was dark, too. But a line of yellow light framed a rear doorway. Probably the same light he'd seen from the back landing.

Once again, he was faced with the problem of passing a series of doorways before reaching the lighted room. An attack could come from any direction except, presumably, up. His eyes raked the ceiling and he smiled at that touch of senseless fear.

He heard a moan. Coming from the lighted room.

He moved along one wall, treading on the edge of the carpet to muffle his footsteps. Finally, he stood before the light-outlined door. His heart racing, he reached for the knob.

He simultaneously opened the door and dropped down to the left of it.

The door swung in on an alcove to a feminine bedroom, the details of which were lost on J.J. His vision was taken up by the woman lying on the floor.

Madeleine's wide eyes stared up at him. She was fully dressed, except for her left penny loafer, which was lying beside her body. The right side of her face was a fierce red and so swollen her eye was nearly shut. Adhesive tape covered her mouth. Thinner strips secured her wrists and ankles.

He moved quickly past the doorway and immediately flipped off the light switch, turning the room as dark as the rest of the house. Keeping watch on the silent hallway, he withdrew a penknife from his pocket and crouched down beside Madeleine. He severed the tape strips connecting her ankles and wrists.

Her arms went around him, hugging him desperately. There were tears of relief in her eyes. He forced himself to look away from her to the hallway.

She drew back and gingerly began peeling the tape from her mouth. It left her lips raw and puffy. A glimpse of them gave J.J. an erotic frisson he did not particularly welcome under the circumstances.

"How badly are you hurt?" he whispered.

"Threw me into a wall," she whispered back. "Knocked out. I'm awake now."

"Where is he?"

"I don't know," she replied helplessly. "I woke up . . . hours ago . . . he wasn't here. Been trying to . . . get loose."

He stood and helped her to her feet. She swayed, steadied herself and nodded. "I'm okay." She slipped her bare foot into the waiting shoe.

He led her to the back door. He unlocked it and was about to step onto the landing when, suddenly, the entire rear of the house was aglow in a blaze of lights.

Shaken, he stared down at the garden, the lap pool. A yellow cat had been caught by the lights. Its eyes glowed for a brief second before it raced away along a flagstone path. Other than that, he could see no movement below.

But a rear escape seemed out of the question now. Even in darkness, the descent along an open stairwell would have been dangerous.

He moved past Madeleine, returning to the alcove. The upstairs hall looked just as empty as it had on his way up. "Stay behind me," he whispered as they stepped through the alcove door.

Music began.

A Dixieland jazz band played a familiar tune. Not one of the upbeat rags but more of a dirge. A piano cut through the brass and a woman's shaky voice sang, *"Marie Laveau, she was a voodoo queen ... an' she walk the streets of New Aw-leen ..."*

It was all stagecraft, he told himself. Shock and surprise. Misdirection, the con man's camouflage. But his heart was still pounding against his chest and the gun in his hand was wet with sweat. If he could just calm down, he could beat this guy at whatever weird game they were playing.

"Where's it coming from?" Madeleine asked, her voice rising in panic.

"One of the rooms," he said. He put his free arm around her, holding her tightly as if to squeeze the fear from her. But he was afraid, too.

Together they made their way to the top of the stairs.

"... she has a red snake she call Ma-man ... and she use her gris-gris like no other witch can ..."

Madeleine leaned into him, crying against his shoulder as they started down the stairs.

"Marie Laveau," the woman sang.

"Oh, Marie Laveau," a male chorus, probably the band members, replied.

"She was a voodoo queen ..."

They were nearing the foot of the stairs when a gunshot from above ripped a hole in the plaster wall not far from J.J.'s head.

He grabbed Madeleine and pulled her over the stairwell. He landed on his side, banging his elbow hard. She fell on top of him.

He pulled her over him, placing his body between hers and the stairwell. Protecting her from any more gunfire from above.

But none came.

Just the slow, mournful song about the voodoo queen drawing to a close with trumpets, piano and singer all ending on the words *"New Aw-leens."*

J.J. stood and helped Madeleine to her feet.

The music started up again. This time the song was "Baby, Please Don't Go." A male voice began to sing along with the woman. Only his voice was not part of the record. And instead of the words of the song, he shouted, *"Please don't go . . . let's end it all right now."*

It came from the top of the stairs.

J.J. stared at Madeleine and pointed to the front door. Obedient but confused, she staggered in that direction. His elbow throbbing, he took a step toward the stairwell, as if drawn by the singer's request.

"Glander?" he called.

"Let's end it all right now," the singer improvised again in time with the music, *"you know I love you so."*

J.J. moved closer to the stairwell. He was within inches of being able to get a clear view of the top of the stairs.

"You know I hate you so," the male singer snarled and two more bullets smashed into the plaster wall six inches in front of J.J.'s nose.

"Screw this," he mumbled, and dived low onto the stairs, aiming up. A second before he shot, he realized that the figure above him seemed to be sitting on the top stair. He lowered his aim and fired. Twice.

The figure bounced backward, then, because of some force of physics that seemed inexplicable to J.J. at the time, it rolled forward and bounced down the stairwell. The detective was barely able to leap back before the body of Theodore Glander landed in front of him, eyes open and glaring. A third eye, high on his forehead, was the result of one of J.J.'s bullets. Blood trickled from it.

The music continued to play.

J.J. stared at Glander, hypnotized by those open eyes. The sounds of Madeleine crying and the female singer's croaking voice broke his trance.

He checked the dead man's empty hands. The gun must have fallen somewhere up above. They'd find it later.

J.J. backed away from the stairs. Madeleine was waiting for him at the front door. He took her in his arms. "It's over," he told her.

From somewhere upstairs, the recorded voice continued to sing.

34

THERE WAS NO question of Glander's guilt. Pen Libideau, the Cajun forger, had found his name among Florine Pousson's customers in her ledger, though her description of him as *"jeune"* was a little off, except that, to a woman in her nineties, a man in his middle years might seem young.

In any case, the unused dolls were still in his home. The police uncovered other circumstantial evidence there, too: the books about Marie Laveau, including one containing information on the original homicidal Meddler, newspaper clippings regarding the murders and, the most incriminating, index cards, neatly filed, containing information about the victims with detailed descriptions of each gruesome death, including his own daughter's.

As Henry Marnet would later sum up the murders:

"Glander had decided some time ago to kill his daughter for her half of his wife's estate. The other deaths had been an effort to confuse the police, to lead them to the false conclusion that all of the murders had been the capricious choice of a homicidal maniac. He had considered himself sane and shrewd, even though he was quite wealthy and his only need for his daughter's money had been in his own mind."

Dr. James Helvig, the psychiatrist who had been advising the NOPD on the Meddler case, labeled it delusional behavior.

J.J. wasn't entirely satisfied with that rather tidy explanation. Why, he wondered, had Glander insisted on getting him assigned to the Meddler squad? Dr. Helvig's response was to question J.J. about his and Glander's previous association.

"Perhaps," the psychiatrist suggested, "Mr. Glander respected you for refusing to speak ill of your fellow officers.

Perhaps he saw you as someone who might be capable of identifying him as the Meddler."

"Why would he want that?" J.J. asked.

"They all want to be caught," Dr. Helvig told him.

"By 'they,' you mean what?"

"Serial murderers, of course."

"But Glander wasn't really a serial murderer," J.J. argued. "He was only pretending to be one."

With infuriating logic, Dr. Helvig replied, "He murdered a number of young women and mutilated their corpses. He may have thought he was only pretending insanity, but I can assure you, those were not the acts of a sane man."

Two weeks after Glander's death, Lamotta called J.J. into his office. "Marty Boyle tells me you're thinking of leavin' us," the lieutenant said.

"Thinking is about as far as I've gotten," J.J. said.

"I fucked up on you, Ca——Legendre," Lamotta said. "We all did. You been playing straight with us all along and we been treating you like Typhoid Mary. I wouldn't blame you if you threw in your shield. I guess you've had some interestin' offers since you took Glander down."

"One or two," J.J. replied. He didn't gloat. He didn't show any emotion whatsoever.

"There are some say you pulled a Wyatt Earp, going after Glander on your own," Lamotta said. "But they don't say it around me. I don't see as how you had any choice. Nobody here would have backed you up. We were satisfied with that poor bastard Raymond Boudreaux.

"Anyway, you got the job done single-handed, and everybody from me to Chief Mathern to the mayor wants to thank you. If you do stick it out with us, I can pretty well guarantee a promotion, which will boost that retirement check a little."

J.J. wished he could enjoy Lamotta's groveling, but he didn't feel comfortable accepting the praise. As he saw it, Glander had done nearly all of the work himself. After eluding the police for so long, leaving no discovered clues, why had he suddenly, at the end, given up? Why had he, with J.J. and Madeleine in his gun sights, shot over their heads? Maybe the psychiatrist had been correct. Glander had wanted to be caught.

"Like to grab some lunch over at Maylie's?" Lamotta asked, bringing J.J. back from his thoughts.

"Could we do it tomorrow instead?"

"Sure," Lamotta said, smiling. "Tomorrow'll be fine."

"There's an errand I have to run today," J.J. told him.

The errand took him to the law offices of Nathan and Burns, where a bored receptionist brightened at his name. "Oh yes, sir. Mr. Billins says you're to go right on back to his office. I'll take you."

She led him past several smiling secretaries eager to get a glimpse at the man who'd killed the Meddler. The door to James Billins's office was open. The neatly attired black man moved from behind his desk, hand extended. "Congratulations on your remarkable achievement," Billins said. "I believe you know Mr. Hart."

Tank nodded to J.J. from a leather chair in the corner of the room.

"I took the liberty of inviting him here, since he is representing the Southern Cross, which I believe to be mentioned in Tyrone's will," Billins said.

"It's your idea that there's a will in the sealed envelope," J.J. said. "But Mr. Hart's presence is all right with me."

"Fine, then," Billins said, staring at him expectantly.

J.J. reached inside his coat pocket and withdrew an envelope. He handed it to Billins, who asked, "And you came by this how, exactly?"

J.J. told them about his visit to Tyrone Pano's cell. "He asked me to locate this envelope and to hold on to it for him."

Tank said, "You tol' me you didn't have the will."

"No," J.J. corrected him. "You asked if Tyrone had given me a will. He didn't. He asked me to locate that envelope and keep it for him. He did not give it to me. And he didn't say what was in the envelope. Mr. Billins thinks it may be a will. For all I know it's Tyrone's laundry list."

"Where'd you get it?" Tank wanted to know.

"It was Tyrone's request that I not disclose that."

James Billins carried the envelope back to his desk and sat down. Both J.J. and Tank sat down, too. Billins removed a letter opener from a desk drawer. Tank leaned forward in his chair. Billins slit open the envelope and removed a sheet of paper. He glared at it and frowned.

"What?" Tank asked. "It's his will, isn't it?"

"It's his will all right," Billins said. "But not the one I witnessed. This one is dated just three weeks ago."

Tank was out of his chair. "The Cross still gets his money, right?"

Billins cleared his throat. "Not according to this," he said. "According to this, his entire estate—all his worldly possessions—go to someone named Shana Washington."

"Lemme see that," Tank said, reaching across the desk and grabbing the sheet of paper. He looked at it briefly, then turned to J.J. "This the Shana you were looking for, otha' day?"

J.J. didn't answer.

"You sure this authentic?" Tank asked Billins.

"It looks like Tyrone's writing," Billins replied.

"What about the other will? The one where he left his money to the Southern Cross?"

"I don't know," Billins said, confused. "Perhaps Tyrone destroyed it. I just don't know."

"I guess you don't know either," Tank said to J.J.

J.J. shrugged. "I'm just the delivery boy," he said. He plucked the will from Billins's hand. "Guess I'd better go find Shana Washington and tell her the good news."

He was getting into his car when Tank caught up with him. The big man was in a combative mood. "You ain't gettin' away with this," he said.

"Getting away with what?" J.J. asked, straightening, facing Tank.

"Tyrone wanted the money to go to us."

"That's not what his will says."

"Fuck what it says. You did this, man. Now you give me that piece of paper and we tear it up right now. Go back to the old will."

He reached out and grabbed J.J.'s coat.

J.J. put his hand on Tank's and said, "Don't be a fool. Look over there."

Warily, Tank shifted his position slightly, so that he could look in the direction J.J. indicated. Across the street, two black men in suits were sitting in a parked tan car, glaring at them.

"What's with them?" Tank asked.

"They're FBI agents," J.J. said. "They'd love to see you do something stupid, so they could lock you up and throw away the key."

Tank dropped his hand and took a step away from J.J. "You're fuckin' with me, Officer," he said ominously.

"I don't want to see you again, Tank," J.J. said. "And I

don't want to hear about you trying to find Shana Washington to give her any grief. If you do, you'll make those guys very happy, because I'll be giving them all they need to close down the Southern Cross and put you out of business."

"Don't bullshit me, Officer," Tank said. "You don't have nothing on the Cross."

"Just a few little things that Tyrone mentioned," J.J. lied. "But I think that'll be enough."

Tank stared at him, studying his face. Then he nodded and took a few steps backward. He turned and walked quickly to the unpainted Pontiac.

After dinner that night, J.J. and Madeleine stopped for a drink at the Perdido Lounge. The bruise on her face had gone from black to purple to a greenish yellow. Sitting at the bar, beside a woman with red, white and blue hair, she touched the bruise and said, "My complexion fits right in."

"It looks like it's healing nicely," he told her.

"What about you? Holding up under all the stroking?"

"I think I can handle it," he said.

"A man named Libideau called the apartment this morning and said he'd finished that job for you."

"I know. He called the office, too. I saw him and it's all taken care of."

"He isn't a jeweler, is he?" she asked.

J.J. smiled. "No. He's a forger. What would I need with a jeweler?"

She stared at him, then shook her head. "You're never going to change, are you?"

"Stick around and see," he replied.

THREE

New Orleans Louisiana

The Present

NADIA WELLS PRESSED the button on the intercom speaker on her desk. "Could somebody please bring me a cup of coffee to soothe my poor, parched throat?" She looked across at Terry Manion. "You want one, too, hon?"

He nodded, and she made that an order for two.

"Well," she said to him, "what do you think about the life and death of Mr. Tyrone Pano?"

Manion glanced at the notes he'd scribbled on a pocket pad during her briefing. "I worked with J.J. day in and day out for two years, and I never heard a word out of him about Pano. I don't even think he mentioned the Meddler."

"J.J. didn't much like tootin' his own horn," Nadia said. "And you know how he was about past history. He only opened up to me because we were having lunch while he was right in the middle of it all and he wanted some advice."

"What specifically?"

"He thought the envelope Pano had given him—the one that contained a will—may have been tampered with."

"Was it?" Manion asked.

"It sorta looked like it."

"What was in the will?"

"He didn't let me see it," she replied. "But later on, it turned out that Pano left everything to my old friend Shana Washington. And I can't see her fakin' any will.

"Anyway, what J.J. told me about Pano, and what you now know, probably is only about half the story. He wasn't the sort of man to bother with details."

Her appraisal was accurate. J.J. had not been completely candid with her about the events of that fateful year. For example, he had neglected to mention his brief interlude with the

159

two FBI agents. It would have helped Manion a great deal if J.J. had told Nadia his theory about Lillian Davis being an undercover agent. But he hadn't.

"I'm beginning to feel I never really knew J.J. at all," Manion said.

"He was not an outgoing man. And neither are you. I think that's why you birds got along so well together. He wasn't comfortable with biddies like me asking him questions all the time."

There was a knock at the door, and then the turbaned Olivette strode into the room and placed a tray containing a pot of coffee and two cups on the desk between Manion and Nadia. "Will that be all, *madame?*" she asked around the cigarette in her mouth.

Nadia raised an eyebrow and said, "I dunno. Sonny, would you care for a sweet roll or something?"

Manion shook his head.

"Then that will be all, my dear," Nadia said.

She smiled as Olivette flounced from the room. "She's been readin' *Cosmo* again, I guess," Nadia said, filling a cup for Manion. "Gets on her high horse about so-called menial labor."

If Manion heard anything she'd said about Olivette, it hadn't registered. His mind was elsewhere. "What happened to Madeleine?" he asked.

Nadia paused, studying him briefly. "You turning into a romantic, sonny? Or have the blues got you down?"

Manion shrugged and pretended indifference.

"I don't know what happened to her," Nadia said. "I never met the woman. She and J.J. were together for a while. But that was when he was workin' Homicide. By the time I threw enough money at him for him to quit the NOPD and join us here, she wasn't in the picture anymore."

"How long was that?"

"Three years, maybe. Fact is, he got bored workin' Homicide. Said he liked it better when they didn't trust him. After he took care of the Meddler, his brothers in blue respected him okay, but they resented him, too. Didn't make it any more pleasant. Anyway, by the time he started with the agency, he was a bachelor man again."

"But they went through so much together," Manion said.

"That don't always warm the bed."

Manion let his thoughts linger on his lost Lucille for a few beats, then switched gears. "I'm still not clear on Pano's death. Did he kill himself or not?"

"J.J. said he thought the suicide note looked legit, but he never believed Pano did himself in," Nadia replied.

"Did he follow up on it?"

Nadia hesitated, then said, "As you know, sonny, J.J. was a damn fine investigator, but he tended to get bored with old cases."

"Even one where he was personally involved?"

"He was a man who moved on."

Manion suddenly realized that what she was saying was the truth. J.J. did have a habit of rushing to shut files and move on. He relished the challenge of a new assignment, but once he'd broken the back of a case, he washed his hands of it. Manion had been happy to tuck up the loose ends of their joint investigations. He'd never for a moment considered his mentor's restlessness to be a professional failing. But impressions change.

"What was it about the suicide that bothered J.J.?" he asked.

"Oh, I forgot that part," she said, and told him about the missing pen and its rather miraculous discovery in Pano's cell.

"Did J.J. mention the name of the cop who conveniently found it?" Manion asked.

"It's an interesting question. If J.J. knew, he didn't say. Or I suppose I could have forgotten that, too."

"The only thing you forget," Manion said, "is to sign your employees' paychecks."

She gave him a wink and, indicating the pad he'd been scribbling on, said, "Maybe *I* should start makin' notes to myself."

"Ever since I stopped drinking, my mind has lost its keen edge," he told her, scribbling himself a reminder to find out who had discovered the pen.

He glanced at the notepad, rechecking the names Nadia had dropped. Madeleine DuBois; Kiel Nathan and James Billins, Pano's lawyers; Patrick Guillory and Martin Boyle, sometime NOPD partners of J.J.'s; Paul Lamotta, who'd been his chief of detectives.

He read the names back to Nadia and asked if she had any idea how he might locate them.

"Well, Lamotta's over in St. Louis Cemetery Number Two," she said. "Stroked out just after J.J. came over here. Copper named Fontineau took his place. He was head of Homicide for a couple of years, then quit and moved back to the country.

"As for James Billins, you must know who he is. Part of the Clay crowd." Magnus Clay, the latest in a long line of the state's oddball politicians, had been a rock star in the fifties, a minor actor in the sixties, a Las Vegas opening act in the seventies, a spokesman for a motor oil in the early eighties and, most recently, Louisiana's favorite son. He was a prime example of the cult of personality, a beaming, handsome performing chameleon who made no mistakes because he did very little except preach (and sing) about the expected upturn in the state's economic picture.

"Does Billins have an official connection to our own combination of Jerry Lee Lewis and Huey Long?" Manion asked.

"Official, I'm not sure. But he's always got a lot to say whenever election time rolls round. I imagine one phone call could provide the specifics of the relationship."

"I hope I won't have to talk with Clay," Manion said. "I find it difficult to concentrate in the presence of greatness."

"But you do it, sonny, and that's why they pay you the big bucks," Nadia said. "Of course, I could probably take some of the load off you. Look into the secret of the gov's platinum hair. Stuff like that. What kind of budget do you have?"

When the television producer Elliott Rubin had given Manion his advance, he'd also supplied him with a business card on which he'd scratched his temporary phone number in Tampa, Florida. Manion got out the card and asked Nadia if he could make a long distance call. She raised one eyebrow and grudgingly nodded.

Rubin was not there. One of his assistants took Nadia's number and promised to have the producer call back within the hour. Twenty minutes later he did, from the auditorium of a Tampa high school, where the segment on teenage hookers was being filmed.

"It's better than we'd hoped," he told Manion. "One of the girls is pregnant. And another one is a dead ringer for Claudia Schiffer."

"Elliott, the reason I called is to tell you that I've decided to proceed with the investigation . . ."

"Great, great," Rubin said.

". . . *but,*" Manion continued, "I'm going to need some help rounding up the people involved in the Pano case."

"What kind of help?" Rubin asked.

"A larger detective agency."

Rubin was silent for a few seconds, then asked, "How much are we talking about?"

Manion put his palm over the speaker and asked Nadia to name a figure for finding the people on the list. She unhesitatingly replied, "Six hundred a day with a minimum of three days."

He relayed the information to Rubin, who asked, "Is your man worth it?"

"She's worth more," Manion said.

"The check is in the mail," he told her after he'd replaced the receiver. "But three grand is their limit."

"Pikers." She grinned. "You don't mind if I work on this myself?"

"I'd be honored," he told her.

"It's a matter of keeping the skills honed," she said. "I don't get much chance these days to get out in the field, and I'm a firm believer in the 'use it or lose it' philosophy."

"Then please use it," he said. "There's one more thing. A favor."

"You're the client."

"Can you phone somebody at police headquarters to okay my digging through department records at the library?" Case records dating as far back as 1965 were kept in a special, climate-controlled section of the New Orleans Public Library.

"What's the matter with your crony Munn?" Nadia asked.

"I'd rather not bother him with this."

She stared at him. "Don't tell me you and his cute little sis are Splitsville?"

He did not bother to marvel at her intuition. "I'd just rather not deal with him right now," Manion said.

"Okay, sonny. Hand me the phone. We've got more than one fish in that particular ocean."

2

IT TOOK A library clerk nearly twenty minutes to locate the NOPD file on Tyrone Pano. Manion spent another two hours leafing through it carefully. Most of it, including Pano's arrest report, was standard copspeak, describing the events as if they'd occurred precisely by the book. The presence of the weapon that killed Lillian Davis in Pano's apartment had closed the lid on the crime. And the additional discovery of notes involving Pano in a terrorist plot against the state had nailed it shut.

Included in the file were reports on the organization that Pano founded, the Southern Cross. A brief history. Surveillance records. A blurred copy of an FBI memo from the field officer, Special Agent Edgar Reel, to Police Chief Mathern, requesting cooperation on the Agency's ongoing investigation of the organization.

Manion added a few more names to his list. Francis Hart (aka "Tank" Hart), co-founder of the Southern Cross. Thayer Coy, president of the League for Negro Advancement, who'd provided a statement damaging to Pano. And Officer Marcus Dudley, who'd been assigned to the Pano investigation and who had interrogated the suspect.

He also found, in a report prepared by Officer Patrick Guillory, that he had been the discoverer of the missing fountain pen in Pano's jail cell.

He put Guillory's name at the top of his list.

Shortly before three, Louis deMay arrived at Manion's office. The boy looked a bit unhappy. Trouble at school or at home, Manion thought. But he chose not to press Louis on it. He had other questions on his mind.

"Let's talk about your great-aunt Shana," he said, when Louis was seated again in the red chair with a Dr Pepper in his hand.

"Like what about her?"

"Can I meet her?"

Louis shook his head. "She passed on two year ago," he said. "She was an ol', ol' woman. But she was real good to me."

"How exactly were you related?"

"She my granddaddy's sister. But he went to live in Chicago and she stay here. He died a *long* time ago. At least five-six years ago."

"Were you born in Chicago?" Manion asked.

"No. I was born right here." He seemed proud of it. "Daddy's the younges' of fo'teen. All my aunts and uncles, they still in Illinois. But my daddy, when he was real young, ran away from home and came down here 'cause he heard Tante Shana had all this money."

"Your aunt was a nurse?" Manion asked.

"Some kinda nursin'. Charity work. But mos' of her money come from Tyrone Pano."

"So your dad came here to live with Shana Washington?"

"Uh-huh," Louis said. "Only, like I say, he was real young, younger than me, even. I'm thirteen and a half. So Shana call *his* daddy to find out what she should do. And my granddaddy tol' her to jus' keep him, that they had more kids than they could handle in Chicago. So Shana raised him."

"I'd like to talk to your daddy," Manion said.

Louis squirmed on his chair. "He's ... not aroun'."

"I don't understand."

"We haven't seen him in a while."

"Your mother, then," Manion said.

The boy looked just as uncomfortable. "Mama, she got nothin' to say about Tyrone Pano."

Manion nodded. "Where do you and your mom live, Louis?"

"Over to Simon Bolivar," he said. "Near Jackson."

"I'm heading that way," Manion lied. "Why don't I give you a lift?"

"That's okay. I enjoy the bus and the streetcar."

"Aw, come on," Manion said. "I like company when I drive. We can talk about Tyrone Pano on the way."

3

THE MORE LOUIS talked as they drove along, the more relaxed he became. And vice versa. Seat-belted into Manion's Mustang, he described Saturdays when his Tante Shana would help him build a tree house in the yard or take him downtown to the Regal movie house for a matinee. "She a smart woman, Shana," he said proudly. "She put some of Tyrone's money in the bank, she give some to the mission she work at, an' she still got enough left over to pay for the house we livin' in now."

As they neared that house, Louis grew tense again, peering through the windshield, studying each pedestrian they passed.

"Looking for something?" Manion asked.

"Just checkin' who's aroun'."

They paused for a red light near an empty lot, where a handful of kids, slightly younger than Louis, were playing a game, tossing a rubbery object that looked suspiciously like a discarded girdle. One of them spotted Louis and called his name. Louis gave him an embarrassed wave.

Then the others picked up the name thing, giving it a taunting, singsong "Loooo-wissss" twist. He faced forward and pretended not to hear them.

The house was a large, weather-beaten gray two-story with a wide front porch. It was set back from the street far enough for the yard to hold two fig trees and a children's jungle gym. Both trees had been picked clean, and the gym was rusted and had an abandoned look.

Manion parked the Mustang behind a purple Mercedes sedan. A white man in a dark suit sat at the wheel, reading a paperback.

Louis thanked Manion for the lift and opened the car door anxiously.

"I'd like to meet your mom," the detective said.

Louis looked at the house and seemed pained. "I don't know if she's—"

The front door to the house opened and two white men strolled out. The larger had the battered and scarred face of a boxer, an image enhanced by his purple warm-up outfit. The other was compact, below average height, with a small, pointy nose that turned his face a bit too handsome. In his casual, baggy, dark gray suit and black knit shirt, he reminded Manion of a Hollywood brat-pack wannabe who hadn't made the cut. He was saying something to the boxer and exercising his boyish grin.

Louis jumped from the Mustang's bucket seat and ran toward the men, forgetting to shut the car door. Manion swung his legs around the shift and slid out after him.

The men paused on the cracked cement walkway staring at the boy.

"Who you guys?" Louis asked.

The too handsome man looked from the boy who was standing in front of him to the approaching Manion and then back to the boy. His face didn't lose its grin. He wasn't much taller than the boy. "I'm Remy," he said. "Who're you, buddy?"

The boy told him his name.

"Well, whadaya say, Louis?" Remy had only a hint of a Southern drawl. Manion thought that accent was like mildew. The longer you stayed in the South, the thicker it grew. Remy hadn't been in town very long.

"You friends of my mama?"

"Sure. Everybody's friends with your mama." Remy was keeping it light, but there was a nasty edge to his delivery. His attention drifted to Manion. "You're his mama's friend, too, I bet."

Manion gave him a bored look and said to Louis, "Let's go inside."

The boy moved past the two men, heading for the front door.

"You're what, a social worker?" Remy asked Manion. "Truant officer?"

Manion cocked his head, but didn't reply. He just stared at the too handsome man, an enigmatic half-smile on his face.

Remy seemed to be unnerved by the half-smile. He shrugged

and said to the boxer, "People today, huh, Cookie? They all got their backs up over something."

"For sure," the boxer replied.

Remy spun on his high heel and headed for the Mercedes. Cookie continued to glare at Manion, his small eyes sunk deep into a face that could have been carved out of a raw potato.

"C'mon, Cook," Remy ordered. The stocky man blinked and turned to follow his boss.

"I bet they *not* friends of Mama's," Louis said.

"Let's go see."

The signs of disrepair Manion had noticed outside the house had not prepared him for the clean, polished interior with its contemporary furniture and bright rugs. The walls were decorated with poster prints, some of which he recognized, and original art that consisted mainly of purposely rough portraiture.

Beside the kitchen door was a large poster for a popular comedy and music review, *Creoles on Parade,* that had been running for the past three years in the back room of a lounge in the French Quarter. The poster was gaudy—reds, yellows, browns, greens. Three men and two women in minstrel garb held up masks to their faces. The masks in their right hands were blackface; in their left, whiteface. Their own faces were milk-coffee-colored. Creole.

Louis ignored the poster as he rushed past it. Manion followed him into a yellow-and-black tiled kitchen where Wanda deMay, an attractive, light-skinned woman in her thirties, sat at a porcelain-top table, scowling at a cup of black coffee. Beside the coffee was a large butcher's knife. As they entered, her handsome face hardened in anger and she began, "I told you—"

The sight of her son stopped her short. "Oh, hi, baby," she said, moving her hand away from the knife. Then she saw Manion. "Who the hell are you?"

"This Mr. Manion, Mama," Louis said. "He's with the *Crime Bustahs.*"

"Didn't I tell you not to get messed up with that craziness?" she said without much feeling, as if she'd lost the argument a while ago. "I oughtta beat knots on Jambo's head for helping you write that letter."

She looked at Manion again, setting her jaw pugnaciously. "Well, what do you want?"

"You're in *Creoles on Parade*, aren't you?" he asked.

Her face softened. "You see the show?"

All he'd seen was her likeness on the poster, but there was no need to tell her that. "You guys are terrific," he said.

"Jambo is working on bringing it to New York soon. So maybe we'll go live there for a while." She winked at her son.

"Who those men just left?" Louis asked.

"Nobody," she snapped. "They're nobody. Gone and forgotten. I went to the A & P today. There's a carton of milk in the icebox." Louis went to the refrigerator. His mother stood up. "Get you some coffee, Mr. . . . ?"

"Terry Manion," he said. "Please call me Terry."

"All right, Terry. My name is Wanda. Wanda, Terry. Terry, Wanda. Sounds like Swahili."

"Coffee'd be fine," Manion said.

She rose, and staggered slightly as she moved to the stove. Manion realized she'd been drinking. Her eyes locked on his too quickly for him to hide his sympathy. She glared at him and said, "Takes one to know one."

She held the pot over a coffee cup. "Want a little something extra in this?" she asked.

"No," he said. "I've been drinking it black for a while."

"I tried it that way," she said. "Didn't improve my life none."

The three of them sat at the kitchen table. The coffee was good. Louis's eyes went from Manion to his mother. The boy could not interpret her mood. Manion was having trouble himself.

"You work for this TV series full time?" she asked him.

"No. I'm just a hired hand. I have my own agency here."

"What have you been hired to do, exactly?"

"Talk to people who know something about Tyrone Pano."

"Too bad old Shana's gone. She'd have been a fount of information."

"Did you know her pretty well?" Manion asked.

"We lived here with her for about six years. Ever since Big Louis quit his brewery job to devote full time to his art."

"Daddy usta be a plant manager at Mardi Gras beer," Louis said with pride.

"Are those sketches his in the front room?" Manion asked.

"From his sketch phase," Wanda deMay said. "In the bedroom we got oils from his oil phase. Last I heard, he was in his neon phase. These phases don't bring in much money. So back then, in his I-ain't-working-in-no-goddamn-brewery phase, I had to dance at this place in Jefferson full of lowlifes just to put food on the table.

"Then Shana took us in. She was getting old, she said, and she couldn't handle the little kids anymore. That's what she used this place for—somewhere workin' women could park their babies.

"Anyway, I helped out with that. And Big Louis started selling a few of his pieces. They didn't bring much and they weren't steady. Lots of galleries around here, but you gotta know somebody to get wall space.

"Anyhow, three years ago"—she almost smiled—"Jambo LeRoux and a couple other friends and I put *Creoles* together and I started making some money."

She glared at Manion as she took a sip of her doctored coffee. "I'll be fine for tonight's performance," she said, a bit defensively.

Manion wanted no part of that discussion. He asked, "How long has it been since you've seen Big Louis?"

"Like I just told that little smart-mouth pretty boy," she said, "he walked out about five weeks ago."

"What did the pretty boy want with him?"

She shrugged elaborately. "He said he gave Big Louis some money for something that Big Louis didn't deliver. I asked if it was a painting and he laughed and said no, it wasn't any painting. I told him to hang loose for a while. Louis be back. He always comes back."

"He's left before?" Manion asked.

She shook her head. "A few times. Usually when some fool puts money in his pocket. But that pocket's got a big hole in it. Shana knew that. It's why she left this house to Little Louis. She also got a lawyer to figure out this trust fund thing, so that the boy gets some cash every month to take care of the upkeep and some of his needs. 'Tween that and *Creoles*, the boy and I, we're doing all right. That's why his daddy'll be back. Because he never does all right."

"Did Shana talk a lot about Tyrone Pano?"

Wanda leaned back in her chair. "She never stopped."

"Then you've heard her theory about him being an FBI agent?"

This time Wanda gave him a full smile. "No. I never heard that. Big Louis would go crazy if he heard that."

"Tante Shana said to never tell him," the boy interjected. "And I never have."

"Why wouldn't she want you to tell him?"

"No way Big Louis could see Pano as anything but a martyr," Wanda answered for her son. "Big Louis takes that black pride stuff seriously."

"And you don't?" Manion asked.

"Like I keep tellin' my boy, black pride don't work with Creoles, because we're not black, exactly. And light brown pride just don't cut it."

She turned to her son. "You hungry, honey?"

He nodded.

Wanda stood, steadied herself and walked to the refrigerator. She opened the freezer compartment. "Got a blackened catfish dinner and a fried chicken with gravy."

"Catfish," Louis told her.

She withdrew the frozen dinner, removed the aluminum top and placed the tray into a small brown microwave oven on a table against one wall. She said to Manion, "Want the chicken?"

He stood. "No, thanks," he said. "I'd better be going."

The news did not make Wanda unhappy.

Louis asked, "You gonna talk to people 'bout Tyrone?"

"That's what I'm being paid for."

"Call me if you need anything," the boy said.

Manion promised that he would.

THE DETECTIVE ARRIVED home, arms filled with grocery bags from the National, to find a big, rough-hewn man sitting on his porch stoop. The man appeared to be asleep. He was wearing a rumpled tan poplin suit. His large jaw was crushing most of his shirt collar. His blond hair looked as if it had just been freshly buzz-cut. As long as Manion had known him, some thirty-odd years, man and boy, Eben Munn's hair had looked that way.

"You awake, Eben?" Manion asked, starting up the steps.

Munn's eyes popped open. "You don't think I'd fall asleep in this cheesy neighborhood? Get my eyeteeth stolen."

He yawned, grunted and stood up. Then he saw Manion struggling with the front-door key and took one of the grocery bags from him. "Let's see what you got in here, podnah," Munn said. "Milk. A six-pack of Dr Pepper. That's good. Raisin bread. Yeah. Imitation crabmeat? What the Christ is imitation crabmeat?"

"A modern miracle," Manion replied, entering his home. He looked down at the pile of mail that had fallen beneath the door slot. None of it appeared urgent enough for him to stoop down to retrieve it. Instead, he carried his grocery bag into the kitchenette at the rear of the house.

Munn lumbered after him, continuing to criticize his purchases. Finally, he said, "Why don't you shove all that imitation crap into the freezer and we'll go out to dinner? On me."

"Promise not to mention your sister?"

"Lucy? I'm thinking of canceling our family ties. I set her up with the perfect guy, my old grammar school buddy—"

"You didn't set us up," Manion interrupted. "And we weren't buddies in school. We just happened to be in the same class."

"So sue me for trying a little male bonding," Munn said. "Lemme treat you to dinner."

"Why?" Manion asked.

"Why? To celebrate my getting on the OCCS." A year earlier, with Manion's help, Munn had put an end to Louisiana crime boss Charlie Benedetto, and sent the gangster's brother, Johnny, on a one-way trip to an Italian exile. Presumably as a result, the police lieutenant had been tapped as a key member of the newly established statewide Organized Crime Combat Squad.

It was the best of all possible situations, Munn thought. He'd just about run out his string on the NOPD. Operating under the OCCS, he was able to retain his lieutenant's rank and seniority within the department, but his orders came directly from the chief of the new unit, whose small, unassuming office was on the first floor of Police Headquarters on Tulane and Broad.

Unlike the other honchos to whom he'd reported in the past, his new boss, Jack Keller, seemed a breed apart, a dedicated professional in his fifties with a lifetime career in law enforcement and no obvious axes to grind. At their first meeting, the graying, ruggedly handsome OCCS chief had explained that he was pursuing no personal or political agendas. He didn't care about publicity. He didn't care about public relations. The only thing he cared about was catching the bad guys and putting them away.

There had been six others at the dinner meeting—four men and two women—culled from the NOPD, the Baton Rouge PD and the offices of the New Orleans and Baton Rouge district attorneys. "There'll be only twelve of us covering the whole state," Chief Keller had told them. "We go where the action is, for as long as it takes. We've got an adequate budget and we can pump that up with confiscated cash and merchandise. I myself am a dollar-a-year man. I've got family money. But I don't expect you to starve. Your pay will be slightly better than you've been getting. But this isn't a moneymaking job. And there'll be damn little glory. I hope to compensate for that with payments of personal satisfaction.

"I want us to be a tight unit that downplays bureaucracy. You report to me and I report to the governor." He paused, saying with a smile, "I may have to put it to music for him.

"Anyway, I expect you to follow my orders. But they're not carved in stone. If you've got a better idea, I want to hear it.

"Finally, let's keep it informal. I'll call you by your first names. And you call me Jack."

Munn had felt he'd died and gone to cop heaven.

"You've been on the job a week," Manion said, forcing the imitation crabmeat into his tiny freezer. "Why celebrate now?"

"Because a week ago, you were too friggin' busy being led down the garden path by my ex-sister. You wouldn't even answer my phone calls. C'mon, let's you and me really do the town."

"I don't do the town anymore," Manion said. "You can't do the town without having a drink, and I'm through with that."

"Then just eat. We'll go to Manale's. Down some raw oysters and move on to one of those shrimp-and-garlic deals."

"Gee, you really whet my appetite," Manion said sarcastically. But he knew that he'd go. Once Munn had his mind made up, it was impossible to change it.

* * *

They were in the policeman's new midnight blue T-Bird, steaming down St. Charles Avenue, when Munn, despite his promise, asked, "What the hell went wrong with you and Lucy?"

Manion made the mistake of changing the subject. "You ever hear of a pretty boy named Remy? Travels with a muscle man, probably an ex-boxer, named Cookie."

The car swerved. Munn gave him a quick, perturbed glance, then went back to studying the avenue. "Remy 'the Muskrat' Ragusa and Cookie Lapicola. Where the hell did you run into that pair of cuff buttons?"

"Just around."

"Around where?" Munn asked. "Something you working on?"

"Kind of," Manion said.

"If Ragusa's involved, it's something I'm working on, too," Munn said. "The little weasel is headed up the organization on roller skates."

"I've never heard of him."

"He's been in New Jersey the last couple years," Munn said, "streamlining the mob's tape-piracy operation. He found some MIT whiz kid who figured out how to dupe a two-hour tape in less than ten seconds. If he'd stayed in Jersey, they'd have probably given him the whole pop stand in a couple years. But he came back home instead."

"Why?" Manion asked.

"Family business," Munn replied, making a sudden turn across the neutral ground, missing a streetcar by two paint layers. "The Benedetto family. Charlie was Remy's uncle. And with Charlie dead and Frankie over in spaghetti heaven, Remy's hoping to pick up all the marbles and keep the game going. He's one of the OCCS's key targets."

Manion looked out of the window. "Eben, unless my sense of direction has left me entirely, we're now headed away from Manale's."

"Yeah. I just thought of a better place."

"Where?" Manion asked, suspiciously.

"Seraphina's."

"Never heard of it."

"It's great. One of the best they got in Jazz City."

"Aw, Christ," Manion said. "I hate Jazz City. I'd rather go visit a gambling ship than Jazz City. It's depressing. Vulgar. Mobbed-up. Full of hookers. The food is always lousy."

"You'll love this place. And while we're driving there, you can tell me how you bumped into the Muskrat and Lapicola."

"Fuck you," Manion replied, and retreated to the far side of the passenger seat.

SERAPHINA'S WAS LOCATED along a restaurant row behind the congested Jazz City shopping mall. The mall was about ten years old, but it looked as if it had just been constructed a month before. The planted trees were stunted. The grass on the neutral ground was an unnatural bright green. Shell dust powdered the smooth asphalt streets.

The restaurants were glass-and-cement eyesores with bright neon names like Mr. Bigg's, Bona Fortuna, Leone's Lighthouse (complete with a miniature revolving lighthouse in front), the Parthenon, the Laff Place on Earth.

They drove past a bar that, under Charlie Benedetto's ownership, had been called Nola Ole. A new flashing pink-and-yellow neon sign out front said it had been renamed the High Rollers Club. A banner proclaimed, "Poker, blackjack and craps lessons! Topless hostesses!"

"I'm not sure that's an improvement," Manion said.

"The owner's name is Harley 'the Rocket' Gazzo, late of Miami. Another of those fluttering Mafia moths," Munn explained, "drawn here by the bright glow of legalized gambling."

Seraphina's occupied nearly half a block on the edge of Jazz City. It had been designed to resemble a villa in southern Italy, complete with outdoor grape arbor. But the wood had a shiny look to it, and the windows of the restaurant-villa were tinted black. And the grapes and vines were plastic. Manion asked, "Do we really have to eat here?"

"Absolutely," the policeman said, turning into the unattended parking lot.

It was chilly inside the restaurant. Chilly and dim. A maître d' in a white linen suit led them into a large circular bilevel room done in dark green and ivory. They followed him around a pathway that looked down on a sunken level crowded with customers. Their destination was a table on the street level underneath a huge watercolor of a Napa Valley winery at sundown.

Almost immediately a waiter with a three-inch pompadour and an attitude arrived with green-and-ivory menus the size of surfboards. He rattled off the specials in a distracted voice, took their orders for drinks—a Cabin Still old-fashioned for Munn and iced tea for Manion—and left them to study the endless bill of fare.

"Some place, huh?" Munn said, grinning at the patrons slightly below them.

Manion scanned the room and asked, "Who's the dowager with the diamond-studded eyeglasses working the cash register?"

The woman seated behind a wooden docket at the rear of the establishment seemed to be in her fifties, sturdy, smiling, wearing a silk dress and diamonds not only around her eyes but on her earlobes, neck and wrists. One of the purposes of the gems, Manion thought, was to distract the eye from the woman's large nose, which, at the moment, was raised in pride as she surveyed the room. When she spied their table her smile froze and that great nose twitched.

Munn nodded to her pleasantly.

Their waiter arrived with their drinks, which he bounced onto the tablecloth in front of them, spilling each. He stepped back from his fine work to discover the woman in the diamond-studded glasses waving at him.

He snapped to attention and loped across the green carpet to her side. She whispered something in his ear and he double-timed it into the kitchen.

He reappeared almost immediately carrying a small serving plate topped by a domed silver cover. The diamond lady lifted the lid, nodded approvingly at the plate's contents and replaced the shiny cover.

The waiter made a grand procession out of his return to their table. As he placed the mystery dish in front of Eben Munn,

Manion realized that the subdued conversations in the room had quieted to scattered whispers. Their table had become the floor show.

"This is just too sweet, isn't it?" Munn said. "Should I be a real prick and not lift the lid? Just ignore the whole thing? Naaaa."

Munn good-naturedly grasped the cover and raised it, exposing the freshly severed head of a chicken resting on a bed of watercress and simmering in its own blood. The chicken's eyes were cloudy, but its beak opened and closed in postdeath jerks. There were gasps from nearby diners.

Munn raised an eyebrow. "Guess they couldn't find a horse's head in the kitchen," he said. Then he bellowed for their waiter.

That worthy stood fast until receiving the go-ahead from the diamond-studded cashier. Then he approached their table. "Yes, sir?"

"Thank Signora Seraphina for the appetizer, but I think I'll have the oysters instead. What about you, Manion?"

"I'm sort of leaning toward the minestrone, assuming there's no chicken in it."

The waiter, considerably more alert now, removed the chicken head with alacrity. Manion said to Munn, "Anytime you want to tell me what this is all about . . ."

"Diamond Lil over there is the owner of this meatball palace. Her full name is Seraphina Ragusa."

"I know you well enough that I shouldn't be surprised," Manion said. "But you really want to eat in a restaurant owned by the sister of Charlie Benedetto? The guy whose death you caused about a year ago?"

"You don't understand how this works, Manion. I'm probably her favorite policeman."

"Then the chicken head was just a little thank-you note?"

"Well, hell, she's gotta make it look good. But the fact is, when Charlie went to that Mafia sauna room down below, Seraphina was able to bring in her little whelp to run things. We'll get the best grub this tourist trap slings."

"But we're not here for the food, right?" Manion asked.

"You were curious about Remy. I figured this would be a good opportunity to get a look at his roots, so to speak."

"He doesn't look very much like his mom," Manion said.

Munn chuckled. "You don't think that's his real nose? The kid had a complete makeover. Where do you figure he got the nickname 'Muskrat'? Used to be a fat little fuck with a schnoz like a macaw."

"What made him change?" Manion asked. "Usually those guys like to flaunt their ugliness."

"Try asking somebody who gives a shit," Munn said. "All I care about is what he can do for me." Then, flustered at having provided Manion with a bit too much truth, he said awkwardly, "Anyway, just wait'll you taste the grub here. You'll love it. I swear."

And he was right. Seraphina's little joke had put Manion off chicken for the night, but the shrimp Italian had just the right touch of garlic and bay leaves. And the cheesecake was a fine substitute for the after-dinner liqueur he would have had in the old days.

"Hey," Munn said, "speaking of Italian shrimp." He gestured with his amazing chin, and Manion turned to see Remy Ragusa in conversation with his mother. The young man leaned forward and kissed her on the cheek.

"Very touching," Manion said.

"Benedetto family values," Munn grunted. "We might as well take advantage of him showing up."

"How?" Manion asked.

"By doing detective stuff," Munn replied.

THEY HAD TO wait only twelve minutes in Munn's T-Bird before Remy Ragusa left his mother's restaurant. As he walked jauntily to his purple Mercedes, the car's back door opened and the sullen Cookie stepped out. He held the door for his diminutive boss, then circled the car to join him on the rear seat.

"I always love to see how these little tin shits spend their leisure time," Munn said. "Remy's uncle Charlie ate too much; his uncle Johnny fucked too much. I wonder what the Muskrat's vice is, besides plastic surgery."

"Music, maybe," Manion offered. "Since he was a cassette pirate."

Munn shrugged. He personally was hoping for an addiction a bit more devastating, crack or heroin maybe, something that would make it easier for him not only to dump the little thug but to control him. As he'd explained earlier to the chief of OCCS, he was into control. It was a waste of time trying to get rid of the cockroaches. What you had to do was to turn one of them into *your* cockroach. Then you could try for two cockroaches. Then three. And pretty soon, you can start putting a serious dent in the cockroach nest.

Jack hadn't been so sure. He'd cocked his big, graying head to one side and asked, "While you pressure your cockroach, Eben, what do you suppose the cockroach's lawyer will be doing?"

"I imagine he'll be at his house, watching *Matlock* on TV," Munn said. "Look, I'm not suggesting we use a rubber hose or anything. You just isolate the roach and let him bump into a few walls and then you offer him the way out and he jumps for it."

"Where does this isolation take place?" Jack was only mildly curious. "Not in any city jail, I hope."

"Nowhere official," Munn had replied. "There's this place I used to go to when I was a kid. Fort Larue. A state park not too far from the city. The fort's built like a big cave. Got all these tunnel-like passageways. You take the wiseguy there after sundown when the park's closed. There's no electricity and it gets real dark in those tunnels at night. And the assholes are paranoid anyway. An hour of damp walls and rat squeaks softens 'em up faster than a rubber hose."

The chief had stared at him for a few moments before saying, "You're a very colorful man, Eben. But, for now, hold off on the kidnapping and terrorizing." He'd leaned forward and poured Munn another shot of Bushmill's. "Don't get me wrong," he said. "I'm not against a little bending of the rules. I just think we'd better play by them until we're sure how free a hand we're going to have."

Munn nodded. Not only was the atmosphere at the OCCS more congenial and the line of authority shorter than at the NOPD, the booze was better, too.

* * *

The destination of the purple Mercedes was a club in the French Quarter called Rowdy's. It was a tourist draw consisting of several entertainment rooms that covered a small spectrum of show business—Dixieland music, soft rock, contemporary jazz and a song-and-dance revue. Munn watched Remy Ragusa and his bodyguard Cookie pause beside the front door, staring at a poster for the revue. Remy grinned at the poster, and made some comment to Cookie before strolling into the club. Munn said, "You mighta been right about this guy havin' a music jones."

Manion thought there was another reason Ragusa was there. According to the poster, the show in the back room was *Creoles on Parade*. Manion wondered what Remy's interest in Wanda deMay really was. She was an attractive woman, a bit older than the mobster. But that still didn't rule out a personal involvement. Whatever, he declined to make Munn a present of the deMay connection. He had no desire to add another problem to the lives of Louis and his mother. For some inexplicable reason he was genuinely fond of Munn, but he did not trust the policeman in situations where members of the Benedetto family were concerned.

Rowdy's proved to be a misnomer. There was nothing even remotely raucous about the bar area, where an assortment of young, well-dressed men and women chatted over cocktails, while three scrubbed college-boy bartenders tossed bottles into the air and performed other feats of manual dexterity before getting down to the nitty-gritty of mixing drinks.

"You been here before?" Munn asked.

Manion started to say no. But, aside from the Santa Fe pastel colors and the soft lighting and the pseudosophisticated veneer, there was something familiar about the oblong bar and the layout of the room. There were a lot of bars he half-remembered staggering through. "Maybe in another life," he replied.

Munn was staring at the doorway through which Remy and Cookie had just passed. "I liked it better when it was the old Perdido," he said.

Manion closed his eyes. The Perdido Lounge, of course. The only part of it remaining was the bar. And maybe the memories. He'd gone there in his Tulane years. And, even after his first dry-out, when he was still struggling to stay on the wagon, J.J. Legendre, who used it as a personal hangout, had dragged him there. Manion had endured the ridicule of bartender and customers by drinking Dr Peppers while J.J. sipped his scotch-and-waters and filled in the gaps of his apprentice's street education.

He stared at the fresh, clean-cut, depressingly ambitious faces and wondered what had become of Wimpy, the incredibly fat black man who insisted on bringing in his own hamburgers and eating them at the bar. Where was Ramona, the nature girl, who cadged martinis for her pet alligator, Leander, who had free run of the bartop? Had the Dubrov dwarfs, formerly of the Moscow Circus, discovered another lounge that would encourage their often lewd gymnastics? Had Lady Morgana, who claimed to be a vampire and dressed accordingly, uncovered another spot that welcomed her red-stained teeth?

Munn chased away the memories by saying, "C'mon, Manion, before somebody tries to sell us a life insurance policy."

They followed a short, dark hallway to a lighted entry, where a young woman in a mock rag-doll costume informed them in a hushed voice that the early show was nearly over. At Munn's insistence, she led them to a small, empty table at the rear.

Louis's mother was sharing the stage with two light-skinned men who were camping it up for the crowd. "Thanks for comin' in late and disturbin' all the other folks who were dumb enough to get here on time," one of the men chided.

Manion was relieved to see that the performer was not addressing them but the other two men who had preceded them and were now seated in the front row. Cookie Lapicola glared at the black entertainer, but Remy Ragusa didn't seem to have heard a word. Ignoring the stage, he took his time giving a waitress his drink order.

The performer continued to stare at Remy, and the audience began to titter. He was joined by a taller, thinner man with a pencil mustache. The thin man leaned over the footlights and gawked at Remy, who slowly realized that he was the center of their attention. The thin man's jaw dropped in mock wonder. "Wait a minute, here. Wait a minute."

"What do you see, bro'?" the other Creole on Parade asked. "You see what I see?"

The shorter performer leaned toward Remy, too. "Oh yeah," he said, grinning, "I surely do."

"We got a Creole brother right here down front doin' the pass."

The shorter Creole asked innocently, "Hey, you passin', bro'? And you think folks don't know?"

Ragusa finally got the drift of their chatter, and his face reddened in a mixture of embarrassment and fury. "What the hell are you talking about?" he asked angrily.

The two actors rolled their eyes. A frowning Wanda deMay moved beside the tall man and whispered something in his ear. He kept his smile, but Manion could see that her words registered. He tapped the shorter man and passed on the whisper.

The shorter man's face was a bit more expressive as the shadow of fear came and went. But he managed a smile as he held up a hand with middle and index fingers forming a "V." "Peace, friend," he said to Remy. "We just goofin' around up here. No offense intended.

"Hey," he cried suddenly, pointing to another table where a young black couple sat. "What we got here? Definitely not Creole, would you say?"

"I would, indeed," interjected the tall performer, following the other's lead.

"You not Creo', are you, bro'?" the shorter man asked.

The customer grinned nervously and replied, "I don't think so."

"Think? I say with certainty," declared the tall Creole. "Possibly even a multiroon, a panaroon. Man, what I'm getting at in my own subtle way is, you ... are ... black." The customer's female companion was not amused. Sensing her displeasure, the tall Creole began a mock flirtation with her. Fluttering his long eyelashes. Making a moue. Winking first one eye then the next. Finally, her angry visage broke and she laughed.

The tall Creole laughed, too. And he said, "Don't get uptight over black. I mean, what do they say about black? That it's beautiful, right? Black is beautiful." He paused, then cast an offstage look. "That might even be a music cue, if anybody's still awake out there."

Suddenly the room was filled with the sound of a small band. Another Creole couple joined the three on stage for what appeared to be the closing number.

They sang:

> "They say that black is beautiful,
> But that don't make it so.
> They say that money can't buy love,
> But just ask any ho'.

They say that justice will prevail,
But that bullshit don't flow,
So take a tip from the Creole crew,
Don't believe what people say.
Just believe what's in your heart . . .
Man, does that sound too ofay?"

The racially mixed audience broke into enough applause for the Creoles to take two curtain calls. Most of the audience left the way they came in. Ragusa and Cookie went through a door beside the stage that led to the back of the house.

Munn led Manion in that direction. But at the door, he paused. "Let's give the Muskrat enough time to get comfortable."

Ragusa must have gotten comfortable right away, because Munn had barely finished his sentence when they heard a scream from backstage. Grinning like a schoolboy, he charged through the door with Manion in his wake. They followed a poorly lit hallway to two bright dressing rooms located side by side at the building's southwest corner.

As Manion approached, he saw that all of the Creoles were in the room to his right. So were Ragusa and Cookie.

The tall Creole was on the floor, rubbing his jaw and glaring angrily at Cookie. "Anybody else have anything to say?" Ragusa asked.

"Here," Munn called, and stepped into the room.

He had their full attention. "Problem?" he asked.

Ragusa grinned at him. "Munn, right? Cookie, this is the gonzo cop who threw my uncle Charlie off the balcony."

"I sent your uncle Johnny off to Sicily, too," Munn said. "You hear much from him these days?"

"No, but Johnny's not big on writing," Remy said. His sleepy eyes turned to Manion. "And Louis's friend. You with Officer Munn?"

"What's going on here, exactly?" Munn asked, helping the tall Creole to his feet.

"Nothing," Remy said. "My associate, Mr. Lapicola, and I just dropped backstage to say how much we enjoyed the show."

"What's your name, sir?" Munn asked the tall Creole.

"So much for fame," the Creole said. "I'm Jambo LeRoux, the creator of *Creoles.* You like the show?"

"What I saw of it looked mean-spirited and goddamned

bitter," Munn told him, "so naturally I liked it. But right now, Mr. LeRoux, I'm a little more interested in that red welt on your face. One of these men do that?"

Jambo barely glanced at Cookie. "Naw," he said. "I tripped."

Munn looked disappointed. He turned to Cookie, his eyes dropping to the man's scarred white hands, which were at his side. Cookie nervously moved his right hand.

With remarkable speed, Munn grabbed the thug's right wrist and yanked up. Cookie halted the yank halfway, putting some strength behind it. He drew back his left fist.

Munn merely stared at him. The other's fist stayed cocked. "Cookie," Ragusa shouted, "relax."

Like an obedient dog, the powerful man seemed to slump. Munn raised Cookie's right fist, studied it and said, "Knuckles are kinda raw."

"That a crime, raw knuckles?" Ragusa asked.

"If the guy was a pro fighter, we might make a case about his fist being a lethal weapon," Munn said. "But nobody seems to be registering a complaint. Of course, if he'd hit me . . ."

"But he didn't," Remy said. "So, I think we'll bid goodnight to all you folks."

He paused at the door. "Officer Munn, I sincerely want to thank you for all your past help," he said mockingly.

Munn winked at him. "Keep your nose clean, Muskrat," he called out, "wherever the plastic surgeon put it."

It took the smile off Ragusa's face. But only for an instant. He nodded and was gone.

Munn turned to the others. "For extroverted show-biz types, you people sure do keep your mouths shut."

"There are certain situations," Jambo LeRoux said, "where it don't pay to improvise."

"Why'd the bodyguard pop you?" Munn asked.

Jambo smiled and said, "You got a problem with that pretty-faced man, you take care of it without putting me in the middle."

"What'd Ragusa want?" Munn asked.

Wanda deMay looked at Manion, puzzled. Munn saw her. "And your name, ma'am?" he asked.

She told him.

"And your association with . . . Ragusa?"

"I don't have one," she said.

"Does anybody have any idea what he was doing back here? Besides beating up on Mr. LeRoux?"

Answer there came none.

Disgusted, Munn turned to go. "You comin', Manion? Or do you have other plans?"

Manion considered staying, talking with Wanda and the others, seeing what he could find out about Louis's father and what Ragusa was really after. But he knew that when he finally arrived home, Munn would be there, expecting a full report. Better to deal with him from a position of almost total ignorance.

Munn didn't waste any time. As soon as Manion was in the car, he said, "Ragusa called you Louis's friend. Who the hell is Louis?"

"A boy. Thirteen years old."

"What's his connection with Ragusa?"

"I don't know."

"Is the kid your client?" Munn asked.

"Not exactly."

Munn showed his frustration by slapping the dashboard with the flat of his hand. "C'mon, Manion. Now's not the time to fuck around. I need this Ragusa bum, and there's something here. I can feel it."

"There's nothing more I can tell you."

Munn gave him a deadpan look. "What about the Creole babe back there, Wanda whatever?"

Manion used his hands to make a helpless gesture.

"I saw the goddamn look she gave you. She's a woman that rings chimes. Is that the deal?"

"What deal?" Manion asked.

"Is that what happened with my sister? Did she find out you were fuckin' around with other women, like Miss Wanda? Is that why she went running back to Boston?"

The evening had been a ride on a merry-go-round, and Manion decided it was time to get off. He opened the door and stepped out. "C'mon, Manion," Munn shouted. "Cut the pouty bullshit. I thought we were pals. You screwin' around on Lucy?"

Manion slammed the door. He didn't know if Munn really thought that he was having an affair with Wanda deMay or if it was just another of the weird games he played as part of his interrogation technique. Either way, he'd had enough.

The T-Bird followed him. In desperation, Manion turned
down a pedestrian alley too narrow for the car. He half-
expected it to be waiting at the other end, but Munn had apparently given up on him. At least for that night.

LOUIS HOVERED, DID a loop-the-loop and then let himself
soar over rooftops. As he approached Long Junior High, he
paused. Down below, at the far edge of the playground, Shoo-
Bear was plying his trade. Louis swooped down, knocked the
packet of drugs from Shoo-Bear's hand and flew upward
again, laughing as the angry crack dealer ranted and cursed.

He was circling for another attack when he felt someone
shaking him and calling his name. He awoke, befuddled, to
find that he was in his living room, curled up on the couch,
still wearing the clothes he'd had on all day. "Hi, Mama," he
said to the woman crouched before him.

"Son," she said, "what did I tell you about the front door?"

He rubbed his eyes. "What time is it?"

"Nearly two. About the front door . . ."

"I'm sorry. I guess I forgot to lock it. Jeral an' his baby sister come by and we watch the movie about the lion king. And
when they lef', I guess I forgot."

There was a noise from the kitchen.

"Somebody in there?" Louis asked.

"Jus' Jambo."

The boy leaped up and ran to the kitchen, shouting, "Hey,
Jambo."

The tall man was standing at a counter, pouring bourbon
into two glasses. He gave Louis a wide smile. "Hey yourself,
tough man," he said, barely getting the bottle down before the
boy jumped into his arms.

Wanda stood at the door, watching them with a crooked smile on her face. "Sorry you two guys don't get along better," she said.

"I watch *The Lion King* again," Louis told Jambo.

"We saw that at the movies," Jambo said. "It's on TV already?"

Louis nodded his head. "On cassette. Jeral brung it over."

"You go on to bed now, son," Wanda said. "It's way too late for you to be bouncin' around."

Jambo tightened his grip on the boy and raced with him from the room, down the hall and into Louis's bedroom. There he plopped him onto the bed.

The room was filled with posters and paper planes and dinosaurs dangling from the ceiling and a neon light sculpture that spelled out "Louis" in bright lime green, a gift from the boy's father. Jambo turned from the neon and said, "Get some sleep and maybe, if you're real good, I'll take you to the radio station with me tomorrow afternoon."

Periodically, Jambo would make the rounds of local radio shows to keep up interest in the revue. Louis always enjoyed the atmosphere of the stations, especially when the DJ or whoever let him sit in the glass room while Jambo did his talking.

"I be good," he said. He hugged the big man and started untying his shoes.

Jambo waited while the boy took off his socks and pants and shirt. Louis asked if it would be all right if he slept in his underwear instead of pajamas, and Jambo said it was fine with him.

He tucked the boy in and bent to turn off the neon light, but Louis stopped him. "I sleeps better with it on."

Jambo looked at him. "You mean you *sleep* better, not *sleeps*."

Louis nodded, aware of the mistake. It was just that after talking with Jeral awhile, he found himself getting sloppy again with his grammar. "Suppose we might have some more el-o-cution practice on the way to the radio shows?" he asked.

"I guess we could fit it in," Jambo said. He gave the boy a wink and left the room.

Louis counted to twenty, then slipped from the bed and tiptoed back in the direction of the living room. He knew from experience just the right section of shadow in the hall to stand in and not be observed from the couch.

From precisely that spot he had caught his mother and

Jambo kissing on the couch a couple of times. And sometimes doing even more than kissing. He wasn't sure how he felt about it. He didn't think it was a bad thing, exactly, because he loved his mama and he loved Jambo. But he wasn't sure what the deal was with his daddy, and that's what bothered him so.

That night, Jambo and his mama were not kissing. They sat with their drinks on the table in front of them. Jambo put some kind of pukey dime-store music on the CD. But they weren't even hugging. They were talking.

"You sure you don't know what the son of a bitch wants?" Jambo was asking.

"Something that Big Louis sold him that belonged to Shana."

"Well, that sweet-faced little ofay is not somebody you screw around with. The man is mean."

She reached out a hand and touched Jambo's cheek. "Still sore?"

He grinned. "My daddy used to whop me harder than that for less reason." Then the grin went away. "But that don't mean those guys are not capable of doing some real damage. I heard about Mr. Remy Ragusa from some people I know in the record business. He scares guys who don't get scared. So if you know where Big Louis is, you damn well better get word to him he's in trouble."

"I don't know where he is," Wanda said. "Probably with some bitch who'll throw him out when his money is gone."

"What do you think he sold to Ragusa?" Jambo asked.

She shrugged and sipped her drink. Then she leaned against the back of the couch and said, "A couple months ago, Big Louis decided to clean out the attic. It was full of old stuff that Shana had been toting around for decades. I suppose he found something up there. But what it is, and how Big Louis knew Remy Ragusa was looking to buy it, I sure don't know."

"What're we gonna do about Big Louis?" Jambo asked.

"Father James says it's just about impossible to dissolve a marriage when there's a child. So I don't know what we do, except what we're doing right now."

Louis thought his mother looked really sad. Her eyes were shiny wet. Jambo looked pretty unhappy, too.

The boy moved away from the shadows. He didn't like seeing his mama cry, didn't like being a party to the unhappiness she and Jambo were experiencing.

He crawled into bed, pulled up the lightweight coverlet and

stared at the glow of his name in neon until his eyelids grew heavy and he fell asleep.

8

STILL IN HIS pajamas at eight-thirty in the morning, seated at his desk, the floor cold against his bare feet, Manion held the telephone to his ear and imagined Nadia strolling from her obscene breakfast into the house to take his call. He stared at the remains of an imitation crabmeat cocktail on his desk. He took a gulp of coffee to put the thought of it behind him.

"Good morning, sunshine," Nadia said brightly. "Up and at 'em, huh?"

"At least up," he said.

"What can I do for you this beautiful day?"

He gave her the new names he'd pulled from the case file.

"I did some work for you yesterday," she said. "Ready with your little notepad?"

"My pencil is poised," he said.

"You can find J.J.'s old flame Madeleine DuBois any day between nine and five at the D.A.'s office, or more likely, in court. She's supposed to be a top killer-diller prosecutor. Name's Madeleine Betterick now, but she and Betterick, whoever he may be, are no longer in domicile. Fact is, she's keeping company with Billy Armand."

"The chief of police?"

"How many Billy Armands are there, sonny? Now, as for the others, Jamey Fontineau passed on in Thibadeaux about seven years ago. Cancer of the colon. Kiel Nathan is in his eighties, on his last leg. Lives over on Arabella, just off the Avenue, with a nurse in attendance." The Avenue was St. Charles. "Nathan's partner, James Billins, is still practicing, but, as we discussed, he's got bigger fish to fry. He's a member of Magnus Clay's inner circle and spends as much time in Baton Rouge as he does in his office here. He single-handedly delivered the black vote to Clay during that first election."

"The guy's tongue must be solid silver," Manion said. "How could he have talked intelligent blacks into voting for a deep-fat-fried Vegas lounge singer over a respected liberal politician like Edgar Dillon?"

"Well, to jog your memory, sonny, our governor got lucky when poor old Dillon got accused of harassing his black secretary."

Manion had forgotten that part of it. "So what's Billins's official title? Keeper of the Golden Guitar Pick? Purveyor of the Honorable Bourbon and Branch Water?"

"Scoff all you want," Nadia said, "but the word is that Billins is pulling the governor's strings like a puppeteer."

"Then he must be pretty lazy. Clay doesn't do anything."

"Not that we hear of," she replied. "But I bet there are lots of little deals being wheeled, and Billins is doing most of the wheeling."

"I need an address for Patrick Guillory," Manion said. "He's the one who found the pen in Tyrone Pano's cell."

"Your wish is my command, sonny." And she provided him with addresses for Guillory and J.J.'s other partner, Marty Boyle. "Now I hope that's worth six hundred bucks of your TV producer's ill-gotten loot."

"How long did it really take you?" he asked.

"About eight minutes' telephone time," she said. "But you gotta know the right person to call. Later, sonny."

Manion thanked her and hung up the phone.

He stood up, drank the last sip of coffee in the cup, tightened the drawstring on his pajama bottoms and went off to get ready for a brave new day.

9

LOUIS DEMAY HAD awakened at 7 A.M. to find that someone, his mother probably, had turned off his neon light sculpture. Sleepily, he wandered into the hall. The door to his
mother's bedroom was closed and he knew this meant that
Jambo had stayed over.

The boy showered, dressed and fed the two goldfish he'd
won at the school carnival earlier that year. Then he poured a
glass of orange juice and used a portion of it to help him swal-
low his vitamin pill.

Louis had plans for the day and regretted they did not include school. He liked school. He returned to his bedroom and
picked up the neon sculpture. There were carvings on the underside of the wooden base. These included his father's signature "LdeM"—the same that Big Louis used on his paintings
and sketches—and the legend "Artwork from Gloworm, Inc."

"Gloworm." That was the word he'd been trying to remember just before going to sleep. Gloworm. The store that mar-
keted his father's neon sculptures. They'd know where Louis
might phone his father and warn him that a strange little dude
and a skull-cracker were trying to find him to do him harm.

He looked up Gloworm, Inc. in the phone book. Unfortunately, its location was in a shopping center across the Mississippi on the west bank. He'd never tried taking a bus over the
river. But he was not lacking in confidence.

Actually, it wasn't very difficult. From the St. Charles streetcar he transferred to the General Mayer bus, which transported
him over the milk-coffee-colored Mississippi and deposited
him near the Oakwood Shopping Center.

Gloworm was on the periphery of the sprawling mall, a
small shop with a window full of brightly colored neon pieces.

Louis smiled at the sailboats and golfers and pennants with the names of football teams—all glowing brightly.

He moved on to the closed glass door, through which he could see an all-white room that smartly displayed an eye-dazzling array of neon objets d'art. The showroom seemed to be deserted. But as Louis entered, an electronic gong sounded and a woman strolled through a rear door.

Some of the dazzle of her smile dimmed when she saw him. But she wasn't unpleasant, like some shop owners Louis had known in his brief life. "Hi," she said. "Can I help you?"

"You have any neons by Louis deMay?" he asked.

She cocked her head to one side and looked at him curiously. "Do you like his work?" she asked.

"Uh-huh," he replied.

"There are some on that wall." She pointed to a grouping of imaginative neons on the wall. In one, a couple danced while a trio of musicians played. The dancers' bodies vibrated as if from some magic glow. In another work, two heads—a man's and a woman's—came together in a kiss.

"I remember that one," Louis said, pointing to a sculpture of a father bouncing a baby on his knee. The baby and the knee moved up and down.

"You remember it?" the proprietor asked.

"That's me. Louis deMay is my papa."

The woman was not comforted by this revelation. She straightened and asked, "Are you with your mother?"

"No," he said, continuing to stare at the father and the bouncing baby. Then he turned to the woman and asked, "You know where I can find my papa?"

She hesitated, then replied, "I'm sorry, but I really don't. I haven't seen him in quite a while."

He frowned. "I was hoping you might know where he is. It's important I talk with him."

"He might call," she said. "I hear from him every couple of weeks. Is there anything I can . . ."

She let the sentence trail off because the boy was staring intently at a large color photograph of a pop art version of the Mona Lisa. The Gioconda's enigmatic lips were in neon, as were the words "Mona's Place," done in matching color.

"When did papa do this?" Louis asked.

"That's not one of your father's," the woman said, too sharply. "That's by . . . another of my artists. Is there anything else I can do for you?"

He wanted to say, "Yes, you can tell me why that picture is up there on the wall next to my daddy's other neons if it was done by somebody else." What he did say was, "No, ma'am, I guess not, 'cept if you hear from him tell him to call me. Louis."

"I'll tell him, Louis."

He could feel her eyes on his back as he walked from the shop. On the sidewalk, he took an abrupt right, counted to fifty and then crossed in front of the shop again.

The woman was still standing by the picture of Mona's Place, but she was holding a cordless telephone to her ear and she didn't look happy.

Louis walked across the street and into the heart of the mall. Eventually, he found a telephone booth with a directory dangling from the end of a chain. Under the directory's yellow pages listing for restaurants, he found "Mona's Place." The address was on Robert E. Lee Boulevard, near the University of New Orleans. Way out by the lake, clear across town. This was a travel day for sure, he thought, double-timing in the direction of the bus stop.

Eben Munn watched the boy hop aboard the bus.

It had been a simple matter to locate Wanda deMay's home. He'd been parked, waiting for anything, when little Louis deMay left the house at 8:55 A.M. At first, Munn had been worried that Manion's little pal might be leading him to a school. But when the boy started to bus-hop, the lawman felt he might just get lucky. And when Louis wound up at the neon shop, Munn was convinced he was on the right track. He had no idea where that track was headed, but he felt it would eventually bring him close to putting the clamps on Remy Ragusa.

He turned on the T-Bird's engine and eased the sedan forward. There was no reason not to follow the bus closely. Bus drivers never thought they were being tailed, and if they did, who cared?

10

BECAUSE NEW ORLEANS is below sea level, a number of pumping stations had to be created to drain off the frequent subtropical rainfalls. Even with the pumps working overtime, the city still floods every now and then.

According to Nadia Wells, former NOPD officer Pat Guillory lived a few blocks away from the London Street station—the one responsible for draining the territory from the French Quarter to Lake Pontchartrain. As Manion's car approached the ex-policeman's address, he was bemused to find that much of the greenery in the area looked parched, as if it hadn't seen water in a year.

Guillory's house was a small white cottage with a small, neatly trimmed yellowing front lawn. No fence. No garden. Just lawn and little house.

Someone was home, apparently. The front windows were open, and Manion could hear the jabber of the radio as he walked up to the door.

He pressed the buzzer and almost immediately the jabber ceased. The floorboards creaked and then the door was thrown open by a sour-faced, emaciated man in pants several sizes too large and a white shirt that billowed on his thin frame. He had a red-and-yellow bandanna wrapped around what appeared to be a bald head. Manion judged him to be in his mid-seventies. "Whadaya want?" the old man asked gruffly.

"I'm looking for a Mr. Guillory," Manion said.

"You found him," the old man said, curiosity mixed with anger now.

"Patrick Guillory."

"Yeah. Right. That's me. Whadaya want?"

"The Patrick Guillory who was a homicide detective on the New Orleans Police Department in the sixties," Manion said.

"Jesus Christ!" the old man exploded. "Identification completed. I'm Pat fucking Guillory. Now what do you want?"

Manion had been expecting a man in his middle to late fifties. He said, "I'd appreciate a minute of your time."

Guillory began coughing. Each racking bark led to one deeper and more devastating. He bent almost in two, his eyes watering, arms flailing.

Manion took a step toward him, then paused. He had no idea how to help the man.

Eventually the coughing subsided. With a deep sigh, Guillory straightened and rubbed his wet eyes and nose on his sleeve. "If you're selling life insurance," he said, "boy, did you pick a wrong number."

Manion told him the half-truth—that he was doing research for the *Crime Busters* television show. Guillory was familiar with it. "We're looking for NOPD cases that the viewers might find interesting, and some of the people at headquarters suggested I talk with you."

"They gave you my home address?" Guillory asked.

"Not exactly. But they mentioned your name and I tracked you down."

"How?" Guillory wanted to know, backing toward an old easy chair that was perched in front of a large vintage TV. He spun the chair around so that he could sit facing his visitor. He was careful not to jostle a nearby coffee table that held fifteen or twenty medicine bottles, a water pitcher, a glass, and a small tape player. There was an empty cassette box on the table. Its cover read, *Accepting Mortality with Reverend Austin Alexander*.

Manion said, "I slipped somebody a tenner to check your jacket."

Guillory began to laugh and the laughter turned into another spasm of coughing. When that subsided, the ill man waved a hand at the thrift-store couch against one wall. "Sit," he ordered.

When Manion had obeyed, Guillory said, "If my address is worth ten, how much is my memory worth?"

"You tell me."

Guillory shook his head. "I don't need money, podnah. What I got money don't help."

"What've you got?" Manion asked.

"You name it, I got it."

"How bad?"

"Why don't we get to why you're here? You want stories about the NOPD?"

Manion nodded. "Different kind of cases. Like the Meddler, for instance. Were you in on that one?"

"That was a beauty, all right," the sick man said, brightening. "I wasn't assigned to the Meddler squad, but I was there to see it come down."

"What about the guy who broke it?" Manion consulted his notebook. "J.J. Legendre. How well did you know him?"

"The Cajun? Hell, I worked with him. Great guy. Great fucking cop. He nailed that son of a bitch Glander."

"What were some of the other things you guys worked on?"

Guillory waved a hand. "A lot of shit. Like I say, we were tight in those days. There was, oh, I don't know . . ."

"The Pano case?" Manion prompted.

"Yeah. The Panther Man. I took over from J.J. on that one. He got reassigned to the Meddler and I was put in charge of building a case against Pano. To satisfy the fucking bleeding hearts, the loot, Lieutenant Paul Lamotta, stuck me with this brain-dead spade . . ." He paused, frowning in concentration. "Name was Tuttle, something like that. Anyway, he was no fucking help whatsoever. But I worked my ass off and then, *poof,* the fucking Panther Man croaks himself in his cell and the whole thing dies with him.

"I mean, J.J. did a helluva job with the Meddler, but if Pano hadn't taken himself out, I woulda got a pretty good pat on the back myself."

He froze, then looked at his watch. "Shit, I almost missed it. My one o'clock." He turned to the table. He began opening one plastic bottle after another, popping pills. "Some of these come from Mexico," he said after he had finished. "They don't sell 'em in this country. Say they don't do any good. But at this point, they sure as hell can't hurt."

He took a gulp of water and began coughing again. When he'd finished, he said, "The fucking fruiters!"

"The who?" Manion asked.

"The fruiters. The fags. They did this to me. They gave me their fucking disease." When Manion made no response, he said, "Oh, you don't believe me? Maybe you think Pat Guillory is queer bait?"

"I hadn't given it much thought," Manion told him.

"It was a couple years after retirement," Guillory said. "I'm in this fucking drugstore and I see this kid lean over the counter and grab a bottle of booze and run out the door with it. I may not be carrying a badge, but I'm still a cop. So I pursue him. He runs into an alley where he's got a motorbike stashed. Puts the booze in his saddlebag. Starts to get on the bike. Then he sees me. He just stands there. This son of a bitch kid, maybe twenty, stands there with his little granny glasses and his nice pressed Levi's. 'Hey, pop,' he says, 'what's your story?'

"My story, I tell him, is that I'm making a citizen's arrest and throwing his fag body into jail for petty theft.

"Now he tells me to go fuck myself and he starts to get onto his bike. I draw my piece and when he sees it, the grin goes and he raises his hands. Starts showing a little respect. But then, I'm not sure what happens, exactly, but I get the idea he's rushing me and I hit him with the gun. I hit him a couple times.

"Maybe I got a little carried away. He's bleeding from the head and he comes at me and takes a swing. I swat it down and bust my knucks on his teeth. Went clear to the fucking bone.

"I bring the guy into the district lockup. A couple days later, a cop calls me and says the fruiter's tested HIV positive. I went in for some tests. Nothing. Then, last year, I started feeling kinda bad and I find out I'm HIV positive, too. That son of a bitch killed me. I'm still walking around, barely, but he killed me."

"It's too bad it had to happen," Manion said.

"Sometimes I feel better than others," Guillory said. "But I don't go to headquarters any more. I'd appreciate it if you didn't mention my . . . condition to anybody over there."

Manion said he wouldn't.

"Where were we, before I . . . oh yeah, Pano," Guillory said.

"Is there any possibility that Pano may have been an FBI agent?" Manion asked.

Guillory's mouth dropped open. Then he began to laugh, a wet, nasty laugh. "Who the fuck you been talking to, boy?" he asked.

"It's a rumor going around," Manion said.

"It's bullshit. Pano was a fucking lowlife murderer and agitator."

"You're convinced he killed himself?" Manion asked.

"Hell yeah, I'm convinced," Guillory replied. "He was all alone in his cell and he hanged himself. Left a note. That's pretty convincing."

"But there was some doubt at the time," Manion said. "Something about a pen."

"That was that goddamned Cajun," Guillory said dismissively.

"What did he have to do with it?"

"I showed him a sheet with the contents of Pano's cell and he asked how Pano could have written a suicide note if he didn't have a pen. But they'd just left the pen off the list. It was found."

"By you?" Manion asked.

He hesitated. "Yeah. I found the fuckin' pen. Buried in Pano's mattress."

"But it hadn't been found when they made up the inventory of Pano's possessions?"

"Nobody was lookin' for it."

"Could somebody other than Pano have put the pen in the mattress?" Manion asked.

Guillory gave him a sour look. "Why the fuck would anybody do that?"

"To make sure that Pano's death stayed a suicide."

Guillory shook his head from side to side. "Jesus. You assholes think there's something screwy about every fucking crime to come down the pike. This was a goddamn suicide, plain and simple. Why don't you get the fuck—"

He started coughing again. Horrible sounds, broken by gasps for breath. When this attack subsided, he waved his hand at Manion.

"Just get out of heah," he said, "before I die all over you."

Manion took the hint.

11

LOUIS DEMAY SPOTTED Mona's Place from the bus. The Mona Lisa sign with its neon smile was hanging in the window. The neon wasn't lighted. The establishment didn't look like much to the boy—a dark, wooden two-story building that needed paint. Two guys who might have been homeless were sitting at a table in front. One was wearing a funny sort of hat or cap that looked like a black pancake on his head. The other's T-shirt was torn. His feet were bare.

It was not until Louis had left the bus and walked past them that he discovered they were playing chess.

He continued on to the front door. It was shut.

"'Scuse me," Louis addressed the men, "but when do they open up?"

The man wearing the pancake hat gave him a stern look. "It's open, kid. Go on in. Gabe's in there."

Louis tried the door. He was surprised at how easily it swung inward.

He stepped cautiously into a large shotgun room running the length of the building. A stairwell along the side wall led to the top floor. The back door was open, letting in bright sunlight that focused on the dirt and sawdust on the floor. There was a funny smell. Like church or something.

A long mahogany bar poked out into the room, dark and ornate. To the boy it seemed gnarled and angry. He was staring at it when a man entered from the backyard carrying a large metal beer keg. He set it on the bar and stared at Louis.

"You sellin' something," the man said, "we don't want any."

"I'm looking for my daddy," Louis replied.

* * *

Eben Munn slouched behind the wheel of his T-Bird across the street from Mona's Place, idly watching the two men frown at their chessboard. He didn't know much about the game, but he thought that people who played it were assholes. He couldn't understand why anybody would spend hours just sitting there, trying to figure out what the other guy meant by his last move. Screw the other guy. Make your move and let *him* do the worrying.

It wasn't long before little Louis was standing on the sidewalk, blinking at the bright sun.

The boy took one long look back through the open door. Then he stepped out into the street and stared up at the second story. But there was nothing up there to see except a row of shuttered windows.

Head down, Louis shuffled glumly to the bus stop.

Once the boy was aboard the Elysian Fields bus and on his way, Munn got out of the T-Bird and crossed the street. The chess player in the beret gave him a hard eye and Munn replied with a cheery wink. "Watch out for his quarterback," he said.

Inside, the bar reminded Munn of a hangout for collegiates who thought they were intellectuals. Austere. Dusty. The smell of stale incense mixing with stale coffee. No big-screen TV. No pinballs. No galactic-battle machines. No foosball, even. Just an old jukebox, a dart target, notices about poetry readings and screen societies tacked to a bulletin board beside the door. A bar, of course. And a bartender, staring at him in a particularly unfriendly way.

"Hiya," Munn said. "How's about a beer?"

The bartender had been prepping the keg. "Draft okay?" he asked.

"Fine," Munn told him.

The bartender was of average height, but the platform behind the bar gave him an extra two or three inches. Munn judged him to be in pretty good shape for a guy of—what? Forty, maybe forty-five.

The glass of beer he placed in front of Munn had hardly any head on it. Munn took a sip and sighed. "First of the day," he said.

The bartender didn't reply.

"The kid who was just in here," Munn said, "what'd he want?"

The bartender raised his shoulders in a shrug. "Who knows?"

"You don't?" Munn looked around the room. "Did he talk to somebody else?"

"He said something about a job."

"Oh? What kind of a job? Dancing? Tending bar?"

The bartender's face hardened.

"Let me make this easy on you," Munn said. He took out his badge and showed it to the man. "Now, what did the kid want?"

"A job, like I said."

Munn picked up his glass and poured the remaining beer onto the polished bartop. "Think you missed a spot," he said.

The bartender got a rag and sopped up the beer. Then he used a cleaner rag to dry the bar completely.

"All this talking makes me thirsty," Munn said. "I'll have another beer."

"Look, mister—" the bartender began.

"Lieutenant. That's lieutenant."

"Lieutenant," the bartender went on, "I don't know you. I don't know what you want. The kid came in, asked me if his father made the sign in the window. I tol' him I didn't know who the hell made the sign. And I sure as hell didn't know who his father was. I'm just the day man. You, I tell the same thing."

Munn looked around the room. "This place isn't much, but still, you'd probably like to stay in business, right?"

"C'mon. Like I say, I'm just the day man. The owner'll be here tonight. After six. He'll be standing right here, tending bar. His name's Jo-Jo. Come back and talk to him."

"What can he tell me that you can't?" Munn asked, slipping from his stool. He circled the bar, stepped up onto the platform. "I like it up here," he said. "You look down on people. I might have one of these installed under my desk."

He lowered his gaze to a tub filled with ice cubes. "What do you know," he said. "A genuine antique." It was an old ice pick resting on the ledge behind the tub. Munn picked it up and rested its point casually on the bar top.

"Hey, c'mon," the bartender begged. "Don't mess up the bar."

"Tell me about the kid's old man."

The bartender's eyes went from the pick to Munn. "Look," he said, "I don't wanna lose this job. Jo-Jo'll bounce me outta here if the bar gets fucked up while I'm on duty."

"So who's fucking up your bar?" Munn asked.

"Jo-Jo told us not to say nothing about the jig."

"By 'the jig' you mean the African-American who's the kid's father?"

"Hell, I don't know if it's his father. All I know it's the same black guy done the sign. Louie."

"What about Louie?"

"He ... visits upstairs."

"He there now?" Munn asked.

The bartender shook his head. "Naw. He went out about an hour ago."

"Who's he visiting? Jo-Jo?"

"Jo-Jo rents out rooms upstairs to a couple of the waitresses. Louie is staying with Celeste. They left an hour ago, like I said."

"Know where they went?" Munn asked.

"I don't keep track. C'mon, huh? Jo-Jo'll be bent outta shape if he finds out I said anything about Louie. Just keep me out of it, huh?"

"Out of what?"

"Whatever's goin' on. I don't need trouble. I don't like trouble. Just keep me out of it."

"All right," Munn said, replacing the ice pick on the ledge. He went back in front of the bar and asked for another beer. While the bartender poured it, he said, "What kind of a guy is this Jo-Jo?"

"He's okay, you don't mess with him. But between you and me, he ain't crazy about cops."

"That doesn't make him different from a lot of people," Munn said. "What's Celeste's last name?"

"I don't know. Just Celeste."

"What time does she start work?"

"The evening shift. After six."

Munn picked up the full beer and drained the glass in a mighty gulp. Then he tapped his chest, issued a tiny belch, threw a few bills on the bar and said, "I'll be back. And I want to surprise Celeste, okay?"

"Like I said, Jo-Jo wouldn't like me talking to cops," the bartender replied. "Far as I know, you ain't been in today."

"Good man."

"Ah ... I got a cousin who's a cop. Maybe you know him. Rawley Louling?"

In Munn's book, Louling was a weasel who always had his

hand out and who took too many weekend trips to Vegas. "Sure, I know Rawley," Munn replied pleasantly. "He's your cousin, huh? Well it's a small old world, isn't it?"

12

MANION WAS IN a different sort of bar. This one, Marty's Irish Heaven, was on Magazine Street in the Irish Channel. Present were half a dozen drunks who looked like they boarded in the place and three tables full of college-age guys eating microwaved cheeseburgers and drinking beer while they watched a videotape of a Saints game with the sound off.

The bar's owner, Marty Boyle, had a ruddy mug and the whitest and most untamed hair Manion had ever seen. He was wearing a bright blue rayon shirt with red and orange polka dots, much of it mercifully hidden by the bib of his white apron.

Manion had been prepared to break the conversational ice by telling the former policeman that he was doing research for *Crime Busters*. But as soon as he mentioned his name, Boyle's face lit up like an electric Paddy mug and he shoved a big, moist hand over the bar. "Lejern used to talk about you," he said.

"So you kept up with J.J.?" Manion asked.

"He'd drop by."

"You knew him pretty well?"

"Well as anybody on the force, I guess," Boyle replied. "He didn't let anybody in Homicide get too close to him, and when he called it quits, the guys down there never heard from him again. Except me. Usually when he needed something in the files and like that. I was glad to help him out. I always liked him. I was sorry to hear about him passing away like that."

Boyle grinned suddenly. "The thing about Lejern, he never

struck me as being all that good-lookin', but the son of a butonna always had women. Beautiful women. And he went through 'em like Sherman went through Georgia. You'da thought that out of all of 'em, he'da found one to stick with for the long haul."

"Like you said, J.J. had a hard time letting people get close to him."

"But you and him musta been real tight, Manion. Whenever he'd come in here, he'd bend my ear with stories about this kid he was working with. He bragged on you the way I used to brag on Marty, Junior, before the little bastard ran off to California with my LeMans."

Manion was surprised. He'd felt very close to J.J., possibly even thought of him as a surrogate father, but he'd never for a moment imagined that the feeling might have been mutual. "That's good to know," he said, though for some reason it made him sad.

"Yeah. Lejern was really somethin'. I liked the man, and I think he sorta liked me," Boyle said. "But he wasn't one to let you know what was goin' on inside. Must have been different with you."

"Not really," Manion said.

Boyle shrugged. "Well, he was a Frenchman. What can I do for you, Manion? A beer?"

"Thanks, no," Manion said. "There was a case J.J. worked on, back when you and he were partners. You remember Tyrone Pano?"

"The Panther Man? Sure. Lejern and me found the evidence that got him locked up."

"Think he really killed himself?" Manion asked.

"Shit, I dunno," Boyle said. "I know Lejern had his doubts. Me, I didn't think about it one way or the other."

"There was something about a missing pen," Manion said. "But another officer, Pat Guillory, found it in Pano's mattress."

"Guillory couldn't find his own dick if he had a hard-on," Boyle said, chuckling. "It was Cady found the pen."

"Guillory's report says he found it."

"Read Guillory's reports and you'll think he found Jimmy Hoffa sittin' in a bar in Jazz City."

"Who's Cady?"

Boyle cocked his head to one side. "Sergeant Edward J. Cady, asshole who was in charge of the lockup. Lucky son of a bitch."

"Lucky how?"

"The guy's got hisself a mansion over the Causeway in Covington. Lives like a fucking king. Lives better than any other ex-cop I know."

"How does he do it?" Manion asked.

Boyle shrugged again. "He was in charge of the fucking lockup. You do an inmate a favor, like bring him a carton of smokes or even a bottle of bourbon, he pays for the service. Cady had that duty for over ten years. You can do a lot of favors in that time."

"You ever hear of him doing any bigger favors than just booze or smokes?" Manion asked.

"Like what?"

"Like maybe helping Pano hang himself?"

Boyle thought about it. Then he shook his head. "That'd be takin' too big a chance. And anyway, who the hell wanted Pano dead that bad?"

"Good question," Manion said.

13

"THE LORD HAS told us to seek happiness here on earth," the Most Reverend Francis Hart was reminding his television flock, as well as those assembled in Studio Seven of Crescent Video on Poydras Street. "And I am here to tell you that happiness has as much to do with satisfying the body as it does the soul. Care for your corporeal form and your spiritual form will glow like it has been touched by the divine flame of the Holy Spirit."

Nadia Wells had to hand it to the reverend. Standing up there in his pink tuxedo, with his white marcelled hair, hand resting on the biggest, shiniest pink Caddy convertible she'd ever seen and backed by a choir of large black women in pink gowns, Hart certainly put on a good show.

"I cannot tell you, brothers and sisters, how downright depressed I was as a young man. Rootless. Aimless. I was concentratin' on saving my soul so hard that my body was being starved of joy. Of happiness. Of the pleasures of life.

"I smile now when I realize what I was doing to myself, doing to my soul. I was cheating myself of my divine obligation to enjoy this life. So I drew out my piddling money from my savings account where it was gathering a miserly five percent interest. Today it'd have been even lower. And I took that money and went out and put a down payment on the nastiest, slickest car I could find. And I got behind the wheel of that machine and I didn't feel . . . *foolish*."

"Oh no, Lord," the congregation replied.

"I didn't feel . . . *guilty*."

"I say no, Lord." This time the response was louder.

"What I felt was . . . *strength*."

"Yes, Lord."

"What I felt was . . . *wisdom*."

"Oh yes, Lord."

"What I felt was . . . *control* over my own destiny."

"Yes, Lord, yes."

"I felt like I could conquer the world, and conquer it I did," the reverend said so quickly his audience did not have a chance to interrupt. "I drove to the home of a woman who I admired greatly, a woman who I had not had the courage to even speak to. And I rang her doorbell and I asked her to take a drive with me in my fine new machine. And, I swear to you, my friends, this woman is here today, my beautiful wife, Latita."

A handsome black woman in her late forties, dressed in a white gown, joined him beside the car. Hart picked up the pace and hardened his pitch. "If you unlock the potential that is in your mind and heart and soul by giving vent to the needs that exist in your body," he said solemnly, "I am here to tell you that the pie in the sky will be on your dinner table this very night. And there is only one way for you to experience these magnificent, God-given rewards. By contributing to and sharing the fruits of this holy ministry, the Heart of Jesus Church of New Orleans, Louisiana."

Nadia looked up as the post office box address of the Heart of Jesus Church appeared on the monitors. She wondered if there really was a church, other than the studio in front of her. If such a house of worship existed in the city, she assumed she would have heard about it and that the reverend's offices would be there, instead of in this video building.

On stage, the singers began a gospel song that sounded suspiciously like "Show Me the Way to Go Home," and the reverend and his wife reached out past the footlights to shake the hands of the faithful in attendance.

Someone touched Nadia's elbow. It was a tall African-American woman in a soft silk shirt and a charcoal suit. "Mrs. Wells, I'm Anika Lane, Reverend Hart's assistant," she explained. "Please follow me."

The woman led Nadia from the studio down a corridor and into an elevator. Two floors up, they stepped into a reception area with molded soft walls painted in pleasant earth shades. Anika Lane ushered the elderly woman past a pretty receptionist at an ultramodern desk module and into a short hallway leading to an office that occupied nearly a third of that floor.

It was big and airy, with lots of floor-to-ceiling windows that looked out over the streets all the way to the Mississippi River. "The view was so much better before they put up the St. Louis Hotel," Anika said, pointing out the hotel and its brand-new, yet-to-be-dedicated casino.

"Well," Nadia replied, "at least the reverend doesn't have to look at the Superdome."

"There is that," Anika agreed.

The door behind them opened and the reverend entered, sweating profusely and removing his coat. He spied Nadia, paused, and slipped back into his jacket.

"Don't keep suited up on my account, Reverend," she told him. "I know how hot those lights must be."

"You are most kind, Mrs. Wells," he said, removing the coat. "Did you enjoy the service?"

"Immensely," she replied. "But if I hadn't already been a convert, I wouldn't be here now to discuss a contribution to the Church."

The reverend smiled. His eyes barely flickered to his assistant, Anika. But Nadia spotted the movement and was not surprised when the tall woman said, "If you'll excuse me, I'd better be getting back to my office."

"Mrs. Wells, do you have a specific area of the ministry where you'd like to apply your contribution?" the reverend asked, as Anika closed the door after her.

"There is one wrinkle I'd like ironed out first," Nadia said. His eyes opened wide. "A wrinkle?"

"I know you were once at the head of the organization known as the Southern Cross."

"I have made no secret of my past history. Not even of things that happened in my youth. I served as leader of the Southern Cross for nearly two years." He smiled. "I was called 'Tank' in those days, a reference to my size. I weighed well over two hundred and fifty pounds. But when I came to love my body, to realize the importance of it to not only life temporal but life everlasting, I knew that I would have to get in shape, as it were."

"You must have lost enough fat to make a whole 'nother person," Nadia said pleasantly.

"Quite," he replied, staring at her long enough to make her wonder if she'd overplayed her hand.

Time to fish or cut bait, she thought. "You took over the Southern Cross from a man named Tyrone Pano, right?" she asked.

He considered the question as if it were a fly buzzing about his face. Then the fly landed. "Tyrone was our leader. After his untimely death, I filled in."

"And the FBI closed you down."

The reverend's smile went away. "The FBI had our organization under close scrutiny, but that was not why the Southern Cross disbanded. I ended it. I saw the error of a life consumed with hatred. I saw the wisdom of a life enriched by all the bountiful rewards this earth offers."

There was a discreet knock at the door.

"Yes?" Reverend Hart called out.

"Me, darling."

The reverend rose from his chair and almost raced to the door. He opened it for his wife. "Come in, dear. Mrs. Wells and I were just chatting."

The attractive black woman nodded to Nadia and smiled sweetly. "I'm Latita Hart. Would I be interrupting if I joined you?"

"Not at all," Nadia said. "The reverend and I were just chewing the fat about an old friend of ours, Tyrone Pano."

Latita raised an eyebrow and looked at her husband, who was frowning at Nadia. "You knew Tyrone?" he asked.

"Oh my, yes," she lied. "I could never understand how he could have taken his own life like that."

"I don't believe he did," the reverend said.

"Oh?" she asked.

"I'd rather not get into it. I prefer not to dwell on the negative."

"But if he didn't kill himself, then who . . . ?"

"The fascist police, of course," the reverend said matter-of-factly. "They killed him and they took his money."

"You must excuse my husband," Latita Hart interjected, with an edge to her voice. "But when one loses a dear friend like Tyrone, not even the passage of so many years can ease the pain."

"What money did the police steal?" Nadia asked.

"There was an officer named Legendre," Hart said, ignoring his wife's glare. "He played with poor Tyrone's mind and won his confidence. And he got him to change his will. This was only a few days before Tyrone . . . passed on."

"And Tyrone left a bundle?"

"Perhaps not a bundle," Mrs. Hart said in a clipped manner.

"Did you know Tyrone, too?" Nadia asked.

"I worked for the Southern Cross," Mrs. Hart said. "I'm curious. How did *you* meet Tyrone?"

Nadia waved an airy hand. "When he was growin' up, I was friends with his aunt, Shana."

Hart and his wife exchanged glances. "Then you must know she was Tyrone's only beneficiary," he said.

"By then, Shana and I had had a falling out," Nadia improvised. "But I thought you said a policeman got his money."

"My suspicion," Hart replied, "is that he and Shana Washington shared it."

"Hmm. I suppose you made darn sure that will was the real McCoy," Nadia said.

"Our lawyer said it was," Hart told her.

The reverend's wife interrupted again. "Forgive me, Mrs. Wells, but I don't quite understand what all this has to do with your donating to Heart of Jesus."

"Please excuse an old lady. I do tend to get sidetracked," Nadia said. "But since the reverend mentioned his lawyer, I wonder if I might know that gentleman's name?"

"Why?" Mrs. Hart asked, fully suspicious now.

"It should be obvious," Nadia said indignantly. "Most charities are set up in such a way as to provide donors with certain tax incentives. I have found that the better the lawyer, the more solid the ground is when you're facing down an IRS audit. So, who's your legal eagle?"

"Our law firm is the best in the city," the reverend's wife said, "Nathan and Billins."

Nadia smiled and relaxed. "Since Kiel Nathan is spending most of his days keeping to that mansion of his, I assume that means Billins is your man. Good." She hopped to her feet and started for the door. "He knows his way around a loophole, sure enough. You'll be hearing from my business guy by the end of the month about the size of the contribution."

She was out of the office and on her way before either the Reverend Hart or his wife could say another word.

14

THE LAKE PONTCHARTRAIN Causeway, covering a distance of twenty-five miles, is reputed to be the longest continuous overwater bridge-highway in the world. Though not normally a fast driver, Manion traversed it in just sixteen minutes. The trip from Boyle's bar to the Covington home of former Police Sergeant Edward J. Cady took a little less than an hour, possibly a record.

Cady's home wasn't exactly a mansion, but it would do until a mansion became available. It was a rustic, sprawling ranch-style construction set among the pine trees, not far from the Pearl River. An enormous satellite dish played hide-and-seek behind shrubbery that hadn't quite filled in enough to camouflage its jarringly unnatural shape.

A black Lincoln Town Car and a silver classic Porsche were parked along the drive. Manion pulled in behind the Porsche. When he stepped out of his Mustang, he could hear the laughter of children from somewhere behind the house.

The man who answered the buzzer was elderly, with a full

white mustache and a white frizz that circled a balding head. He was plump, nut brown from the sun, and depressingly cheery. He introduced himself as Ed Cady and grabbed Manion's hand in his large paw, giving it a hearty shake. Then he invited the traveler inside.

"You sure didn't take your time gettin' here, son," he said. "You must have jets on that Mustang. Seems like I just hung up the phone and here you are." He led the young man down a hall past an open door. The room beyond was occupied by two small tow-headed children, obviously a brother and sister, yanking on the arms of a wobbly sawdust clown that hung from a thick wooden rafter.

"Place is full of kids," Cady said. "It's grandpa's week. Once a year, I give my sons and daughters a break by lettin' 'em deposit their Munchkins here for five days. Got half a dozen of 'em now. Four boys. Two girls. I gather that number'll be increased by two this time next year. Couple of nannies help out. Hell, they do most of the work. I just sit around looking like a proud grandpa and pretend I'm an expert on child-rearin'."

"This is a great place for it," Manion told him. "Lots of space."

"Yeah. My wife and I used to live in a little two-room apartment on Louisiana Parkway in New Orleans. That's where we raised *our* kids. By the time I could afford to build here in Covington, the kids were on their own and Lula—that's my wife—took sick and we lost her. But I went ahead and had the place built anyway. I never regretted it. Not even when property values dipped lower than a snake's belly."

"Even then," Manion said, looking out of French windows at a yard man scooping pine needles from a long rectangular swimming pool, "I couldn't have come close to scraping up the down on a house this big and beautiful."

Cady grinned and led him further along the abruptly angled hall. "Know what you mean, son. If I hadn't been moonlighting when I was on the NOPD, I'm not sure I could have swung it, either. And then I was fortunate enough to have a job waiting after I put in my time."

"Something in law enforcement?"

"Sort of. I was a consultant for the best law firm in the city."

"Which one is that?"

Cady paused as if trying to decide if he should name his

former employers. Apparently he saw no reason not to. "Nathan and Billins," he replied. "Only it was Nathan and Burns, then. Billins wasn't made a partner until about nine years ago, when Calvin Burns died."

He opened the door to a surprisingly modern den with leather chairs and a sofa facing a floor-to-ceiling video wall like the pews in a church facing an altar. A boxing match was taking place on the huge screen. Orange padded gloves as large as pumpkins plowed into sweat-slick flesh. "A mite early for this sort of entertainment," Cady said, picking up a remote power stick and pressing the screen into darkness. "The Small-Tyner fight from Vegas," he said proudly. "I taped it off pay-per-view couple nights ago. What are you drinkin'?"

"Coffee'll be fine," Manion said.

His host wobbled to the door and called out, "Carmelita, a couple black caf-fays, *por favor*." He retraced his steps and waved a hand at a chair not far from his favorite. "Now, tell me exactly what kind of police stories you're lookin' for."

"As I said on the phone, Mr. Cady . . ."

"C'mon. Eddie, please. Even the kids call me Grandpa Eddie."

"Well, Eddie, I'm looking for stories about what crime was like in New Orleans back in the sixties."

"Same as now, only maybe a little less violent," the elderly man said. "Naw, that's not true. It ain't the same at all. There are some sick son-bitches out there these days. Way back when there were sickos, too, but not nearly so many of 'em."

"What about race-related crimes?" Manion asked.

"There's a lot of that goin' on today," Cady said. "More than you read about. Just one more reason I'm happy to be here in Covington.

"Back in the fifties and sixties, though, it was different. Jew lawyers and blacks comin' down South, stirrin' people up, pittin' white against black, black against white, then going back home to Jew York or wherever and letting us clean up the mess."

"The law firm you worked for had a Jewish partner and an African-American partner," Manion said. "Was that a problem for you?"

Cady stared at him for a few seconds and replied, "No. I got no problems with Jews and blacks."

"You recall a group called the Southern Cross?"

Cady's eyes dulled, and he hesitated a few more seconds.

"Yeah. I remember 'em. They had big plans to blow up the capitol, or something. But they never quite got around to it, I guess, 'cause the capitol's still there."

"Their leader was a man named Tyrone Pano," Manion said. He waited for Cady to react. But the old man didn't say a word.

The silence was broken by an elderly Latin woman in a black dress with a white collar entering with a tray holding two cups of coffee. Her face was entirely without expression as she handed the cups to Manion and her employer.

"Carmelita makes the best coffee this side of Morning Call," Cady said. The woman gave him a wintry smile and silently withdrew from the room.

"You must remember Tyrone Pano," Manion said, after sipping the coffee.

Cady nodded his tanned head. "Yeah. I got my fill of him when he was staying in my lockup. Mean little bastard. Arrogant. The worst kind of nigra. Troublemaker. A murderer, too. Killed some nigra gal. The best thing he did was to save the city the price of a trial."

"What made him kill himself?" Manion asked.

"Who knows? Maybe he was in love with the woman and was sorry for what he did. Maybe he didn't want to stand trial. Maybe he got religion. Maybe he was just tired."

"There's a rumor it might not have been a suicide."

Cady's eyes narrowed in suspicion, and his cheeriness gave up the ghost. "Meaning what?" he demanded.

"That he was murdered, I suppose."

"In my lockup?" Cady asked, reddening. "I don't think so."

"Couldn't a visitor—"

"No!"

"There was something about a fountain pen," Manion said.

"That was that stupid son of a bitch Guillory. 'Where's the pen?' he asks me. Okay, we missed it the first sweep of Pano's cell. But it was there, stuck in his mattress."

"How'd he get it? I understand pens or any pointed objects weren't allowed."

"He had visitors. One of them must have slipped it to him."

"Visitors have always had to log in, haven't they?" When Cady nodded, Manion continued, "Could those logs still be around somewhere?"

"Shit, they keep everything. But I wouldn't know where to look for it. What are you wasting your time on Pano for, anyway? There been all kinds of stories. The Meddler case, for example. Or that sniper on top of the motel. Or that society kid, the one who got his boyfriend to help him bump off his mom and dad. Now those are stories for your TV show."

"The thing about Pano . . ." Manion began.

"Enough about him," Cady snapped, his face flushing a strange orange shade. "I don't have anything more to say about him."

Manion stood and thanked him for his cooperation.

"Yeah, right," Cady grumbled cynically, leading him toward the door.

Outside, as Manion headed for his Mustang, a little girl with bright golden hair, dressed in a tiny pink warm-up outfit, ran to the old man and hugged his legs.

Even that didn't take the scowl off Cady's face. He bent down and disengaged her tiny hands and continued staring at Manion, ignoring her pleas for Grandpa to come play.

Manion called out his goodbye and got into his car. He received no reply. When the Mustang left the drive and bounced onto the macadam leading to the highway, he took a last look back. Cady was still standing in front of the house, staring his way, making sure he was truly gone.

MUNN RETURNED TO Mona's Place at a little after six.

It was dusk, and the neon smile was brightening the window.

The chess players had long since given up the table in front to the cockroaches, mosquitoes and other night companions.

Inside, thanks to soft lighting, the room had a slightly warmer atmosphere. But to Munn, who had grown up over a tavern and who had seen his father beaten senseless by members of the Benedetto family in a similar surrounding, it was not a place that cheered his soul.

A few early diners sat at wooden tables munching large, ungainly hamburgers and drinking coffee from mugs plastered with a print of La Gioconda. They looked to Munn like bikers and ex-cons. But in his book, anyone who dressed in leather vests and Levi's and whose hair went past the collar was somebody you kept in front of you at all times.

There were two waitresses on the floor trying to out-blasé one another. They were dressed in black leather skirts, black tank tops and black stockings. One was brunette, a hardbody with acne scars. The other was blond and voluptuous, with a face that was almost pretty under the pale white makeup.

Behind the bar, a smiling, gap-toothed fellow with an eye patch was caressing a fat yellow tabby that seemed to be enjoying the attention. The man was wearing tight black trousers and a black-and-white striped shirt with the sleeves ripped off. He had a tattoo of the Mona Lisa on his right bicep. He bid Munn welcome without missing a cat stroke.

Munn sat down on a stool at the bar. "You the owner?" he asked.

The man rolled his one eye around the room. "A poor café but mine own," he said, placing the cat on the bar. "You want to take it off my hands?" he asked as the animal darted away. "It's a solid moneymaker."

"I'll just have a brewsky," Munn said.

"I bet I could find a Dixie back here somewhere," the man said. "I keep 'em for the carriage trade. We're more of a coffeehouse, you see."

"You have beer on draft, don't you?" Munn said, pointing to the spigot that the day bartender had used.

"Oh yeah. I forget about that sometimes. I don't recommend it."

It had tasted fine that afternoon, but Munn said, "The Dixie'll do, as long as it's not any of that Blackened Voodoo stuff."

"Just plain ol' Dixie," the bartender said, uncapping a bottle from the fridge and placing it before him. "Need a glass?"

"Save it for your next customer," Munn said. He sipped the beer and let his eyes roam to the mirror behind the bar that reflected the whole room. A couple came in and joined one of the diners. The brunette waitress slithered over to the table and took their order. Then she relayed it to the bartender, who carried the information through a door at the rear of the bar.

"You Celeste?" Munn asked the brunette waitress.

She gave him a bored look and didn't reply. When the bartender returned, she told him, "Mr. Slick here is asking for Celeste."

The bartender was wiping his hands on a dirty rag. "Celeste isn't on duty," he said to Munn.

"Too bad," Munn said. "I made a trip for nothing. But I've had beers in worse places."

The bartender's eye shifted, and Munn turned to see the cat leap onto a table occupied by a guy munching a burger who didn't seem to mind the company. The cat gave him a look of utter contempt, then sprang to a shelf just below the ceiling, where it curled around a plaster bust.

"Leonardo," the bartender said.

"The bust?" Munn asked.

"No, friend, the cat. The bust is Liszt. And I'm Jo-Jo." He poured hot coffee into a thick mug and handed it to the brunette waitress, who carried it away to a table.

Munn sat there drinking his beer slowly.

A few customers strolled in. A few strolled out. The cat stayed on its shelf. From time to time, it yawned. Munn yawned, too. "Leonardo looks bored," he said to Jo-Jo.

"Mellowing out now," the bartender crooned. "But he can be something fierce when riled. Played tic-tac-toe on the back of a Great Dane about a month ago. What do you want with Celeste?"

"Friend of the family," Munn said.

"And you forgot what she looks like?"

"It's been a long time."

"I don't expect her in tonight," Jo-Jo said.

"Doesn't she live here?"

Jo-Jo smiled. "That don't necessarily mean she'll be here tonight. Celeste's a popular lady. Another Dixie?"

"Guess not," Munn said, and paid for the beer. As he started for the door, a woman descended the stairwell from the floor above. She was attractive, if a bit plump, a blonde with a pleasant, unremarkable face.

Jo-Jo was staring at Munn with his good eye. Munn winked at him and headed for the blonde. "Celeste?" he called out.

Her green eyes widened and she began to backtrack up the

steps. Munn was aware of a silence in the room. Then Jo-Jo shouted, "Leonardo, attack."

The cat seemed to appear out of nowhere, leaping onto Munn's left leg and hooking its claws into his thigh. Munn staggered against the wall and grabbed the animal by its skinny neck. He tried to pry it loose. Jo-Jo was out from behind the bar, rushing toward him with a baseball bat in his hand. Munn yanked the cat from his leg and threw it at the bartender. He didn't wait to see where or if it hit him.

The blonde was somewhere above, clicking a key into her door lock. When Munn reached her, she paled, brought her hands close to her chest and squeezed her eyes shut. "Please, no . . ." she begged.

Munn's leg hurt like the fires of hell. His pants were ripped. He pried the key from her fingers and opened the door.

Staring into the small, dim bedroom, he sensed a flurry of movement. Before he could focus on it, the blonde was on his back, screaming and trying to claw his face. "Jesus," he shouted and stumbled. They both fell hard into the room.

Munn pushed the woman from him and struggled to his feet. He cursed himself. He should have played it straight from the jump, showed Jo-Jo his badge and bulled his way into Celeste's room. It had been the other bartender's talk about Jo-Jo being a cop hater that had convinced him to keep the badge in his pocket. As a result, he'd been clawed by a cat that was probably rabid and he was in the middle of a situation.

Jo-Jo's thudding footsteps were approaching.

Munn brought out his badge and drew his gun. "Police," he said firmly. "Everybody just relax."

The room was a mess. Art canvases—nude studies of Celeste, mainly—rested against the walls. Damp bloody towels were bunched on the floor. A black man was huddled in a corner of the room. Shivering. His face was plastered with homemade bandages. One eye was swollen shut. His bottom lip was split and newly scabbed over. He sat on the floor, cowering in his underwear, shaking like the fit was on him.

Munn said "Police" again and showed the man his badge. It didn't seem to help.

"Your name deMay?" Munn asked.

The man's head jerked in what looked like a positive reply. When deMay's teeth began to chatter, the policeman ordered the woman to get him a blanket.

She picked herself up slowly from the floor and moved toward the bed in a daze.

Jo-Jo charged through the door wielding a baseball bat. His cat followed him in. The cat began to stalk Munn.

"Nice kitty want a lead furball?" Munn growled pointing his gun.

The one-eyed man grabbed his pet with his free hand and pulled it close to his body protectively. Leonardo didn't like that idea. He raked his paw over Jo-Jo's arm, leaving four red lines through the Mona Lisa tatoo. "Don't you hurt these people, you bastard," Jo-Jo snarled at Munn.

"I'm a cop, damnit," Munn said.

"So fucking what?" Jo-Jo wanted to know.

"So I'm not here to hurt anybody," Munn shouted, pointing his pistol directly at the cat's face. "Except him, maybe. Put the cat out—now."

Jo-Jo backed out of the door. Leonardo didn't want to go. He scratched his master once more. Munn slammed the door on them and turned to see that the blonde was wrapping the black man in a rough woolen blanket.

Munn holstered his gun and slipped the badge back into his pocket. As he approached them, the blonde drew back in fear.

"I'm not gonna hurt anybody," Munn said. "It looks like that's already been done. Let's get him onto the bed."

DeMay was stiff as a plank, his teeth chattering. Munn and Celeste awkwardly transported him onto the rumpled bed.

"Who beat him?"

"I . . . don't know. He came in like that about three hours ago. We had lunch together. Then he went off. Said he had some business to take care of. I don't know where he went or even how he was able to get back here like that. I fixed him up best I could."

"He's been staying here?"

She nodded. "For five or six weeks," she said. "Told me he needed to get away from things for a while."

"He didn't say why he had to get away?"

"No. But he does that sometimes. Usually, it's trouble at home."

"You think his wife did *that*?"

She didn't reply.

"He mention a guy named Ragusa?" Munn asked.

She said nothing, but deMay jerked back. Munn reached out

a hand and held the battered man's head still, staring into his eyes. "You better get him to a hospital."

"He wasn't this bad until you busted in."

"My bustin' in sure as hell didn't give him a concussion."

"Will you drive us?"

Munn gave her a derisive snort. But the fact was he felt guilty about the stupid way he'd played this scene. "Yeah, I'll drive you," he said. "I better get this cat scratch looked at anyway." He stared at the pathetic deMay. "But I'm sure as hell not gonna help you put his pants on."

Munn left the room to find the bar owner standing beside the door. Jo-Jo said, "I agree with you about Louie needin' a doc. I told her that."

"Your friggin' cat got any diseases I should know about? Rabies, anything like that?"

"The animal leads a cleaner life than I do."

Munn could believe that. "What do you know about Romeo and Juliet in there?" he asked, his eyes searching the hall for any sign of the suddenly absent feline.

"Like she told you, Louie's been stayin' here."

"Any idea who scrambled him?" Munn asked, pressing on his throbbing thigh.

"If I did, I'd be figuring out a little payback," Jo-Jo said. "I like Louie. He's a real ar-teest. He did our sign."

"He and Celeste been together long?"

"Old friends. She used to model for him when he was in his pastel stage. He'd drop by once, twice a week. Lately, he's been comin' in for longer spells."

"Must make it a little rough on the wife and kid," Munn said.

"How a man treats his family is his business. But real ar-teests don't live by the standards of squares. Maybe you heard of Mr. Paul Gauguin?"

"He into neon, too?" Munn asked.

Jo-Jo gave him a one-eyed stare.

"Remy Ragusa come around here?"

"Who he?"

Munn gave him a disgusted look. "Friend of Gauguin's," he said.

Celeste came to the door with the news that Louis deMay was ready.

The three of them got the black man down the stairs. If the customers of Mona's Place were too disturbed by the sight, they didn't show it. Maybe they thought it was a warm-up to the poetry readings.

Leonardo the cat sat on the bust of Liszt. He'd lost interest in all of them. That was fine with Munn.

16

"WHO IS THIS?" Madeleine Betterick (née DuBois) asked.

Her telephone voice was low and husky. It also had a slightly artificial, professional sound, as if she'd spent time losing an accent and acquiring a broadcast quality. The better to sway juries, Manion thought.

Standing in a pay phone in an Eckert Drug Store a block away from the courthouse, he repeated his name.

"And you want to talk with me about J.J. Legendre? Why?"

"I'm researching one of his cases and I hope you might be able to help," Manion answered.

"Oh God. Not that Meddler business again," the woman moaned in mock, or perhaps genuine, despair. "I'm sorry, but I closed the book on all that years ago."

"No, it's not the Meddler," Manion said quickly before she could hang up. "It's about a man named Tyrone Pano."

She was silent for a second. "I remember the name, of course. But I'm still a bit confused as to why ..."

"I'm contacting every possible source," Manion told her. "But, frankly, it's not only Pano I want to talk to you about. I ... worked with J.J. for a while."

"Really?" she said, giving the word an interested, not doubting, inflection. "When was this?"

"A few years ago," Manion said. "I'd just like to talk with someone who knew him."

"And precisely what aspect of J.J. did you want to discuss?"

"I'm not sure," Manion said. "I worked with him, and I felt

close to him, but I don't think I really knew him. I guess I'd just like to get a clearer fix on the kind of man he was."

Again there was momentary silence from her end before she said, "I don't think I can help you with Pano. J.J. didn't talk much about his cases. But if you'd like to dish the French son of a bitch, I might be on for that."

"I'm not far from the courthouse," Manion said.

"It's not convenient for me to see you here," she replied. "I've a meeting in ten minutes. And then I have to be across town. I'll be free at six-thirty."

Manion looked at his watch. An hour and a half away. "Fine," he said.

"Then meet me in front of Holy Name Church on the Avenue. I'll be the gray-haired matron with a bulging briefcase, wearing dark brown and a holier-than-thou expression."

She'd been to confession, she told him, as Manion drove them up the Avenue to the Carrollton section. Then she added, "That should act as a good warm-up for our little *parlez-vous*."

He had spotted her at once as she left the church, an extremely attractive woman dressed for success in a dark brown coat suit that managed to show off her rounded figure without making a point of it. She wasn't really gray. Silver strands among the blond.

He'd taken the time to study her carefully before approaching her. Her patrician, seemingly unruffled, beauty and her graceful stride gave her the appearance of someone in control of her emotions and perfectly at peace with the world. But in the car, listening to her barbed and sarcastic references to the late J.J. Legendre, that first impression kept slipping away. He had to cast frequent sidelong glances to convince himself that she wasn't undergoing some physical metamorphosis as well.

She was famished, she'd informed him as soon as the introductions were complete. Would he mind if they ate while they talked?

He'd admitted being hungry, too, and suggested they dine at Charlie's Steak House.

"I'd rather go to Camellia Grill," she'd replied with a mysterious smile.

On the way there, she solved the mystery. "When J.J. and I were . . . whatever we were," she said, "we'd invariably start out going to Camellia Grill and end up at Charlie's. Care to guess whose choice Charlie's was?"

"Did he always get his way?" Manion asked.

"Oh yes," she replied. "I've discovered an important fact about relationships: the ones who care the least always get their way."

Manion wondered where that left him and Lucille Munn. Who was getting their way now?

"I even converted to Catholicism for him," Madeleine said.

"I didn't know he was Catholic until his death," Manion told her.

"That's because you and he never discussed marriage," she said bitterly. "It wasn't as though he went to mass or anything. In retrospect, I imagine he made a big thing about his religion only because he knew my family hated Catholics and he thought that would end the marriage talk.

"My conversion let him know how serious I was and that scared him away, I suppose. Something did."

"He moved out?" Manion asked.

"No. I left. I told him there was this associate in the law firm where I worked who was showing interest. He was attractive and ambitious, and while I wasn't exactly panting with desire to go out with the guy, I felt I had to consider all my options. I wanted J.J. to tell me not to go out with him, that I was *his* woman and would be his woman for the rest of our lives. But he didn't do that. Instead, he said, 'Guy sounds like a good catch.' And that was that."

"Maybe he was waiting for you to decide for yourself not to see the other man."

"Right," she said sarcastically. "And maybe his little finger was too tired for him to lift it. If he had, I would have dumped the lawyer in a New York second."

"How'd you and the lawyer get along?" Manion asked.

"It was doomed," she said, chuckling. "First affairs after the rebound are doomed before they start."

Lucille had been on the rebound when she and Manion met.

"In any case," Madeleine said, "I'm glad I became a Catholic. It's one of the few things keeping me going these days. Three minutes in a darkened confessional with a faceless priest is easily worth an hour with a bored shrink. It's about the only good thing that came from my relationship with J.J."

"Literally, the only thing?" Manion asked.

"Of course not," she said. "I loved the man. I may have been a young idiot at the time, but I wouldn't have let myself get involved with a cipher. He was strong and silent and always seemed to know precisely what he was doing. He was goddamned Gary Cooper."

"He said he always wanted to be William Powell."

"Powell? You mean slick, suave. Debonair." She smiled. "J.J. was about as suave as flannel pajamas. That was another of his appeals. He was comfortable to be around.

"And for a while, he was in love with me, too. I'm sure of that." She looked up and gave Manion's profile a rueful smile. "But nothing lasts."

"He never seemed very happy," Manion said. "It was as if he knew too much or had seen too much to just kick back and enjoy himself."

"I remember him loosening up once," she said. "On a short trip to Destin. It was the best time we ever had together. The grim nightmare was behind us. I'd done well on my finals. J.J. was Homicide's fair-haired boy. And he'd been offered some ridiculously lucrative position with a bank and he didn't know whether to take it or not.

"That reminds me—Pano," she said. "J.J. had met with this bank president because of something Tyrone Pano asked him to do. I have no idea what. But the banker liked J.J. and offered him this incredible job."

"Which bank?" Manion asked, too casually.

She paused to consider the question. "Century National, I think," she said.

She couldn't have surprised him more if she'd pulled a knife on him. His father had offered J.J. a job? He'd had no reason to think they'd ever met. Certainly J.J. had not mentioned it. And their meeting involved Tyrone Pano.

"You sure you don't know what Pano asked J.J. to do at the bank?" he asked.

She shook her head. "In any case, J.J. decided to stay with the NOPD and he turned the banker down. It wasn't that he was unambitious or that he didn't care about money. He just had his own odd set of priorities. And for him, staying on the force was at the top. I suppose I was a few rungs down from there."

Manion heard what she was saying, and reacted with a polite mumble, but his curiosity about the Jack Manion—J.J. Legendre connection was pushing all new information to the rear of his mind.

* * *

By the time they reached Camellia Grill, where, miraculously, they had to wait only a few minutes before being seated at the spotless counter, Manion was once again concentrating on his companion.

At the moment, she was watching their burgers being prepared with the delighted anticipation of a schoolgirl. "I've loved this place ever since college," she said.

"I come here pretty often myself," Manion told her. He had, in fact, been there only the week before. With Lucille Munn.

"I'm sorry I can't provide the key that will unlock the secret of J.J.," Madeleine said. "And I know even less about Tyrone Pano. So dinner's on me."

"J.J. must have told you something about Pano," he said. "Something about a will, maybe?"

There was no spark of memory in her eyes. "As I said, he rarely talked about police business. And when he did, I was never sure if he was being truthful or making fun of me because I was so gullible. But . . ." She stared at the counter as if hoping for a videotape from yesteryear.

"Something?" Manion asked hopefully.

"There was this odd, milk-skinned man who came by the apartment. . . ."

"Can you fill in the description?"

"Unusually pale. Maybe five foot nine. Dressed casually. Losing his hair. A long nose and hollow cheeks. Like Punch. He dropped by one night after dinner. J.J. wasn't surprised to see him. He fixed the man black coffee and bourbon and they took their cups out on the porch while I did the dishes.

"They stayed out there for a while, talking and laughing. Then, they left the apartment together. J.J. was back in half an hour. He seemed inordinately pleased with himself. He said that the pale man had helped him make sure that Pano's death served at least one good end."

"Do you recall the pale man's name?"

"I think it was Penn, like the comic magician."

Manion closed his eyes and tried to think back through J.J.'s acquaintances that he knew. Penn had a familiar ring to it. Then it hit him. One of J.J.'s few friends was an artist named Pen Libideau. He'd been in the office a few times, meeting J.J. for lunch. But he was neither milk white nor thin. Still, people change over the years. He knew that Libideau had changed professions. J.J. had told him that the man had once been a forger.

What sort of work might Pen the forger have done to put a positive spin on Pano's death? It must have involved the will.

The counterman placed their burgers in front of them and for a few minutes neither spoke. Madeleine broke the silence by ordering a grilled doughnut, and Manion followed her lead. When they'd done away with their sticky desserts, she dabbed at her lips with her napkin and asked, "Was it a big funeral?"

"I was out of town," Manion replied, "but I heard it was a small turnout. Just a few friends."

"A widow?"

Manion shook his head.

"But he had . . . someone?"

"Yes."

She smiled, not pleasantly. "Let me guess. In her twenties?"

"Barely," he answered.

"That old bastard," she said softly.

"I guess I'd better get you back to your car," Manion said.

As they drove down the Avenue, Madeleine turned on the Mustang's radio, tuned in a jazz station, then lowered the sound until the music became nearly subliminal. "How much do you know about Theodore Glander?" she asked.

"The Meddler, you mean?"

"I prefer to call him by his real name, Theodore Glander."

"Well, I know that he butchered five women he didn't know to disguise the fact that he murdered his own daughter for her money. I know he used you to draw J.J. into some sort of showdown and that you and J.J. came out on top."

"Did he talk much about it?" she asked, almost hopefully.

"No," he replied. "I've been reading up on it. And one of J.J.'s old partners filled me in. Marty Boyle."

"Oh my God, the cop with the wild hair and the hideous clothes."

"He's got his own bar on Magazine. His hair is white, but still wild. Clothes still hideous."

"I met him the same day I met the monster, Glander," she said.

"How'd that happen?" Manion asked.

"I paid a surprise visit to Homicide. This was when police headquarters was on Loyola and Tulane. Boyle escorted me past the front desk and deposited me at J.J.'s cubicle. My dearly beloved and some other detectives were talking with Glander and his son-in-law. When their confab finally broke

up, the son-in-law—his name was Keller—strolled over and
began talking to me.

"I thought he was hitting on me until I realized who he was.
Then Glander joined us and Keller—was his name Jim?
John?—introduced us. I remember him saying, 'Dad, this is
J.J. Legendre's ladyfriend.' It was all so bloody polite. Only
Glander was running the information through his twisted brain
to see what he could do with it."

"He got you to come to his home?"

"Under the pretense of having an apartment for rent."

"How did he know you needed an apartment?"

She frowned. "I'm not sure. I suppose I may have mentioned it. I'd been circling ads in the paper when we were introduced."

"What happened at Glander's home, exactly?" he asked.
And she, without a moment's hesitation, did the thing she had
said she wouldn't. She recalled for him the terror of her en-
counter with the Meddler.

They arrived back at Holy Name Church before she finished. Manion parked in a slot next to her Camry and was
pleased to see that she did not seem inclined to cut short her
grim reminiscence. He was fascinated by every detail.

When she did finish, he began to question her. Why had
Glander pushed the department into putting J.J. on the case?
Why had he gone to the trouble of using her as bait to lure J.J.
to his home? What was he planning? To kill them both? Why
at his own home? He'd killed his daughter. He'd gotten away
with it. Why did he want a confrontation with J.J.?

She held up her hands. "I've asked myself the same questions. So did J.J."

"And?"

She shrugged. "The prevailing opinion was that Glander
simply wanted to be caught. I didn't believe it then and I don't
now."

"And J.J.?"

"He thought it was nonsense, too. But he was able to turn
his back on it and get on with his life. I tried, but there are still
things that bother me. As you may imagine, a mountain of information about serial murderers has been collected over the
past thirty years. And according to the stats, they rarely feel
guilt or remorse for their crimes. So it's doubtful that Glander
wanted to get caught. On the other hand, he did kill his own

daughter. And if that doesn't at least give a man second thoughts about what he's done, nothing will."

"Sounds like you've become an expert on serial killers," Manion said.

"I've spent a great deal of time—probably too much—researching various case studies, as well as digging into Glander's biography. It was either that or try to pretend that that day and night never happened. And according to my psychologist, embracing the experience was the right way to go."

"What did you find out?"

"That Glander fit the serial-killer pattern like a hand in a glove," she said. "With a few tiny gaps. He was male. White. From a working-class background. Father ducked out on the family early on. Glander was a likable young man. Some found him charming, if overly ambitious. Often acted on impulse. Was resentful of the upper class. Even after he married into it, he felt that his wife's friends snubbed him. They did, of course.

"When the city council decided he'd done his job in cleaning up the police force and refused to renew his contract, it hit him hard. Thanks to his wife's wealth, he was able to contribute to the right political campaigns and eventually establish a little power base that allowed him to throw his weight around. But he remained very bitter about the dismissal."

"Psychological emasculation," Manion said.

"Oh, oh," she said. "Sounds like somebody else is in therapy."

"Have been," he said.

"Anyway," she went on, "here's something you may not know. Many serial killers are law buffs—ex-cops or cop wannabes."

"Glander was an ex-lawman."

"Exactly," she said.

"Any anomalies?" Manion asked.

"If he really did suffer guilt pangs, that would have been one. And most serial killers fall into the twenty-five- to thirty-five-years-old bracket. Glander was considerably older. Other than that, he was definitely in the picture."

She looked at her watch. "My God, I've been yakking away for hours."

"I wasn't at all bored," Manion said. "What made you decide to tell me about Glander?"

"I . . . I'm not sure," she said, opening her door. "I've tried to let go of it. It's been years since I've given in. But, like an alcoholic who can't pass a bar, here I am having one last drink."

Manion understood the analogy. "It was something quite out of the ordinary that you were a part of," he said as she reached back over the seat for her briefcase.

"Some women my age dote on their first lover," she told him, as she tugged the case free. "Or their first marriage. My strongest memory is of my first serial murderer."

She stepped from the car, then turned and smiled at him. "I guess it's true what they say," she told him. "Nostalgia just ain't what it used to be."

17

THE RED LIGHT on Manion's answering machine was blinking frantically when he arrived home, but he ignored it until he'd put away the small bag of groceries he'd purchased. A quart of milk. Coffee. A loaf of French bread. A pound of butter. Pickapeppa sauce. The essentials.

He sawed a few slices from the loaf, slathered them with butter and sauce and carried them into the office.

According to the blinking light, there were four messages. One of them had to be from Lucille. He took a deep breath and rewound the tape.

Message number one was from his employer, Elliott Rubin, the ponytailed producer of *Crime Busters*. It was a rather frantic plea for Manion to call him immediately at an Atlanta, Georgia, number. It had been recorded at four-ten that afternoon.

The second message was also from Rubin, conveying pretty much the same sentiments. Recorded at five-fifteen.

On the third message, Rubin sounded as if his world were

cracking apart. "I cannot fucking believe you don't check your messages," he shouted. "This is serious, goddamnit. Call me immediately."

Manion stopped the machine before the last message could play out. He wanted to savor the possibility that it might be Lucille, though he knew damn well it would only be Rubin, jacked up another notch.

"GodDAMNIT, Manion. Of all the irresponsible fucking . . ."

Manion stopped the tape and rewound it.

He sat eating his bread and sauce and staring at the phone for about ten minutes. Then he dialed Lucille's hotel in Boston.

"I don't see a Munn," the clerk said. "Oh, here we are. Ms. Munn *was* staying with us. She checked out earlier today."

"Did she leave a message for me? Terry Manion?"

"No indication of any messages."

Manion broke the connection. At the dial tone, he punched in the number of Lucille Munn's apartment in New Orleans.

After fifteen rings, he gave up and dialed another number.

Eben Munn answered on the third ring. His voice was heavy with sleep. "This better be good," he growled.

"Tough day?" Manion asked.

"Scratched by a cat, pounded on by a woman, attacked by an asshole with a baseball bat. About average, I'd say. What's your story? Still in a snit over our little disagreement?"

"I can live with it," Manion told him. "Have you heard from Lucille?"

Munn took his time replying. "Yeah," he said, finally. "She left word on my box earlier today."

"Is she back in town?"

"No. She said she was driving to Cape Cod or some such shit."

"She leave a number where she can be reached?"

"Sure. Got it here somewhere." It sounded as if he were throwing beer cans on the floor. "Yeah, here goes." He read the number carefully, then asked, "You thinkin' of callin' her?"

"Yes."

"Might not be such a good idea," Munn said. "She's with Benton at his parents' house."

"I see."

"Don't go jumpin' to any conclusions," Munn said.

"No. She probably just wanted to see Cape Cod."

"Exactly," Munn said.

"Screw you," Manion said.

"Not tonight, podnah," Munn said. "I'm too wiped out by the cat scratch or the Percodan, or both of 'em."

Manion was left listening to a dial tone.

He sighed, ate his last piece of bread and sauce and went upstairs to bed.

Across the street from Manion's apartment, the man once known as the Meddler weighed his options. Should he enter the apartment and kill Manion in his sleep, as he'd been requested to do? Or should he merely monitor the situation until murder proved to be the only solution possible?

He hated being pressured and decided not to yield to it. He started up his car and drove away.

WHEN MUNN AWOKE the next morning, fuzzy-headed and cotton-mouthed, the scratches on his thigh were both itching and stinging. His first inclination was to pop another pain pill and chase it down with a cold Sam Adams. But it was nearly nine o'clock and he wanted to give his new boss a buzz-free verbal on Louis deMay. He grabbed the phone.

The OCCS chief was already in his office. He listened while Munn presented a considerably edited version of his discovery of the battered deMay, then said, "I assume you have recommendations."

"Sure," Munn said.

"How fast can you bring 'em down here?"

"I, ah . . . maybe I could just tell you now."

"You okay?" the chief asked, suddenly concerned.

"Fine," Munn said. "I can be there in an hour."

Cursing, he got out of bed and staggered to the bathroom. A

shave and hot shower cleared his head but did little for his disposition. There was no food at all in his apartment, except for the remains of a two-day-old muffuletta. He washed it down with instant coffee.

On his way out, he gave the bottle of pain pills a soulful look, but left it behind. He didn't think he'd make such a good impression on the chief if he showed up Perked.

As it was, his boss took one look at him and said, "What the hell's wrong with you?"

"White night," Munn replied. "Insomnia."

"Happen often?"

"Rare as a fat doper," he replied, paraphrasing a line from one of his favorite novels.

"So tell me your ideas about Ragusa," the chief said.

"Louis deMay reneged on something that Remy wants, big time," Munn said. "The Muskrat's muscle, Cookie Lapicola, beat the bejesus out of deMay, but he didn't get what he was lookin' for."

"How do you know?"

"On the way to the hospital last night," Munn said, "deMay woke up long enough to fill me in. Cookie plucked him off the street and drove him to a garage somewhere to work him over. The muscle came down a little too hard and deMay took a pass before he had time to tell Cookie whatever it was he wanted to know. DeMay woke up an hour or so later on the cold, cold ground, all alone. So he stumbled back to Mona's Place, where I found him."

"DeMay didn't give you even a clue what Lapicola was trying to squeeze out of him?"

Munn shook his head. "I stayed with him for a while at the hospital, hoping he might mumble something while he snoozed. But he didn't."

"And his girlfriend didn't know?"

"She's pretty convincing on that score."

"Well, I suppose we could pick up Lapicola on assault."

"I doubt that deMay will press charges," Munn said.

"So what have we got?" the chief asked, frustration starting to alter his vocal pitch.

"What we've got," Munn said, "is a staked goat, Jack. Let's use deMay to draw Ragusa out of the tall grass."

The chief shook his head. "What good'll that do? If we grab Ragusa on a lame-o charge like assault, his lawyer will spring him within the hour."

Munn was feeling pretty frustrated himself. "Forget the assault," he snapped. "Bump that up to attempted murder, kidnapping. Ragusa isn't exactly Carlos Marcello. He's a showbiz hustler-thief with a nose job. He'll be as hard to bend as Silly Putty."

"What do you mean 'bend'?"

"Like I've been saying all along. Don't arrest these guys. Turn 'em and keep 'em out on the streets workin' for us."

The chief stared at him for what seemed like an eternity, then said, "I think you're probably right that Ragusa will take a run at this goat of yours. I'll assign a round-the-clock on deMay. But if Ragusa goes for it and we nail him, we don't screw around. We book him on the strongest charge we can, legally. We don't get too cute. We're not the goddamn S.S. We put the asshole away. Then we can play with his head a little, and if he agrees to do some odd jobs for us, that'll be the icing on the cake. In return, maybe we give him cable in his cell. But he stays off the streets for as long as the law allows."

Munn slumped back in his chair, obviously unhappy with that decision.

"Imagination is not highly prized here at the OCCS," the chief cautioned. "This is a meat-and-potatoes operation, Eben. We want to keep it as simple as we can. We catch the bad guys and lock 'em up. You with me?"

Munn nodded halfheartedly. He wasn't at all sure he *was* with the chief, but he didn't think the moment was right for confession.

He rose to leave, but the chief stopped him with a question. "The other night when you confronted Ragusa, you said a civilian was with you?"

"Right."

"Why?"

"We were having dinner together when I eyeballed Ragusa," Munn said. "We both followed him to the nightclub."

"So the civilian isn't involved? No connection to Ragusa?"

Something about the tone of the question bothered Munn. It was as if the chief knew the answer and was testing him. He said, "If he has one, he didn't mention it."

"Are we talking about a private eye named Manion?"

Munn smiled as if he were impressed. Actually, he was highly pissed off. "Somebody following me around?" he asked.

"Nothing like that. The reason I picked you for the Combat

Squad was the way you took care of the Benedetto brothers. A p.i. named Terry Manion assisted you. I just assumed he might be 'assisting' you again."

"Manion's not assisting me on anything," Munn said, the throbbing cat scratch adding to this discomfort.

"Fine. But I definitely don't want outsiders muddying up our pond. You'd better make sure Manion's a real innocent. If you find out he's working on anything that involves Ragusa, squeeze him for whatever he's got. Then do whatever you have to to keep him out of our way."

Munn stood up. "I'll see to Manion as soon as I've arranged for the deMay surveillance."

"I'll take care of that," the chief replied. He looked at his watch and then back up at Munn. "You clear on this?"

"Like crystal."

Munn walked through the silent building to the front door, then out to the lot and his parked car. He felt as if he'd lost two battles. He was being aced out of the Ragusa bust and he was now responsible for making sure that Manion kept out of it, too.

He started the car, his thoughts darkening. This Combat Squad gig wasn't turning out to be all that sweet, after all.

WHEN LOUIS ARRIVED at school that morning, Shoo-Bear's black Jaguar was in its usual space under an oak tree near the corner. The plump dope dealer was sitting against a fireplug, handing a glassine packet to a boy in Louis's class named Jose Alfonso.

It was not the first time Louis had witnessed Shoo-Bear plying his trade. But usually he sold to, well, the kids you'd think might take dope. Jose was a nice, quiet boy who kept to himself. Louis liked him. He knew Jose was having troubles at home. His father had been out of work for nearly two years and his mother, who'd been to college and used to work in the library before it closed down, was cleaning people's houses. Using his antenna for new prospects, Shoo-Bear was cultivating Jose.

"Hey, Jose," Louis called out. "Don't take none of that shit from that lowlife."

Startled, Jose Alfonso began to back away and Shoo-Bear trained his dark glasses on Louis.

"He's selling you that stuff cheap, Jose. Trying to hook you. Ask around what he charges later, when you got to have it."

Shoo-Bear pushed himself off the fireplug, but Louis stood his ground. "Give him back his dope, Jose," he said.

"You keep it, boy," Shoo-Bear told Jose. "On the house. Get happy for a while."

The school bell rang. Louis grabbed the glassine packet from a startled Jose's hand and threw it at Shoo-Bear. Then he and Jose ran for the entry gate.

Shoo-Bear paused to pick up the glassine packet. "You done, boy," he called out with more weariness than passion.

The boys didn't stop until they were inside the school building. Then Louis began to laugh away the tension. Jose stared at him angrily. "I don't need you to tell me what to do, deMay," he said.

"You don't want to mess yourself up with that stuff," Louis replied.

"What makes you think it's for me?" Jose shouted in full fury. Then, wet-eyed with tears of frustration, he strode away.

The door behind Louis opened suddenly, but it was just another almost late student. Before the door closed, however, the boy could see the plump dope dealer back on his fireplug, froglike, biding his time.

Great way to start the day, Louis told himself.

20

FOR THE SECOND time that week, Manion nursed a glass of orange juice and a sweet roll through a magnum breakfast at the Wells home. He waited until the others had waddled from the table before telling Nadia why he'd come.

"This lawyer, Billins, seems to be the link between Pano and everybody else," he said. "I need to see him as soon as possible. But the trick is going to be finding him in town and then getting him to sit still for an interview."

Nadia sighed, picked up her cup of coffee and replied, "Well, I suppose I might as well earn my daily pay."

Approximately two and a half hours later, they were in the presence of James Billins. He was smaller than Manion had expected, and he looked younger than he did on television, except for a sprig of wiry gray hair near his temples. His round face broke into a smile easily and his trim, well-dressed body moved in a comfortingly relaxed manner as he sent his assistant off with orders for coffee for his "guests" and Perrier for himself.

Accompanying his composure was an affected attempt at elegance that Manion found a bit off. Maybe it was the way the lawyer cocked his head as if listening to tinkling bells, with a knowing grin on his face. Or the way he touched his silk tie and adjusted his French cuffs, as if he'd spent time studying Cary Grant movies. Maybe it was just that he wore polish on his fingernails.

Billins smoothed down the hair at the back of his head and said to Nadia, "Congressman Pannet is a fine old gentleman. He allowed as how you've been friends for a long time."

"Since we were young and innocent," Nadia replied. It had not surprised Manion to discover that she was able to cajole

235

the respected politician into providing their introductions to Billins.

The lawyer waited for her to continue. When she didn't, he settled back in his chair and lost a bit of his grace. His brown eyes darted to Manion before returning to the elderly woman. "The congressman said you wanted to speak with me on a matter of some delicacy?" he asked.

"Well," she said, "I don't know how delicate it is, exactly, but it's important."

The assistant returned with their liquids. Nadia took that opportunity to open her purse and remove a checkbook. She reached out and snatched a pen from its holder on Billins's desktop.

The lawyer didn't notice his assistant glide from the room. He was staring at Nadia as she signed her name to the check, then tore it from the book and pushed it across the desk.

Billins picked it up, puzzled.

"Jube Pannet says you charge three hundred dollars an hour. That's high as a cat's back, but he says you're worth it. In any case, we have no choice. My associate, Mr. Manion, needs to ask you some questions. Shouldn't take longer than an hour, but if it does, I'll tear that up and write you a new one."

Billins let the check float to his desktop. His brown eyes focused on Manion.

"What kind of questions?"

"About Tyrone Pano."

Billins showed no sign that the name meant anything to him. He asked the detective, "Were you related to John Manion?"

"I'm his son," Manion replied, vaguely annoyed as he always was when a relative stranger brought up the subject of his father. "You knew him?"

Billins adjusted a cuff and said, "He was a client of the firm."

"You didn't handle his succession," Manion said.

"No. Actually, our tie was to the bank, not your father." He smiled suddenly, for no reason that Manion could see. "And you're here to talk about Tyrone Pano. Might I ask why?"

Manion's mind was playing with the information about his father, moving in on it and backing away. Nadia said, "We're researching Pano's life for a television program, and it's sorta like a jigsaw puzzle. We're hoping you might have a few of the missing pieces."

"Television," Billins said with a feckless smile. "What do they hope to stir up by doing Tyrone's story?"

Nadia started to reply, but Manion had pushed his father back out of his thoughts. "I don't know their precise plans," he said, "only that they're interested in what happened to him."

"So long ago. Well, what can I tell you about poor Tyrone?"

"You were his lawyer. What sort of man was he?"

"I think he was an honest man whose intentions were misinterpreted by many," Billins said. "He saw the cruelty and injustice that African-Americans were being subjected to and he tried to do something about it."

"And the murder?" Manion asked.

"You mean the Davis woman?"

"Was Pano involved in any other murder?" Manion asked.

"Actually," Billins said, his enigmatic smile back in place, "I don't believe he was involved in any murder. He knew Lillian Davis, of course. They worked together. But I've never believed he killed her."

"The note he left indicated—" Manion began.

"It indicated nothing, except that Tyrone was either tricked or otherwise forced into writing it," Billins said sharply.

Manion pushed his glasses a fraction of an inch higher on his nose and asked, "Tricked by whom?"

"The police, of course."

"Was he also tricked into taking his own life?"

"That would follow," Billins said, regaining his professional cool.

"I'm sure the *Crime Busters* show would be interested in airing your views," Manion said.

"Thirty years ago," Billins replied, "I'd have leaped at the chance to go on record. But now, I don't think my appearance with Mr. Pierre Reynaldo would be of any benefit to Tyrone or myself."

Manion greeted the statement with a smug smile that he hoped was just the least bit maddening. He said, "Perhaps you wouldn't mind telling us what happened to Mr. Pano's possessions after his ... death."

"Abiding by his final will, I saw to it that they were turned over to a Miss Shana Washington. She was his sole heir."

"Do you recall a diary?"

"Tyrone didn't strike me as the sort to keep a diary."

"All sorts do. But you have no knowledge of any diary?"

"We have an inventory of his possessions in our files. If it's important, I could get someone to root around in the warehouse where we have them stored."

"Not at three hundred dollars an hour," Nadia said.

Billins shrugged. "It would take considerable searching."

"How close were you to Mr. Pano?"

"I'm not sure what you mean."

"Was it more than a lawyer-client relationship?"

"I thought it was. But toward the end, he seemed to be getting all sorts of odd ideas, prompted, I suspected, by a policeman he befriended. They like to do that, the police. Erode a suspect's confidence in his attorney. I'm afraid it worked in Tyrone's case. With tragic results."

"Any specifics on the odd ideas that the police put in his head?"

"It was so long ago. I never knew exactly what the policeman—an Officer Legendre—did to ingratiate himself with Tyrone. But suddenly, my client—my friend—refused to see me. Didn't want to hear about my plans for his defense. This was a man I'd known for seven years."

"You mentioned his *final* will. How many others were there?"

"Only one that I prepared."

"Prepared when?"

"Oh my. Let me see. Two or three years before his death."

"Do you recall the name of the original beneficiary?"

"I don't know as I do. . . ."

"Might it have been Francis Hart, who was then Pano's second-in-command in the organization known as the Southern Cross?" Nadia asked.

Billins's eyes opened wide. "What possible bearing could . . ."

"Isn't the Reverend Hart presently your client?" Manion wondered.

"Many influential members of the African-American community are my clients."

"I'll take that for a 'yes.' Was he your client in sixty-five, when Pano died?"

"Our firm represented the members of the Southern Cross who were being persecuted by—"

"Including Lillian Davis?" Manion interrupted.

"We would have represented her, had she needed us. But I don't recall her ever availing herself to our services." He consulted a wafer-thin gold wristwatch and looked imploringly at Nadia. "I really am sorry, but I have an appointment. . . ."

"Just one other question," Manion said, rising. He paused. "Did you ever hear it rumored that Tyrone Pano might have been working for the FBI?"

Billins smiled patronizingly. "That's one of the more inane rumors about Tyrone."

"Were there others?"

"Oh my, yes. That he slept with every woman who was in the Southern Cross. That he was as bloodthirsty as Adolf Hitler and Josef Stalin combined. Some said his goal was total, violent revolution. Others thought he was merely trying to line his pockets."

"What do you think?"

"I think he was a man who was tired of being deprived of his rights because of the color of his skin."

Manion nodded.

"Thank you for the check, Mrs. Wells," Billins said. "I'll donate it to the Reverend Hart's cause in your name."

"That's up to you," Nadia said, her purple eyes growing as hard as sapphires. "By the by, you say your pal Pano was probably murdered in his cell?"

"Such was my feeling at the time."

"Then the guy in charge of the lockup should know something about it, right?"

Billins blinked. "I . . . I'm not sure—"

"There was a fella named Cady who worked for you for a while," Nadia went on.

Billins blinked again, then cocked his head in thought. "Yes. Ed Cady, I believe. Did some investigative work for the firm."

"What kind of investigative work?"

"I'm not sure. I was only a junior partner in the firm then. I never used him myself. Why do you ask?"

"Ed Cady was the cop working the lockup when Pano took his long nap."

"I can't believe that," Billins said.

"You're sayin' you didn't know?" she asked.

"If I had, I certainly would not have—"

"What sort of gig could Cady have had here that'd pay him the kind of loot it takes to buy a place like he's got?"

Billins shook his head. "If Cady accumulated any great wealth, I can't believe he did it here. At best he was a part-time employee. Now, I really must ask you to excuse me."

"Could we get a little look-see at his employment record?" Nadia asked.

"I'm afraid our employee files are confidential."

"Heck. I should have guessed that."

Manion paused at the door. "If Pano didn't murder Lillian Davis," he asked, "any ideas who did?"

Billins raised his elegant shoulders an inch in a helpless shrug. He was through talking. Friends of Congressman Pannet or not, their time was up.

As soon as he was alone in his office, James Billins visited his private bathroom. Amid the marble and mirrors, the Meddler was sitting on the lidded toilet, shaking his head at him. "Jimmy, Jimmy, Jimmy," he said. "You fucked the duck on Cady."

"I told them nothing substantive," Billins said.

The Meddler stood and looked at himself in the mirror. He sighed and patted the slight sag under his chin. "I used to be such a good-looking son of a bitch."

Billins was nervous around the man. It was impossible not to be. They'd known each other for a long time, but the fact was, the man was a flake. And dangerous. There was no telling how many people he'd killed. Twenty. Thirty. Maybe more. "It doesn't matter what I told them anyway," Billins said. "Since you're going to be taking care of them."

The Meddler shook his head. "Maybe not," he said. "Maybe there's a simpler way."

"The old lady has very powerful friends. She's dangerous."

"My point exactly," the Meddler said. "Why stir up that hornet's nest needlessly? Do you have any cologne?"

Billins pressed on a section of the mirror over the washbasin and a door opened on an assortment of bottles and tubes. "God," the Meddler said, "I love this sort of self-indulgence."

"You could afford it if I can," Billins said.

"It's not just affording it. You have to enjoy buying all this crap." He selected a bottle with a pale green liquid, unscrewed the cap and splashed a little on his hand. He sniffed it, sighed. "Damn, but this is a heavenly scent." He slapped the cologne on his slightly sagging cheeks.

His eyes suddenly locked on Billins, and he said, "Sometimes I get the feeling you hate me, Jimmy."

"I don't hate you," Billins lied. "You've helped me a great deal over the years."

"Oh, I've done some dirty little tasks for you. But as long as we've known one another, I've always had the feeling you don't really think of me as a pal."

In spite of himself, Billins had to smile. A pal? The bastard had been blackmailing him for thirty years. True, he'd helped out with a few things that the lawyer would have been incapable of handling himself. Nasty things, not the least of them a murder or two. But there'd been a quid pro quo.

"No, I don't think of you as my pal," Billins said. "I think of you as something rarer—someone I can trust."

The Meddler smiled. "Then trust me on this, Jimmy. Let me take care of things my way."

"As if I had a choice."

"We always have a choice," the Meddler said. "Fortunately for you, for three decades now you've made the right one."

"Then you'll take care of Manion and the Wells woman?"

"One way or another," the Meddler said, slipping the bottle of cologne into his coat pocket.

21

"WHAT'S YOUR TAKE on Mr. Billins?" Manion asked, as Nadia guided her Jaguar through mid-morning traffic along Canal Street.

"Oh, the natural result of some brains and education, a little luck and a whole mess of ambition."

"Enough to make him sell out one client in favor of another?" Manion wondered.

"Hell, sonny, the man's a lawyer." She grinned and gunned the engine. "Regardless of what he says, he gave the policeman Cady a sinecure. What'd Cady do for him?"

"Murdered Pano?" Manion asked. "And, if so, why?"

"Do we really care?" Nadia asked. "Unless there's something

you're not tellin' me, all we're supposed to do is fill in the background, not solve any thirty-year-old murders." She braked the car in front of Manion's home-office.

He was reaching for the door handle when she said, "I'm damn sure it's just a coincidence."

"What is?"

"The thing that's been bugging you."

He nodded, but remained frowning. "J.J. went to see Dad because of something that had to do with Pano," he said.

"He told me he needed a safety deposit box," Nadia said. "I sent him to your father."

"Dad offered him a job."

"How'd you find out?"

"Madeleine Betterick."

"Ah," Nadia said. "Well, J.J. turned him down."

"So he needed a deposit box? For Pano's will?"

"Sounds logical."

"You say you thought the envelope containing the will may have been tampered with. And now we hear Dad and Billins—"

"One of the big problems in this country today," Nadia said, "is the pervasive conspiracy mentality. It's making everybody too damn cynical."

"The pot calling the kettle black," he told her.

"Hell yes, I'm a cynic," she replied. "But at my age, havin' been witness to six or seven decades of human frailty, I figure I've earned the right.

"Anyway, if you're thinkin' that your daddy and Billins and the Reverend Hart conspired to mess around with Pano's will, or some such nonsense, sonny, you better save a place for me in there, too. I was the one who told J.J. to use Jack's bank, and the beneficiary was a friend of mine." She winked at him and added, "I bet we can find somebody who'll remember seeing Lee Harvey Oswald in the bank, too, waitin' for Clay Shaw to cash a check."

Manion nodded. "I hear you," he said. "I just can't . . ." He paused. "I can't figure out why Dad . . . took his life."

"None of us can. But I sure as hell don't think it had anything to do with Tyrone Pano. And I'm the least bit disappointed that you're even considering it." On that note, she put her car in gear and left him with a squeal of tires and a plume of exhaust.

* * *

Manion strolled into his office and dropped the mail onto his desk. He brushed through it, idly wondering if it might not contain a letter or card from Lucille Munn. But it was just the usual collection of bills and advertisements and notices about million-dollar magazine sweepstakes.

He leaned over the desk to dump the junk mail into the wastebasket and saw the blinking light on his answering machine. He rewound the tape and heard the mildly furious voice of Elliott Rubin. "I've been trying to get you all week," Rubin whined. "Where the hell are you? On vacation? Look, it's nine o'clock. Pierre is on his way to New Orleans. He decided to fly in for the day for some promos for WCAJ. Wants an immediate face-to-face briefing. If by some stroke of luck you get this message and still give a shit, and if you're able to hook up with him, fine. If not, consider yourself canceled."

With a sigh, Manion sat down at the desk, removed his glasses and rubbed his eyes. He probably should have returned Elliott's previous messages, but the producer's attitude had annoyed him. It still annoyed him. And now, Pierre Reynaldo was in town, probably frothing at the mouth. Well, he thought, screw them if they can't take a joke.

But the fact was that there was still nine thousand dollars to be earned. And, he had to admit, he certainly didn't want to walk away from the Pano investigation.

He got out the phone book and turned to the "W"s.

WCAJ-TV, until the late 1980s, had been merely a blip on the UHF dial where old movies went to die. But a change in management and an open band on the cable system sent the station's signal across the country, repackaged as the Cajun Channel. It flourished for a few seasons. Then, when the craze for Cajun food and song ground to a halt, the station's swinging doors saw an exodus of country chefs carrying all their filé powders and boudin sausages with them. Some of the music makers stuck around just to keep the channel a little different from the seventy or more others. But even they began to be shoved out by an assortment of syndicated talk shows—conservative, liberal, religious, salacious. The content of the psychodramas seemed to matter not, as long as stories and opinions of some sort or other were being spewed out into America's heartlands and sponsors ponied up the cash to keep the cameras' eyes glowing.

The station occupied a relatively small portion of a block in the heart of the French Quarter. A two-story red brick building housed WCAJ's business offices and the promotion and advertising people. There, Manion was told that Pierre Reynaldo was taping his spot announcements in the studios.

A lovingly tended patio separated the front building from its mirror image. But what seemed to be an identical two-story rear edifice was, in fact, a large, warehouselike space that had been divided into television sound stages.

Pierre Reynaldo was in Studio B, but he wasn't taping spots. He was shouting at a short, balding man who was on the phone.

Reynaldo was short himself. He looked as if he might have been tanned under the makeup. His hair was brushed straight back on his rather square skull. He was wearing his signature bow tie, in this case a yellow polka dot. "This was supposed to have been all fixed," he said with a snarl. "Tell them I don't give a damn about permits. Permits can be bought."

The balding man was trying to talk to the party on the other end and ignore Reynaldo's loud voice without offending him. A young woman was standing beside the talk show host. She was brunette, several inches taller than Reynaldo, with a pretty, heart-shaped face and a full figure. She was wearing a loose black pantsuit that might have been silk.

She draped an arm over Reynaldo's shoulder and herded him away from the balding man. "Let Les handle it," she told him. "They're his people and they'll be ready for us by the time we get there."

She looked up and saw Manion. "Yes?" she asked.

"My name's Terry Manion," he said.

They were both looking at him now. Reynaldo frowned and said, "Jesus, you sure don't look like a private eye."

"That's the secret of my success," Manion replied with a straight face.

"I'm Mickie McCormick," the young woman said, extending a hand that Manion shook. Reynaldo obviously did not feel the necessity for such formalities.

"Five minutes more and we'd have been gone," he said.

"Mr. Manion is a detective, Pierre," Mickie McCormick said. "I bet he could have tracked us down."

The balding man, Les, replaced the receiver and said, "They're ready for us."

"You got a car, Manion?" Reynaldo asked. "Good, then

Mickie can ride with you. I'll go with Les. I wanna chew his ass a little for this screw-up. We'll talk later."

Mickie McCormick had barely begun extolling the virtues of working for a genius like her boss when they arrived at their destination. A WCAJ camera crew was set up in front of an old, not particularly well-cared-for building on South Rampart. Down Home Donuts occupied the ground floor. Above it were apartments. Some curious residents were gathering around the cameras. A few recognized Reynaldo as he strolled toward the center of activity.

Manion found a parking spot a block away. By the time he and Mickie returned to the scene, camera crews from other stations had arrived and were setting up. "I thought your boss was doing spot announcements," Manion said.

"He doesn't like to waste an opportunity," she told him. "C'mon."

As they moved through the gathering crowd, Reynaldo was talking into several cameras. " . . . Pano's last address as a free man," he was saying. "The police dragged him down those steps. We'll be returning to town shortly to begin filming the Tyrone Pano segment of our show. And I can guarantee you that it will be the definitive account of the man's life and death."

A short, blond woman pushed her station's mike toward him and drawled, "Are you suggestin' there's more to the story than was told thirty years ago?"

"More? With the police and the FBI and who knows who else involved? Oh, I think it's safe to say there may have been a little cover-up."

Reynaldo saw Manion in the crowd. "And here's someone who has been working . . ." He paused because Manion had turned and was walking away. Smiling and regaining his composure, he went on, ". . . working with me, Mr. Les Donald, of superstation WCAJ."

The conference, such as it was, went on for a few more minutes. Then, satisfied that hidden within the self-promotion there lurked a usable sound bite or two, the news crews departed. Reynaldo did a quick spot for WCAJ and scanned the area for Manion and Mickie.

They weren't far away. The detective had moved his car directly across Rampart from the activity. He'd remained in it to dissuade Reynaldo from making another try at drawing him into camera range.

The little man gestured imperiously. They were to join him at once. Nine thousand dollars, Manion thought as he crossed the street.

"What the hell were you doing walking away like that?" Reynaldo asked him. "That kind of exposure you can't buy."

"Exposure isn't exactly what you want in my business," Manion said.

Reynaldo inspected him critically. "If you say so," he commented, but he clearly thought Manion was an unambitious idiot who didn't know the value of promotion and publicity. "Well, come on into my office and tell me what my money has bought so far."

Reynaldo walked into Down Home Donuts. Manion and Mickie exchanged looks and followed him in.

The shop was relatively clean, with a warm red tile floor and walls so thick with white paint they'd begun to resemble the inside of a cave. Reynaldo was at the counter, looking at a display of pastries of various sizes and shapes. A plump black woman observed him with patience and a blank face.

"I'll have two of those," he said, pointing.

"Baih paws?" the woman asked.

"If that's what they are, yeah. What about you, Manion? A baih paw?"

"No, thanks," Manion said. "I'm a vegetarian." He noticed that the little man didn't extend his offer to Mickie.

"Coffee, then?" Reynaldo asked.

"Sure," Manion said. "Café au lait."

"Two of those," Reynaldo said.

There was only one other customer in the shop, an ancient black man at a table off to the side, who was sipping coffee and reading a tabloid newspaper that looked as if it had been printed in someone's basement. Its headline read, "Exalted Mustafa Claims Throne." Manion wondered what it was all about, but he didn't feel like bothering the old man.

Reynaldo picked a table beside the front door. He carried his purchases to it, and Mickie and Manion joined him. "Would you like something?" Manion asked the woman before he sat down.

She shook her head.

"Okay, detective, give," Reynaldo ordered, between bites of bear paw.

Before meeting Reynaldo, Manion had decided to be guarded in reporting his findings. Having seen the little man's fondness for press conferences, he scaled back even more.

He told them that young Louis deMay might have had a point when he wrote his letter. "Tyrone Pano's death does seem to have its suspicious aspects."

"Like what?"

"Like maybe he didn't kill himself," Manion said.

"Not bad. What've you got?"

"What do you mean?"

"Physical proof," Reynaldo said, annoyed. "Food for the camera's eye."

"No physical proof at present."

"Okay, then tell me about the FBI tie-in," Reynaldo said. "What'd you get out of them."

"I explained to Elliott Rubin that I wasn't going to approach the FBI. So far, the people I've spoken with who knew Pano think that his being an FBI plant is pretty silly. But if I come up with anything indicating otherwise, you'll be the first to know."

"Let's get the FBI office here on record," Reynaldo said. "Get them to deny or admit that Pano was a Fed."

"If you want to rattle their cage, feel free," Manion said. "I can think of more amusing ways to complicate my life."

"Then what the hell am I paying you good money to do?"

"Gather information."

"So what've you gathered?"

"The officer who arrested Pano was suspicious of his death," Manion said. "The guy in charge of the jail where Pano died is now a wealthy man. Pano's lawyer doesn't believe he was guilty of murdering Lillian Davis."

Reynaldo looked at him. "That's all?" he asked indignantly. "That's *bubkes*. That's nothing."

"It's what you get after just a few days' work."

"Okay, give it to me straight," Reynaldo said. "Are you gonna come up with anything I can sink my teeth into?"

Manion considered the question, then said, "I can't guarantee anything. But there's something off about Pano's death. And I'm going to do my best to find out what it is."

The look Reynaldo gave him was not one of confidence. "Okay, Mickie stays here to give you a hand," he said.

"I'm using the Wells Agency for whatever help I need," Manion said.

"Okay, then she stays here to keep me posted on your progress."

Manion shook his head. "I don't work with someone looking over my shoulder."

Reynaldo turned to Mickie. "Sorry, babe. But the man says 'no.' Good luck in your next job."

The woman looked at him, confused. "What's that?" she asked.

"You screwed up with Les," he told her. "I had to pick up the pieces and get the press conference back on track myself. I figured I'd give you one more chance, keeping an eye on Manion. But he says no go. So you're history."

Mickie looked from him to Manion pleadingly. The detective wondered if this was a game they'd played before.

"She can stick around," he said.

Pierre Reynaldo grinned at him. "Good man," he said patronizingly. He looked at his watch. "Damn," he muttered. "What time do they get out of kid school here, Manion?"

The detective shrugged. "It used to be three o'clock. I don't know what it is these days."

"Three. I wanted to say hello to the kid, Louis deMay. But my plane leaves at two."

"They'd probably let him out of class for a few minutes," Mickie said.

"Naw. No time. I'll catch him next trip." He stood up. "Get to sleuthing, Manion. Gimme something to work with."

It was his exit line.

When he'd gone, Manion turned to Mickie. "He's a real sweetheart," he said. "I can see why you're so loyal to him."

"Okay, so he's just another showbiz asshole," she said. "At least he's left me one of his bear paws."

22

JUST BEFORE THE English teacher, Miss Latrobe, dismissed the class for the day, she asked Louis to wait at his desk. Concerned, he watched his schoolmates rush from the room. When they'd gone, Miss Latrobe, an angular, large-boned woman who reminded Louis of an athlete he'd seen on TV, turned to him with a frown. "I missed you yesterday, Louis," she said.

Oh, man! He'd forgotten all about his promise to meet with Miss Latrobe after school the day before. "I . . . I was sick."

"No you weren't," she said sternly. "I tried to reach you at your home."

"Oh."

"Nobody answered the phone."

"There was somethin' I had to do, Miss Latrobe."

"If you're serious about wanting to go to the State Rally, you're going to have to work."

"Yes, ma'am," Louis said.

Each year, schools throughout Louisiana sent their top students to compete for honors at the State Rally in Baton Rouge. At the start of the term, Louis had been the favorite in chemistry and math as well as English lit. But, because of his concern over the rending of his parents' marriage, he had found it more and more difficult to concentrate on the sciences, which were not his favorite subjects. Literature was another matter. Reading let him escape his problems. But he was in need of tutoring.

Miss Latrobe suggested they meet the following day after school.

"Don't disappoint me again," she warned.

If he hadn't been thinking about the Rally, he might have noticed the car keeping pace with him as he started for home.

It was not until it swerved in and stopped at the curb that he sensed danger.

By then, the passenger door had been thrown open and Shoo-Bear was out of the car, grabbing at Louis.

Louis backtracked, but the crack dealer's hand clamped on his arm and jerked him forward. "Come on, boy," he almost whispered. "You gonna get some special learnin' today."

Louis began to scream as Shoo-Bear dragged him toward the waiting automobile.

Then, suddenly, a white man was standing near the car, slamming the door shut before Shoo-Bear could get there. It was that mean-looking baldy who'd been at his house the other day. Then the other white guy appeared. What was his name? Remy.

He said, "Let the kid go, asshole."

Shoo-Bear was having trouble with the situation. The driver's door of his Jaguar opened and a giant got out. "Problem?" he asked.

"Not if the asshole lets the kid go," Remy said.

"Get these white trash out of my way, Nydo," Shoo-Bear ordered.

Louis forgot to keep screaming as Nydo moved in on the baldy, taking a gravity knife from his pants pocket. He flicked his wrist to shake the blade into place, and the baldy made his move. He took a funny hop and planted the toe of his shoe into Nydo's kneecap. There was an ugly snapping sound and Nydo let out an awful howl.

Baldy pivoted on one foot and drove his heel into Nydo's other knee. The big man plummeted to the ground where he lay, moaning, arms stretched out like he was playing airplane. He was still holding the knife. Baldy brought his heel down on the knife hand and Nydo let out a yell they could hear in Biloxi.

Then the baldy reached down and took the weapon from Nydo's lifeless fingers. He held it up daintily, like a girl might hold something up for show and tell.

Remy took a few steps closer to Shoo-Bear. "You wanna let the boy go now?"

Shoo-Bear did not let him go.

The baldy was moving in on Shoo-Bear now. "Mr. Ragusa says to let him go," the baldy said.

"Ragusa?" Shoo-Bear repeated, and Louis was suddenly free.

"What you messin' with me for?" Shoo-Bear asked.

"Because I know Louis's family and I consider him a special friend of mine," Remy said, winking at Louis. "But even if he wasn't, I just don't like you and your *bros* sellin' drugs to kids."

"Don't gimme that bullshit," Shoo-Bear said. "You want the little bastard, you got him. Now go on outta here."

"No," Remy told him. "Like I say, we don't care for the business you're in. So you're gonna be our poster boy. Got it?"

"More bullshit." Shoo-Bear moved to his fallen friend. Louis saw Remy nod to the baldy. The baldy grabbed Shoo-Bear's arm and spun the plump man around, smashing him into the side of his black Jaguar.

"C'mon lad," Remy said to Louis. "This isn't anything you want to see. Let's us go sit in my car and listen to some CDs while we wait for Cookie to finish up."

Deep down, Louis would have liked to stay and see bad things happen to Shoo-Bear. But he didn't want to seem ungrateful, so he went along with Remy's plan. He couldn't wait to tell his mama and Jambo how wrong they were about Remy. The man was their friend.

23

WHEN MANION AND Mickie McCormick parked at the curb in front of his home-office, a familiar stocky figure was sitting on the stoop grinning at them. Eben Munn stood up, gave his back a twist and emitted a grunt. He placed the remains of a po'boy sandwich into a greasy white bag and dropped the bag on the ground beside the steps.

He looked from Mickie to Manion with a raised eyebrow. "Early date?" he asked.

"Not so early," Manion told him, picking up the sandwich

bag and depositing it into a small, battered metal garbage can hidden under the steps.

Munn shook his head, staring at Mickie. "It's hard to believe you used to be a rich kid, Manion, the way you forget your manners."

"I'm sorry," Manion said. "Did you want to save that sandwich?"

"Naw. I meant you forgot to introduce me to the lady."

"In this case, chivalry outweighs manners," Manion said. But he performed the introduction. Munn took the woman's hand daintily and bowed. Manion thought it was the same bow they'd been taught when they'd been in a grammar school play together.

Inside the building, he opened the drapes and turned on lights. "What can I do for you, Eben?" he asked.

Munn looked at Mickie. "You and Manion old friends?"

"Terry and I just met. We work for Pierre Reynaldo," Mickie said, as Manion ducked into his kitchenette.

"That shitheel? Work for him how?"

"Terry is doing research on the Tyrone Pano case for the shitheel," Mickie said. "And I'm helping him."

"Then I guess the thing I really want to know is this, *Terry*—where the hell does Remy Ragusa fit in?"

Mickie snapped to attention. "The organized-crime guy?" she asked.

"The selfsame," Munn said.

"I'm not sure what the connection is," Manion said from the kitchen. "Iced tea okay for everybody?"

"See?" Mickie said to Munn. "Manners. Iced tea would be fine."

Manion returned with three glasses, a sliced lemon and a sugar bowl. "No doilies?" Munn asked as he picked up one of the glasses.

"We're roughing it," Manion said.

"Look, podnah, I was a little out of line the other night," Munn said. "Can we get past that and be schoolmates again?"

"Why not?" Manion said. "Pano left everything he owned to a woman who is related to the deMay family. Ragusa paid the deMay boy's father money for some unspecified reason and deMay reneged on the deal. That's the only connection I know of."

Munn sipped at his tea. "This is a real novelty," he said.

"Doesn't taste like flowers or cinnamon or anything. Just real tea. Who the hell is this Pano and what team did he pitch for?"

Manion was glad to let Mickie provide a brief description of the short, unhappy life of Tyrone Pano. When she'd finished, Munn said, "Do you suppose it was something belonged to Pano that Ragusa tried to buy off of deMay?"

"The diary," Mickie announced.

Manion winced. It was not smart to feed Munn's imagination.

"What diary?" the policeman asked him.

"There's rumor that Pano had a diary, but no one has actually seen it."

"What's so hot about it?" Munn wanted to know.

"He wrote in it that he wasn't really a revolutionary," Mickie said eagerly. "He was actually working for the FBI."

"Yeah, those undercover guys are well-known diary writers," Munn replied with heavy sarcasm.

Manion nodded.

Mickie looked crestfallen, then brightened. "Maybe he kept the diary just in case he got into trouble and needed to prove who he really was."

"It's not proof, babe," Munn told her. "It's still just his word. Has anybody checked with the Feds?"

"Terry says he doesn't want to rattle their cage."

"Terry has these brief flashes of intelligence," Munn said. "Let's forget the diary and get serious. Is there anything else of Pano's that would interest Ragusa? Buried loot? Blackmail information? Some kind of political dynamite that's taken thirty years to heat up?"

There was a chirping noise coming from Munn's belt.

"A beeper?" Manion asked, and laughed.

"Standard Combat Squad issue," Munn announced, blushing. He squinted at the digital number on the top of the beeper.

"Can I use the phone?" he asked without bothering to wait for Manion's reply.

The number was answered by a nurse on Ward Four of the hospital where they'd taken Louis deMay. Munn gave the nurse his name and almost immediately Celeste was on the line, talking a mile a minute.

The gist of it was that deMay had left the hospital and wouldn't let her go with him. "Some lilies were delivered to him. With this card. It says, 'Please take care of my object of great value and I will take care of yours, big daddy.'

"Louis, the poor man, is barely able to keep his eyes open, but he sat up in the bed and grabbed the phone. He called his wife and she told him his boy hadn't come home from school. He got out of bed, threw on his clothes and ran out of the hospital. I wanted to go with him, but he told me no. He had to go alone. Please help him."

"Any idea where he's gone?"

"There's this place in the Oakwood shopping center, over the river where—"

"Gloworm," Munn said. "I know it."

"I think that's where he's headed. It's where the book is."

"What book?"

"I . . . it's what Ragusa wants. I guess I should've mentioned it before, but Louis told me not to say anything to anybody about it. Some book that Louis's aunt had. He keeps it locked in his workroom."

"At Gloworm?" Munn couldn't remember there being enough space for a workroom.

"Next door. It's like a warehouse or something. The woman who runs Gloworm turned it into a studio for her artists."

"Okay," Munn said. "I'll check it out. Is the Combat Squad guy still there?"

"What are you talking about?" she asked.

"Maybe it's a woman. Whoever's been keeping an eye on Louis."

"Nobody's been here, except doctors and nurses."

Munn scowled. Maybe the OCCS guard had been on the job outside the hospital. In any case, the point was now moot. "I'll see to Louis right now," he said, and replaced the receiver. "You two want to take a drive?"

"Where to?" Manion wanted to know.

"Over the bridge to Oakwood," Munn said. "On the way, you can tell me everything you know about this Pano diary."

24

THE MEDDLER SPOTTED Louis deMay the moment he burst through the front door of the hospital. The wounded and limping black man flagged down a Yellow cab and got in, moving with amazing speed, considering his condition.

The Meddler waited for Remy Ragusa's purple Mercedes to leave the curb in pursuit, then he joined the procession, keeping back far enough to escape detection from Remy's driver. The man looked like a dimwit, but driving *was* his profession.

The chase continued through the city, down Claiborne Avenue to the I-10, and eventually over the river to the west bank, a twenty-seven-minute trip.

DeMay's destination was a shop called Gloworm. The black man paid the driver and limped quickly to the shop. It was closed.

Ragusa's Mercedes idled at the curb for about a minute. Then its driver cut the engine. No one got out.

The Meddler watched both the purple sedan and the black man from his car, parked across the street.

He saw deMay hop from the showroom to a building next door. It was square, windowless. No identifying sign that he could spot. A warehouse of some sort. DeMay raised his arm and ran his hand over the door frame. He stepped back, looking puzzled.

Remy Ragusa got out of his sedan and waited for Cookie to join him. Then they both strolled slowly toward the black man. He didn't see them until it was too late.

Cookie grabbed Louis's arm. Remy took a step to face him. Then, suddenly, the warehouse door opened.

From the Meddler's vantage, he could not see who had

opened it, only that Ragusa and his thug were frozen in their tracks. Then they and deMay entered the building.

A second later, Ragusa exited and, staying near the door, turned to his sedan. He raised his hand, using a wiggling index finger to tell the driver to join them.

The driver, whose vapid appearance was not deceiving, stepped from the car slowly as if unclear about what Ragusa wanted. He had his hand under his coat. Holding a gun?

Ragusa shouted, "Come here, putz!" so loudly that the Meddler could hear him clearly.

The driver loped forward, keeping his hand where it was. He, too, entered the building.

The Meddler was confused. The plan couldn't have been simpler. Ragusa snatches the kid. Ragusa uses the kid to trade off for the diary. So simple. So clean. Now there might be a mess.

Unless . . .

He got out of the car and walked toward the warehouse. The door was still ajar. He stood and listened.

Inside the warehouse, Ragusa, Cookie and their driver stood a few feet to the right of the door, leaning toward a bare wall, their arms straight out in front of them, hands pressed against the cement. Munn was just behind them, police special in hand, a broad smile on his face. Louis deMay slumped on a folding chair while Mickie and Manion sat on top of a work-table, their legs dangling. The three of them watched Munn's tableau expectantly.

"Look, I dunno what you're talking about, kidnap," Ragusa was saying past his armpit. "I like little Louis. Cookie and me, we was drivin' by the school and saw he was in trouble with some bad dude who sells dope to the kids."

"My boy doesn't mess with drugs," Big Louis said. His eyelids were fluttering, the adrenaline finally losing out to bone-tired weariness and damage.

The interior of the building was one long room. Boxes were piled at the far end. The rest of the space had been cut up into sections that were being used by a variety of neon artists. DeMay's area suggested that he was deep in a multimedia period. There were four completed oil portraits and maybe three or four others in various stages, each enhanced by a touch of neon and an actual, three-dimensional object.

"Did I say your boy was messing with drugs?" Ragusa

asked indignantly. "The way little Louis tells it, he interrupted a sale between the dealer and one of his schoolmates and the dealer was into payback. So, naturally, me and the Cookster had to explain to the dealer the error of his ways."

"Like Robin Hood," Munn said, not without sarcasm.

"Yeah," Ragusa replied. "Look, can we turn around and talk like human beings?"

Munn took a few steps back. "I'm not sure about the human beings part," he said. "But turn around. Just keep a little distance between you and the fire power." Two guns, taken from the driver and Remy, rested on the table next to Mickie.

The diminutive hood wiggled blood back into his fingers as he faced Munn. "You got me all wrong, Munn."

Manion's attention drifted to Louis deMay's paintings. Some were hanging on the wall, others rested against it. He slipped from the table for a closer look. There was a nude of a pale blond woman sitting on the edge of a bed. The woman's eyes looked apprehensive, though her bright red neon mouth was open in a smile. She wore a thin gold chain on her wrist, a real one that had been glued to the canvas.

A painting of Wanda deMay found her looking very small on a huge, unfurnished stage, pages from a real script stuck to the bottom of the canvas. The words "Nobody Allowed Backstage" were in neon, on the wall over the woman's head. The final two pieces were of a jolly plump black woman in her later years wearing neon reading glasses and holding a real, three-dimensional book on her lap, and of little Louis carrying what appeared to be a real rose in his right hand. His sneakers were outlined in neon.

"Where is the boy?" Manion asked Ragusa.

"With my mom," the mobster said. "At the restaurant. Last I saw of him he was in the kitchen, scarfing up some pasta and playin' Gameboy with the sous-chef's daughter."

"There's a phone on the wall, Ragusa," Munn said. "Why don't we arrange a little father-and-son connection?"

The mobster strolled to the phone and dialed a string of numbers. The call was answered immediately. He whispered something and handed the phone to deMay, who winced when he pushed himself up from his chair. He swayed slightly as he took the phone. He asked, "Louis?" with apprehension. Then they all saw his face break into a wide smile.

"See," Ragusa said. "This is just a big misunderstanding, Munn."

"What about the flowers and the note?" Munn asked. "You sayin' you weren't tryin' to threaten deMay into turnin' over the diary to you?"

"So maybe I was taking advantage of the situation. But I never claimed I was gonna do anything to the boy. Hell, I don't play like that."

"Why were you driving around the school?"

Ragusa smiled, showing a hint of his former self. "Actually, we were there to talk with the dealer, a real lowlife named Shoo-Bear. We don't like him fuckin' up kids with drugs."

"What do you think, Manion?" Munn asked.

"If I had a vote for this year's Nobel," Manion said, "I know who'd be in the running." He was studying the portrait of the plump woman.

Louis deMay replaced the receiver. He found his folding chair and dropped onto it.

"Boy okay?" Munn asked.

DeMay nodded. "Said Ragusa saved him from a beatin' or worse."

"Maybe they were holding a gun to the boy's head."

"Naw. Little Louis is too smart for that. A gun to his head, he'd've figured out a way to let me know." He glared at Ragusa. "Louis says he likes the son of a bitch."

"See? No fucking kidnapping. I don't hurt kids."

"But you aren't very nice to adults," Manion said, indicating the battered deMay.

"Louie took my cash, then tried to hold me up for more." Louis was silent.

"So, Louie. You owe me one, huh?"

"Don't owe you nothin'. You took it out of my hide."

"Screw that, Louie. We had a deal. Come across."

"I don't have it."

"That's why you ran all the way here in your condition," Ragusa said flatly. "Come on. I got things to do."

"You're not makin' any demands here, Fake Face," Munn informed Ragusa.

"Why do you want the diary?" Manion asked.

Ragusa stared at him, as if trying to decide if it was worth answering his question. "Favor for a friend," he said.

So it *was* the diary he was after.

"What friend?" Munn asked.

* * *

Standing just outside the door, the Meddler tensed. If Ragusa dropped Billins's name, there would be no alternative but to clean house. He checked his pockets. A gun. Seven shots. And a knife. Not *the* knife of old, but good enough. No problem.

But Ragusa didn't say a word, except to inform his men that they were reclaiming their licensed weapons and leaving.

"You're not going to object, are you, Officer Munn? I mean, where's the crime, huh?"

The Meddler took a few backward steps, so that he was safely out of sight behind the building when Ragusa and his men made their exit. The punk didn't know anything about him—what he looked like, who he was. You never knew when you might want surprise on your side.

25

MUNN STOOD IN the doorway and watched Ragusa's purple Mercedes drive away. To make sure it wasn't doubling back, he walked out to the street and continued to mark its progress along the outskirts of the shopping center until it mixed with the evening traffic heading toward the bridge.

Reentering the building, he walked directly to deMay and demanded, "Okay, Louie, where's the diary?"

"What diary?"

"Your paintings are interesting," Manion said.

"Gimmicks," Louis deMay said glumly. "You wanna see art, look over there at Morgan Dumas's stuff." He pointed to a section of the room where even in shadows they could see large neon lights twisted into the shapes of naked, muscled men. "Morgan's a little one-track, but the man is definitely an artiste."

"What's with the neon lips?" Munn asked, perusing deMay's paintings now, too.

The black man frowned as if he didn't understand the question.

"The lips," Munn prompted. "On the sign at Mona's Place and on the painting of Christine right here? Your pal Morgan likes muscles. You like lips."

"It's the neon thing," deMay said. "I mean, it goes on and off. Just like people turn smiles on and off. Turn feelings on and off."

"I like this one," Manion said, indicating the plump woman with neon glasses.

"Yeah. Well, that's not one of my better neons. This one over here . . ."

"I really like it," Manion said. "I imagine the neon glasses are meant to indicate that when she puts on her glasses to read, her whole being is illuminated."

"Something like that, but . . ."

"Probably by what she's reading," Manion went on. He reached up and touched the binding of the book that the plump woman had in her hand.

"Wait, now."

"Forgive me, Shana," Manion said, and tugged at the book. It slipped from the niche that had been cut into the canvas to house it.

"You fucker," Louis deMay growled at him. But he was too worn out to offer any physical protest.

Munn moved beside Manion and took command of the book. "I'll be damned," he said. Then, "Wait a minute. This says it's somebody named Coalsack's diary."

"It's a name Pano used," Manion said.

He looked over Munn's shoulder at diary entries in precise Palmer penmanship. The policeman started to read aloud, " 'June 2, 1963. Made plans to meet with J.G. about setting fire to Perez barn. . . .' I'll be damned," he repeated. "This could be the genuine article."

"It's genuine," deMay said gloomily.

Mickie McCormick had been observing them silently, trying not to draw attention to herself. But she was too ecstatic to remain quiet any longer. "Pierre's going to flip his rug. There *is* a goddamn diary. And we've got it."

Munn raised an eyebrow, but he was in no mood to explain the situation to the woman, that she and her sleazebag boss might get the diary in a year or so when it was no longer of any interest to the Louisiana Organized Crime Combat Squad.

He closed the book and forced it into his coat pocket, ripping the material.

"Time to go, Louie," he said. "Need a hand?"

"I'll carry myself."

They filed out. Manion locked the door and placed the key back over the door molding. Munn's T-Bird was parked across the street in the Oakwood shopping center lot. Before they reached it, all the lights in the lot suddenly blinked on. Munn went immediately into a crouch, his hand inside his coat.

"It's just nighttime, Eben," Manion said, "not quite Armageddon."

Munn straightened. He said to Mickie, "Remember, honey, when Armageddon comes, I'll be the only guy ready for it."

With the arrival of night, the traffic was snarled and noisy, blocking the bridge to New Orleans. Munn grumbled something about amateur drivers and braked the car. He made an illegal U-turn and headed in a northerly direction, away from the bridge.

"What's your plan?" Manion inquired.

"Take the goddamn ferry," Munn replied, and headed for Algiers Point.

Manion yanked the diary from the lawman's pocket, straining the material even more. "Jesus," Munn yelled, "try not to rip the coat off my back."

Manion ignored him and snapped on the interior car light.

"I can't stand driving with the light on," Munn complained. "I can't see the goddamned road."

Manion began turning pages. The diarist's penmanship was extraordinarily clear and tiny, and the notations were dense with event.

Munn looked into the rearview mirror at deMay. He was resting against the back seat next to Mickie, his eyes shut. "Hey, Louie," Munn called. "Why'd you pick Ragusa to sell the diary to?"

DeMay's eyes opened to slits. "I didn't," he said.

"Then who did you approach?"

DeMay didn't answer.

"We have the diary," Manion told him. "We'll know every word that's in it. Eventually. Save us some time and effort. What makes it so valuable?"

"It ain't just the book that's valuable," deMay said.

"Then what . . . ?"

"Something my aunt told me," deMay explained. "The diary reminded me. Hell, I was only a little kid, much younger than my boy, when Pano was supposed to have killed his woman. But the diary fills in some blanks. And then Shana told me what Tyrone said about his lip slippin' in the wrong place, well . . ."

A blue sedan was advancing on the right, moving faster than it should have at that time of night. Suddenly, its headlights lit up the T-Bird just before it smashed into them.

The crash propelled Munn's car to the left onto a foot-high concrete ledge. Below the ledge was a walkway leading to the ferry landing. On the other side of the walkway was a wooden guardrail and the Mississippi, glittering hungrily in the night.

The T-Bird teetered on the ledge for a few seconds, head-lamps sending their light out into space.

Manion experienced the giddy sensation of looking out and seeing nothing but sky and the lights along the opposite bank.

Then the sedan smashed into them again and over they went, rolling and rolling until they landed with a terrible scraping noise on the walkway. The car rested on its left side. Its front had smashed through the guardrail and was sticking out over the water.

Shoved backward by an opaque air bag, Manion seemed to lose consciousness during the spin. But he awoke to the reality of someone pushing the bag aside, trying to pry the diary from his fingers.

He held on tight.

The man was standing beside the wreck, his arm reaching in and down through the open door. The man tugged mightily, but Manion refused to let go. The struggling figure was a blur in the night. It took Manion a second to realize that he'd lost his glasses. Munn, on the seat next to him, was a blur, too.

Sirens sounded, moving near.

Manion heard someone say, "Fuck it." The arm was with-drawn and the door raised and slammed shut.

Manion began to move his free hand under the air bag. His glasses had been snared at chest level. He fumbled the temples open and shoved them into place. He seemed to be the only one conscious in the car. As he looked up through the side window, he saw a lighted match floating through the dark toward the sprung hood of the car.

It was followed by a *whoosh* of flame. Panicked, Manion dropped the diary and pushed the car door open. He tried to move through it, but he'd forgotten the seat belt. He unlocked it, scrambled up through the open door, and leaped clear of the car.

The front of the machine was in flames. He struggled back up on the T-Bird's side. Mickie was slumped against her seat belt. Manion reached in, unlocked the belt and untangled it from her. As he dragged her through the door, she opened her eyes, muttered something that sounded like a bird's coo.

He draped her over the side of the car, hopped down to the walkway and lowered her. Then he carried her unconscious body away from the vehicle.

A thick black smoke was rising from under the hood. Manion climbed onto the T-Bird's side again and looked in. Munn's seat had been shoved back, trapping Louis deMay, who didn't seem to be breathing.

The car was heating up as Manion leaned in through the door. He could see smoke rising from under the dash and he thought he could actually hear the crackle of the fire. He pressed the release of Munn's seat belt, but it was jammed.

His face was about a foot from Munn's ear when he began to shout the policeman's name. Munn opened one eye. "What?" he growled.

"A knife, goddamnit," Manion shouted.

"Yeah, sure. Anything." Munn managed to raise a hand to point to the key in the ignition. A small penknife was hanging from it.

The car shifted a few inches. Manion wondered if it wouldn't be better if the car did fall into the Mississippi. Was drowning an easier death than burning? He shook the thought from his head and yanked the key from the dashboard.

It was hot.

He sawed away at the safety belt. It wasn't quite parted when Munn began to push his bulk toward Manion. With a pop, the belt separated and the policeman drew up his legs, grunting.

Manion backed away and Munn lifted himself through the door. They both jumped to the walkway just as there was the muffled *whomp* of an explosion, and the whole car was ablaze with Louis deMay still inside.

Manion rushed forward, but it was too late. Flames engulfed the car.

He and Munn scurried down the walkway to where Mickie was staring at the blazing car, crying.

Munn looked at the burning T-Bird, too, and muttered, "I hope the poor son of a bitch didn't wake up."

The firemen sprayed the car and the surroundings. The paramedics treated the three of them for smoke inhalation and lacerations.

Munn swore vengeance on Ragusa.

"It wasn't his car that hit us," Manion said. "And it wasn't he or Cookie who set us on fire."

"You think the little fucker's got only one car? Or one set of bozos?"

Manion shrugged.

Munn gestured toward a police car parked near the fire truck. "The guys offered me a ride to the city. You comin'?"

"The medic still isn't finished with Mickie," Manion said. "I'll wait around and go back with her."

"She's a temptin' little thing, isn't she?" Munn said.

"You tell me."

Munn grinned. "Yeah. I still get the calling every now and then. Anyway"—he started toward the police car—"watch your back, podnah. Maybe the Muskrat was after deMay, but just maybe he's decided to take care of *all* of us."

Ten minutes after Munn's departure, a fireman approached Manion with a charred, soggy mess. "This yours?" he asked. "We found it a few feet from the car."

In spite of the soot and scorch marks and water stains, Manion recognized the binding. "Yeah," he said. "I guess it is. Thanks."

26

THE COPS LEFT Munn at the Fairmont Hotel, where he caught a cab to Jazz City. If the cabbie thought it weird that a battered guy in a torn suit smelling of smoke wanted to be dropped off in an alley near Seraphina's Ristorante, he didn't mention it.

Remy's sedan was parked in the lot behind the restaurant. Approaching it from the rear, Munn could see by the moonlight that it looked intact. No major dents. It was not the vehicle used to bump his T-Bird off the road.

He moved to the car quietly.

Ragusa's driver was behind the wheel, head resting on the seat, smoking a cigarette and listening to music on the car radio, an old Louis Prima record that Munn had always liked.

He hummed along with it as he stuck his police special in the man's ear. "Out of the car," he ordered.

He walked the hapless driver around the sedan. "Unlock the trunk," he said. Ragusa's driver looked past Munn to the rear of the restaurant. But there was no hope on his face.

He opened the trunk. Fortunately for him, he'd taken good care of the car. The spare tire and the tools were neatly packed and in place.

"Hop on in," Munn commanded.

Twenty minutes or so later the back door of the restaurant opened and Remy Ragusa exited with Cookie Lapicola and the deMay boy. They'd taken a few steps from the building when Remy's diamond-studded mom appeared in the doorway. She said something, and her son returned to kiss her on the cheek. Satisfied, she went back to work, and Remy, his bodyguard and Louis continued on to the sedan.

They were a few feet from the car when Munn, who'd been

265

sitting behind the wheel, waiting, opened the door and slipped out, his gun in his hand.

Remy clutched his chest in mock terror. "Jesus! Munn, you almost made me drop a load."

Cookie looked bored. Louis's eyes were saucers, focused on the gun.

"We were just driving the kid back to his house," Remy said. He squinted at the tape and bruises on Munn's face. "What the hell happened to you?"

"Car trouble."

"What're you doin' here?"

"Hitchin' a ride."

Ragusa shrugged. "Where'd Frankie run off to?" He frowned at Munn. "What'd you do with him?"

There was a pounding noise from the rear of the sedan.

"You trunked him?" Ragusa said. "I swear, Munn, but you are a blast from the past. The keys?"

"I don't have 'em. Frankie must."

Ragusa shook his head pityingly. "Okay, Cookie, open the trunk."

Cookie moved to the rear of the car. He made a fist and brought it down like a piston on the trunk lid just above the lock. With his free hand, he yanked up on the lid.

There was a metallic snap and the trunk lid flipped up, exposing a frenzied Frankie. He crawled out, glaring at Munn.

Cookie bent the trunk latch back into place with his thumbs and closed the lid. He tested it to make sure it didn't rattle.

"We gotta be going, Munn," Ragusa said. "It's almost curfew time and the kid's mama is waiting."

"I'll ride with you," Munn said.

"Your gun is making Louis nervous. Isn't it, Lou?"

The boy swallowed and nodded.

Munn shoved the gun into his belt. Then he slipped into the front passenger seat beside an understandably surly Frankie.

"What's goin' on, Munn?" Remy asked as they glided through the night. "What really happened to you?"

"You don't know?"

"Last I saw you were at the art place with Louie."

"You with my daddy?" Louis asked.

Munn nodded. He kept his eyes on Ragusa. If the hood knew anything about what had happened to the T-Bird and Louis deMay, senior, he was wasting his time as a wiseguy. He should have been in Hollywood.

"Daddy comin' home?"

"We can talk about it later," Munn told him.

Leaning against the passenger door, the lawman was able to watch the driver and the three people on the back seat. The driver just did his job. In the rear, Ragusa made quarters dance across his knuckles for Louis, told him jokes and, finally, gave him a ten-dollar bill. "Little Pris tells me you slaughtered her at Gameboy. Went all the way to Space World. This is your win."

"I was just playing for fun," the boy said.

"Pris wasn't. She never plays for fun."

Grinning, Louis took the ten-dollar bill. Then he nestled his head against Ragusa's shoulder and closed his eyes. Remy winked at Munn, who felt like throwing up.

Louis awoke when the car stopped in front of his home. "Lieutenant Munn can take you inside, Louis," Remy said. "Your mom don't exactly approve of me."

"If you've been lyin' to me, Ragusa," Munn said, "I'm gonna give you your old nose back."

Remy looked at him in genuine confusion.

Jambo opened the front door of the house and scooped little Louis up in his arms. The boy wiggled around anxiously. "I want to see Mama."

"In the kitchen."

The boy scampered off.

"Louis called and said he was with the gangster," Jambo said with an edge. "When did you join the party?"

"I wanted to make sure he got home safely."

"Fine. You did that." Jambo started to shut the door.

"I better come in."

Jambo's expression said he was expecting that and he wasn't happy about it.

"Have the police called?" Munn asked.

"Look, it's okay. Little Louis is home now."

"I'm talking about big Louis," Munn said.

Jambo backed from the door. "Maybe you better come in."

The tall Creole led Munn into the deMay kitchen, where Wanda was hugging her son, eyes full of happy tears. "No show tonight," Jambo said to Munn. "First time we missed since we started."

"My boy's home," Wanda deMay said. "Everything's fine now."

Munn was sorry to have to contradict her.

27

MICKIE MCCORMICK'S HOTEL room was painted in cool pastel colors—lavender and sky blue—with white trim. Manion stepped out onto a wrought-iron balcony that faced the foot of Canal Street, the Aquarium and the Mississippi. A passing gambling ship made lights dance merrily on the dark water of the river. To his left, across Canal, the top floor of the St. Louis Hotel was aglow. Behind a glass wall, workmen on golden time put the finishing touches on the hotel's new casino. Manion yawned and reentered the suite.

Mickie was on the phone, relaying the afternoon and evening activities to Elliott Rubin. She unconsciously touched the plaster on her forehead as she animatedly described the descent down the embankment.

She paused, then said, "We have the diary." Another pause. "I don't know. It's pretty badly damaged. I think we'd better have an expert look at it before we try—"

As Rubin interrupted her, she looked up at Manion and, covering the phone, whispered, "You want to talk with him?"

Manion shook his head and opened a little refrigerator filled with every imaginable type of booze, as well as nuts, candies and crackers. They'd ordered dinners from room service, but he didn't know if he could wait. The boutique bottle containing pistachio nuts seemed to be calling to him.

He closed the door with the call unheeded.

Munn had been right, of course. Until they knew precisely what they were dealing with, caution was advisable. He wasn't going to return to his apartment that night. His intention had been to get his own room in the hotel.

Mickie had called that idea stupid. "Mine has this huge bed. Or if you're shy, you can take the sofa. And it'll keep your expenses down." She paused and lost most of her perkiness. "The bottom line is I don't want to be alone tonight."

Manion agreed to stay. But he suspected the invitation had more to do with the diary than with his company.

He waved his hand at Mickie until he caught her eye, then moved his index finger in a fast circle. She recognized the television hurry-up signal and brought her conversation with Rubin to a close.

"What's up?" she asked as Manion took the phone from her.

"Something I nearly forgot," he said, dialing.

He recognized the male voice that answered the phone at the deMay home. Jambo.

Manion identified himself and asked to speak with Wanda deMay.

"She's busy now with your friend Lieutenant Munn," Jambo said without emotion.

"Little Louis get home all right?"

"He's here now."

"Good, tell him I called."

Manion replaced the receiver on its cradle.

"What?" Mickie asked.

"I just felt a passing fear that nothing was going to be all right."

Their dinner arrived, wheeled in by a tall black man dressed like an Arabian Nights genie. He made a big production out of removing the dish covers and describing in minute detail the edibles before them. They were, in fact, so artfully presented that some identification was necessary.

Manion and Mickie were both past caring about what they were eating, as long as it didn't fight back. Once the genie was returned to his bottle, they dined heartily. Mickie drank wine from a carafe she found in the portable bar. Manion settled for tomato juice.

"I'm sorry I didn't let you talk me into a dessert," he said, when his meal was a memory.

"Have a bite of my pecan pie," she suggested, and was amused by how quickly he did.

When they'd finished, she yawned and said, "Time for bed."

"I'll take the couch."

"You in a relationship? Gay? Or just not interested?"

"Number one, I guess," he said.

"Where is she?"

"In Boston."

She stared at him. "Living there?"

"Visiting."

She raised an eyebrow. "Another guy?"

He didn't answer.

"But you feel you should keep yourself pure?" Mickie said. "That's so uncool it's almost contemporary."

"I guess I'm a Henry James sort of guy in a Howard Stern world," Manion replied.

"Good thing I packed my vibrator," she told him.

28

IN THE MORNING, Manion showered, shaved with a pink plastic razor he found in the bathroom, dressed in his old clothes and left without waking the suite's other occupant. He took the diary with him.

The police lab would have been the logical place to get its condition appraised, and Munn could have arranged that. But Manion wanted to know more about the diary's contents before Munn got a look at them.

As usual, Nadia knew just the man for the job—Dr. Kermit Pressman, of the Louisiana Library of Antiquity.

The library was in City Park, not far from Delgado Museum, a stone-and-glass building constructed in the 1930s by the WPA. Dr. Pressman was, contrary to Manion's expectation, a man in his early thirties as big as a linebacker. His private office was a lofty space where scarcely an inch of floor or desk or table top was visible, thanks to an assortment of musty books, yellowed pamphlets, manuscripts, flaking prints and notepads marked with odd scribbles.

On the desk, in counterpoint, was a Sony Discman and a scattered collection of CDs featuring rappers and rockers Manion had never been exposed to.

Dr. Pressman casually cleared a section of desk and began poking at the diary with a long, pointed instrument. "Some of the entries at the front of the diary were lost to the fire and water. But the rest of it looks salvageable. The diarist used a ballpoint pen, which is good. Its ink is less soluble than those used in fountain or soft-tip pens."

"Would it be possible to Xerox the remaining pages?" Manion asked.

"Something like that," the big man said genially.

"When might I be able to pick up a copy?"

"Let me poke around at it awhile," Dr. Pressman told him. "Call me this evening and I'll be better informed."

"Is there a way of checking its authenticity?" Manion asked.

"If you have something else that the diarist has written, we can make a pretty good comparison. And there are ways of testing the ink elements to see if they conform to inks that were used during the periods in question."

Dr. Pressman saw him out. They shook hands and Manion said, "You look like you might have played college football."

The doctor smiled. "How do you think I wound up taking a crip course like Library Science?" he asked.

29

WANDA DEMAY WAS still in her robe when she answered Manion's ring. She stared at him through the screen door without saying a word. He wondered if her eyes were red from lack of sleep or because her husband had died the night before. "I'm sorry to bother you," he said.

"By now, you'd think I'd be used to it."

She walked away from the open door. Manion took that as an invitation for him to enter.

She sat down on her living-room sofa and picked up the coffee cup she'd left to answer the door. A telephone rested on the coffee table. And a sheet of yellow paper with names and telephone numbers.

"Little Louis home?" he asked.

"Jambo took him out for a drive. Give me time to take care of the funeral arrangements."

She noticed the bandage on his chin. "Were you in the car when it crashed?"

He nodded.

"Was big Louis still alive when it caught fire?" she asked, her eyes staring into his.

"No," he said, though he wasn't really sure.

"That's what that policeman said, too. Munn. He's a weird one."

"What makes you think so?" Manion asked.

"He asked me if I knew Tyrone Pano," Wanda said. "I said, man, I woulda been three or four years old when he died. And I wasn't even livin' in New Orleans at the time. I grew up at the Bay." Bay Saint Louis, Mississippi, was a small town on the Gulf.

"My sister and I used to spend summers there when we were kids," Manion said. "I drove through the Bay last year and didn't even recognize the place."

"Gambling fever," she said. "Turns things to crap. Why should the Bay be any different?" She sipped her coffee.

"You said your husband had been sifting through Shana Washington's possessions. I'd like to do a little sifting through them myself, if it's all right."

"Why not?" Wanda said, and got to her feet. "There's a steamer trunk in the attic. Feel free to snoop through it."

Manion thanked her and climbed the steps, then the wooden ladder that led to the attic. In the warm, dusty storage space, he found a large footlocker that was brim-full of Bibles, books, knickknacks. There was correspondence from a wide variety of people, mainly connected with missionary work. It took him a while to locate three items involving Tyrone Pano. Two were letters written by him when he was in New York, presumably on business for the Southern Cross.

The first described the city, focusing on the conditions of the tenements and the treatment of Harlem blacks. The second was lighter in tone and told of a cocktail party he had attended at the home of a wealthy theater producer. It had been in honor of a black militant who had just been released from prison, and the white hostess had spent the evening bragging to everyone about how the collards and black-eyed peas for the hors d'oeuvres had been flown in that morning from Alabama. Regardless, the soul food had remained virtually untouched.

The other item of interest was the will leaving all of Pano's worldly possessions to Shana Washington. Manion was no expert, but the meticulous penmanship of the letters seemed to resemble what he'd seen of the entries in the diary. The will's handwriting was looser, less disciplined. Unless Pano had been using his other hand to write, the will appeared to be a rather poor job of forgery. If Pen Libideau had done the job for J.J., he'd been smart to get into another line of business.

Manion tucked the three items into his coat pocket and put everything else back into the trunk, closing the lid.

Downstairs, Wanda deMay was no longer in the living room. Her coffee cup was in the kitchen, empty. He walked down the hall to the rear of the house.

He paused at the open door to the master bedroom. Wanda deMay stood by the bed, facing a painting on the wall. It was a portrait of her and her son. Her back was turned to him, but Manion could tell by the rocking of her body that she was crying.

He moved away, praying that the floor would not creak under his feet and draw her attention. Then he left the house, closing the front door behind him quietly.

30

IN THE MID-1970s, Larry Libideau, former forger, turned his life around. A family man with a cheery wife and two more or less happy children, he bought the print shop where he'd been working for more than a decade. He and his brood were occupying half of a refurbished duplex on Annunciation Street not far from the shop. Life was pleasantly uneventful.

He missed the thrill he once got from a perfectly duplicated signature, of course, but he had taken up a hobby that nearly matched that artistic satisfaction—oil painting. After just a few night school lessons, it had been obvious that he was a natural. Before long he was able to copy even the most intricate old master so convincingly that all but expert eyes would be fooled.

Old habits die hard, but Larry the family man had no real desire to use his art forgeries for illegal gain. Nor did he wish any less scrupulous soul to be so tempted. So, having completed a remarkable recreation of a Rembrandt, say, he would add a special touch—a tiny hot pink alligator staring up at the seated physicians with a slightly demented smile.

The little alligator was added to re-creations of Gainsborough, of Toulouse-Lautrec, even of Titian. Since the Libideaus' friends were amused by these whimsical oils, Larry started putting them in the window of his print shop. And passersby began inquiring if they were for sale.

He had his first art show in 1981 in one of the better galleries in the French Quarter. Twenty-six of the thirty paintings sold during the cocktail party. The remaining four were snapped up as soon as the review of the show appeared in the *Times-Picayune*.

Thanks to the little pink alligator, eventually christened the

Goofygator, Libideau and his wife currently resided along a lovely tree-shaded boulevard in the suburb of Metairie, within walking distance of the country club.

The house itself, Manion discovered, was a two-story Italian-style villa set well back from the boulevard and surrounded by a natural wall of tall bamboo. On the pale orange tile of the open front porch, a sculpted stone replica of the Goofygator guarded the front door. Its slightly crossed eyes seemed to follow Manion as he approached and pressed the bell.

The door was opened by a matronly woman in her late fifties with dark rings under her eyes. She introduced herself as Larry's sister, Marcella Zabisa, and led the detective into a surprisingly bright nook filled with white rattan furniture covered by cushions of forest green.

"Larry'll be with you in a minute," she said. "Can I get you something? A Coke or a beer?"

Manion declined.

"Well, if you'll excuse me, I'd better get back to work."

Not more than ten minutes after his sister had walked brusquely from the room, Larry Libideau entered. "Hiya, Manion," he said, offering his hand. "Long time."

It had been five or six years. Libideau looked about ten years younger. It took Manion a few seconds to realize why. He now had a fine head of light brown hair, or a very expensive wig. In addition, he seemed relaxed and self-satisfied in his lime-green slacks and a Hawaiian print shirt with short sleeves.

"You're looking like the world's treating you pretty well, Pen."

"Can't complain. Getting ready to take a tour with the new book. And, Manion, I use the name Larry these days. Pen . . . you know, that's sorta past history."

"Sure," Manion said. "So you're an author now?"

Larry Libideau shook his head. "Just a doodler. It's a kids' book—*Meet the Goofygator.* Sort of a spinoff from the comic strip. You got any kids?"

"Not married," Manion said.

"You gotta get married. I kept tellin' that to J.J., but he wouldn't listen. I was sure sorry to see that old boy go."

"Me, too," Manion said.

"You weren't at the funeral," Libideau said, more a question than an accusation.

"I was out of town."

"I miss the poor son of a bitch." Libideau's voice cracked. He cleared his throat. "Anyway, you said on the phone you had something to show me."

Manion reached into his pocket and withdrew Tyrone Pano's last will. He was using a plastic Baggie to preserve it.

Libideau glanced at it and his face went slack. "What's on your mind?" he asked flatly.

"Nothing that'll cause you any problems," Manion assured him. "As I said on the phone, I just need some information." He took another plastic-covered sheet from another pocket. It was one of Pano's letters to Shana.

Libideau frowned at the letter. "I don't get it."

"The will is something you did for J.J."

"That's your story," Libideau said.

"Pe—ah, Larry, this isn't a shakedown," Manion told him. "The letter was written by Pano. I just want to know why you had so much trouble copying his handwriting."

Libideau looked at both pages. He said, "Come with me."

He led Manion through French windows and past a cobalt blue swimming pool to a room over a three-car garage. His work area. On the bleached white hardwood floors were four easels holding paintings in progress, a draftsman's table and chair, a butcher-block floating chest, bright yellow file cabinets and a state-of-the-art stereo tier.

Libideau placed the two sheets on the table and sat down. He opened a drawer in the floating chest and took out a sheet of blank paper. He picked up a pen from a collection in a coffee mug on the top of the chest. He glanced at the Pano letter and began to scrawl on the blank paper.

He worked quickly and without hesitation. When he'd finished, he handed the page to Manion. It was another version of Pano's last will, this time perfectly matching the penmanship of the New York letter. "When I copy something," Libideau said, "I damn well copy it. If this will is something I did, and it doesn't resemble Pano's handwriting, then the will I was using as my guide must've been bogus, too."

"Is that what you were using? Another will?"

The artist was plainly discomfited by the discussion. "What's this all about, Manion?" he asked.

"I'm trying to put together the events that led to Pano's death."

"Why, for Christ's sake? Isn't there enough happening on the streets today to keep you busy?"

"Sometimes you have to take the jobs you get offered."

"Is somebody coming after me?" Libideau asked.

"Nothing like that," Manion said. "As far as anybody else is concerned, you're not involved at all."

Libideau looked doubtful.

"Larry, it's important I know about that early will. You wouldn't still have it?"

"Me? I would have burned it as soon as I was finished with it. And a smart guy like J.J. would not only have burned it, he would've ground up the ashes, too."

"You wouldn't remember what it said?" Manion asked.

"This is gonna get me in trouble."

"No. It isn't," Manion said firmly.

"This guy, Pano, left everything to that black group, the Southern Cross."

Manion thanked the ex-forger and took back his bagged samples.

"Don't thank me," Libideau said. "Just keep away from me with this kind of stuff. The old days are dead. I'd just as soon leave 'em buried."

MANION ARRIVED AT his apartment to find that Munn and Mickie had broken in and were sitting at his desk drinking beer and wolfing down muffulettas. Mickie had the good grace to look vaguely embarrassed as she lowered her sandwich and said, "I hope it's all right, us just coming in here like this."

Manion stared at Munn, who feigned sudden interest in his food.

"I was standing outside," Mickie went on, "wondering what

to do next, since you weren't here, when Eben drove up. He took me to this little place where a tattooed man with three rings in his nose makes sandwiches...."

"Deakey's," Munn said merrily. "Don't worry, Manion, we got one for you. And some root beer in the fridge."

"You broke the lock again," Manion said. He couldn't remember if it was the third or fourth time.

"It's for your own good. You gotta get a better setup," the lawman chided him. "A mad-dog crackhead with absolutely no hand-eye coordination could pop that lock with a toothpick."

Manion sighed. He noticed that the Xeroxed newspaper articles about Pano little Louis deMay had given him were sitting in front of Munn. The lawman looked down at them and said, "I like to read when I eat."

Manion poked into the brown bag that was leaving an oil slick on his desk top. He removed a monstrous round sandwich at least three inches high at its center, eyeing it with some dismay.

He carried the muffuletta into the kitchenette, halved it and poured a glass of Barq's root beer. When he returned, Munn had finished his sandwich and was looking longingly at the remains of Mickie's. She said, "That wasn't a very friendly thing you did this morning, Terry, sneaking off without waking me."

Munn rolled his eyes.

"I didn't sneak off," Manion said. "It was nine o'clock. I had things to do."

"Speaking of which, where's the fucking diary?" Munn asked.

Manion looked accusingly at Mickie, who said, "Well, you took it and I didn't know what your plans were, so I sort of mentioned it to Eben...."

"And we wasted a couple hours poking through your files and underwear. You're not carryin' it. You wouldn't just leave it in your car. What'd you do with it? It's evidence."

"You break into my house and search it and you're giving *me* attitude."

"Well, hell, I bought you lunch," Munn told him. "Besides, I had a lousy morning."

"Get up on the wrong side of the cave?"

"No. As a matter of fact, I visited Louis deMay's girlfriend to let her know what happened to him. She only cried for about an hour. I had to go home and change my coat. But you go ahead and eat, Manion. We got nothing better to do than to sit here and watch you."

Which is what they did.

Finally, when he had put the untouched half of his muffuletta in the fridge, Mickie asked, "What now?"

"I'm going upstairs for fresh clothes," Manion told her.

He took his time, but when he descended the stairs he saw they were seated exactly where he'd left them.

Munn checked out his white silk shirt and pressed brown trousers. "You look snappy, Manion. Goin' to a cotillion?"

"The library," the detective replied. Actually, he wanted to drive to Nadia's, to talk over his discovery that Tyrone Pano almost certainly was murdered. But first he had to shake Munn and Mickie. And there was something he wanted to do at the library anyway.

"Why there?" Munn asked. "If you're lookin' for winos, you can find all you want down the street in the Pelican Catch."

"People go to the library for other reasons, Eben," Manion said. "But it helps if you know how to read."

"You can be my guide," Munn said.

32

AT THE LIBRARY off Tulane Avenue, where they found no winos and not even very many of the homeless, Manion led them to the periodicals section. Armed with a collection of microfilm boxes containing all the *Times-Picayune* newspapers for the year 1965, he found an empty viewer and began spooling.

His goal was to cover the period from the murder of Lillian Davis to Tyrone Pano's death in his jail cell. He wanted to make sure that little Louis hadn't missed some key information when he had done his Xeroxing.

As he approached the date of the Davis slaying, the front pages of the papers made clear the impact that the Meddler murders were having on the city. Actually, it was the second death that made the front page. That's when the pattern was discovered. A photo of the first victim, barmaid Mae Rita Downs, who had only rated a brief notice on the day after her grim passing, appeared under the banner headline side by side with a picture of the unfortunate insurance agent Leslie Jeanaud, victim number two.

Then came the information about the voodoo dolls being left at the crime scenes, and historian Henry Marnet's moment in the limelight, dredging up memories of Marie Laveau and providing the serial killer with his infamous nickname.

After the discovery of the third victim, Lee Ann Keller, a reader would have had to work hard to find news of anything else. Lillian Davis's death occurred the same night as the Meddler's victim number five, Theresa Liverdais, a clerk at a French Quarter hotel. Her story was front-page material. The Davis shooting took place only a few blocks away, but the coverage of it was in another section altogether, a single paragraph sharing the page with all of the other run-of-the-mill crimes and misdemeanors of the previous twenty-four hours.

While Manion paged through the rest of the paper, Munn, who'd been reading over the detective's shoulder, yawned and got to his feet. "Think I'll go chat up the librarian."

Manion watched with curiosity as he sauntered across the room, jaw jutting pugnaciously, heading for the information counter and an elderly woman in a cardigan sweater who seemed engrossed in whatever she was reading.

Munn reached over the counter to tap the librarian's shoulder and the woman jumped a foot. When she calmed down, Munn smiled at her and mumbled something that Manion couldn't hear. The microfilm beckoned, and he turned back to the news of 1965 New Orleans.

"Just look it up in the NOLSIS," the elderly librarian instructed.

"The What-sis?" Munn asked.

"Our catalog system that displays all the titles the library possesses," she explained, pointing a mildly arthritic finger at a line of computer terminals against a far wall. "Just operate it as you would any computer."

"Oh sure," Munn said, not bothering to mention that he stayed clear of computers and thought anybody who used one was a geek.

It wasn't as difficult as he'd imagined. You just pressed the arrow buttons until you found the word you were looking for—in this case an author's name—and you pressed the key marked "Enter." Hell, he was computer literate. Maybe he'd even buy himself one. Then he could get fitted for glasses and start wearing white T-shirts and baggy Levi's and a baseball cap with the bill turned around so that it served no useful purpose. Just like the fucking computer.

He found the "M"s, then zeroed in on "Marnet, Henry." He hit the "Enter" button and was rewarded with four listings:

"Marnet, Henry: *To Catch a Meddler;* 1st ed., 1967; Harvest House, New York; 342 pp.; nonfiction account of the capture of New Orleans' serial murderer Theodore Glander written by the man who named him the Meddler. 873.2M. ON LOAN."

"Marnet, Henry: *To Catch a Meddler;* 1st paperback ed., 1968; Panda Books, New York; 342 pp.; nonfiction account of New Orleans' infamous Meddler murders. AVAILABLE."

"Marnet, Henry: *Red Magnolias;* 1st ed., 1959; Raynebeau Press, Rayne, Louisiana; 301 pp.; nonfiction survey of communism in Old and New South. 873.2M. AVAILABLE."

"Marnet, Henry: *Voodoo Queen;* 1st ed., 1962; Raynebeau Press, Rayne, Louisiana; 267 pp.; biography of Marie Laveau, her life and times. 873.2M. ON LOAN."

Munn followed the instructions and cleared the screen, then strolled back to the woman in the cardigan. She watched his return with a face that registered no emotion known to him. "Where are the paperbacks?" he asked.

She extended her arm stiffly to point the way, like a stern father sending his unwed pregnant daughter into the snowy night. Munn grabbed the tip of her finger between his thumb and forefinger and shook it, saying "Thanks."

He found the book, a small paperback with a cover depicting a nearly naked woman being dragged into an alley by a slavering beast of a man wielding a huge knife. The library had sent it out to be rebound in a more permanent form, but it still looked as if it had come close to the end of its tawdry life.

Munn scanned the first couple of pages, then, fascinated,

carried it to a reading table where he began to devour it with much the same dedication he'd shown to his muffuletta.

An hour later, when Manion and Mickie told him they were ready to go, Munn waved them away. He'd cab back to his car. Manion moved closer to get a look at the book, but the lawman drew it to his chest like a poker player hiding his hand.

Manion shrugged. "Well, happy reading," he said.

"Yeah," Munn said. "These things you call books are okay. Some day they may even replace television."

"Eben's kind of cute," Mickie said as they were driving away from the library.

"A regular teddy bear," Manion said.

"He's much hipper than he'd like you to think. Is he involved with anybody?"

"No. He sorta lives for his work."

"Who doesn't?" she replied. She looked at her wristwatch and asked, "How much further to the hotel?"

"Ten minutes."

"Good. Pierre wants me to report in at three-thirty. That's when they wind up taping."

"You'll make it."

"You coming up?" she asked.

"Errand to run."

"What about later?" she asked. "Are we going to be roomies again tonight?"

He hadn't thought about it, but the danger hadn't lessened. He probably shouldn't spend the night at his apartment, especially with a broken front-door lock. There was a spare room at Nadia's he could use. "We'll figure it out over dinner," he said. "I'll be back by five. If the teddy bear finishes his book before nighttime, maybe I can convince him to join us."

"I was hoping you would."

33

THE MEDDLER SMELLED the pine and listened to the breeze rustle the leaves of the trees. Only a few miles away, traffic whizzed by along the Causeway, but in the sylvan section of the Louisiana countryside, all was quiet and still, except for the occasional squirrel, snake, muskrat or nutria.

He picked up a pinecone and lobbed it into a little brook that babbled several yards away. The brook didn't mind at all. This was, he thought, the life. No worries. No cares.

Suddenly, birds fluttered from the trees to his left. He was facing in that direction when a dog emerged from the forest. He stood maybe a yard high, a good-sized dog of a slightly ghostly gray color. The Meddler thought it might be a weimaraner.

It moved gracefully on full alert, staring at him with pale eyes. The Meddler dropped to one knee and said, "Howdy, boy. What's your name?"

"Butch."

Edward J. Cady stood a few feet to the right of the dog. A shotgun, broken, was draped over his left arm. The portly man looked annoyed. He was panting. The dog wasn't at all winded. He approached the Meddler and accepted a pat on the head.

"What the hell is so goddamned important?" Cady demanded.

"It's the Pano thing," the Meddler said, scratching Butch behind the ear. "Weimaraner?"

"So his papers say," Cady grumbled. "Who are you and where do you come into this deal?"

"Just a friend of Jimmy Billins's." When the Meddler stood, his knees popped. "Getting old," he grunted.

"No fun being old," Cady informed him. "But, like the man says, it ain't so bad when you consider the alternative. Now, what's so goddamned important it's made me take a two-mile hike when I should be home with my family?"

The Meddler looked at the shotgun. "Do much shooting around here?" he asked.

"Some. That's the beauty of having all this land. You can do what the fuck you want. And what I want now is to hear you out and get back home."

"Right. Well, it seems Pano has come to the attention of some TV people and they're poking around—"

"Yes, yes," Cady said impatiently. "I know all that. Guy named Manion came out here to see me. I told Jimmy about it."

"That's why Jimmy asked me to touch bases with you."

"I'm not worried about this TV bullshit. Why is he?"

"Well, you know Jimbo," the Meddler said, closing the gap between them. "That *is* a beautiful gun."

"It's a Krieghoff Crown," Cady said proudly.

The Meddler moved closer, staring down at the shotgun. "Beautiful," he said. "Beautiful grain and polish on the wood. And the engraved figures—that hunting dog looks like Butch."

"Yeah," Cady said, letting his pride in the gun mollify his annoyance. "That's all gold. Jim gave me that six years ago."

"He's given you a lot, hasn't he?"

"It's gone both ways," Cady said, snapping the shotgun closed, cocking it and positioning it between them. The dog was suddenly alert, watching them both closely.

"No," the Meddler said. "It's been strictly a one-way deal. Jimmy gives, you get."

"The deal's our business," Cady said, slipping his finger into the trigger guard of the shotgun. Butch let out a little happy yip at the prospect of action.

"And all you got in return," the Meddler said, "was thirty years of living like a millionaire. Better than a millionaire. I know, because I don't live as well as you."

"That's your problem," Cady said. "Take it and your million off my property and all the way back to New Orleans."

"A long time ago, I told Jimmy he was stupid to keep paying you."

"Shove off," Cady said. "Before I get really mad."

The Meddler nodded. But instead of leaving he took a quick step closer to Cady. The old man raised the shotgun, but his target ducked suddenly and came in under the gun. He pushed up on the barrel and yanked down on the stock.

Cady's finger was trapped in the trigger guard. It pulled off the first round when the shotgun was pointed straight up. The Meddler continued to twist the weapon until the barrel bounced against Cady's nose.

The old man squealed and tried to yank his finger from the trigger. "Consider the alternative," the Meddler told him, and pulled the shotgun forward with a jerk.

Butch was not a guard dog. He was trained to be a hunter. He was, however, protective of his master. The stranger was struggling with his master, which meant he should help. But his master was using his weapon, which meant he should stay ready to go after game. Mixed signals.

He waited.

And when the first shot was fired, Butch looked away from the two men to search the ground for falling game.

The second shot drew his attention back to the struggle just as his master was thrown backward onto the ground. His master did not rise again. His face looked very strange. Wet with something dark. Messy.

Butch turned to the stranger and bared his teeth.

"Easy now, Butch," the stranger said calmly. "Just let me do this."

Butch watched the stranger get out a white cloth and bend over his master. Butch had decided to attack if the stranger touched his master. But the stranger was more interested in the weapon in his master's hand. He wiped it with his white cloth.

Then he looked around. He found a broken tree branch. Using the cloth, he carried the branch to his master and placed it at his feet. Then he put away the cloth and said to Butch, "Good dog. Run back to the house, now, and go 'Woof-woof.' Do the Lassie bit."

The stranger laughed and walked away.

Butch looked at his fallen master. He didn't know what to do.

34

GEORGE WELLS, EIGHTY if he was a day, stood on one foot, arms extended, and began to twist his body so methodically it reminded Manion of a slow-motion movie. The old man was performing his afternoon exercises on the bank of the bayou that flowed beside the Wells home. Manion was on the screened porch, having tea with George's wife, Nadia.

"He started that oriental stuff about nine years ago," she said, "when his knees began hurtin' after his five-mile jog. It looks sort of loopy, but it doesn't scare the animals and, Lord knows, George is in better shape than"—she stared at Manion—"than most people I know.

"Anyway, suppose you review the bidding on this Pano murder theory of yours."

"According to my source—" he began.

"And you're not gonna tell me the name of your unimpeachable informant," she said testily.

"You know I trust you, Nadia. It's just that I promised—"

"Yes, yes. Get on with it, Terence." She was angrier than he'd thought.

"All right. My source says that when J.J. opened Pano's envelope, it contained a will leaving all of the Panther Man's possessions to the Southern Cross."

"That sounds pretty logical to me. J.J. didn't know what to do about it. He didn't want to hand over the loot to a group that would probably use it to buy guns and dynamite. So he decided to fake up another will favoring Shana. Good for him."

"The problem is, the Southern Cross will was a forgery, too."

She grinned. "That's lovely," she said. "That crooked lawyer

286

Billins had to sit there with egg on his face, knowing full well J.J.'s will was as bogus as the one he signed as witness. But I don't see how we get from there to Pano's being a murder victim."

"You said that when J.J. and you had lunch, you suggested he compare the will to—"

"Pano's suicide note," Nadia exclaimed.

"And they were close enough for J.J. to think the note was real. The thing he didn't consider was that both will and note were forgeries, done by the same hand."

"At the behest of Billins," Nadia said.

"He was certainly a party to it. And if somebody went to the effort of concocting a suicide note for Pano, then it is doubtful that the Panther Man merely went along with the plan and did himself in."

"Good work, sonny. Now the question you've gotta ask yourself is this: Is Pierre 'Golden Throat' Reynaldo gonna plunk down any more loot if you give him a murder on a silver platter?"

"One would hope," Manion said.

"What do you suppose was in the envelope before Billins and Company made their substitution?" Nadia wondered.

The smile left Manion's face. "More important, where was the substitution made? At Shana Washington's, when she had the envelope? Or at Dad's bank?"

"Get off that track, sonny," Nadia warned him. "Jack wouldn't have been party to anything like that."

"How can you be so sure?"

"Because I knew him too well."

He stared at the elderly woman. "What *was* it with you and Dad?" He had asked her similar questions from almost their first meeting. But she never provided anything even approximating a satisfactory reply.

Nadia smiled and said, "We were very close."

"How close?" he asked.

"You mean, what was the nature of our relationship?"

"Exactly."

"It was one that warmed my heart until the day he died. Now, may we get back to business?"

Manion began to object, but she was determined to say no more about her relationship with his late father. Instead, she said, "We can assume that whatever was in the envelope is lost to the ages. Pano thought the envelope was safe with Shana—"

"Or with Dad," Manion interrupted peevishly.

"Damnit," Nadia said, "you have a head like marble. Okay, let's address that point. Here's the progression. The Reverend Hart, then known as Tank, tells J.J. that Pano wants to see him in his cell. Hart doesn't know what Pano's gonna say to J.J. Certainly, he doesn't know that the Panther Man is gonna send J.J. after an envelope. Anyway, J.J. goes to see Pano and less than an hour later, Billins is on the horn, griping about the visit. So we know there was a leak in the jail. And we can assume that the man responsible for the leaked information was the former Sergeant Cady.

"In all likelihood, Cady saw or heard Pano tell J.J. about Shana having the envelope and he passed that on to Billins. The switch took place before J.J. had a chance to take possession of it."

"We don't know that for sure," Manion said.

"No. But if we look at your theory, that the envelope was exchanged in the bank, there are two problems. One, they couldn't be sure that J.J. hadn't opened the envelope before he banked it. More important, the person who got J.J. to take the envelope to your dad was me. And I'm not the one who got the cushy job at Billins's law firm. But let's really nail it down. Let's go talk with your pal Cady."

"He's a tough nut," Manion said. "I couldn't scratch the surface."

"Well, hell, sonny, let's go see if the two of us can't crack him open."

She stood and looked out over the lawn at her husband, who was in the midst of a one-legged squat. "At his age. Amazing, isn't he?"

Manion nodded.

"Let's make sure Mr. Cady's at home before we drive all the way to Covington. At this time of day, the Causeway'll be packed tighter than a sardine can."

She strolled to her office, where her assistant, Olivette, sat at a computer preparing the weekly schedule for the field operatives. She was wearing her pale green turban and blouse combination with what appeared to be leopard-skin tights.

Nadia asked her to phone Edward J. Cady in Covington and tell him to stand by for a call from James Billins at precisely five-thirty. "By then we should be at his doorstep. Say that Billins will be in meetings until that time and it's vital they speak exactly at five-thirty."

"Gotcha," Olivette said and picked up the phone.

Manion poked around the office, noting something new on the wall, a photo of Nadia taken with the current First Lady. He looked at the elderly woman with a raised eyebrow. "It was at one of her Health Care soirees. I like her. She's tough."

Olivette waved her hand to attract their attention. "Oh my God," she said, "when did it happen? The poor man." She paused, listening to what was being said on the other end of the line. While she did, she scrawled something on a sheet of paper in front of her. She held it up to them. It read:

"Cady blow head off."

IT WAS A busy day for the Meddler.

He arrived back from Covington just before the traffic picked up. He had two calls to make and would have stopped at the nearest pay phone, but some of the old ex-cop's blood had sprayed his shirt and coat. So it was home again, home again, jiggidy-jig.

He exchanged his stained clothes and made the first phone call. Checking in with Billins. Yes, everything went smoothly. No, he did not think Cady had any hidden signed confession or backup plan in case of his death. Not after thirty years of peace in the valley.

The second call was to set up his next task of the day.

That accomplished, he drove downtown via St. Charles Avenue. He parked the car and entered the hotel lobby just as the woman he was meeting stepped from the elevator. She paused, looked at the passing parade and frowned.

Her height was above average. She was curvaceous, with a lovely face. There was a scratch above her right eye. Probably from the car incident. He was glad now she had escaped the fire, though that escape was making more work for him. In this case, he thought it was going to be work he'd enjoy.

He approached her slowly, saw her bite her lip and look at her watch. Oh yes, he was attracted to her all right. He was old enough to be her father—her grandfather, given the right set of circumstances—but he definitely was going to have fun with her. He'd almost been tempted to dust off his old friend the razor-sharp knife he'd retired so long ago when that very exciting period of his life ended. In the end, he'd settled for a very ordinary blade that he'd just as soon not have to use. There would be other enjoyments, maybe even ... but enough idle speculation.

"Miz McCormick?" he asked.

She turned and looked him squarely in the eye. Then she smiled and it warmed him. "You must be Sergeant Gannon."

"Yes, ma'am, Frank Gannon," he told her. If she hadn't been so young she might have recalled that a Frank Gannon once helped Joe Friday seek out criminals on the *Dragnet* television series.

She extended her hand. It was firm and warm, and he realized it had been entirely too long since he'd indulged himself with a young woman. "I can't tell you how impressed I am by the way you located me," she said.

"It was simple, ma'am. Your name was in the *Picayune*, along with the story about Mr. Reynaldo searching for information concerning one Tyrone Pano. So I just phoned a few hotels to see if you'd checked in. This was the third on my list."

"But how did you recognize me just now?" she asked.

"I just looked for the most beautiful woman in the lobby."

She smiled. "So what's this information you have, Sergeant?"

"It'd be better if I show you," he said.

"Is it far?" She seemed hesitant.

"Ten-minute drive."

"And it will positively change the whole thrust of our story on Tyrone Pano?"

"As I told you on the phone, Miz McCormick—"

"Mickie, please," she said.

"As I told you on the phone, Mickie, this will be a startling revelation."

She positively tingled at the news.

"I'm sort of expecting someone to drop by," she said. "Would you mind if I left them a note?"

"Please."

"Where is it we're going?"

"Basin, across Canal. The building used by Pano's group, the Southern Cross. Tell him we'll be back in thirty minutes."

"What makes you think it's a 'him'?" she asked, smiling.

"Beg pardon. I didn't mean to imply . . . it's just that you're so attractive, I assumed it would be a man."

"Why, Sergeant Gannon, do all you New Orleans policemen say such nice things?"

Damn if she wasn't flirting with him! Oh yes. And he was going to flirt with her, too. In his own unique way.

"We New Orleans policemen only speak the truth," he said.

He watched her cross the lobby and scribble a note at the front desk. She handed it to a clerk, said something to him. The clerk nodded and put the note into a slot marked with her room number.

Mickie looked a little flushed as she raced back to him. "Let's go," she said.

He led her through the front door, then down a walkway between the hotel and the building next door. At the rear of the hotel was a quiet alley. A dark sedan was parked, facing them, hugging the back wall of a men's clothing shop.

They walked to the car. He used his key to unlock the passenger door. He glanced up and down the alley. Then he opened the door. As she bent to get in, he removed a leather sap from his belt and brought it down on a precise spot at the base of her skull.

When her legs buckled, he grabbed her and eased her into the passenger seat. He strapped her seat belt in place. Her head lolled forward. He eased it back against the headrest.

Satisfied that she had the appearance of a woman catching a few z's, he locked the car. He had something to take care of at the hotel desk and he didn't want her to be disturbed by anyone with evil intent.

36

DR. KERMIT PRESSMAN of the Louisiana Library of Antiquity ushered Manion into his cluttered office. He was in high spirits. "This Coalsack diary is fascinating," he said. "I hope you don't mind my making a copy for myself."

"I won't tell anybody if you don't," Manion said.

"We were able to salvage a total of two hundred and eighty-five pages from what I assume to be a three-hundred-page diary," Dr. Pressman said, picking up a stack of Xeroxed sheets about an inch and a half thick. "The handwriting is clear and precise, rather like that of a grammar school student. The dates covered are from September 3, 1962 to March 29, 1965. Some of the entries are quite intriguing.

"For example, look at December 2, 1962."

The towering archivist flipped through the stack eagerly, then handed the proper sheet to Manion.

"Met with J. on city council. T. threatened to stage traffic jam on Willow before game. J. promised to consider demands for more work from Canal Street stores. Could smell the bullshit. Fuck him and his wait-and-see. Sugar Bowl gonna be a little late getting started this year."

The archivist exchanged that page for another. It had an entry for a fateful date in November of 1963. "JFK got shot in head. Some brothers and sisters walking around like it has meaning. Say JFK on our side. I explain no white man on our side. No Kennedy. And, now, definitely no damn Texan. These people preach white man politics. There is no black man politics except the politics of revolution. I am a black politician."

"Interesting, huh?" Dr. Pressman asked.

"How much of the diary did you read?"

Pressman managed to look a bit sheepish. "All of it. Kept me awake most of the night."

"What were the final entries like?" Manion inquired.

"The diarist and several members of his organization were formulating plans for a demonstration in Baton Rouge," Dr. Pressman replied. "If the specific plans were discussed, it must have been on the page that was torn out."

"What do you mean?" Manion asked.

"The last page in the diary was torn out. Some time ago, judging by the color and texture of the torn edges."

Manion took the stack of pages and looked at the last one. The final, March 29, 1965, entry began: "Decision made to go forward with the plan. Will give warning to make sure building empty. No sense killing anybody, since FBI knows. Big problem there and what to do? Can't talk to B., he's letting his dick think for him. Real possibility we been set up. Know for sure tomorrow night. If the bitch . . ."

The rest of the sentence was continued on the missing page. Dr. Pressman was saying something, but Manion couldn't hear him. He was too busy building blocks. Could the missing diary page have been what Pano sent J.J. to keep for him? Perhaps it had information that would show how Pano and the Southern Cross had been "set up." By the FBI? "If the bitch . . ." he'd begun. The bitch being who? Lillian Davis? Yes, Lillian Davis.

Dr. Pressman was pacing the floor, nattering about the archival importance of the diary, when Manion interrupted him. "Did you come across anything in here about Pano working with the FBI?"

The big man gave him a wide grin. "Hardly," he said. "This guy hated all forms of law enforcement. Particularly the FBI. In fact, if you look at some entries near the end, you'll see he was trying to bug the local FBI office."

"Any mention of a woman named Lillian Davis?"

"He doesn't use names," Dr. Pressman said. "Only initials. I really can't remember if there are any L.s or L.D.s. I do plan on going through the diary again, though."

Manion asked him to call if he found any reference to the initials. The archivist promised he would. "But before you go . . ." he said, opening a drawer to his desk. He removed the diary. It was encased in clear plastic. "Judging by my eye, this is an authentic diary of the period. But we should put it through some tests to be sure. And you said you'd provide me with a sample of Pano's handwriting."

Manion patted his coat pockets. Fortunately, he still had one of the letters written to Shana Washington.

Dr. Pressman studied it and said, "I'd be willing to say this is a match. But we'll make one hundred percent sure." He hesitated and then asked, "What plans do you have for the diary? Any chance of its becoming a part of the library's permanent collection?"

"It's not mine," Manion said.

"Then who . . . ?"

Manion had to stop and think. Shana had given it to little Louis deMay. "I'll ask the owner," he said. "My guess is that he'll agree. Especially, in return for unlimited access to the library."

"Of course, if that would appeal to him."

"I'll get back to you," Manion said, heading for the door.

"Don't forget your copy," Dr. Pressman called.

Manion wasn't ready to share the contents of the diary with Munn or Mickie. He asked Pressman to hang on to it for a while.

Even with the evening traffic, he arrived at Mickie McCormick's hotel room only a few minutes later than he'd planned. But she was gone.

The desk clerk had a message for him. "Exciting news about Pano! No time to lose! Waiting in alley behind hotel in rented dark gray Buick. Hurry up. It's hot out here." It was signed "Mickie."

Manion was puzzled. He knew she could be impatient, especially when it came to getting her job done. But why had she gone to the bother of renting a car when he had one they could use? And why wait in the alley instead of the lobby or the room?

He decided not to use the walkway to the rear of the hotel but to circle the block instead. She'd asked him to hurry, but a little caution was worth a few extra minutes.

From the side street he spotted the Buick parked midway down the alley, facing away. Someone was in the passenger seat, but it was impossible to tell who.

He entered the alley warily.

The rear door of Mickie's hotel clanged open suddenly, making him jump. Two black men carried out a huge metal

Dumpster and deposited it in the alley. They went back inside the hotel, slamming the door shut behind them.

No one else seemed to be in the alley.

"Hey," a male voice whispered behind him, "got any spare change?"

He turned to find a beggar standing less than two feet away. He hadn't heard a footstep. He studied the man. Dressed in rags and an ancient Saints cap. Dirt was crusted on his hands and face. One of the hands was held out to him. "Help the homeless. A Vietnam vet."

"Why'd you sneak up behind me?" Manion asked.

"Didn't sneak, man," the beggar said and pointed to his feet. He wasn't wearing shoes.

Manion pulled a few loose bills from his pocket and handed them to the man.

"Goddamnit, you get the hell out of here!"

A middle-aged man in a dark blue suit was running toward them from the direction of the hotel. "Don't give him any money," he commanded.

The homeless vet ran for the street, money in hand.

The suit, panting, stopped by Manion. "You want to throw your money away, don't do it around the hotel. Those people are like stray dogs. You feed 'em and they keep comin' back. You must have shit for brains."

"You work for the hotel?" Manion asked.

"Yeah. So what?"

"So do you insult all your guests like this?"

"Oh, look, I'm sorry, sir," the man said, backing away. "It's just we been having so much trouble with bums . . ."

"You hotel security?"

"Yes, sir. Corey's the name. Don Corey."

"Well, Don, I'd like you to do me a favor," Manion said.

"Favor?" The man looked suspicious.

"Walk me to the Buick."

"Sure. Why?"

"You never know. Back alleys. We might meet another panhandler."

The two men moved to the car. Mickie was visible now. Eyes closed. "Your wife takin' a snooze?" the man asked.

"Let's see."

Manion reached out to open the car door. It was the last thing he remembered, except for a brief second of pain.

37

HE AWOKE ON the back seat of the Buick, sitting upright, held in place by a safety-belt harness that crossed his chest and traversed his waist. His feet were bound by adhesive tape. He assumed his wrists were, too; they were secured behind his back. The car was moving, being driven by the man who'd called himself Corey. At first, Manion thought he'd lost his sense of hearing. Then he realized that the sedan's windows were keeping out all exterior sound, while keeping them from being heard by the other motorists.

Mickie sat beside Corey. She was apparently bound, too. She was wide awake and terrified. "And to our right," Corey was telling her in the manner of a tour-bus driver, "the remnants of one of the most famous old plantations, Redneckland, brought to devastation by the yam blight."

She was not amused.

Manion tested the ties on his wrist and found them to be more than sufficient. His head throbbed. He stared out of the window at the passing landscape. It was familiar-looking swampland. Much of Louisiana was familiar-looking swampland.

"The water with the light green scum to your left is so stagnant," Corey said, "mosquitoes come here to die. They call it the Mosquito Graveyard. Paul Theroux wants to write a book about it."

Manion saw a rough wood marker that read "Ft. Larue—2 mi." and knew immediately where they were. Thirty miles or so out of the city on highway 90, heading for the Rigolets, where he and his father used to fish for tarpon.

"Look who decided to wake up," Corey merrily informed

Mickie. "The boyfriend. Don't tell him about the little liberties I've taken."

Mickie turned her head and gave Manion a wan look.

"What's going on?" Manion asked.

"I'm introducing the lovely Miz McCormick to some of Louisiana's living history," Corey said.

"Where are we going?"

"You know Fort Larue, Manion?" Corey asked.

"I know what it is, but I've never actually seen it," Manion lied. He'd taken many school trips there. Unpleasant outings with the bigger boys like Eben Munn waging mock battles with bamboo popguns, using the hard fruit of the chinaberry trees for projectiles. But if no other good came from those terror-filled jaunts, they provided Manion with a firsthand knowledge of every nook and cranny in the old fort.

"Well," Corey went on, "I understand it's a nice quiet spot to hold a little chat."

"What sort of chat?"

"This and that. About J.J. Legendre, for example. I was hoping you could tell me if he was happy in his later years."

"You knew J.J.?"

"Our paths crossed. He did me a favor once."

"Before he became a private investigator?" Manion asked.

"Private investigator," Corey said with disdain. "Waste Particle Manager. The titles we think of to bring a sense of dignity to an undignified profession. Yes, I knew Legendre when he was a genuine lawman, the best the NOPD had. I touched base with him only once after he became a *private investigator.*

"So I ask you, Manion, was he happy being a *private investigator?*"

"Reasonably."

"Do you remember a lunch you had with him at Brennan's seven years ago?"

Manion's head hurt. "Seven years ago? No. We ate at Brennan's at least once a month."

"Sitting in the corner of the room. Looking like an old queen and his kept lad. Anyway, I was there, as was, at a separate but equal table, a longtime business associate. As I was there to pass along an item to him on the q.t., we were not mingling.

"Legendre left your table, probably to go to the rest room. He paused to bid me hello and continued on. As he passed my associate's table, words were exchanged. Not friendly ones.

Later that night, I got a phone call from my associate. He wanted me to kill Legendre.

"There was little chance of that. Once before, I'd toyed with the possibility of ending the detective's life. I decided not to, and those decisions stick with you. So J.J. lived and eventually somebody else killed him. Do you believe in Kismet, Manion?"

"No," Manion replied. "I think we can change our destinies."

"Some of us can," Corey said, chuckling. "And the others might as well rest their heads on the block."

Manion stared at him. Middle-aged. Salt-and-pepper hair. Expensive suit. He didn't think he'd ever met him before, certainly did not remember the incident at Brennan's. But he knew with chilling certainty who the man was and what he had done. And what he was capable of doing.

38

FORT LARUE'S PARKING area was empty except for a new Mercedes convertible and a Previa van. "Looks like some visitors are staying past the time limit," Corey said. "Too much longer and I may just have to bust them."

A family of five came over the ridge beside the fort's roof, the kids romping in front of parents who'd obviously had a long, wearying day. "Cry for help," Corey told his hostages, "and there will be blood on the ol' camp grounds tonight."

"Why'd you bring us *here*?" Manion wondered.

"Everybody's gotta be someplace. Whatever happened to Myron Cohen?"

"Who?" Mickie asked.

"Myron Cohen," Corey said. "Comedian. That was one of his punch lines. 'Everybody's gotta be someplace.' Used to call himself a monologist. Another of those smarmy profession upgrades. The man was a comic. Told Jew jokes. Must be dead by now. Back when he was on the Sullivan show he looked like he had one foot in the grave."

"Why are you doing this?" Mickie asked.

Corey ignored her. "You know, I think I watched too much television in the sixties. There wasn't anything else to do. Then I got a hobby. Killing people. It certainly puts TV way in the shade." He looked at Mickie. "Even your show."

Manion watched the family pile into the Previa and drive away. Going on with their lives.

"This must be a terrific place for children," Corey said. "All those passageways and tunnels. You could play hide-and-seek forever. Okay, kiddies, let's go see the fort."

Manion looked at the remaining sports car and wondered where its owner was.

Corey didn't seem to care. He got out of the Buick, circled it and opened Mickie's door. He removed a buck knife from a sheath strapped to his calf. He pressed it against the soft underside of her chin while he released the seat belt. He stepped back to let her swing her legs out. He guided his knife through the adhesive bindings around her ankles.

Then, prodding her with the blade, he moved her near Manion's door.

He repeated the process there, being careful not to give Manion a chance to kick him once the detective's ankle bindings were severed. "We'll just leave the wrists tied for a while," Corey said, replacing the buck knife with a handgun.

In the century or so since Fort Larue had been built, utilizing a natural stone foundation, layers of loamy topsoil had covered the structure and filled in the places between it and the hillside until they had become one, covered over by a thick grass. This made it seem as if the fort existed underground, carved into the side of a hill.

Corey ordered them to precede him down the sloping walkway to the entrance. "Journey's end is near," he told them, urging them past the fort's open door into a claustrophobic room that resembled a cave. Several passageways split off from it.

Corey indicated the nearest one on the right.

That led them to a slightly larger, darker room. The only light was the dusk filtering through bull's-eyes in the boarded-up windows.

It was enough for them to see the short man dressed in white slacks and blue silk shirt. He was pacing up and down in a state of extreme impatience. Remy Ragusa.

He was as surprised to see them as Manion and Mickie were to see him. "What's going on?" he asked Corey. "Why're *they* here and who the hell are you?"

"A man with a plan, Remy."

"Where's Jim Billins?"

"He won't be coming."

"What? He said this was supposed to be some fucking ultraprivate meeting between him and me. Leave Cookie at home and drive yourself, he says. Through all the goddamn traffic."

"Sorry about that, chief," Corey said. "He got a call from the gov. Some shindig at the St. Louis Hotel."

"Yeah. They're dedicating the casino," Remy said. "A grand a ticket is what I paid." He started for the door. "You can bet I'll give Jimmy a piece of my mind, when I see him there."

"But you won't," Corey said matter-of-factly.

"You don't think so?"

"No. I need you here."

Ragusa looked at him in disbelief. Then he smiled. "I'm gonna pass on a party I paid two grand to go to because you need me here. Gee whiz, guy. It's nice to be needed, but what's so important?"

"I want you to kill them." Corey indicated Manion and Mickie.

"You're a nut case, brother," Ragusa said. "I don't kill people."

"It's Jimmy's idea."

"The favors I owe him ain't that heavy. I don't even touch a gun these days." He turned and started for the door.

"Hold up, partner," Corey said evenly.

"Fuck you."

"One more step and you're a dead man."

The mobster turned. "You're threatening me, you asshole?"

"There's gonna be a shoot-out at the old fort," Corey replied, removing another gun from under his coat. "You and Manion. One of those tragedies with nobody surviving."

Ragusa frowned. "What're you talkin' about?"

"Jimmy wants me to close down a few lanes on the information highway. Manion. The beautiful Miz McCormick. And you. There's a fourth, but I'll figure out something for him later."

Ragusa looked no less puzzled. "I still don't get the drift of . . ." He leaped suddenly at Corey, fingers reaching the gunman's throat.

Corey was caught off guard. But he managed to get one of his weapons between him and Ragusa. He fired once and the little man was flung backward onto the dirt floor.

By then, Manion and Mickie were entering a tunnel leading away from Corey. A bullet pinged against the wall near Manion's head as they ran awkwardly, hands still tied behind their backs.

Manion's memory of the pitch-black passageways proved accurate, but it was a child's memory. Rounding one corner, he banged his forehead against a low ceiling and was momentarily dazed. Mickie stumbled into him. "What happened?" she asked.

He shook some of the dizziness away. Too many blows to the head can slow a man down. Or they can clarify his situation. He backed against a wall, feeling for a rough edge of broken stone. Then he began rubbing his taped wrists over the rough spot.

He'd sawed through one strand of the tape when from somewhere down the passageway came the familiar, taunting call, "Ready or not, here I come."

"I want you to feel my wrists," Manion whispered to Mickie.

"Huh?"

"Find the end of the tape and unwind." He was perspiring. The fears of childhood mixed with the much more legitimate fears of his present situation.

It took precious seconds for her to locate the tape edge, then unwind enough of it for Manion to free his own hands. "Am I getting warmer?" the gunman's voice echoed down the tunnel.

Manion led her away.

As they passed through a small room something rustled in the dark. "God, what is that?" Mickie asked.

His night vision told him it was some sort of animal. More than one. The animals were hissing at them. Rats? Three huge rats, standing on their hind legs. Too big to be rats.

Manion fumbled with the tape holding Mickie's wrists. "Nutria," he whispered to her. "Nesting in here."

"What the hell are nutria?"

"Rodents."

"Oh God," she said.

The hissing nutria circled them and raced from the room. "They were afraid of *us*," Manion told her, as he unwound the last of her tape.

From the passageway not far away, they heard Corey shout, "What the hell . . . ?"

"I hope they bite that bastard in the balls," she said, rubbing her wrists.

They ran onward. The young Manion's favorite hiding place was behind a narrow doorway so strangely angled that the big boys racing down the tunnel, if they saw it at all, assumed it was an odd shadow along the unbroken wall. The doorway led to a tiny room that a normal-sized man would have to bend to enter and a fat man could not enter at all. At Manion's urging, Mickie backed into the space, ducking her head. There was so little light in the tunnel that the gunman would surely pass it by if Mickie could stay perfectly quiet.

He ran on noisily, hoping the sound would move the gunman quickly past Mickie's niche. Eventually, he reached the front of the fort. Using his shoulder, he pushed out two boards that had been blocking a window. Outside, the night was starless. Good. In darkness, the advantage was his. Especially since he knew that the designers of the fort had included an emergency exit, the window before him.

He sat on the rough sill and drew his legs up. There was a thirty-foot drop from the window to a gravel bed below. It looked as dangerous then as it had when he was a kid. Maybe more so.

A foot or so above the window was the first of a series of iron rungs attached to the fort's outer wall that could be used to climb to the grassy top leading to the parking lot. From there it would be a simple matter of finding a phone.

He reached up, felt the rust-covered rung. He remembered that one of his classmates had slipped from the rungs, breaking an arm and a leg and ruining that school trip to the fort.

He was about to pull himself up when he heard Mickie scream.

He crouched on the sill, looking back into the fort. There was a faint but steady glow in the passageway. Corey, the son of a bitch, wasn't stumbling in the dark. He had a light. And he had Mickie.

39

MANION CONSIDERED HIS options. If he ran, Corey would probably kill the woman. But if he stayed, what use would he be against a man with a flashlight and a gun?

Mickie screamed again, and he realized he had no choice. He dropped to the dirt floor of the fort, feeling for a rock, a branch. Something. But the room had nothing. Except dirt. He grabbed a handful and moved beside the doorway.

The light drew nearer.

Manion tensed.

The light entered the room. A small penlight. Manion leaped forward and tossed the dirt into the gunman's eyes, then grabbed the man and fell with him to the floor.

His opponent was weaker than he'd expected. And softer. And when crying out in surprise, sounded remarkably like Mickie.

Manion felt something cold touch his neck.

From behind him, Corey said, "Ooops. You're IT."

He'd given Mickie the flashlight and sent her into the room ahead of him. He reached down to retrieve the penlight which was lying in the dirt. As his two captives picked themselves up and dusted off, he said, "Let's go back to where we left poor Remy."

"I think I'll stay here," Manion said.

"As you wish. I'm easy. I can do it here."

His gun was aimed point-blank at Manion's chest. His finger tightened on the trigger. And a voice close behind him called out, "Yo, asshole. Think fast."

The gunman whirled. "Remy?"

"Naw, it's only me," Munn said, and fired his police special.

* * *

The first shot hit the gunman in his chest like a punch, sending him toward the center of the room. He stood there a second and dropped the flash. Manion scooped it up and turned it on the wounded man as he tried to lift his gun. Munn, framed in the doorway in dusty pants and rolled shirtsleeves, fired again. The bullet sent the gunman back another two steps, but, somehow, he remained standing, glaring furiously at Munn.

"Talk about die hard," Munn said.

"Wait," Manion called out. But Munn fired twice more and the gunman danced backward and finally fell to the dirt.

"I thought I was gonna have to beat him to death," Munn said, moving forward and kicking the gun from lifeless fingers.

"We could have used him alive," Manion said.

"Picky, picky," Munn replied, bending down to search for a pulse in the man's neck. "He's gone this time for sure."

"That's what they thought thirty years ago," Manion said.

"I'll be damned," Munn exclaimed, looking at Manion in astonishment. "So you know who he is?"

"John Keller. Thirty years ago, he was a young assistant D.A. who figured out a way of getting rich quickly. He murdered several women, including his wealthy wife, and he tricked J.J. Legendre into laying the blame for all the deaths on his father-in-law. You just killed the Meddler."

Munn shook his head in admiration. "Once a brainiac, always a brainiac. My old schoolmate still knows all the answers. Maybe you can tell me what Keller's been up to lately."

Manion cocked his head. "He's carrying a badge. He was talking about 'busting' late visitors to the fort. I'd say he was in some form of law enforcement. Since you seem to know something about him, I imagine he might even be a member of the NOPD."

Munn opened his mouth, but Manion interrupted. "No. Make that a member of the Organized Crime Combat Squad. Am I close?"

"On the nose," Munn said. "Except for one thing. He wasn't just a member. He was the head honcho, good old Jack Keller, the great guy I been working for. I hitched my wagon to some star all right."

He turned to Mickie, who was shivering, and put his arm around her. "You okay, babe?"

"I thought you'd never ask," she said. Then she rested her head on his shoulder. "My hero."

Just as Munn moved to kiss her, Manion turned the penlight on them. "Time to go," he said.

40

"THIRTY YEARS AGO, I was in kindergarten," Munn said as they worked their way back to the fort's entrance. "Who knew from the Meddler? But you were right, podnah, about the library being a place of enlightenment. I spotted the name John Keller in the newspaper: the husband of one of the Meddler's victims. I wasn't sure it was *my* Jack Keller, of course. He hasn't been goin' around spreading sea stories about how his old lady bought the farm. But the guy said he was loaded. So fat, moneywise, he wasn't taking any pay for heading up the squad."

"Inherited wealth," Manion said.

"You bet. According to the book about the murders, the wife's money didn't go to him when she died. It went to her old man. So Keller had to figure out a way to get it *and* the old man's loot as well. He conned Glander into making him his heir and then repaid him the kindness by setting him up to take the fall for the murders."

"Wait a minute," Mickie said. "If this guy's father-in-law was found guilty of murdering his daughter, he wouldn't have gotten her money. Criminals can't profit from their crimes."

"I'm not so sure they couldn't in Louisiana in 1965," Munn said.

"In any case, Glander was never officially found guilty," Manion said.

"The Meddler book made the final shootout seem a little weird," Munn said. "Glander was supposed to have shot at your pal, Legendre, and missed. Legendre looks up a stairwell and sees Glander sitting on the top step. He fires. Glander rolls down. They found Glander's gun up where he was sitting."

"He was probably unconscious the whole time," Manion said. "J.J. told a friend that there was music playing, no doubt to cover the noise when Keller dragged Glander to the stairs and propped him up. Then he shot at J.J. again and, as he hoped, J.J. returned the fire."

Munn nodded. "If a bullet hits a guy, it usually throws him backward. But Glander rolled down the stairs."

"Keller probably pushed him down. He didn't want J.J. coming up to look at the body before he could make his getaway down the rear stairs."

"Anyway," Munn said, "Keller fixed it so that Legendre plugged the old guy. So Glander was never declared legally guilty. Dead men don't stand trial."

"Sounds like the title of a murder mystery," Manion said.

"But if Keller was that wealthy," Mickie asked, "why was he still killing people today?"

"Maybe he liked it," Munn said.

"He was doing it for his friend James Billins," Manion said.

"Billins? The lawyer?" Munn asked. "How does he fit into this?"

"We could have asked Keller if you'd held those last shots."

"Gee whiz, Manion. I call that a cockroach's gratitude. I save your life and you pimp me about knocking the guy off."

"How'd you get here, by the way?" Manion asked.

Munn didn't answer at first. The truth was that he'd become suspicious of Keller because no guard had been placed on Louis deMay at the hospital. When Munn discovered that the chief had called the office, saying he'd be out the rest of the day, he'd become curious. He camped out near Keller's Garden District home. At the tail end of the afternoon, Keller had driven up in a rented Buick. He'd rushed inside, changed his clothes and returned to the rental. He drove off and Munn followed.

He could not tell this to Manion and Mickie. They'd realize that he'd seen Keller knock them out, tie them up and drive off and he hadn't lifted a finger to help. In point of fact, the OCCS chief had attacked Mickie so quickly, Munn hadn't had a chance to stop him, even if he'd been so inclined.

His decision to wait and see was born of two reasons. First, he wanted to know what the hell Keller was up to, and second, he was certain that he was in control of the situation and that

Manion and Mickie were never in any serious danger. Unfortunately, he had momentarily lost track of Keller's rental in the flood of traffic as they were leaving the city.

But he knew where his chief was headed. After all, it had been he who'd told Keller about the solitude of Fort Larue.

"How *did* you find us, Eben?" Mickie asked.

"I dropped by your hotel to see you, precious," he said. "And I spotted Keller driving away in a car that wasn't his own. Naturally, that made me curious. Then I saw you and Manion were in the car with him. So I hung a U-turn and tried to head him off. We kinda got separated in traffic, but I followed my nose and made it here in time to save the day."

"And kill our last source of information," Manion said.

They were approaching the room near the entrance to the fort. "Yeah? Well, I think I know how we can find out about Keller's connection to Billins."

"How?" Mickie asked.

"We'll just ask Billins."

"Without Keller we don't have any leverage," Manion said.

"Maybe just a little," Munn replied, and led them into the fort's final room.

" 'Bout time you got back, Munn," Remy Ragusa said from the floor. "I only lost another quart of blood."

He was propped up against a wall, with Munn's jacket rolled into a pillow behind his head. He blinked in the dim glow of the flashlight. "There were some big rats running around in here," he complained.

"Must've made you feel right at home," Munn said.

"We'd better send for an ambulance," Mickie suggested.

The bottom of Ragusa's silk shirt was wet with blood, as was the front of his white slacks. Munn had briefly examined the wound when he found the little man. It had looked like a clean in-and-out shot through the side. Not fatal. Unless some crucial organ or other had been punctured. "We got some questions to ask you, Ragusa," the lawman said. "And you don't have a lot of time to try stallin' us. The quicker you talk, the quicker the men in white get here, assuming you've got a phone in that male menopause special parked topside."

Ragusa nodded his head. He didn't look well. "Did you get him?" he asked. When Munn nodded, the little man grinned and began to cough.

"We'd like you to help us take down the man who ordered your death," Manion said.

Ragusa glared at him. "Help you how?"

"Tell us what you know about James Billins. Particularly why he's so desperate to get Tyrone Pano's diary."

"Sure. After this, I don't owe the fucker any loyalty."

"I better go order up that ambulance," Munn said. He grabbed Mickie's hand. "C'mon, we can neck in the car between phone calls."

"As nice as that sounds," she said, "I don't want to miss any of this. It's the crime story of a lifetime."

Manion and Munn exchanged looks. "The problem is," the lawman told Mickie, "depending how all this shakes down, it may not be a story for public consumption."

"What do you mean?" she asked indignantly.

"I mean, first things first," he said. "If we get our facts straightened out and we nab the bad guys, then maybe we'll let you run with your story. But right now, you and me are going to the parking lot."

She frowned at him. "I almost got killed here. I deserve . . ."

"You know why you didn't get killed?" Munn asked. And he grinned at her. She couldn't resist the grin.

"You are my hero," she told him. "And I'll go with you. But if you try to stonewall me on any of this, I'll carve 'Liar, Liar, Pants on Fire' across that big chin of yours with a rusty razor blade."

When they'd gone Ragusa asked, "She as tough as she sounds?"

"Could be," Manion said.

"And she's Munn's broad?"

"I think so."

"Good," the little man said.

41

UNFORTUNATELY, REMY RAGUSA did not know very much. Sure, he'd heard of Keller. "Supposed to be in charge of some new bunch of state cops looking into the rackets. Never met the guy, though, and don't plan to."

Manion didn't bother to enlighten him. Instead, he asked about James Billins. "Jimmy's a power player. I needed his help with something. In return he asked me for a favor. This guy deMay was hitting him up for serious dough because of something in a diary. Billins asked me to grab the diary for him. I could sure use a drink of water."

Manion left the fort and headed for the picnic area. He looked over at Remy's Mercedes and saw that Munn and Mickie were still seated in it. Were they kissing?

He found a fountain near the rest rooms. He fished a paper cup from the trash bin, rinsed it and used it to bring water back to the wounded man. Remy gulped it greedily.

"What was in the diary that made Billins want it so badly?" Manion asked him.

"I dunno. I never even got my mitts on it."

"What did Billins do for you?" Manion asked.

After some hemming and hawing, the little mobster said, "It was Mama's restaurant. It belonged to my uncle Charlie. When he went down there were about five or ten bastard fed and state law–enforcement agencies trying to get their hooks in everything. Billins had the deed to Seraphina's changed so that Mama's name was on it. And he did it with one phone call. So I owed him."

"Was the beating of deMay your idea or Billins's?"

Ragusa ducked his head when he answered. "I tried to do it the easy way. Paid deMay ten fucking grand and the bastard reneged on the deal. Wanted another ten, he said, to go live in New York where the real artists are. Fuck him. A deal's a deal. Cookie punched him a little to find out where the diary was. But he wouldn't give.

"So, no. Billins didn't say to beat him. But he asked me later to chill the guy. I told him I don't play that game. Look, you sure the medics are on the way? I hurt bad and I'm getting light-headed."

"They'll be here soon," Manion said. "We're going to need a statement from you."

"Statement? An official statement? No fucking way."

"Billins tried to have you killed."

"Fine. I'll take care of that or I won't. Guys like me don't go into any courtrooms voluntarily. Statement!" He began coughing.

The paramedics arrived a few minutes later. The fort was in Orleans Parish, and the first lawmen on the scene were two state policemen from Troop B. The ranking officer and Munn strolled away from Manion and Mickie for a few minutes. Then Munn returned and said, "We're all gonna have to spend some time with the stenos tomorrow, but, for right now, *amigos,* let's went."

The two men deposited Mickie in front of her hotel, but not without a fight. Finally, Munn told her, "Look, we're on the brink of something, you and me. And I think we ought to see where we're going with it. Play it out. But I don't want to get that mixed up with business. And what Manion and I are doing tonight is business."

"What about my business?" she asked angrily. "News is my business."

"And no news is mine," Munn said, putting the car in gear and driving away.

"Solid way to start a relationship," Manion told him.

"Listen to who's giving advice," Munn said.

Munn sat at Manion's desk, gnawing on Popeye's fried chicken. Manion slouched in his visitor's chair, sipping Barq's. For over an hour they'd pushed and pulled at the skimpy and disjointed information they possessed in an effort to build a case against James Billins.

"The Muskrat was about as much help as a hernia," Munn said, rooting in the box for the last piece of breast. "Without his statement, we got nothing solid on Billins. But at least we know how Keller fits in. When Ragusa refused to do the button on deMay, Billins must have asked his bloodthirsty old buddy Keller to do the job. And he took his work very seriously."

Manion leaned forward and swished the soft drink around in the bottle. "The two questions we have to answer are these: What specifically is in the diary, or, more precisely, what does Billins think is in the diary? And what's the tie that bound Billins and Keller? It wasn't money. Keller could have bought and sold the lawyer."

Manion stood up and shooed the policeman from his chair. He had to make a phone call. Dr. Pressman at the Library of Antiquity answered on the second ring. The detective quickly explained what he wanted—references in the Pano diary to lawyer James Billins, or as Pano would have it, J. and/or B.

"If Billins is a lawyer, then Pano was using the initial from his last name, 'B.' Let me get my notes."

Manion could hear him shuffling papers. Munn asked, "You gonna eat your red beans?" and chuckled when Manion said he wasn't.

"Here we are," Pressman said. "There are maybe two dozen references to 'B.' Most of them have to do with legal matters. But here's one from October 7, 1964. 'B.' has more to him than I thought. Smart. Committed. Knows how to work the system.' Pano may be talking about the legal system, but I think it's a broader comment than that. In the same entry, Pano is discussing the difficulty he's having in getting explosives. It almost sounds as if 'B' is helping him with that problem, too."

" 'Almost sounds' isn't going to be good enough," Manion said.

"It's very likely that the missing page contained some mention of 'B.,' " Pressman said, "since he's mentioned in the preceding page."

Manion asked him to refresh his memory of that entry.

"The date is March 29, 1965. It reads: '. . . No sense killing anybody, since FBI knows. Big problem there and what to do? Can't talk to B., he's letting his dick think for him. Real possibility we been set up. Know for sure tomorrow night. If the bitch . . .' "

Manion thanked Dr. Pressman for the information and replaced the receiver. Munn looked at him hopefully. "See any more red beans in the box?"

Manion handed him the box and relayed the diary's last entry verbatim. The lawman said, "Sounds like 'the bitch' might be the woman who was murdered, Lillian Davis. Pano thought she was working with the FBI."

"Shana Washington got it wrong," Manion said. "Or maybe Pano lied to her. It made no sense for him to have been an FBI plant. Davis, on the other hand . . ."

"But if she was a Fed," Munn said, "and Pano knew about it, that makes *him* the number one suspect for her murder. Not Billins."

Manion grinned suddenly. "Maybe I do have all the answers," he said. "What did Louis deMay tell us that night before the car crash?"

"Something that his aunt told him. I can't remember what."

"He said, 'Shana told me what Tyrone said about his lip slippin' in the wrong place. . . .' That was what got him to blackmail Billins with the diary. His lip slippin'. His lawyer making a mistake."

"This lawyer, B., is the same one who was letting his dick think for him," Munn said, getting it. "Billins had a thing going with Lillian Davis, who was probably an FBI plant."

"That gives Billins an even better reason to have her killed than Pano," Manion said. "He had a lot more to lose—his reputation, his promising career. And he'd been in love with her and she played him for a fool."

Munn looked at Manion. "Just that last might make any guy think about murder, right?"

Manion smiled at him. "If the guy was inclined to violence. Anyway, if Billins had Lillian Davis murdered, that gives us his link to Keller."

Munn scowled. "I don't follow."

"You should have paid more attention at the library," Manion said. And made the connection for him.

"Real thin, podnah," Munn said. "Billins is a VIP. You try putting him away with what we've got and we both will have to move to Texas. Unless we play this one real nasty."

"It's already nasty," Manion said.

"Then hardball it is," Munn said eagerly. "But we have to swing by my place first for a few items."

42

THE DEDICATION FESTIVITIES at the penthouse casino atop the Hotel St. Louis were in high gear when Munn and Manion stepped from the elevator. The domed room, featuring a floor-to-ceiling unrestricted view of the city and old man river, was brightly lit by a dozen or more cut-glass chandeliers. To their right, the cream of New Orleans society rubbed elbows with politicians, celebrities, gamblers and criminals as they "tested" the electronic slot machines and poker and card games.

To their left, in the main casino, the more adventurous party-goers were trying their luck against flesh-and-blood dealers and croupiers. The men and women were in evening clothes. Manion often thought that New Orleans was the only city left in America where formal dress was donned with regularity.

He and Munn, in their somewhat rumpled suits, were raffish-looking enough to raise the eyebrow of the haughty young woman seated at the end of a reception table blocking their entry. Behind her were two hulks who, even in black tie, looked like French Quarter bouncers. On the sparkling white tablecloth in front of her was a clear plastic clipboard containing a list of names, most of which had check marks next to them.

"Can I help you *gentlemen*?" she asked rather sharply. The bouncers glared at them.

"Sure, honey," Munn told her. "My name is Ragusa and this here's my significant other"—he winked—"Mr. Lapicola."

She scanned her list. Manion was sure she was praying that the names not be there. But they were. The bouncers shifted their weight. The beauty gave them a cheesy smile. Before she could send them to the elderly dowager type with the orchid corsage to her left, Manion asked, "Is Jimmy Billins here yet?"

She seemed surprised at the question but didn't hesitate to answer. "Mr. Billins arrived with Governor Clay about half an hour ago." Her eyes shifted to an approaching couple, and Manion was no longer part of her mural.

The dowager was waiting with a stack of five poker chips. Munn already had his. "The first five hundred dollars are courtesy of the St. Louis," she informed them. "After that, you're on your own, gentlemen."

The last woman at the table was a diminutive type with a dark cocktail in front of her. Her tongue was slightly thick as she reminded them in rote monotone that "All proceeds from tonight's gala go to Hope for the Homeless, a charitable organization founded by the Heart of Jesus ministry, to provide health and medical care for the state's needy."

"A noble cause," Munn said.

"You are encouraged to contribute whatever you'd like."

Munn took the chips from Manion and handed them and his to her. "With our blessings."

They stood at the periphery of the action, scanning the crowd. "I see the mayor is partial to craps," Manion said.

"There's Billy Armand with his old lady."

The chief of police who was sleeping with Madeleine Betterick was a thick-chested man in his early fifties wrapped in a tight tuxedo. His wife was a thin, pursed-lipped woman in a pale green gown. They both looked very bored, with the casino and with each other.

"Do you see Billins?" Manion asked.

Munn shook his head. "Might as well mix and mingle."

They found the lawyer in a small bar area one level down from the casino. Several partygoers were gathered around the Steinway while Governor Magnus Clay entertained them with one of his own compositions.

"It's love love love love, billygoat love," the leonine-haired governor sang. "Love love love love, sillygoat love."

"The guy's a musical genius," Munn said. "And dig his backup singers."

There were four young, clean-cut men positioned at various key spots in the room, all of them wearing headsets and lumps near their left armpits.

Billins was seated at a table next to the piano, tapping away on a small notebook computer. Before Manion and Munn could reach him, Governor Clay ended his ditty, stood and carried his drink to Billins's table. His bodyguards closed in on him a bit, but kept their distance.

The governor and Billins were looking at the computer screen as Manion and Munn approached. Munn circled the table and positioned himself next to the lawyer, careful to keep a pleasant smile on his face and his hands visible and empty. "Could we have a minute, Mr. Billins?" he asked.

The lawyer looked up at him and then at Manion, who was hovering a few feet away. Vaguely puzzled, Billins said, "I'm sorry, but the governor and I are going over his speech right now."

"Only take a minute," Munn insisted. "It's about Jack Keller."

"Jack Keller?" the governor asked. "I know that name, don't I, Jimmy?"

"Yes, sir. The man heading up our Organized Crime Squad."

"Right," the governor said. "A damn fine lawman. What about Keller? Is he here?"

"Nope. Not present. Fact is, he's dead meat, sir," Munn said with a straight face.

"What?" The governor jerked back against his chair, spilling his drink. The bodyguards took a few steps closer.

"Crab bait. Worm food. Stone cold dead in the market."

"What the hell's this guy talking about, Jimmy?"

Billins rose from his chair. "Let me go chat with these gentlemen, Governor. Find out what I can. May we use your suite?"

Governor Clay nodded, and the lawyer and Manion started away.

"Go on. I'll catch up," Munn told them. He took the chair Billins had been using. The lawyer hesitated, then walked away with Manion.

The governor stared at Munn, who suddenly tapped the side of his nose with a forefinger and lowered his voice. "A word to the wise, Governor. Jimmy's in shit up to here. And it can rub off on anybody."

"What the hell are you talking about?"

"Billins has been using Keller as his own private hit man. And he's gonna be nailed for it. I'd start backing away from him as fast as I could, if I were you."

"Who the hell do you think you are?" the governor asked. "Comin' to me with these wild-ass rumors."

Munn used two fingers to slip his ID from the breast pocket

of his coat. He showed it to the governor. "I worked with Keller on the Crime Combat Squad. Just a few hours ago, I personally witnessed him trying to kill three innocent civilians."

Munn was conscious of the bodyguards surrounding him, waiting for the governor to give them a sign. "I'm going to reach into my inside pocket," Munn told all of them, "and remove an envelope."

It was small and square. He presented it to Governor Clay. In it, the governor discovered two items: a negative and a photo of him, taken years before. Probably in Las Vegas. Probably when he was still active in show business. He was seated at a table near a swimming pool. There were two naked women in the pool. But they weren't what had turned the governor's face suddenly pale. It was the man sitting at the table with him, a short beach ball of a man with a crocodile grin. He was Charles Benedetto, Remy's uncle, who until his recent death had been in charge of the Mafia's holdings in the Texarkana area. He and Clay were laughing like old pals.

"Where'd you get this?" Governor Clay asked, shielding the photo from his bodyguards.

"In a metal box that Keller kept in a niche behind the wood paneling of his office," Munn lied. Actually, he'd found the photo in Benedetto's safe a year before, on the day that the crime lord died. He'd kept it and a few other little mementos that he thought might come in handy in the course of his career.

"Is there more?" A layer of perspiration lined the governor's upper lip.

"I used the shredder. It's all gone. Unless Billins has dupes. He and Keller were buddies."

Clay's eyes had turned to stone. "You're not holding anything out?"

"If I was, it would have been that negative."

The governor nodded and shooed the bodyguards away. "Okay, Mr. Munn," he said, "let's say you got my attention. Now what?"

"Why don't I go see what I can shake out of Billins? How do I get to your suite?"

"One flight down. There's a little brass plaque on the door, says 'Governor's Suite.' "

"If I can't find it, I'll ask somebody," Munn said.

"When you're finished, come back up here and give me a report."

"You'll be the first to know," Munn told him.

THE GOVERNOR'S SUITE was a lavish, four-room affair complete with all the amenities, including a redhead sitting on the sofa watching a movie on HBO.

"The governor's . . . niece," Billins explained to Manion as they entered the room. "Jenna, this is Terry Manion."

". . . and Eben Munn," the lawman said from the door behind them.

The redhead moved her eyes from the screen to regard the newcomers. She gave them more of a grimace than a smile, nodded, and turned back to her movie. Billins blinked and asked, "Why aren't you at the party, Jenna?"

"I don't like to gamble," she said, pouting. "Besides, it's Mel Gibson."

"You can rent the video," Billins told her, a bit harshly. "Leave us alone."

Something about the way he said it made her grab the TV's remote control and flick off the set. She stood and walked from the room without another word. When the door to the suite clicked shut, Billins turned to Munn. "What's all this about Keller being dead?"

"Oh yes, sir," Munn said. "He's dead all right."

"Where? How?"

"At Fort Larue. Four or five bullets entering his body, disrupting organs, letting his blood leak out."

"How did it happen?" Billins was barely maintaining his calm.

"I just pointed my gun at him," Munn said. "And went bang-bang-bang. Bang."

"You? In God's name, why?" Starting to fray a little.

"Because he was gonna shoot Manion."

"Why?"

"I guess because Keller was what we call in the trade a stone killer. That's what he did best. Murder people."

"This is shocking news," Billins said. "But I don't understand why you've come to me."

"We thought you'd want to know, you and Keller being so close," Manion told him.

"Close? I barely knew the man."

"A partnership that lasted thirty years," Munn said, raising his eyebrows, "but you barely knew him."

"What partnership? What the hell are you implying?"

"That you and he go way back," Munn said.

"All I know about Keller," Billins snapped, "is that he is . . . *was* a dedicated lawman who served this city and state well. But I wouldn't call the man a friend or a long-term associate."

"You seem pretty cavalier about your old friends," Manion said.

"What's that supposed to mean?"

"The last time we discussed Lillian Davis you didn't mention that you'd had an affair with her."

Billins stared at him. "An affair? I knew her, of course. I . . . was very fond of her. But an affair? Nonsense."

"You weren't in love with her?" Manion asked.

"In love? That's absurd. I've been in love with and married to the same woman for thirty-four years."

"Maybe it was just the sex, huh?" Munn said.

"What . . . no . . ."

"It doesn't matter," Manion said. "You trusted her. You thought she loved you."

"And all the time," Munn added, "she was just doin' her job for the FBI. Playing you for Mr. Chump. Gathering the goods so she could nail your butt to the jailhouse door right next to Tyrone Pano's."

"No. You're wrong." Billins's normally modulated voice had gone up a few octaves. "Lillian was a dedicated—"

"You remember the serial killer they called the Meddler?" Manion asked, not waiting for the lawyer to finish his platitude.

"What? The Meddler? Of course," Billins said.

"The night Lillian Davis was murdered," Manion told him, "the Meddler killed another woman just a few blocks away. That put him in the neighborhood where he actually witnessed the Davis murder. Out of professional curiosity, he became interested in the case. He discovered the man behind the murder. You."

"This conversation is over," Billins said. "I don't have any idea why Jack Keller should have tried to link me to some long-forgotten murder—"

"I didn't say Keller linked you to the murder," Manion told him. "I said the Meddler did. Are you telling us that Keller was the serial killer known as the Meddler?"

Billins froze. "Of course not," he said finally. "The Meddler died thirty years ago. I . . . we were talking about Keller. You're purposely trying to confuse me."

"Keller was the Meddler all right," Manion said.

"That's ridiculous. How—?"

"I think we all know how. We also know that you and he became secret sharers. He knew your murderous past. And you knew his. And together you helped one another through the years. You did what you do best, wheel and deal. And he took care of the rougher aspects of political expediency."

"I've known marriages that weren't so nurturing," Munn said.

Billins was staring at the wall somewhere between the two men. "Your accusations are ridiculous," he said tonelessly. "Where's the proof?"

"Tyrone Pano's diary," Manion said.

Billins's head snapped back as if he'd been slapped.

"It's all in there," Manion said. "Conversations you and he had linking you with the most militant acts of the Southern Cross. Your affair with Lillian and the discovery that she was an FBI plant. The last page of the diary is missing. I think Pano tore it out himself just after Lillian Davis's murder. He was afraid. Afraid that he'd be blamed for her murder. Possibly afraid that you might murder him. That page of the diary would have put the cops on your doorstep. It was his life insurance. He gave it to Shana Washington to hold for him.

"But he had second thoughts. Maybe he was worried that he was putting her in danger. Maybe he just wasn't confident that she'd know how to use the information if anything happened to him. In any case, he asked J.J. Legendre to become its new custodian."

"This is all meaningless," Billins said. "What torn page? Show it to me."

"Somehow you switched envelopes. You took the diary page and left a bogus will."

"How clever I must be," Billins said, gaining strength.

"Where was the switch made?" Manion asked. "At Shana Washington's? Or was there a way you were able to break into the safety deposit box where J.J. was keeping the envelope?"

Billins smiled. "I don't know what you're talking about. And I think it's time you were going."

They'd almost cracked him. But he'd been too tough for them. Munn winked at Manion. Time for the fallback plan.

"Keller had this little tin box," Munn said.

"Well, who doesn't?" Billins asked, smirking a little.

"He had the goods on a lot of folks."

"But not on me, I can assure you," Billins said.

"No. But it's not going to look so good for the governor, him giving a key law-enforcement position to an assassin who gets off on mutilating young women."

"They might even say," Manion added, "that Governor Clay knew that Keller had been guilty of dirty tricks that aided his election."

"The governor's a big boy who can take care of himself."

"His only contact with Keller has been through you," Munn pointed out. "If Clay is implicated, he'll most certainly drag you into it."

Billins smiled. "I wouldn't hold my breath," he said. "Whatever harm Keller's little box can bring the governor is nothing compared to what my little box can do to him. Now, are you gentlemen going to leave, or must I get the governor's security staff to toss you out?"

Manion and Munn left the room, apparently dejected.

At the door, Billins said, "You're going to be sorry you tried to fuck with me." He turned to Manion, "And that goes for the old whore you work with. Things are going to get pretty rough in this state for all of you. I'd think of moving very far away."

He slammed the door.

Munn turned to Manion, and his glum face broke into a grin.

As they ascended the stairs, Munn said, "If he weren't such a prick, I'd feel sorry for him."

Manion didn't reply. He was not delighting in the moment.

"Cheer up, goddamnit," Munn said as they entered the casino, where the governor was getting ready to make his dedication speech.

Manion couldn't cheer up. Nor could he explain to Munn why he felt no satisfaction from the way they were handling the situation. He didn't believe that the end justified the means.

He stayed on the outskirts of the crowd as Munn worked his way to the governor. The lawman whispered a few words in the governor's ear, then opened his coat and carefully removed the mini-recorder from his inside pocket. He handed it to Governor Clay, who pocketed it and excused himself from the crowd. He and his security team went off in the direction of the bar. The dedication speech would be a little late.

Munn returned to Manion, as happy as a lark. " 'Love love love love,' " he sang, " 'billygoat love.' "

MANION NURSED A Dr Pepper for forty-five minutes at the bar at Rowdy's waiting for the early *Creoles on Parade* revue to end. The room was crowded with couples who'd come in together, couples who'd met just that night and a scattering of stags who had failed to meet. To Manion, all of them seemed young and slightly foolish, and he envied them.

When the crowd poured out of the back showroom, he bucked the traffic and went in. Wanda deMay was in a dressing room with the other women, fixing her makeup. Her son was asleep on a cot against the far wall. She saw Manion's reflection in the mirror and rose to greet him.

They walked out into the hall. Jambo stood in the other dressing room, sipping from a coffee cup and staring at them, as if waiting for a signal from Wanda.

"What now?" she asked Manion.

"It's all over," he said.

"What's all over?"

"Nobody'll be bothering Louis or you," he said.

She didn't seem convinced. "The only person who won't be bothered again is Louis's father," she said. "We're burying him tomorrow."

Jambo couldn't stay away. Joining them, he put his arm protectively around Wanda's shoulders. "Everything all right?" he asked.

Manion nodded. "The man who killed Louis's father is dead," he said. "His name was John Keller."

Wanda nodded and moved closer to Jambo. "Do you know why big Louis was killed?"

"No," the detective lied. "I don't think we ever will."

"That man who took little Louis . . ."

"He's in the hospital. Keller tried to kill him, too."

Jambo shook his head. "Nothing makes much sense, does it?"

"Sometimes that's better," Manion said.

45

SHORTLY AFTER ELEVEN that night, Manion's phone rang. Eben Munn. "Turn on the news now. Channel Three," he ordered and hung up. Manion got out of bed, stumbled downstairs and clicked on the small black-and-white TV in his office. When the picture flopped into place, a remote camera was panning the exterior of the building that housed James Billins's law firm. Police cars were parked at its base along with mobile news cars and an ambulance. The crowd of gawkers was starting to disperse.

The camera zoomed in on a balcony near the top of the building. Manion could barely make out a lighted office, curtains fluttering.

A female reporter was saying, ". . . unclear as to what might have led Mr. Billins . . . Just a minute, I understand that the police have found a note. A suicide note has been found."

The scene returned to the studio where the anchor couple, a blandly handsome man and woman, sat at a desk, staring into the camera. A large photo of James Billins was on display behind them. The man said, "As soon as the police release the contents of that suicide note, you'll hear it here on Three. Until then, James V. Billins, one of the state's power brokers, adviser to four Louisiana governors, dead at fifty-seven, an apparent suicide."

Feeling oddly detached, Manion turned off the television and climbed the stairs to his bedroom. The phone rang again. Munn. "Well, I guess that means we won't have to get out of town."

"No?" Manion asked. "What makes you think Governor Clay's suicide squad won't be coming for us next?"

"Suicide squad? Jesus, Manion, what books you been reading? Sure, Clay sent some folks to talk with Billins. They had to get a little rough with him, but he turned over his file on the governor and they left him in his office all alone and feeling blue. The big jump was strictly his idea."

"Maybe he just forgot to tie his bungee cords," Manion said.

"Fact is, he was despondent because he knew he was about to be hauled in for ordering the murders of Lillian Davis and Tyrone Pano. I got this straight from Clay himself. The big guy and I are thick as thieves."

"An apt metaphor."

"Hey, lighten up. Rejoice. Good times are ahead. I got a hunch I'm gonna be the next chief of the Crime Combat Squad."

"Congratulations," Manion said dryly.

"Look, why don't we come over there and cheer you up?"

"We?"

"Me and Mickie. She's in the kitchen breaking dishes."

"She unhappy about something?"

"Are you kidding? She's a member of the media. She's the enemy. Of course she's unhappy. The gov wants a filter on Billins's bad behavior and she's gotta go along with it."

"You mean he's sweeping the little peccadilloes like murder under the rug? What about Lillian Davis? Do we just let the world keep thinking that Tyrone Pano killed her?"

"You're right," Munn said. "I see your point. You got to give that leech Reynaldo something for his money."

"That's not it at all," Manion said heatedly. "Screw Reynaldo. I'm talking about justice."

"Oh, that," Munn said dismissively. "Well, try this on. Keller killed Davis because she saw him murdering one of his Meddler victims. Then, later on, he visited Pano in his cell and killed him and made it look like suicide."

Manion didn't respond. He was thinking about all the suicides he'd known. How many of them had been genuine? He relaxed his grip on the phone and said, "Good night, Eben."

"Why don't we come over there and celebrate the ten grand?"

"What ten grand?"

"The loot you'll get when you give Reynaldo the diary."

"If Pierre Reynaldo gets his hands on that diary, there's no telling what conclusions he might come up with," Manion said. "He might even start to wonder who the lawyer, J.B., was and that might lead him to . . ."

"Okay, okay. Then just tear out those pages and . . ."

"The diary isn't mine, Eben," Manion said.

"But . . ."

"Look, it's late and I'm tired. You and Mickie have a good night," he said, and replaced the receiver.

He picked up the phone again and dialed the Cape Cod number Munn had given him. A sleepy and annoyed man told him that Lucille and his son Markham had gone back to Boston. "Who is this?" the man thought to ask finally, just before Manion broke the connection.

She was at her hotel. She answered with a yawn.

"I was wondering how you were doing," he said.

"I'm sleeping."

"Sorry. I've been trying to reach you for a few days."

"We were at the Cape."

"I know. Eben told me."

There was a pause. Then she said, "Mark's getting a divorce."

"Are you going to marry him?"

There was silence on the line.

"Is he there?" Manion asked.

"No. He's spending tonight at his place with his children."

Manion thought about J.J. Legendre, the man he'd idolized.

The man who'd been wrong about so many things. The man who'd grown old without a mate.

"I love you," he told her. "I don't want to spend another minute without you."

"Oh?" she replied softly.

"I want you to pack your bags and catch the next available flight. I don't care when it gets in, I'll be waiting at the airport."

"What's been going on there?" she asked suspiciously.

"The usual. A thirty-year-old murder solved. A Jack the Ripper taken off the streets. Political empires shifting and shaking. Your brother behaving badly."

"Have you been drinking?"

He smiled. "No. Thinking is what I've been doing. It's the opposite of drinking. I was a fool to let you go back to Boston."

"Yes, you were," she agreed.

"I should have done everything in my power to make you stay."

"Everything like what? Are we talking marriage here?" she asked.

"Absolutely," he replied.

"I'll call you right back with my flight number," she said. "By the way, I love you, too."

Feeling a bit woozy, he hung up the phone. He leaned against the bed's headboard and waited for Lucille's call. And wondered if he was doing the right thing.